Scarred

THOMAS ENGER

Translated from the Norwegian by Charlotte Barslund

FABER & FABER

First published in this edition in 2014
by Faber and Faber Limited
Bloomsbury House
74–77 Great Russell Street
London WC1B 3DA

Originally published in Norway as *Blodtåke* by Gyldendal Norsk Forlag in 2013

Typeset by Faber and Faber Ltd
Printed and bound by CPI Group (UK) Ltd, Croydon, CR0 4YY

This translation has been published with the financial support of NORLA

The right of Thomas Enger to be identified as author of this work has been asserted in
accordance with Section 77 of the Copyright, Designs
and Patents Act 1988

A CIP record for this book
is available from the British Library

ISBN 978–0–571–27248–8

FSC
www.fsc.org
MIX
Paper from
responsible sources
FSC® C101712

2 4 6 8 10 9 7 5 3 1

Prologue

Werner is dead.

He really is; he knows that now.

He needed to stand beside the small, rectangular grave before he could grasp it. Properly take it in. He had to see the coffin first, see the mourners. Their dark clothes, their dark eyes.

Werner is gone.

For ever.

Fluffy snowflakes fall to the ground around him; some are caught in a never-ending, whirling spiral. The snow makes his eyes water, but he doesn't mind. It makes it look as if he is crying.

He turns to his mother. There are cold trails down her cheeks. She continues to stare at the glossy, brown coffin. And beside her his father, who could barely tie his own tie this morning because his hands were shaking so badly. Who needed help shaving. Who ran outside last week in only a T-shirt and underpants though it was the middle of the day and big, white snowflakes were falling. Who screamed while he clawed through the snow like a maniac. Who pulled Werner out of the heavy whiteness.

But Werner's lips had already turned blue.

They'd done it before, Werner and him, built caves inside the snowdrifts and dug tunnels connecting them. They would crawl through them though they knew they could collapse at any moment. And later – the thrill of emerging out into the light, still in one piece. They would dice with death and win.

Until that day.

*

Everyone is here. All of Werner's classmates. Even some of his teachers have come to the funeral. There are people here he has never seen before. Family friends. Friends of friends. Everyone is sad. Or maybe they're just pretending, like him.

They lower his brother into the black void. They sing with voices that can barely be heard. But he doesn't want to sing. Or talk to anyone. Later, people gather in his house. He has something to eat and drink. He's the only member of his family who does.

In the afternoon he sneaks up to his room, plays a cassette tape and flops down on his bed. Music usually makes him feel good, but not today. It takes him a while before he realises why.

Something in the room has changed.

He gets up from the bed and wanders up and down while he tries to work out what it is. And then he sees the photograph on the wall, a picture of Werner staring down at him, a picture that wasn't there before, but hangs there now. His knees almost buckle.

He hasn't told anyone how he watched the roof cave in on his brother. How he didn't lift a finger, not for a long time, but relished the sensation surging through him. He was master of life and death. He was the only one who could save Werner.

The apple of their father's eye.

He knows who put up the photograph, obviously; he remembers his father's screams when the doctors said there was nothing more they could do. You can't give up, he begged them, please, please don't give up! And the look on his face when they came home from the hospital later that day, when they sat around the dinner table in the time that followed and no one said a word. There was no mistaking it. Was it because he wasn't crying?

No.

It was because he hadn't said sorry.

It had been his idea. His game. And he knows taking the picture down won't help. His father will keep putting it back up, again and again. Making it impossible for him to forget.

Werner always used to smile when he had his picture taken, but he doesn't on this one. He just looks straight at the camera. His hair is combed to one side and almost covers his eyes, but not enough to extinguish the light in them. The muffled screams he let out under those white, lethal masses come back. Like an echo.

By the time he sits down on his bed again, it has grown dark outside. It stopped snowing a long time ago, but the snow could have swept right through the room without him noticing anything but the light in his brother's eyes. The light that can't be snuffed out.

Werner isn't dead.

He isn't really; he knows that now.

But next time, he thinks. *Next time will be different.*

September 2009

Sunday

Chapter 1

Ole Christian Sund puts down the glass on the bedside table with a soft thud.

'There,' he says, smiling to the resident whose moist, stiff eyes stare out into the room. Sund wipes away a trickle of water from the corner of the man's mouth, meeting resistance only from the stubble on his chin. The skin is so pale it's practically transparent.

'Do you need anything else?' Sund says in a loud voice.

The lines in the man's face remain unchanged. Sund looks tenderly at the resident, a man who has been with them for eighteen months, but who keeps death waiting. There's not much left of him, only lifeless skin and bones, hair detaching itself from his scalp, a glassy stare that rarely changes focus. Not even the eyelids seem to be working any more.

Sund thinks, *he looks like my dad. He spent the last years of his life like this; barely aware of his surroundings. Most of the time his eyes would seek out the ceiling or some object in the room, lost in a world of their own. It's six years since he died, but it still feels like yesterday.*

Sund leaves quietly. In the corridor he meets a resident with a relative, a grandchild possibly, out for some gentle exercise. He smiles to them and takes out his mobile: it's just after five in the afternoon. A sinking feeling starts in the pit of his stomach.

Soon she'll be here to pick Ulrik up and yet another week will come and go without him being a part of his son's life. At most he'll get to hear about it – if Martine can be bothered to reply to his text messages.

He knows he's pestering her, but as he can't be there every day and hear the news from Ulrik's own mouth, at least he can hear it from hers. How the boy is, what he learned in school that day. Friends he played with at home or visited. All the things he misses out on because Martine and he stopped loving each other. Or rather – because she stopped loving him.

And though he thinks he has found a new love, he hates the thought that another man might have taken his place not just in Martine's bed, but also in Ulrik's life. That Ulrik might start to love his new dad while his real dad is just someone who makes him come to work with him when they were supposed to be having fun together.

If he could afford to turn down the extra shift, he would have. Fortunately he managed to find a fully charged electric wheelchair in Ward 4 for Ulrik to play with as long as he promised to look out for the residents. And he did, of course he did, he's such a good boy. He loves zooming around the care home. The last time Sund saw him he was doing precisely that.

But where has the little tyke got to now?

Sund's shoes make a steady sound against the floor as he starts checking passages and common rooms. In the television lounge he finds only Guttorm and a couple of the other residents embroiled in a heated argument over which channel to watch. Sund carries on looking, but can't see a happy, whooping nine-year-old in a wheelchair anywhere. He searches the corridors on both sides of the building's long H-shape. And finally, outside one of the resident's rooms, he spots his little boy who no longer seems quite so small in a place where death waits around every corner.

Sund smiles to himself as he always does when he watches his son without his being aware of it. But something is wrong with the boy in the wheelchair. His hands are wedged between his thighs. His feet are crossed. And he's rocking back and forth while his eyes seek out something on the floor, but there's nothing there except the cold light from the fluorescent tubes in the ceiling.

'Hi, Ulrik,' Sund says and stops. 'What is it? What's wrong?'

Ulrik makes no reply; he just carries on rocking. Sund bends down and strokes his hair. For a brief moment he wonders if one of the residents might have hurt him, but dismisses the thought instantly. At times they act up and lose their temper, but they would never take it out on a young boy. They all adore him.

'Hello, son,' Sund continues. 'What is it?'

No response.

Sund looks up and reads the name plate outside the room. Sees that the door is ajar.

'Have you been visiting Erna again?' he asks.

The boy just carries on rocking.

He has seen something, Sund thinks. Or heard something.

His knees are shaking as he gets up. He walks past the wheelchair and pushes open the door to the resident's room. Erna Pedersen is sitting in her chair, straight up and down as she always does. But that's not why Sund pulls up short and takes a long step backwards. It's her face, usually white and cold. Now it's discoloured. Dark, rust-coloured trails run from her eyes down her wrinkled face like a river delta. He just has time to realise what her smeared glasses are hiding before the stench of death comes rolling towards him.

Chapter 2

Henning Juul leans forwards on the cold, rough seating planks below Dælenenga Club House. Above him the clouds have dressed the sky in layers of grey that move across the city as if they have somewhere special to go. The wind, which earlier that day whipped up dust and rubbish in the streets of Oslo, has started to settle, but still contains a hint of anger.

Henning comes here as often as he can whatever the weather. He finds the place conducive to thinking, though it hurts him to see children, young and old, do the things Jonas would have been doing if he'd still been alive.

A football bounces towards a boy of eight or nine years. It rolls right past his football boots. Another boy with hair so blond it's practically white takes possession of the ball, runs towards the goal and scores.

'For Christ's sake, Adil. What do you think you're doing?'

The coach, dressed in a black tracksuit, screams till he is red in the face.

'You were supposed to stop the ball!'

The boy who has scored the goal runs past Adil and sends him a look of triumph.

'Good work, Jostein. Well spotted.'

The coach blows his whistle. The game resumes. Henning follows Adil's movements. There is something resigned about them, a sense of hopelessness. As though he'd really rather not be there.

Henning has seen Adil before. Usually he is alone. No one ever picks him up after football practice. Sometimes he is with one of the other boys from the team, but his friend isn't there now. Henning imagines he probably has better things to do on a Sunday evening.

And, strictly speaking, so do you, Henning says to himself, only he had been desperate for a change of scenery, something to distract him. But no matter how hard he tries to clear his head, the questions keep returning. What did former enforcer Tore Pulli know about the fire that killed Jonas? And was that the reason why Pulli himself had to die?

Henning's mobile goes off in his inside pocket. He takes it out and groans. The name on the display tells him something has happened and that the rest of his evening is most probably ruined.

Even so he answers it.

'Hi, Henning, it's me. Have you heard the news?'

Henning holds the mobile away from his ear. Kåre Hjeltland's voice is so loud he doesn't need a telephone. He is the most fanatical news editor Henning has ever met, he operates exclusively at a super-octane level and it doesn't help his somewhat comical appearance that he has been saddled with an aggressive form of Tourette's. Tonight his random swearing has temporarily eased off, but Henning knows that his boss's head makes sudden jerks while he talks. Hjeltland continues before Henning has time to say anything.

'An old woman has been killed in a care home right around the corner from where you live. Do you think you could go over there? I'm a bit short of people tonight.'

You're always short of people, Henning thinks, but doesn't say it and checks his watch at the same time. He had planned to go home and try to sleep for more than two hours in a row for once. But he also knows that Hjeltland doesn't have many journalists who can cover a murder right now. Iver Gundersen is still on sick leave after being beaten up in Josefinesgate a couple of weeks ago, and the Sunday evening shift at the offices of *123news.no* comprises just two staff: a duty editor who has to keep on top of everything happening in the whole world with just a keyboard and only ten fingers, and a sports journalist reporting the latest football results.

Henning takes a deep breath and looks up at the gathering clouds. *Another killing*, he thinks, with everything that that entails: more time at work and less time to look for whoever torched his flat.

And yet he sighs and says: 'All right, then.'

Chapter 3

Inspector Bjarne Brogeland parks near the entrance to the care home and steps out into the autumn evening. He slams the car door shut and takes a look around.

A narrow one-way street winds its way through towering buildings with dark windows that reach for the sky above Grünerløkka. The streetlights reflect on the wet tarmac. The road has been closed off to traffic, but curious onlookers walk slowly past on the pavement.

It's the same everywhere. People like to rubberneck, catch a glimpse of death, a hint of tomorrow's headlines so they can boast that they were there, that they saw it. Death in a body bag. Death in the eyes of a crime scene investigator dressed in white coveralls.

Bjarne has never understood the fascination with gore and wrecked cars, the desire to deliberately inflict trauma on yourself. People don't know that the image of a broken body or the smell of a crushed skull doesn't just disappear while you get on with your life, go to the cinema, to the café or drink yourself senseless. Such memories can return without warning. And once they're in your head, they'll stay there for a long time.

Bjarne's father, who was an engineer, once told him that his team killed a female polar bear when he was working on a research project near ESRO, the European Space Research

Organisation, in Ny-Ålesund in the sixties. They enticed the polar bear with food and as she stuck her head inside the wooden box where the bait was lying, she triggered a mechanism that fired the fatal shot from a sawn-off 12 bore shotgun. The polar bear had two small cubs, which were running helplessly around their mother when the team came to pick her up, Bjarne's father said. He never forgot their screams. 'They sounded just like human children, Bjarne. It might as well have been you screaming.'

*

It's a little over half an hour since Bjarne got the call. He had just put his five-year-old daughter Alisha to bed and sat down on the sofa with his wife. The message made him shudder and the feeling returns as he approaches the care home. There's something about the murder of old women.

Bjarne glances at the clouds and pulls his collar up tighter around his neck. Darker and colder times are coming.

A sign to the left of the main entrance warns potential intruders that the area has CCTV. *Good*, Bjarne thinks. Perhaps the killer was caught on camera. He turns around and looks up at the buildings opposite. Closed curtains in the flats. Closed shops and a hairdresser at street level. A café called Sound of Mu also appears to be empty though a dim light seeps out from inside. Sunday is the big day for café visits and walks in Grünerløkka so several people might have seen the killer as he left – if he left through the main entrance.

Bjarne goes inside and doesn't meet anyone until he gets out of the lift on the third floor. He stops at the red and white police tape outside Erna Pedersen's room and hears the crackling and beeping of a police radio nearby while he slips bright blue plastic covers over his shoes.

He pauses before he enters. As always he hopes the walls will talk to him, that the chaotic landscape that awaits him will show him which path to follow. And he knows that he mustn't look at the victim immediately, but concentrate on the other information in the room. He also tries as far as that's possible to ignore smells, but it's hard to block out the scent of death. He often wakes up in the middle of the night with a sense of being surrounded by this very smell.

Bjarne nods to Ann-Mari Sara, the crime scene technician, as he comes in. She is squatting on her haunches at the feet of the dead woman, her face hidden behind a camera. She lowers it and nods in return.

It took a while before Bjarne learned to appreciate Ann-Mari Sara. She is petite, barely more than 1.58 metres tall. Short, messy hair. Never wears make-up. He doesn't recall ever seeing her smile and he has noticed that she doesn't seem particularly bothered about personal hygiene. She is also immune to any attempt at charm or small talk. She rarely replies to questions that aren't work-related.

But she is undoubtedly one of the best crime scene technicians Bjarne knows. Always thorough, always alert. Always respectful. He has never seen her chew gum or try to lighten up the tense atmosphere at a crime scene with a snide remark about the victim's appearance or lifestyle. She is the most dedicated colleague Bjarne has ever come across and she is especially good at putting herself in the mind of a criminal and imagining what might have happened. If she hadn't been so brilliant at analysing a crime scene, he would have liked to recruit her as part of his own investigation team.

Now she gets up, raises the camera to her face again and presses the shutter release. Then she points to a Bible on the floor.

'I think he started with this one,' she says. 'Used it to bang . . .'

Bjarne raises his hand to stop her.

'I haven't examined it fully yet,' Sara continues. 'But it would appear to have thirteen dents on it.'

Thirteen dents, Bjarne mutters to himself. The killer must have been very angry. And he thinks that this particular book is responsible for many deaths, but never quite like this.

The room is exactly as he had imagined. Small, oppressive and cold. A bed neatly made-up, anonymous yellow curtains, speckled lino on the floor and soulless furniture. Withered flowers on the table. A TV magazine with a programme circled in red, others crossed out. Red wool. Knitting needles, some big, some small. A shot glass, unused. A glass of water on the bedside table.

The place reminds Bjarne of a prison cell. And he realises how much he dreads old age. Squashing his whole life into a room measuring three metres by three metres.

There is something oddly pleasant about the victim in the chair. She is sitting on a cushion; Bjarne can just make out a pattern of yellow and green flowers. In her lap lies the start of a sock. A small, red sock.

Bjarne leans towards her. Although he has prepared himself for the sight, he still feels a prickling sensation behind his forehead. From behind the smeared glasses, trails of congealed blood have spread across the wrinkled, eighty-three-year-old face like the branches of a tree. And where her pupils should have been, he can see something shiny; something that just about sticks out.

Two of Erna Pedersen's own knitting needles.

'Did you see the marks on her throat?'

Bjarne leans closer, moves some hair out of the way with a pen he takes from his jacket pocket.

'You're joking,' he says.

Sara raises one offended eyebrow.

'As there's not much blood at the scene, her heart must have stopped beating before the killer forced the knitting needles into her eyes.'

'So he strangled her first,' Bjarne concludes.

Sara nods.

'But there are another couple of interesting things.'

Bjarne turns to her.

'We haven't got a murder weapon,' Sara says.

'What do you mean?'

'You can't force knitting needles through someone's eyes just by hitting them with a book. The nasal bone gets in the way, as does the forehead. He must have used something else. Something heavier. Take a look at this.'

Bjarne follows Sara's index finger, which stops at the victim's brown, knitted cardigan. A fine layer of white powder has settled on her shoulders.

'I don't know what it is yet, but I'm sure that the knitting needles dented whatever it was the killer used to bash them into her head.'

'Did they go right through her skull?'

'No, that requires more force,' she says, tapping her own head with her knuckles. 'The skull is thick. And it gets thicker with age, especially in women. But it looks as if he tried.'

Bjarne pulls a face.

'Is there anything else I need to know?'

'Yes.'

She steps past him and goes over to the wall behind the chest of drawers. Points to a picture frame lying on the floor. The glass is smashed and the picture is unclear, but Bjarne can still make out a seemingly happy and contented family of four.

He asks who they are.

'Don't know,' Sara replies. 'But the odds are they're the victim's son or daughter and his or her family. I'm more interested in why the picture is on the floor and why the picture hook on the wall is bent.'

Bjarne looks up.

'If you take a look at the floor, you'll see that it's clean. You can almost see your own reflection in it.'

'So the picture was torn off the wall,' Bjarne concludes. 'Possibly today.'

Sara nods.

'If I were you, I'd ask myself why.'

Chapter 4

It takes him only ten minutes to walk from Dælenenga Sports Park to Grünerhjemmet, the care home at the bottom of Markveien. It's a redbrick building that blends in effortlessly with the rest of the architecture in Grünerløkka. Few people walking past it would know that many of the neighbourhood's most vulnerable residents live here. The exceptions are on 17 May, Norway's Constitution Day, when schoolchildren stand outside to sing the national anthem, *Ja, vi elsker dette landet*, or otherwise when an ambulance or hearse is called.

A small crowd has gathered outside the main entrance, a subspecies of *Homo sapiens* that Henning would recognise anywhere, any time. And it takes him only a moment before he spots her among the other journalists.

Nora.

The woman he once loved with every fibre of his being. The woman he failed to love like she should have been loved. The woman who was ill on the day his flat burned down and who will never forgive herself for asking Henning to look after Jonas that very night, even though it wasn't his turn. The woman who finalised their divorce shortly after that fatal night when he needed her most.

To say that being around Nora since he returned to work has been awkward would be an understatement. Their shared past as parents and the fact that they work for rival newspapers is just for starters. Another complication is that she is now dating Iver Gundersen, Henning's closest colleague at *123news*.

Nora waves and slowly makes her way towards him; she stops a metre in front of him and says 'hi'. Henning nods and smiles, sensing immediately how a protective bubble forms around them where the wind, the air, the care home – the whole world – cease to exist.

'How are you?' she asks.

Henning tilts his head towards his shoulder, first to one side, then the other.

'Not too bad,' he says.

Henning hasn't seen Nora since the end of the Tore Pulli case, but she sent him an email a couple of days ago after reading an article he had written about how and why Pulli was killed. It wasn't a long email, just two sentences, but it has been on his mind ever since.

> *Bloody good article, Henning. You're still the best.*
>
> *Hugs*
>
> *Nora*

He should have replied and thanked her for her kind words, of course he should, but he couldn't bring himself to do it. What he definitely ought to have done was to thank her for saving his life as he lay unconscious in that grave, hovering between life and death just over one week ago. Nora had realised that something was wrong when she called at his flat and got no reply. She contacted Bjarne Brogeland who took action so that Henning was eventually found and saved.

He hasn't managed to thank her for that, either.

It doesn't make things any less awkward that her voice is gentler than it used to be and that he can detect genuine concern.

'My head still hurts a bit, but I'm all right,' he adds. 'How is Iver?'

Nora imitates Henning's shrug.

'He says hi,' is all she says.

'Is he out of hospital yet?'

'Mm,' she says and nods. 'Bored rigid on the sofa.'

Nora's skin is still smooth. Her dark, shoulder-length hair falls in waves down her blue anorak, an anorak Henning has seen her wear before. He can even remember when. Between Gjendesheim and Memurubu when they hiked Besseggen Ridge on a day that started as summer, but ended in full-blown winter. The wind gusting towards them now holds some of the same promise.

'So what's happened here?' he asks.

Nora turns to the redbrick building. Again she shrugs her shoulders.

'We don't know very much yet other than the victim is an old lady.'

Nearby a journalist bursts out laughing. Henning glares at him.

'No statements yet?'

Nora shakes her head.

'I imagine the police will hold a press conference tomorrow morning,' she says with a sigh.

'Yes, I suppose they will.'

Press conferences, however, are open to everyone and tomorrow is too far away. So Henning takes out his mobile and texts Bjarne Brogeland asking him for a quick chat about the case. The reply comes in a couple of minutes later:

> *Rushed off my feet. Will call when I have two minutes.*

Just as I thought, Henning thinks. In other words: no reason to hang around.

He looks about him. It's getting late. The deadline for printed newspapers is imminent, which means that duty editors everywhere are now screaming for copy. But there is a limit to what field reporters can write tonight. The investigation has only just begun and no one knows the name of the victim or how she died, so it's still possible to be the first reporter to break the story tomorrow. All he needs is a detail or two that no one else knows yet.

Henning uses his mobile to check out the online competition and sees that none of them is reporting anything other than the obvious. Nor is anyone going to let him into the care home this late in the evening and possibly not tomorrow, either. The residents and the investigation take priority. Standing here watching police officers come and go is a waste of time.

And that gives him an idea. What about the staff? And the visitors? How will they get out of the building tonight?

Henning catches Nora's eye and he signals that he's off. But going home is the last thing on his mind.

Chapter 5

A care worker in a white uniform sits on a chair outside the television lounge picking his nails. He flicks away a bit of skin that lands on the floor. Then he jumps up as though the seat has suddenly got hot.

Bjarne Brogeland is standing in front of him.

'Ole Christian Sund?'

The man nods and rubs his neck with his right hand. Sund has a sparse, blond moustache on his acne-scarred face. His eyebrows meet in the middle. His thin arms stick out from the loose-fitting sleeves.

'How is your son?' Bjarne says, finding himself a chair and indicating to Sund to sit down again.

'I don't know,' the care worker says, looking glum. 'He's with his mum now, but she's not replying to my texts. But I'm sure he's fine with her.'

'Yes, mums are great at that sort of thing,' Bjarne says, smiling sympathetically. 'I presume you've been offered counselling?'

Bjarne takes out his notebook and pen.

'We have. But Martine, Ulrik's mum, is a psychologist and no one knows Ulrik better than her, so—'

'I understand,' Bjarne says. 'But we'll want to talk to him as soon as possible. He might have seen something important.'

Sund nods and rakes a hand through his long, blond fringe.

'I've never seen him like that,' he whispers. 'He seemed almost in a trance.'

'How do you mean?'

'He just sat there. Rocking back and forth. His eyes were all glazed and distant.'

Sund's face takes on a sad, anxious expression.

'Did he say anything to you?'

'Not straightaway. But when I came back out from Erna Pedersen's room, he muttered something about fractions.'

'Fractions?'

'Yes. He kept repeating it. Fractions, fractions, fractions.'

Bjarne notes down the word in capital letters.

'Now he's been very excited about his maths homework recently so it might have something to do with that. What do I know?'

'How old is he?'

'He's nine.'

Bjarne nods.

'I won't keep you for very much longer,' he says. 'But do you have any idea who might have done this?'

Sund heaves a sigh.

'No.'

'Can you think of anyone who didn't like her?'

Sund mulls it over.

'I don't think so.'

'Have there been any disagreements here recently? Did someone get angry or upset with her?'

Again Sund racks his brains.

'Sometimes our residents get agitated and their discussions heated. But I really don't think that anyone would hurt Erna Pedersen. She never made a fuss; she was quite frail and unwell. And if she hadn't died like . . . like this, she would have died soon, anyway.'

Bjarne scratches his head with the pen. A female care worker walks past them. Sund takes out his mobile and checks for new messages. Then he turns it off and puts it away.

'Did you notice if anyone went to her room today?'

Sund shifts slightly on the chair.

'I was working mainly at the other end of the corridor. A lot of staff are off sick at the moment.'

Bjarne nods again.

'I can see from the visitors' log that no one visited her today. Do you know what it was usually like? Did she have a lot of visitors?'

'You're better off asking Daniel, Daniel Nielsen. He was her primary care worker. But, no, I don't think they were queuing round the block, to be honest.'

Bjarne writes down Nielsen's name and circles it.

'Are you aware of any relatives who might have visited her from time to time?'

'If they did, it can't have been very often. I barely know what her son looks like.'

'So she has a son?'

Sund nods.

Bjarne writes 'son's family in broken photograph?' on his notepad.

'The camera outside the main entrance,' he continues. 'Do you happen to know if it records?'

Sund shakes his head.

'It's only there so we can see who rings the bell outside regular visiting hours.'

'So people can come and go as they please?'

'They can.'

Bjarne nods again.

'Did something unusual happen here today? Anything out of the ordinary?'

Sund thinks about it.

'The Volunteer Service people were here in the afternoon to play and sing for the residents.'

'Go on?'

'They come once a fortnight.'

'I see. Are they popular?'

'Yes, very.'

'Did Erna Pedersen usually join in?'

'Yes, but I don't think I saw her there today.'

Bjarne makes another note.

'How many people usually come from the Volunteer Service?'

'Five or six, I think.'

Bjarne has met members of the Volunteer Service before, people of all ages who help others in return for no money at all. They're unlikely to be the type to force knitting needles into the head of an old lady, Bjarne thinks, but he still makes a note of the name of the service in capital letters with an arrow pointing to it.

'Okay,' he says, getting up. 'I can imagine that you want to get home and check on your son. But please think about what you saw here today, especially if something strikes you as a little odd or unusual. Anything that might be of interest.'

'Will do,' Sund says, taking the card Bjarne hands him. Then he hurries towards the lift while switching on his mobile to check for new messages. It doesn't even have time to beep before he shakes his head in despair.

Chapter 6

In the old days Henning used to go running along the River Aker late at night, though he would sometimes come across people he would rather not meet after the hours of darkness. He would always jog straight past them and ignore their offers of all sorts of dubious merchandise. Even so, it was never a very pleasant experience.

A similar unease comes over him as he walks past Riverside, the café at the bottom of Markveien, to get round to the back of Grünerhjemmet. But there are no unsavoury characters around tonight, only the river, which winds its way down to Oslo Fjord under a bridge.

It could have been a picture postcard of the city. There are old ruins and tall trees on the far side of the river. On warm summer days people sit in Riverside or on the grassy bank leading down to the water and let life and the river flow past. But the area around the mouth of the Aker has become a haven for drug dealers and their customers. Once upon a time such people would have hidden in the shadows because it was shameful both to sell and to buy drugs, but now everything is out in the open and no one seems to care. The police know what goes on, but don't have the resources to do anything about it. And if one dealer is arrested, another will take his place the next day.

Henning follows the road around the care home where

bushes as lifeless as the residents inside have been planted along the walls. He knows how hard it is to get a place in a care home these days. You practically have to have one foot in the grave already. It means that many vulnerable people in Oslo and in the rest of Norway have to rely on self-sacrificing relatives or visits from care workers in their own homes.

Henning wanders around the car park while he waits for someone to emerge from the back entrance. For the first fifteen minutes nothing happens. He looks at his watch. Slowly 9 p.m. turns into 9.30. In his former life he might have lit a cigarette – or fourteen – while he waited, but he stopped smoking completely after the fire. There's something about flames and embers. He can't look at them without seeing his son's eyes in all the red and orange.

The door opens and a woman comes out. She has brown hair and is wearing a beige coat.

'Excuse me,' Henning says, rushing towards her. She instinctively slows down.

'Do you work here?' he asks.

The woman's expression immediately becomes guarded as she reluctantly replies 'yes'. Henning knows that the burn scars on his face can make him look scary, especially in the dark, so he follows up his assertive opening with a smile that's intended to be disarming. The woman walks off.

'Sorry, but you'll have to talk to someone else,' she calls out.

'I—'

'I don't talk to people like you.'

Henning is left standing with a reply that withers on the tip of his tongue.

Ten minutes later a man appears. He is happy to stop, but neither speaks nor understands Norwegian terribly well. It doesn't, however, prevent him from chatting and smiling. Henning eventually works out that the man has washed the floors on the ground and first floors tonight, but he doesn't know anything about what happened on the floors higher up.

'Who lives on the third floor?' Henning asks him.

'All the mad people,' the man says.

Henning frowns.

'The mad people?'

'Yes, the ones who've gone gaga.'

The man smiles and reveals a row of bright white teeth.

'Right,' Henning says.

The man gives him a thumbs-up before he gets on his bicycle and rides off.

So the victim suffered from dementia, Henning concludes. It's not a story in itself, but it's a useful detail to include. He needs more.

Henning knows that care staff have a duty of confidentiality, but it's not a rule that has bothered him before. In his experience some people simply enjoy chatting. It's just a question of finding them. Working on them.

Not so easy on a Sunday night.

A woman in a hijab comes out. Again Henning smiles, but she ignores him. A little later he tries a man with dark stubble, but learns only that he has been to visit his mother and is annoyed that he missed the Brann versus Vålerenga match on TV.

Henning is about to call it a day and crosses his fingers that *6tiermes7* – his secret Internet source in the police – can give him some information when a man in a black leather jacket and trousers comes out. His hair, long and blond, swings rhythmically from side to side as he quickly crosses the car park. Henning thinks he recognises him from somewhere and goes up to him.

'Hi, my name is Henning Juul. I work for *123news*. Could I have a word with you?'

The man glances at Henning.

'I'm busy,' he says.

'I can walk with you if that's more convenient?'

The man still doesn't say anything, but Henning can see there are signs of recognition in his face too.

'What's going on up there?' Henning asks.

The man looks at him quickly.

'I won't quote you. I'm just trying to find out what happened. I hear someone killed a demented old lady?'

The man glances at him again.

'Sorry,' he says. 'But I have to get home. My son—'

The man breaks off halfway through the sentence and his eyes flicker. Henning continues to follow him.

'Okay, fine,' Henning says. 'But here's . . . '

He starts to jog as he produces a business card from his pocket. 'If there's anything you want to tell me, on or off the record, then just give me a call. Any time. Okay?'

Reluctantly the man takes the card Henning is holding out.

'Thank you. Then I won't keep you any longer. I hope your son isn't asleep yet.'

He smiles after the man who looks over his shoulder several times before he disappears in the night. There, Henning thinks, was an interesting person, someone who stands out from the crowd. A staff member who didn't look exhausted after working, but upset. Or possibly frightened.

For the next hour Henning tries to speak to more people, then he goes home. He sits down in front of his laptop hoping to chat to *6tiermes7*, a hope that gradually diminishes as the clock approaches midnight. A little desperate now, Henning sends Bjarne Brogeland a few more text messages. He doesn't give up before his police contact rings him back.

'You're a pest,' Brogeland says.

'You said you'd call when you had two minutes.'

The roar of traffic mingles with the sound of Brogeland's exasperation.

'Are you on your way home?'

'Wow, you should've been a detective, Henning. It's five to one in the morning.'

'Then let's make it quick. Demented old woman found killed. What happened?'

'Your version is fine.'

'Mm. But she wasn't shot or someone would have heard it. And it would've been messy. So, for the same reason, I don't think she was stabbed, either, because then you would already have arrested the killer.'

'Who says we haven't?'

'You do. I can tell from your voice. You're exhausted. You sound defeated. You wouldn't if the case had been solved.'

Brogeland sighs.

'I can't give you much, Henning. Tactical considerations, you know.'

'Mm. What if I were to tell you that I spoke to a staff member tonight, a man with long, blond hair who looked like he'd seen the grim reaper—'

'Did he talk to you?' Brogeland interrupts him.

Henning makes no reply.

'I hope he didn't say anything?'

Henning doesn't reply immediately.

'He said he had to hurry home to his son.'

'Damn,' Brogeland hisses softly down the phone. Seconds pass. Henning knows better than to ruin a moment like this with more questions.

Finally Brogeland heaves a sigh. And when he pulls over at a bus stop and starts talking, Henning fills a whole A4 sheet with a story that, back in the old days when he was a cynical and less sensitive reporter, he would have summarised in three words:

GRANNY BRUTALLY SLAIN.

Monday

Chapter 7

She chose the ring tone because it reminded her of a fabulous party with a deluge of presents. Even so the sound of her mobile is never a welcome intrusion.

Trine Juul-Osmundsen, Secretary of State for Justice, flings out her arm towards the bedside table and tries to silence her phone before the noise wakes up Pål Fredrik, who often complains that she always gets up at the crack of dawn. She is too tired to open her eyes while she fumbles for the rectangular instrument of torture. Finally she gets hold of it and slides her thumb across the screen. Peace at last.

Trine sinks back on her pillow. How many hours of sleep did she manage this time?

Far too few.

She had woken up in the middle of the night, soaked in sweat. In her dream she had found herself in a big, open space surrounded by a large crowd. She knew she couldn't move her hands or her arms, but she still tried to free herself, calmly at first then with rising panic. She turned her head to one side and gasped as she looked up at the grey sky. Something metallic was gleaming above her and she could see that it was sharp. Cheers broke out just as she saw the rope being cut and the huge blade come crashing down towards her. She knew it was the last thing she would ever see; the feeling was so strong, so vivid that she thought she must have died and was still clasping her neck when the terror of her nightmare woke her up and she had to remind herself to breathe.

Trine turns over to look at Pål Fredrik who is snoring away with his mouth half open. Sometimes he will ask what her night terrors were about and every time she gives a vague answer or tries to make light of them before she asks him a question in return in the hope it will distract him. And every time he replies: 'I dreamt about you, darling. I only ever dream about you.' And then he smiles, that remarkably charming smile of his that she couldn't help falling in love with one evening God knows how many years ago when they met in Lillehammer at a conference about economic crime.

She resists the urge to sneak a couple of minutes in his embrace before the day claims her. This tall, slim, muscular man who when he is awake is a bundle of energy, never happier than when he is on a bike or climbing a mountain. Now he is far away in a carefree slumber.

Trine smiles tenderly; she has always envied her husband his ability to sleep. She can't remember when she was last able just to close her eyes and drift off. She lies awake at night, though she tries not to think about that day's events, the people and the stories she encountered, tomorrow's challenges and how she will meet them. Her brain refuses to go into hibernation mode. There is rarely or never room for personal reflection even though Pål Fredrik is good at giving her something to smile about during the night before he turns over on his side and goes to sleep.

Another reason Trine dreads sleep is that her nightmares seem to have a recurrent theme. Things she doesn't want to dream about. Things she doesn't want to remember.

She can see that it's light outside, but it's not as bright as it was yesterday. Autumn is upon them and the mere thought of it makes it harder to leave the bed. But she forces herself to sit up, stretches out her arms and opens up her lungs, exhaling slowly in a yawn. Naked, she shuffles out into the passage, into the bathroom and steps under the shower where she ponders what lies in store for her this week.

She is off to Sandvika Police Station later today where the police's IT support and purchasing services department is presenting a technical solution for electronic monitoring of people who have been served with non-contact orders. This will be followed by lunch at the Prime Minister's office and a Cabinet meeting. Tomorrow she is making a visit to Bruvoll Prison and later she will open a new children's home in Oslo. She's also going on a trip to Kongsvinger in eastern Norway to discuss initiatives to strengthen border control. And she has a feeling she is due to speak about police preparedness in this Wednesday's question time in Parliament.

It's going to be a busy week.

When she has dried herself, applied body lotion and not too heavy make-up, she returns to the bedroom to select today's skirt, blouse and jacket. On her way to the kitchen she picks up her mobile, wakes the screen up purely out of habit, but stops in her tracks when she sees that she has already received a call from a *VG* journalist. Before 6.30 in the morning.

The same man had tried to call her last night, but she never answers calls or requests from the fourth estate on Sundays. Or before she has had her first cup of coffee.

So she goes to the kitchen, turns on the coffee machine and adds ground coffee and water. She waits until the light stops flashing and presses a button with a picture of a miniature cup. Soon she is inhaling the aroma of an espresso, something that usually wakes her up.

Then her mobile rings again.

Trine puts down her cup. This time it's a reporter from *Dagbladet*. She sighs and ignores the call. When will they learn that all requests must go through her press office? Trine decides to get a new mobile number – again. Far too many people in the media know it even though she changes it regularly. Someone in her department is clearly keen to curry favour with the press. As if the press has ever done anything to help her.

Trine has gone over to the fridge to get some orange juice and cream cheese when her mobile starts ringing again. *Nettavisen* this time.

She stops and stares at the display. Three calls this early.

Something must have happened.

Trine is about to go to her study to check the Internet newspapers when her mobile lights up again and beeps. A text message. A moment later another one arrives. And another one. Trine is in the process of opening the first message when the ringing of the doorbell makes her jump.

A visitor at this hour?

Trine pulls her jacket tightly around her, goes into the living room and peeks out from behind the white curtains. There is a reporter outside with a pen and notepad in his hands. A photographer stands right behind him with the camera ready at head height.

But what piques her curiosity, what makes her particularly anxious, is the sight of many cars arriving outside the house she and Pål Fredrik bought in Ullern in west Oslo for almost eighteen million kroner last year. She sees that several of the cars bear the logos of NRK and TV2. A slightly bigger car with a satellite dish on its roof pulls up and parks outside her front door.

Not only has something major happened, Trine realises. Something is terribly, terribly wrong.

Chapter 8

Late to bed, early to rise.

That's how it has turned out, Bjarne Brogeland concludes, as he sits in his car on his way to work – again. And sometimes that is just the way it has to be. He resigned himself to it long ago and usually he loves giving his all to his work as an investigator. Use his body and his brain to solve a case and then move on to the next one. Do his bit to help make Oslo a city that's safe to grow up and live in.

But even Bjarne, who has been fit and healthy all his life, who has always watched his diet and rarely poisons his body with alcohol, has started noticing how life as a police officer in the capital takes its toll on him. More importantly it takes its toll on those about him, his family, because he is seldom with them when they get up or go to bed. And when he finally gets home, he is usually so tired and worn out that he can't be bothered or doesn't feel like doing anything. He just wants to relax. Enjoy some peace and quiet.

He hasn't told anyone, not even Anita, that he has written but not yet sent off an application to Vestfold Police. They have a six-month vacancy for a Head of Investigation starting in just four weeks. The current post holder is taking leave to write a book; a crime novel, Bjarne believes. Bjarne thinks this job could give him an opportunity to gain valuable management experience. Everything is about experience.

And that's the rub. He hasn't been a detective for very long, but he has been with the police force all his life and is regarded as a safe pair of hands. He has studied management and he has recently made a name for himself with his analytical skills. Previously he always felt he had something to prove whenever he spoke up in a meeting, especially to his boss Arild Gjerstad, Head of Investigation, but he has got over that, thank God.

He has no idea how Anita would react if he were to get the job. It would mean him being away from home, from her and Alisha even more; it would take him further away from the ideal of family life that is so important to his wife. Isn't he making enough sacrifices as it is?

He can see it in his daughter's eyes and hear it in the conversation around the kitchen table on the rare occasions they are all there at the same time. He has absolutely no idea how she is getting on. What she learns at nursery, who her friends are. Who is mean to her and who is nice. It's not easy being a kid, he remembers that from his own childhood. But it's not easy being a dad, either. Or a dad and a policeman at the same time.

Alisha deigned to let him put her to bed last night as long as he played with her first. Playing covers everything that makes her laugh out loud. He read to her from a Karsten and Petra book, scratched her on the back with sharp nails, something she loves. But he wasn't allowed to lie next to her when she finally settled down. Only Anita gets to do that.

And maybe it makes no difference how much he plays and reads and scratches. He will always come second. And, yes, that's still a spot on the podium, but Bjarne has never enjoyed not being first. He has always loathed the thought that someone might be better at something than he is.

I need more hours in the day, he thinks, and turns off towards Grønland. If you could buy time, he would have ordered it by the shed load. Then there would be time for trips to Legoland, a seaside holiday to Sørlandet, he could have gone camping in the mountains, caught those fish. He could have given Anita the children she always said she wanted.

But if he's going to do his job properly, if he's going to be as good a policeman as he wants to be, then he has to live the job. He has to be the job. And the job has to be him. All of him.

And soon they will turn forty, both him and Anita. And even if time isn't running out for him, then it is definitely running out for her. Exactly what that means they haven't yet sat down to discuss. They haven't had the time.

Bjarne met Anita at Idretthøgskolen, the Norwegian School of Sports Sciences, in the mid-nineties. She was in the year below him and not really his type; she was into Aerosmith and TV soaps such as *Beverly Hills 90210* and *Melrose Place*, she was twenty-two centimetres shorter than him and played football from time to time. But with her shoulder-length blonde hair, a slightly crooked front tooth and her echoing, infectious laughter, she grew increasingly irresistible to him. He was happy to ignore the fact that she had grown up in Hamar and kept declaring her intention to move back east, to the home of the Hamar Olympic Hall even though she was born in the beautiful scenic fishing village of Henningsvær in the Lofoten Archipelago. She had charm. The raw charm of

Arctic Norway. He simply had to have her.

At first she resisted him, primarily because she already had a boyfriend, but she surprised him by going for what she could get, rather than holding on to what she had. Six years later they got married, and because of Bjarne's job they now live in a semi-detached house on Tennisveien in Slemdal. Their car is a Volvo estate with a fan belt that never stops complaining. They don't have a holiday cabin and they don't have a dog, either, but they have a daughter whom he would happily throw himself under a bus to protect. Even if he is only second-best.

You've been lucky, he tells himself, and watches the grey band of tarmac that stretches out in front of him. He sees people going to work, cyclists jumping a red light and grim-faced pedestrians. The wind urges them on. Bjarne can feel the gusts against the car. A new spell of bad weather sails towards the city over the pointed roof of Oslo Plaza Hotel.

It's going to be a cold day, Bjarne forecasts, but hopefully a productive one, even though they didn't learn much about the eighty-three-year-old victim last night. A widow, retired teacher, born and raised in Jessheim, moved to Oslo in the early nineties. She has a son who doesn't visit her very often, but it was him in the photograph, Tom Sverre Pedersen, and his family. He is a doctor and lives in Vindern. And the photograph of him and his family had indeed been torn down and smashed.

I'm sure it's important, Bjarne thinks, but for reasons he has yet to find out. What he finds most peculiar about the case so far is that no one seems to have seen or heard anything. Neither the care workers nor any other staff had noticed if anyone entered or left Erna Pedersen's room that afternoon. And no one Bjarne spoke to had had a bad word to say about the victim. She never made a fuss, barely communicated with anyone and spent most of her time knitting. An old lady who kept herself to herself and did what little she was capable of.

However, we still have lots of people to interview, Bjarne thinks. Her primary care worker, for example. Daniel Nielsen. The man who looked after her most of the time. The people from the Volunteer Service. And not least – the little boy playing on the wheelchair who discovered the body. He might have bumped into the killer. Someone must have seen something. People in the street. Residents in neighbouring buildings.

We've only just scratched the surface, Bjarne predicts, as Oslo Police Station appears to his left with its dirt-grey walls and shiny clean windows. And he feels genuinely excited at the prospect; he is looking forward to getting stuck into a new case.

Oh yes, he thinks with a smile as he drives into the underground car park.

You still love this job.

Chapter 9

Trine Juul-Osmundsen runs to her study, flips open the screen of her laptop and keeps hitting the Internet icon until the computer finally finds the network and downloads the front page of *VG Nett*. What she sees makes her gasp.

There is a huge close-up of her face under the headline:

ACCUSED OF SEXUAL ASSAULT

Justice Secretary Trine Juul-Osmundsen accused of sexually assaulting a young, male politician.

What the hell?

Trine clicks on the article while her heart starts to pound. The opening sentence merely repeats the lead-in. What the hell is going on, Trine thinks again as she reads on.

The incident is alleged to have taken place at the Labour Party conference in Kristiansand last autumn where earlier that day Juul-Osmundsen had given a firebrand speech. Several commentators later said that the Justice Secretary was starting to look like prime ministerial material, but the question is now if that is still a realistic prospect. *VG* has spoken to sources who claim that on the night in question Juul-Osmundsen assaulted a young politician, who later is said to have tried to resolve the incident with her – without success.

'What's going on?'

Trine jumps and spins around, slamming shut the laptop a little harder than she intended. She positions herself in front of the desk and looks at her husband who has come into her study dressed in only blue and black striped pyjama bottoms. His short grey hair stands up and he still has sleep in his eyes. A fine layer of stubble covers his cheeks with a mask of something grey and dark, while the skin on his face reveals many active hours spent in the open air. The muscles in his throat and neck are taut like steel wire.

Even after four years of marriage Trine still feels warm all over whenever she sees him like this, rough, unshaven and shirtless. But his inquisitive eyes, still sleepy, bore into her and leave an open, stinging wound.

'I thought I heard the doorbell?' he says.

Trine looks at him, but her gaze soon slips away and fails to find anything to settle on. Now she knows why there is a pack of journalists outside. And why more are bound to turn up.

'Yes,' she says.

'This early?'

'M-hm,' she replies, absent-minded, but she still can't bear to look at him; she has no idea what to say. How can she explain to him what has happened and what they are about

52

to be subjected to?

Trine starts to walk past him when he puts out his arm to stop her.

'Hey,' he says. 'Good morning.'

He smiles and tries to hug her, but Trine can't cope with it. Not now. So she frees herself from his strong arms and says she is running late. Fortunately he buys her story.

Trine goes into the kitchen where she stops and rests her palms heavily on the worktop while she mutters curses under her breath. She continues swearing until she hears her husband's voice again.

'I'm just taking a shower.'

He is on his way to the bathroom when Trine says his name and straightens up. Pål Fredrik stops. She takes a step towards him and sees the look in his eyes, which she knows will change as soon as she starts talking. The doorbell rings again, but Trine doesn't take her eyes off him.

'Aren't you going to answer that?' he asks her, sounding baffled.

'No,' she says quietly.

He glances at the front door.

'Do you want me to get it?'

Trine shakes her head. She can feel her throat tighten.

'I need to ask you a favour,' she whispers and faces him.

'Okay?' he replies slowly. 'What is it?'

Words, sentences – even the air – stop their journey across Trine's lips.

'What is it?' he repeats.

She clears her throat: 'Don't read anything they write about me in the papers today.'

Trine waits until she can hear the sound of running water before she goes back to her study, closes the door behind her and hits a key on her mobile.

'Pick up, Harald,' she says as she paces up and down the floor.

Harald Ullevik has been Trine's closest and most important sparring partner for the almost three years she has been Secretary of State for Justice. Always wise and knowledgeable. Always warm and friendly. Some of the speeches he has written for her have been brilliantly insightful and rich in persuasive arguments that she was proud to take the credit for. Several times his elephantine memory has rescued her from embarrassing situations. In fact he has been as much of an adviser to her as a Junior Minister. At times he has practically been acting Secretary, willing to stand in for her whenever she needed it. If anyone can help her out of this mess, it's him.

'Hi, Trine.'

As always Ullevik's voice sounds bright.

'Have you seen today's *VG*?' Trine says immediately.

'No,' he says after a brief hesitation. 'But they've just called me with a summary. I told them to get lost, obviously. We have to draw the line somewhere.'

Trine flings out her other hand.

'Half of Norway's media is in my doorstep, Harald. I don't know what to do.'

'Trine,' Ullevik says. 'Calm down, it'll be all right.'

Usually his rock solid voice can convince her that

everything will indeed be all right. But right now she struggles to believe him.

'They're going to bombard you with questions once you leave your house, but for God's sake don't start arguing with them. Don't say anything until we've looked at this together and agreed a strategy.'

Trine heaves a sigh and thinks about Pål Fredrik, wondering if the water can wash away some of the shock and the disbelief she saw in his eyes. When she took another step towards him to assure him that the accusations were not true, he simply turned away.

'It'll be all right,' Ullevik reassures her again. 'You get yourself to work in one piece and we'll deal with this together.'

Trine continues to listen to the echo of his voice before she utters an 'okay' and hangs up. When the silence returns, she realises that her knees are threatening to buckle under her. She orders them to lock. Then she swallows something viscous and thick that is stuck in her throat, disconnects the laptop, puts it in her bag and hurries out into the hallway. She stops in front of the hall mirror, smooths a crease in her jacket and studies her face, her hair and her eyes. She decides she is wearing too much make-up and starts to wipe off the lipstick she applied earlier, but she is desperate to get out of the house, and she doesn't want to wait for Pål Fredrik to come out of the shower so she can stare into the depths of his shocked and horrified eyes.

She quickly checks her shoes to see if they are clean. Then she braces herself. *Put on a brave face. And keep your mouth shut.*

Chapter 10

The morning is still only a pale outline over the roofs when Henning wakes up from his usual spot on the sofa. His face is squashed into one of the cushions and he can almost feel the imprint on his cheek.

He stayed up later than he had planned, but he didn't need coffee to keep him awake. The story he had ready for publication at 8 a.m. practically wrote itself. He said only that the victim was killed and mutilated, a headline he knew would attract hits. He had agreed with Bjarne Brogeland to keep back the grotesque details and he isn't sure that he will ever make them public. The readers don't need to know what was done to Erna Pedersen's eyes.

Henning gets up to check that the story has been uploaded and taken its rightful place at the top of the front page.

It's not there.

Instead he is shocked to read what his sister Trine Juul-Osmundsen has been accused of. He quickly gets dressed and finds the telephone number of Karl Ove Marcussen in Helgesensgate. It takes a few seconds before a man's voice answers with a sleepy 'yes'.

'Hi, my name is Henning Juul. I'm Christine's, your neighbour's, son. You're the building's caretaker, aren't you?'

'Yes.'

'Great. I've a massive favour to ask you.'

*

Trine steps out into a roar of voices that stops her in her tracks. A thousand words and sentences are hurled at her, but even if she tried, she wouldn't be able to tell the questions apart.

Her bodyguards manage to clear a narrow path for her and she keeps her eyes firmly on the ground. She is aware of the presence of a photographer who has climbed a tree in her neighbour's garden. His camera is aimed at her. It feels as if he is about to shoot her.

Trine would never have believed there was room for that many people outside her house. Her black government car appears in front of her. She aims for the open door on the right-hand side while her bodyguards try to keep the press at bay. They are fairly successful, she manages to get inside, but even though the window behind which she is hiding is tinted, the flashlights continue to go off.

The car pulls away. Trine turns around to see if they are being followed.

'Yep, they're after us,' Trine's driver says and looks for her eyes in the rear-view mirror.

Trine has always liked her driver, a middle-aged man who hasn't had a single day off sick during the three years she has been Justice Secretary. No matter what has happened, he greets her with a calm and pleasant voice. The car is a safe haven where she can take some time out. She likes being in the car, talking to him, inhaling his warm smell, but she doesn't know if he has seen today's headlines yet and she doesn't have the energy to discuss them with anyone before she has to.

Trine clutches her mobile, which vibrates and beeps every two seconds. She feels like kicking a hole in the seat in front of her. Her mood worsens when she realises that her tights have laddered below the knee. *Trine in a hole* will probably be the headline in some newspaper soon. And how they'll laugh at the editorial offices. Fortunately she is not due in Parliament until later today and she knows they sell tights in the Parliament shop.

Trine usually spends her time in the car catching up on the news, but not today. She dreads the moment when the car stops and she will have to get out and face the vultures. She spots the media the moment the car pulls up in front of H Block in the government district.

Trine tries to focus on the sound of her own footsteps as she walks the short distance to the entrance. Click, click, quick and hard. Words and predictable questions rise and fall before rising again because she doesn't answer. The sound waves follow her even after the security guard has admitted her. As she enters the lift and the doors close behind her, the noise instantly disappears. It is like wearing noise-cancelling headphones. Suddenly she can hear her own hectic breathing.

Trine closes her eyes as the lift sweeps her upwards. She doesn't open them again until it pings and the doors slide open.

*

As soon as she steps out into the corridor, she feels the probing looks of people coming in the opposite direction. Normally she would have met them with her head held high and a friendly nod. But not today. She is burning up inside and her rage expresses itself as angry lines around her eyes. *Your feet*, she thinks. *Concentrate on your feet.*

At the door to the wing where Trine and the administration of the Justice Department have their offices, she is met by Katarina Hatlem, her Director of Communications. She ushers Trine in while she continues to talk on her phone.

'I understand,' she says. 'But Trine isn't here yet. We'll have to get back to you—'

Hatlem rolls her eyes.

'Fine,' she says eventually. 'The people's demand has been duly noted. I'm going into a meeting now. Goodbye.'

Then she hangs up and shakes her head so her long red curls bounce from side to side.

Over time Katarina Hatlem has become one of Trine's closest friends. Trine can talk to her about anything, but the main reason she wanted Katarina as her Director of Communications was that she had worked for the Norwegian Broadcasting Corporation, NRK, for many years. She knows the media inside out.

Trine rushes down the corridor leading to her office, but slows down when she reaches the portrait wall where former Justice Secretaries smile at her from gilded frames. It is a world dominated by men, but with a stronger female presence in the last two or three decades. The pictures act as a reminder of how quickly a life in politics can change. Many of the Ministers resigned under a cloud, Trine remembers, and some of them fell hard. She knows that her department has already prepared a framed picture of her in case her departure turns out to be sudden. They have even bought her leaving present. It is like working under the sword of Damocles.

She speeds up, enters her office and hangs her jacket on a coat stand behind her desk.

'Is everyone in yet?' she says brusquely.

'Everyone who needs to be here, yes,' Hatlem says.

'Okay, let's start the meeting.'

Hatlem leaves the moment Harald Ullevik enters. He stops and says 'hi' to Trine with a warm gaze that, like the sound of his voice earlier, makes her throat feel tight and raw. She forces herself to look at something other than the elegant man in front of her. With his short, greying hair and his perfect posture Harald Ullevik could easily feature in a Dressmann ad. At a party once Katarina Hatlem compared him to Harrison Ford and the forty-six-year-old Junior Minister is probably the man in this building who attracts the most attention – also from other men.

'How was it?' he asks. 'Was it as bad as you feared?'

'Worse,' Trine snorts and turns away from him.

'But it went okay? You didn't say anything?'

Trine shakes her head.

'Good,' he says and steps closer to the large boardroom table. 'The other Under Secretaries are out of the office today, not that it makes much difference. And you won't be needing these,' he says, picking up a pile of newspaper cuttings that the press office has left for her on the table. 'The only thing the media are interested in right now is how you're going to respond to the allegations. So we need to find out what you're going to say – if, indeed, you're going to say anything at all.'

Ullevik tosses aside the pile, takes a seat at the table and pours some water into a glass. Trine doesn't feel like sitting down until everyone else has taken their places. It doesn't take long before she hears more footsteps approaching.

Permanent Secretary Hilde Bye enters with Trine's political adviser, Truls Ove Henriksen, at her heel. They nod to Trine and mutter an almost synchronised 'good morning'. Then they take their usual seats around the table and have time to pour themselves coffee before Katarina Hatlem enters and closes the door behind her.

Trine sits down and puts her hand on today's diary print-out. Everyone around the table looks as if they are waiting for Trine to say something, but she doesn't know where to begin. She grabs hold of the press cuttings and stabs her finger so hard at the top sheet that it bends.

'Is this really legal?' she says.

'Is what legal?' asks the Permanent Secretary, a woman who has been in charge of the Justice Department's administration for many years, interrupted only by a three-year period when she was District Governor on Svalbard. Trine has never got on with Hilde Bye, but has never quite understood why. Perhaps it's just a difference in age. Trine has always detected a hint of scepticism in Bye's eyes and it hasn't faded now.

'I haven't read everything yet,' Trine says. 'But in its lead story, *VG* refers to sources its reporter has spoken to. Can you really publish any allegation as long as two sources are prepared to back it up? No matter what the subject matter is?'

Trine looks around the table for an answer.

'Are you saying the story isn't true?'

Trine looks daggers at the Permanent Secretary's raven black hair.

'That's exactly what I'm saying.'

Trine had been asked to say a few words at Hilde Bye's recent fiftieth birthday party. She had sweated over her keyboard trying to think of something nice because it was so much easier to mention all the things Hilde Bye wasn't. Not especially friendly, not especially talented – jobwise or with people. Too enamoured with being in charge.

'But if that's the case,' says Truls Ove Henriksen, 'then that's what you say. That the allegations are false.'

'If that's the case', Trine snarls to herself and glares at the bald man. She knows what he is really thinking, this wet rag of a political adviser who was foisted on her when she was made a Minister three years ago. She had been so overcome by her unexpected appointment that she had agreed to everything her party wanted. Such as having a political adviser, a man she didn't know very well, but who was part of the political horse-trading after the election – because he had previously been the secretary of the Labour Party's branch in Trom.

'I'm not going to dignify this tabloid tosh by commenting on it,' she says, jabbing her finger on the file again.

'But you're going to have to,' Katarina Hatlem argues. 'The media won't stop clamouring until they get something and you won't be able to go anywhere or do anything without this becoming the story.'

'I'll talk to the Prime Minister's office and get them to drop you from question time on Wednesday,' Ullevik says.

'That's probably wise,' Hatlem says and nods. 'I also think we should issue a press release as soon as possible—'

'No,' Trine interrupts her and clenches her fists so hard her knuckles go white.

'No to what?'

'We're not going to issue a press release. If I have to refute these allegations, then they've already won. I'm being accused of something I haven't done, and I can't respond without knowing the source. Nor has the matter been reported to the police.'

'Not yet.'

'What are you saying?' says Trine, glowering at her political adviser.

'I'm just saying that could happen before we know it. There'll certainly be a public demand for it.'

Trine snorts.

'This is bullshit,' she shouts. 'I've no idea where it's coming from. But I can promise you, I'm going to find out.'

Harald Ullevik clears his throat.

'Let's take this one step at a time,' he says, calmly. 'This incident is supposed to have taken place at last year's party conference in Kristiansand. Everyone who has ever attended a party conference knows that things go on there, all sorts of things.'

'Are you saying that—'

'No, no, Trine, I'm not saying anything, but I know what people will think. That's why I'm asking you: what do you remember from that day?'

Trine exhales hard through her mouth while she thinks back. She has been to so many party conferences that they all blur together.

'Not very much. But I know what I didn't do.'

Silence falls around the table. Her Permanent Secretary sips her coffee while she glances furtively at Henriksen across the table. *She has doubts*, Trine thinks. *That woman doesn't believe me.*

'Okay, I have a suggestion,' Katarina Hatlem says. 'Even though this story is very much about you, we won't involve you at this stage. We'll deal with each press request in turn and repeat the same message: that you refuse to respond to anonymous allegations, you're not going to waste your time on this, and blah blah blah. If that doesn't take the sting out of what's coming towards you, we'll select one or two journalists we know are sympathetic towards us and give them a little more.'

'There *is* nothing more,' Trine insists. ' I didn't do it.'

'No, no, but we can say something about your work in recent years specifically to crack down on sexual assaults and domestic violence. We can probably produce some statistics to prove our commitment to these particular issues.'

Trine nods, so far so good.

'If the allegations remain vague, I don't think it'll do us any harm to take the moral high ground,' Hatlem continues.

'*VG* refers to a "young, male politician",' Truls Ove Henriksen says. 'Could the alleged victim have been someone from the Party's youth branch?'

Trine shrugs her shoulders.

'I assume most people would think so, yes. But I've no idea how *VG* got its story. I've been married to Pål Fredrik for four years and I've never been unfaithful to him. I haven't even been tempted.'

Henriksen makes no reply. His shiny head is now sprinkled with beads of sweat.

'But at some point you may have to provide an explanation,' Ullevik says.

'We won't say anything about that now,' Hatlem maintains.

'We don't want to create expectations that Trine will make a statement.'

'No, no, of course not,' Ullevik says. 'I'm just saying that you need to review your movements that day very carefully. Who did you sit next to during dinner? Who did you speak to? When did you go to bed? Can anyone give you an alibi – things like that. The more details you can provide about what you actually did on 9 October last year, the better. And if you do say something, you must be absolutely sure that it's true. If you make even one little mistake, the press will question everything else you've said and done.'

Trine makes no reply, she just closes her eyes and disappears into a world of her own. Then she opens her eyes.

'What did you just say?'

'Hm?'

'Did you say 9 October?'

'Yes?'

And she suddenly feels hot. Terribly hot. *That's not possible*, she thinks. *It's just not possible that anyone would ever find out about that.*

'What is it?' Katarina Hatlem says. 'You've gone white.'

Trine continues to stare into space while her jaw drops. *This is a trap*, she thinks to herself.

I've been set up.

Chapter 11

Henning takes a quick shower, eats some baked beans straight out of a tin and makes his way to Grønland where the offices of *123news* are based. It's a grey morning. It's yet another day when the city tries its hardest to seem even less attractive than it does in the winter.

While he walks he thinks about his sister and the media witch hunt she will be subjected to in the coming days. Working on any other news item is almost pointless. The front pages of every newspaper will be plastered with stories about Trine for the foreseeable future.

Even so.

The police are giving a press conference at 10 a.m., an event Henning under normal circumstances would have ignored except that Assistant Commissioner Pia Nøkleby is likely to be leading it. Henning has a bone to pick with her.

The sight that greets him as he steps on to the grey carpets in the *123news* offices reminds him of an anthill. People are scurrying back and forth, they are practically running. Henning can see it in their eyes, expressions verging on panic. Stressed fingers flying across the keyboards. It's the same, it's the usual. And he knows why, of course.

National news editor Heidi Kjus spots him in the commotion and walks up to him, addressing him in a bossy, metallic voice that always makes him think of dog training. Heidi is wearing a short, dark blue skirt with a matching jacket. If she hadn't been a journalist, if she hadn't been middle management, she would have looked at home in a solicitor's office.

Henning had hoped that she would comment on the story he filed last night, but she simply stops and looks around. The pumping vein on her neck is working hard. Her cheekbones are – if possible – even more pronounced than usual.

'I've been wondering about something,' she begins.

Henning waits for her to continue.

'As you probably know the—'

Heidi looks across the room as if the atmosphere will justify what she is about to suggest. Henning has a pretty good idea of what is coming next.

'No one can get hold of your sister,' Heidi then says.

She fixes him with a look again. In the past the expression in her eyes has been icy, but not today. Now they are dark brown, verging on black. They match her personality.

'Have you spoken to her today?' she asks him.

He snorts and bursts out laughing.

'Heidi, I haven't spoken to Trine for years.'

'No, but—'

'And even if I had been in contact with her, I couldn't ring her now, you know that. I can't work on a story that involves Trine.'

'No, but I thought that maybe you could—'

Again her gaze disappears out into the room.

'You thought that I might try to get a comment from her all the same,' he says and checks her face for a reaction. And it comes. Her gaze is sharp, a little offended at first, then it changes to aggressive.

He shakes his head.

'Even if I did have Trine's number, which I don't, then I highly doubt that she would pick up if I called. Trine and I haven't seen each other for a long time. She didn't even attend Jonas's funeral. Nor was I invited to her wedding.'

Henning sits down and switches on his computer.

'Yes, but at least you could have tried,' Heidi says, showing no signs of leaving. 'That's the problem with you, Henning. You won't even try. You can never do as you're told, you always have to argue. Is it too much to ask that you show a bit of team spirit just once in a while?'

Henning looks up at her again.

'Team spirit?'

He spits out the words as if they had a bad taste.

'If your sister has screwed up, then it's our duty to report it, Henning, you know that.'

'Yes, I know. But there's a difference between—'

Henning stops, checks himself.

'It's a waste of time, Heidi. I don't like wasting my time.'

'No, I know,' she snarls. 'Just imagine if you actually had to work with other people.'

'I work with Iver.'

'Yes, but Iver isn't here. And he's not coming back for a while.'

Henning makes no reply, he can't think of anything to say. Neither can Heidi. So she storms off in a huff.

Chapter 12

'I need a moment to myself,' Trine says in a low voice.

She is aware of the looks being exchanged in the meeting room, but right now she is focusing mainly on not throwing up.

'Please,' she says. 'I need a few minutes alone.'

Chairs are quietly pushed back. It takes half a minute, then only Katarina Hatlem remains. She stops with her hand on the door handle.

'Is everything okay?' she asks.

Trine turns around, but doesn't look at her friend; she just nods quickly while her eyes well up. Everything is not okay. When the room is silent, she sits down again. Buries her face in her hands. Sniffs and shakes her head.

9 October.

With hindsight it's not difficult to list the reasons why she could and should have acted differently. But she remains convinced that she did the right thing. And she would do it again, should the same situation arise. She would just have been more careful about covering her tracks. Because that must be what happened. Someone must have seen her and talked. It's the only logical explanation.

Why on earth did she ever say yes to this job?

When the Prime Minister called, her first thought was the opportunities opening up to her. A chance to achieve more, more power, bigger budgets. But also more publicity, more disapproving voices, more criticism. There will always be someone who wants more, who thinks your priorities are wrong, that your strategy is a mistake, that you're not up to the job. Even so, she said yes, she didn't consider the offer for more than a few seconds before she jumped at the chance. Prime Minister William Jespersen wanted her to work for him. *William Jespersen.*

She knew it was a thankless task, but that was part of its appeal. Norway hadn't had all that many strong Justice Secretaries in the post-war period. The chance to put her name on the map, writing herself into history as an effective Justice Secretary, was too tempting. She wanted to be a respected Minister whose visions were implemented. She imagined that life as Justice Secretary would be about prevention, response, investigation and rehabilitation.

And now – it's all gone.

Her dreams, her ambitions, her visions. All gone. This is what they'll remember her for. Not for any of her achievements.

The Prime Minister had warned her what to expect. He said that everyone's eyes would be on her because she wasn't an obvious choice. She hadn't even been in the reserve, he said, and hey presto, suddenly she is playing in the first eleven. Trine didn't understand what he meant, nor did she ask, after all it was the Prime Minister who was talking to her. Later she realised it was a football metaphor.

Jespersen also warned her that there was bound to be gossip 'because you're a beautiful woman', and he wanted to know if she had the guts to handle it. She had responded by giggling like a little girl.

What she wouldn't give to be a little girl again. She feels so vulnerable, so unprotected against the media scrutiny that has already begun and so scared of what else might surface in the next few days. The consequences it can have. For everyone.

But will they really manage to dig that deep?

Trine wakes up the screen in front of her. Her mailbox comes up. Countless emails appear, the unread ones marked in bold. Her gaze stops at an email that was sent less than ten minutes ago. She doesn't recognise the sender; it's the text in the subject field that attracts her attention.

> **9 October**

She clicks on it against her better judgement. And the message makes her clasp her hand over her mouth.

> *I know what happened on 9 October last year. Or should I say – the next day?*
>
> *Consider this a warning. Resign or the truth will come out.*

Chapter 13

The radio is on, but Bjarne Brogeland isn't listening. His eyes scan the city that glides past him. There is a muffled sound of tyres against wet tarmac.

They finished the morning briefing only fifteen minutes ago. Today's tasks were explained and allocated under Arild Gjerstad's skilful management. Now a large number of officers, led by Emil Hagen, are on their way to Grünerhjemmet to continue interviewing everyone who was there yesterday. At the police station Fredrik Stang is doing background checks on all the staff members at the care home, focusing on those who worked on Erna Pedersen's ward. Crime scene officers are supporting the investigation by taking fingerprints and looking for matches on record.

Bjarne was tasked with visiting Ulrik Elvevold Sund, the boy who discovered Erna Pedersen's body; a job he was happy to accept since Ella Sandland, the station's femme fatale, was coming with him. Bjarne has been smitten with her for a long time, but none of his flirtatious remarks or come-ons has ever provoked as much as a shrug. That, however, Bjarne thinks, only makes working with her all the more charged.

He gazes at her, at her discreet make-up, the elasticity of her cheeks, her chin, her lips slightly dry right now, but normally moist and soft. Her eyelashes arch up over her eyelids. Sandland is like the sun. It's always warm wherever she is.

'So,' he says, exhaling hard. 'What do you make of all this?'

Sandland, who sits straight upright and looks out of the window with an alert expression, turns to him.

'I don't know what to think. Who would do something like that? I mean – even thinking of pushing knitting needles through the eyes of an old lady in the first place? How sick is that?'

As always her west Norwegian accent tugs at his heart-strings. She shakes her head; her short, blonde hair doesn't even move.

'Someone must have really hated her,' she concludes.

'Do you think it's symbolic that he used the Bible to whack the knitting needles through her eyes?'

'I don't know,' Sandland replies. 'Was she a Christian?'

'Or perhaps it was about her eyes,' Bjarne speculates. 'Perhaps she'd seen something. It's a very symbolic action, targeting her eyes.'

Sandland makes no reply, she just nods to herself.

Bjarne switches on the sat nav and takes a right, finds where he is going and parks facing the direction of traffic in Jens Bjelkesgate, right outside the entrance to an apartment block with the number 43. The wall is yellow with white painted windowsills and render below them. The door to Entrance B is blue.

Bjarne has phoned ahead to say that they are on their way, that Martine Elvevold should prepare both herself and her son for a chat. When Sandland rings the bell, they are admitted immediately, and are met on the ground floor by a woman with a gaunt face who greets them with a 'hi'. Her face is pale and drawn as if she hasn't slept well. Her brown hair lies messily on her shoulders.

'Come in,' she says when they have shaken hands. They enter a living room filled with film sounds. Bjarne recognises it immediately as one of the *Shrek* movies. Ulrik, a boy with blond, longish hair – just like his father – sits slumped on the floor in front of the TV.

'Can I get you some coffee or something?' Martine offers.

'No, thank you,' the officers reply in unison.

'How is he?' Bjarne says.

Martine Elvevold hesitates for a few seconds before she answers.

'It's difficult to say,' she begins. 'I've kept him at home from school today, but he seems a little – how can I put it – detached. There are moments when he's his old self, but every now and then he'll stare vacantly into space. Ulrik has always been a rather fidgety boy. Always a little on the anxious side.'

Bjarne nods.

'Has he said anything about – about what happened?'

Elvevold shakes her head.

'I haven't pressed him, either. I decided it might be good to give him time.'

'Unfortunately time isn't a luxury that we can allow ourselves,' Bjarne says. 'Do you mind if I have a word with him?'

'No,' Elvevold says, but her eyes immediately assume a worried expression. 'Only – go easy on him.'

Bjarne smiles empathetically.

'Of course.'

He signals to Sandland that he will take this chat on his own.

'I think I would like that cup of coffee after all,' she says.

Martine Elvevold smiles and leads the way to the kitchen. Bjarne waits until he and Ulrik are alone. He sits down on the floor, not too close to him, but a little to the side.

'What are you watching?' he says, looking at the boy's flitting eyes, which follow the images on the screen. Fiona is busy beating up a guy pretending to be Robin Hood.

'Holy cow,' Bjarne says. 'That's one tough lady.'

Ulrik makes no reply.

'My little girl loves this film,' Bjarne says after a pause. 'I think I must have seen it thirty times.'

Ulrik still hasn't got anything to say. Bjarne lets his gaze roam around the room while he thinks about how best to approach this nine-year-old boy. DVD boxes for several films are piled up in front of the television. There is a crate of Lego under the coffee table. Marbles lie scattered around. There is an indoor football on the floor near the sofa.

'Ulrik,' Bjarne says, turning to the boy. 'My name is Bjarne. I work for the police.'

The boy doesn't take his eyes off the screen.

'I'm trying to find out what happened at the care home yesterday. I know that you were the first person who saw that Erna Pedersen had died.'

This time the nine-year-old looks at Bjarne.

'Can you tell me what you saw?'

Ulrik's eyes return to the TV.

'Would you mind if I turn down the volume?' Bjarne says, pointing to the remote control. 'Makes it easier to talk?'

Ulrik says nothing, but Bjarne takes it as an indication that it's fine. He reaches out for the remote control and turns off the sound. Immediately they can hear noises coming from the kitchen. Muffled talking, a cup clattering.

'We know that somebody hurt her,' Bjarne continues. 'And it's my job to stop anything like that from happening again. I'm hoping you might be able to help me.'

Ulrik meets Bjarne's eyes.

'Did you see someone hurt Mrs Pedersen?'

Ulrik lowers his gaze and fidgets. This time Bjarne waits.

'She was just dead,' Ulrik says eventually.

'You didn't see what happened when she died?'

Ulrik shakes his head fiercely. Bjarne nods and tries to think of another way to ask the same question. Can't think of one.

'Did you see anyone in her room?'

Same response. Again there is something brooding and sad about Ulrik.

'Was she nice, Mrs Pedersen?'

The boy nods.

'She used to give me toffees.'

'Toffees? That was nice of her,' Bjarne says. 'So you knew her?'

'Not very much.'

'But a little?'

Ulrik stares down at the floor again. Bjarne doesn't know if there is any point in continuing the interview. Though he doesn't know the boy, it's clear to see that he has retreated deep inside himself. If that is for any other reason than having seen a dead body, a murdered body at that, it is hard to say.

'Okay,' Bjarne says and gets up. 'Thanks for talking to me, Ulrik. I hope we can talk some more another time.'

The boy says nothing and Bjarne gives him the remote control. The room immediately fills with song. It's a pretty melody, totally unsuited to the moment.

Bjarne finds the others in the kitchen.

'He's a great kid,' he says to Martine Elvevold. 'I think he's going to be all right.'

Ulrik's mother smiles tenderly.

'Was he any help?'

'He was,' Bjarne says and nods at the same time.

'I think perhaps I should let him spend some time with his friends after school today. If he wants to. It might be good for him to do something normal again.'

Sandland smiles and puts down her cup.

'That sounds like a good idea,' she says.

Chapter 14

The words in the email hit Trine so hard she starts to hyperventilate. It is as if the room begins spinning and she has to sit down in order not to fall. At her desk she rests her head in her hands and leans forwards on her elbows. Her hair falls over her eyes and forms a shield around her face, but one that offers no protection.

She raises her head and notices that the email was sent by biglie0910@hotmail.com. She splutters at the sender's name and guesses that whoever is threatening her isn't using an IP address that will prove easy to trace. Nor will she tell the Security Service about it either; she doesn't want to involve anyone else.

Then she remembers that her secretary automatically receives copies of all emails that go to the Justice Secretary's email address. Trine gets up, a little too quickly and instantly feels dizzy again. She clutches her head and regains her balance. Then she goes to the door and opens it. Sees that her secretary isn't at her desk right now.

A stroke of luck.

Trine rushes outside, glancing quickly up and down the corridor; she can hear voices and noises from every direction, but even so she races around to the back of the reception counter, wakes up the computer mouse and finds the email program and the email from biglie0910. She deletes it, both from the inbox and from the deleted items folder. She hurries back to her office before anyone sees her.

When she has shut the door, she leans against it, closes her eyes and hyperventilates. Again she has to concentrate hard not to cry. But how can anyone know what she did? Who is trying to set her up?

There is no shortage of enemies, neither in the Ministry of Justice itself, the police force or the Labour Party. Several people felt overlooked when she was appointed Justice Secretary three years ago. Words such as quotas for women were mentioned, there were hints that Trine would never have got the job if the Prime Minister hadn't had to appoint a woman. *I bet my enemies are gloating now*, she thinks. But who could have found out what she did? She didn't tell anyone, did she?

Trine shakes her head, goes back to her chair and sits down. She checks her mobile. Sixteen missed calls in only the last twenty minutes.

How quickly things can change. When she first appeared on TV or in the newspapers, she would get heaps of supportive text messages from people she knew and quite a few she didn't. It hardly ever happens now. That's why she makes a point of sending sympathetic messages to Ministers or other politicians, especially women, when they have been involved in a controversy. Quite simply because nobody else will. Not a single one of her government colleagues has texted her their support. Nor have any of her friends.

Maybe she doesn't have any. Not any real friends.

Her thoughts are interrupted by a knock on the door. Trine sniffs, straightens up and blinks hard a couple of times. The door opens and Harald Ullevik pops his head around.

'Hi,' he says softly. 'Can I come in?'

Trine feels incapable of saying anything yet, so she simply nods. Ullevik opens the door fully, enters and quickly closes it behind him. Takes a slow step forwards, presses his palms together and looks at her.

'Please,' she whispers. 'No pity. I don't think I can handle that right now.'

Ullevik says nothing, but nods gently.

'I just wanted to ask if there's anything I can do for you.'

'You can sue *VG*,' she says half in earnest, half in jest. 'No,' she sighs. 'I don't know.'

Ullevik doesn't move. The walls radiate silence.

'Trine, I—'

Ullevik lowers his gaze and digs the toe of his shoe into the floor.

'What is it, Harald?'

It takes a few moments before he looks up at her.

'I just wanted you to know that I ... that you have my full support. No matter what. You've done a brilliant job as Justice Secretary. You're the best one we've had for years.'

Don't cry, Trine tells herself. *Don't you dare start crying now*.

'If there's anything you need, then ... Don't hesitate to ask. Okay?'

Stupid eyes.

'I will,' she stutters while the corners of her mouth start to tremble. 'Thank you, Harald. It means a lot to me to hear you say that.'

Ullevik smiles warmly. Eyes meet eyes and she could have hugged him if there hadn't been a desk between them, as well as her knowledge that she would most certainly burst into tears.

'Okay,' he says. 'I'll leave you in peace.'

She watches him go and soon she is alone in the silence once more – normally a welcome friend on a noisy day. But not today.

Eventually Trine gets up and rings an internal number. Katarina Hatlem shows up in her office less than one minute later.

'What is it?' she asks and closes the door behind her. And before Trine has time to respond, she says: 'How are you?'

'I can't handle this on my own,' Trine says. 'You have to help me.'

Chapter 15

Emilie Blomvik can't sit still for one minute. It's almost like being back at school and waiting to get the results of a test you know you have done well in. She is quivering with anticipation, but it's still a welcome sensation. She can only imagine how Mattis must be feeling right now.

Before he left work last Friday, the partners told him they would like to meet with him Monday morning. You've been doing very well recently, they said, but that was all they told him. Emilie has asked him several times during the weekend why he thought they wanted to meet with him. And even though he only shrugged and replied 'I don't know', she could tell from looking at him what he was thinking. The way a small smile would curl up at the corners of his mouth though he tried very hard to suppress it.

Is it finally his turn to be made a partner?

Emilie isn't quite sure what being made a partner entails, but she is absolutely sure that it's a good thing. It holds out a promise of better times to come. Nicer holidays. More of everything. Before Mattis went to work today, he promised to ring her as soon as the meeting with his bosses was over. She doesn't know what a Monday morning means for a lawyer, but surely it can't be that long before he calls?

Emilie smiles to herself when she remembers how she met Mattis, or rather how he met her. He came up to the check-in counter at Gardermoen Airport where she worked and asked if she had ever been reindeer hunting. Emilie was lost for words after this unexpected question and when she didn't reply immediately, he said: 'Would you like to try?'

She didn't know what to say; she is quite sure that she blushed as she sat there behind the counter. She had had her fair share of chat-up lines over the years, but the word 'reindeer' had never featured in any of them. And she was instantly attracted to the idea of leaving everything behind, eloping with a total stranger to a foreign place. He looked almost ruggedly handsome as he stood there, even though he is really quite skinny and not particularly attractive or brave, but Emilie had never been drawn to men with film star looks. And she had no trouble imagining how much tougher he would look with a hunting rifle in his hand. Had she been ten years younger, she might have thrown caution to the wind and gone off with him.

But she remembered him the next time he came to check in. She spotted him in the crowd, saw him wait until her counter was free. She got butterflies in her stomach and felt hot all over. She is quite sure that he noticed the warmth in the smile she flashed him. And there was something appealing about his confidence when he asked her if he could buy her a cup of coffee when he came back. Or a beer. Or a Strawberry Daiquiri.

Now the latter might have been a fluke, but at the time she loved Strawberry Daiquiris. And one Strawberry Daiquiri turned into two and three when he called her one month later. Now they have been living together for three years and been parents for two and a half. And she would have to agree that they're happy.

But she is not sure that he is Mr Right.

Mattis is kind, funny and sociable. He is a great father to Sebastian – when he is at home, that is. He gets on very well with Emilie's mother, with her friends, he even says that he likes or indeed 'absolutely loves' Jessheim, where they live. But sometimes it's as if they are on different planets. One fortnight every year he goes hunting up in Finnmarksvidda in northern Norway. In the summer he prefers to go to rock festivals with his friends, while she prefers sun loungers and all-inclusive holidays. They don't spend very much time together these days. He is busy with his work in Oslo; she with hers at the airport. Emilie had thought that living together, being a family, would be about more than just simple logistics, the organisation of everyday life. And the question she has been asking herself more and more often recently is: does she really love him?

Fortunately deciding where they were going to live required little discussion. Mattis wasn't particularly bothered. Nor was he worried about how the house should look. Interiors, choice of sofa, the colour on the walls, the dinner service, none of that mattered to him and he was happy to leave all the decisions to her. So they bought a house that Emilie plans to redecorate over time, once she gets a clearer idea of what she wants.

Her only regret is that Johanne didn't move back home to Jessheim once she had finished her studies. It would have made it so much easier for them to meet, or at least they would be seeing each other more than they do now. A whole summer has come and gone since the last time. And that is why Emilie is particularly excited about having lunch with her friend tomorrow.

But tomorrow is twenty-four hours away. Right now it is about the usual morning routine. Give Sebastian his breakfast, clean his teeth, brush his hair, make his packed lunch, help him into his coat and wellies, pack a spare set of clothing in case – no, not in case – because he inevitably gets dirty or wets himself.

She can't wait until that stage is over. Sometimes she wishes it was possible to press the fast-forward button, as if life was a DVD series where you could skip all the boring episodes. But then Sebastian will smile or laugh or say something that gives her a warm glow all over, and she wishes she could change the pace of life to slow motion instead.

*

It is just past 8.30 in the morning when Emilie parks outside Nordby Nursery, a long flat building that has never been painted any colour other than red. She went there herself when she was little. She doesn't remember very much about it except that they spent most of the day outdoors regardless of the weather – a tradition that seems to have endured. The nursery has a large outdoor space with plenty of playground equipment and a hill where the children can toboggan and roll down in winter.

Emilie gets out of the car, adjusts her clothing slightly, lifts Sebastian out of his car seat and puts him down carefully on the ground. Then she holds out her hand to him and he takes it. Slowly they start walking towards the entrance, a tarmac footpath where prams are lined up all the way to the wall. A father she meets practically every morning smiles to her. Emilie smiles back. It's a fine morning and it's important to enjoy it while it lasts. The sun breaks through the trees, which are craning their necks towards the sky. An autumnal morning mist has wrapped the branches and leaves in candy floss.

Her attention is drawn to a man standing close to the fence behind a fir tree. He is holding up a camera and isn't moving. Emilie slows down and narrows her eyes to get a better look at him. She can't see much in the drowsy morning light other than that he wears a khaki army jacket and that his face is obscured by the camera. When he lowers it, he seems to be staring right at her. At them.

'Mummy,' says a small, squeaky and impatient voice at her side. She looks down at Sebastian who is pulling at her.

'I'm coming, darling, I was just—'

She turns again and looks towards the fir tree. The man is no longer there. She tries to work out where he could have gone, but all she can see are branches swaying in the wind and clouds of dust whirling up from the ground.

How strange, she thinks. *Was he taking pictures of us?*

She looks around. Right now they are the only people outside. And she thought there was something familiar about him.

She brushes the idea aside. He might just have been taking pictures of the beautiful light. Nothing to worry about.

Emilie carries on walking to the entrance while she glances at her watch. And it comes back, this twitchy, nagging feeling. Surely Mattis has to ring soon?

Chapter 16

The reporters gathered around the big staircase at Oslo Police Station instantly fall silent when Pia Nøkleby arrives. She is usually accompanied by Chief Inspector Arild Gjerstad, but this time she is alone.

Henning has to be honest: he has grown to like Pia Nøkleby since he returned to work in the spring. He likes her dark hair, the fringe that she always brushes behind her right ear even though the hair instantly falls back over her eyes again. And her eyes – brown with a fleck of green, eyes that never look tired. The little beauty spot left of her nose, which gives him yet another reason to look at her heart-shaped face. Her lips always moist, not too red, as if she deliberately stops herself from being too beautiful. Her cheeks, soft and rosy with only a hint of pale, delicate hairs, are tempting to touch.

She is always very serious when the microphone is switched on, behaving like she thinks she should and ought. But as soon as the cameras are turned off, her personality changes and she will come out with quick and insightful comments. She has always had this professional acuity that rarely or never leads her astray in interviews.

Henning has seen something in her eyes, not often, but every now and then she drops her facade. True, it's some time since he last felt a woman's warmth, or even interest, but he hasn't completely lost his touch. Pia's voice tends to soften when she speaks to him, also when other journalists or police officers are present.

But Henning also remembers how Pia's replies became more and more evasive when he started asking questions about the police investigation into a murder of which ex-torpedo and property magnate Tore Pulli was found guilty. At first he had put her behaviour down to work-related stress, concluding that she might not be inclined to answer questions from someone who was clearly critical of an investigation she had headed. But ever since Henning discovered that Pia had redacted a report in the police investigation program, Indicia, a report that stated that Tore Pulli was outside Henning's flat on the night of the fire that killed his son, it's tempting to think that her less than forthcoming answers were prompted by other motives.

All Henning knows about the Pulli report is that Pulli was sitting in a car outside Henning's flat in Markveien 32, on 11 September 2007, and that he had been there several nights in a row. But why was he there? Was he waiting for a meeting? Was he planning to beat someone up – after all, he had previously made his living as one of Oslo's best-known enforcers? Or was he simply observing?

Henning has been asking himself those same questions in the last few weeks. Last month Pulli contacted Henning and told him he had information about what happened on the night that Jonas died. But before Pulli was able to tell him, he was murdered in Oslo Prison. Because of what he was about to tell Henning? And what did the original Indicia report say about Pulli's movements on the night in question? Who might that information have incriminated – unless it was damaging to Pia Nøkleby herself?

Henning was tempted, of course he was, to confront Nøkleby when he discovered what she had done, but he has since had second thoughts. He decided to protect his source who had told him Nøkleby had edited the report and find another way to proceed. There must be others who know something.

He looks at Nøkleby as she stops on the fourth step from the bottom and surveys the crowd. TV camera lights are switched on. Microphones are stretched out. Mobile telephones switched to recording mode.

Henning knows the police are not about to disclose anything that he doesn't already know. They might release a photograph of the victim, tell them a little about her background and confirm the information that Henning has already included in the article he filed earlier today. But Nøkleby won't say anything about *how* the victim was maimed. Instead she will say that the investigation is looking at every aspect, technical as well as tactical, and that they have solid evidence that they are following up. But no one will be told what that solid evidence is, obviously.

Henning is there mainly to see how Nøkleby behaves, if her face gives anything away. He tries to catch her eye, but her gaze glides across the large room and the reporters assembled there.

When she has finished her statement and everyone has gone their separate ways, Henning sends her a text message asking politely for a private chat. He sits down on a bench outside the police station from where he has an uninterrupted view of Oslo Prison and waits for her to reply. This is the place they usually meet. Occasionally she invites him to her office, but only when she has information she officially wants the media to know about.

While he clutches his mobile waiting for her to get back to him, life in Oslo rushes by on the roads below. The sky is just as restless as satellite images played back at high speed. And he wonders how long it will be before another gigantic bucket of water will be tipped over the city.

He thinks about the murder of Erna Pedersen. Given the number of potential witnesses it's odd that no one saw anything. On the other hand – all the patients on Ward 4 were suffering from some form of dementia, so even if they had seen something, there is no guarantee that they would have remembered it. It is even possible that one of them might have killed her and not even know it.

He tries to visualise Erna Pedersen, old and grey, in her wheelchair when she met her killer. He must have been known to her. No stranger would enter the room of an eighty-three-year-old woman, strangle her and then proceed to whack knitting needles into her eyes afterwards.

But why do it when the woman was already dead?

The killer must have suffered an enormous, pent-up rage. Killing her wasn't enough. This gives Henning an idea. The murder is unlikely to have been planned in advance. Not in detail, at any rate. Then the killer would have used something other than the victim's own knitting needles – unless he knew that she always had them by her side.

There can be no doubt that this was a crime of passion. And everyone who commits a crime of passion is affected by it one way or another. It takes time to recover from such raw emotions. How can the killer have found an outlet for such tremendous pressure without anyone noticing a change in him?

Since no one at the care home saw the killer, they must have been distracted. Or did the killer switch from being Mr Hyde one moment to Dr Jekyll the next? In which case they are looking for a killer who is extraordinarily callous.

Henning ponders the most important question in every murder investigation. Why? Several motives can be eliminated immediately. Jealousy. Desire. Some people kill for the thrill of it, but it's rare. Neither is there anything to suggest that this murder was committed to cover up another crime. Nor is loss of honour a likely motive, since it mostly occurs between gang members or people with extreme religious convictions. Personal gain? It's possible, of course, since no information has yet been published about the victim's financial circumstances, be it anything she might have kept in her room or any money she might have had in her bank account. No more alternatives exist, except the usual one:

Revenge.

And in view of the killer's unbridled rage, revenge is the most obvious motive. But what could an eighty-three-year-old woman ever have done to anyone? Nothing, probably, in the last few years. Not much happens at a care home. So we need to go further back in time, Henning reasons. But how far back? To the time before she was moved to a care home? Or even further back? Surely there is a limit to how much evil a woman can do after she turns seventy?

At the police press conference they learned that the victim was originally from Jessheim – where Henning also grew up, incidentally. Perhaps the answer lies there? In which case he knows exactly who to ask for help.

Henning is so completely lost in thought that he doesn't hear the footsteps behind him, and when Pia Nøkleby sits down next to him, he spins around so fast that she starts to laugh.

'I didn't know you scared so easily.'

'Oh,' Henning says and blushes. 'Occupational hazard.'

Nøkleby laughs again.

Henning likes laughter. He especially likes *her* laughter. And it's hard to believe that Pia Nøkleby would have been able to sit here with him and act as if nothing had happened unless she had a clear conscience. She knows Henning's story, knows what happened to Jonas. So could she really have tampered with the Tore Pulli report in Indicia and still sit here joking with him?

'I should have brought you a strawberry ice cream,' he says.

Nøkleby smiles and brushes some hair behind her ear.

'I'm still feeling sick from the last one you gave me.'

Henning smiles and watches her lips stretch out, moist and perfect, as if she put on fresh lipstick just before she came down to see him.

'Nice summary you just gave us,' he continues. 'Nice and professional, as usual.'

'Hah,' she snorts. 'There wasn't much for you lot to go on. Or, at least, not for you.'

He lowers his gaze.

'Sometimes, Henning, your sources are a little too well informed.'

'So you don't fancy becoming one of them?'

This time they both smile.

'I thought I *was* one of your sources?'

'Yes, but on-the-record sources are boring, Pia. You know that.'

She laughs again.

'But I won't lie – you're my dream source. No doubt about it.'

'Oh?'

'But more than anything, I wish I had a source who could grant me access to the information held in Indicia.'

Henning looks up at her.

'Now that would be worth having,' he continues.

Nøkleby doesn't reply immediately.

'Yes, I can imagine that's every journalist's wet dream,' she then says.

'Mm.'

Henning had expected that her eyes would start to flicker the moment he mentioned the word 'Indicia', especially if she understood why he was bringing it up. But there was no hint of a change. No quick, nervous glance. Not even a twitching in the corner of her mouth.

Perhaps it was too much to hope for. Pia has worked for the police for years; she is used to keeping secrets, to keeping a straight face in front of the media.

But would she be able to conceal something as big as that?

'How easy is it for an outsider to gain access to Indicia?'

Nøkleby turns to him.

'How do you mean?'

'Could I, for example, log on to Indicia if I knew your user-name and password? From the outside?'

Nøkleby's mouth starts to open, but she hesitates before she replies.

'I hope you're not about to make me an indecent proposal?'

'You know me better than that, Pia.'

Her face darkens slightly. Her gaze sharpens.

'But could I? I mean, purely hypothetically, of course, just to be clear.'

Nøkleby doesn't reply. She simply stares at him with searching eyes.

'I thought you wanted to talk to me about the murder of Erna Pedersen?'

'That too.'

Her eyes probe him so hard that her gaze pricks him.

'The functionality of a program such as Indicia isn't something we share with the public, Henning. Not even with off-the-record news-hungry journalists.'

'Sorry,' he says and smiles.

'Tell me, why do you want to know?'

He shrugs his shoulders.

'I'm just curious.'

'Yeah, right,' she says, sarcastically. 'You always have an agenda.'

True, Henning thinks and pauses before he replies. Then he holds up his hands in defence.

'There's an exception to every rule,' he says and smiles again, hoping that will be enough to lift the veil of scepticism over her eyes.

He isn't that lucky.

'Well, if there's nothing else, then—'

Nøkleby stands up.

'There is.'

She stops and looks down at him.

'How far back in time are you going to have to go to find the reason for the revenge killing of Erna Pedersen?'

Nøkleby looks at him. She shakes her head almost imperceptibly.

Then she leaves.

Chapter 17

Bjarne has only just stepped out of the lift on the third floor at Grünerhjemmet when Emil Hagen sees him and signals for him to wait. Bjarne duly stops halfway between the two corridors that run parallel like an H with the TV lounge to the right and the nursing station to the left. Behind a large glass window a woman is concentrating on a computer screen. Its green glare reflects in her glasses.

Hagen, a police officer with short legs and brown spiky hair, ends the call and snaps shut his mobile, then comes towards Bjarne with bouncy trainer steps that squeal against the shiny, polished floor. His jeans fit snugly around his thighs. A black leather jacket envelops taut upper body muscles that strain against a plain white T-shirt.

Emil Hagen joined the Violent Crimes Unit less than three years ago, straight out of the police academy. At first his youthful enthusiasm and naivety might give people the impression that he was head over heels with the profession and the status it gave him. But Bjarne soon realised that there was an entirely different reason for Hagen's dedication.

Hagen had been brought up in a home without any boundaries, where his parents were rarely present or, if they were there, were rarely sober. Hagen rapidly realised that if he wanted to escape, he had only himself to rely on. He would need to take responsibility for his own life. Work hard at school, look out for himself. And he did it, that wasn't the problem.

The problem was his sister, Lise Merethe.

Boys quickly discovered her; she would often come home drunk late at night and at the age of sixteen she was well on her way to becoming a fully paid up member of the intravenous drug user community. Hagen grew up as he walked the streets of Oslo trying to save his baby sister from ruin. To no avail. One autumn day in 2005 she was found under a bridge near Oslo's Stock Exchange. Killed by an overdose. But instead of burying himself in grief, Hagen set to work systematically; caring little for the tough guys he encountered on the drugs scene or how he spoke to them, he just wanted to find the answer to the question of who had sold Lise Merethe the fatal dose.

The dealer in question turned out to be a small fish in a big pond, but Hagen realised something about himself: he had a gene or two that made him well suited for investigative work. The course of the rest of his life had been set. Every day he turns up for work with a resilience and a spring in his step that Bjarne envies him. As if he is still trying to save his sister.

As far as Bjarne is concerned, the reason for his choice of career was nowhere near as noble. For him being a police officer made you a tough guy. As did wearing the uniform, being where the action was, speeding away in a car without worrying about losing your licence. And it was also about the women. For a while everything was about them. He worked out and knew that he looked good; he had the uniform, the handcuffs and the gun – three attributes you can never go wrong with when you're trying to become an alpha male. A test, however, he has yet to pass when it comes to Ella Sandland.

Now she comes up alongside him while Emil Hagen pushes two pieces of chewing tobacco under his upper lip.

'The pathologist says the victim was killed sometime between three and six yesterday afternoon,' he begins. 'I've gone through the visitors' log and eliminated everyone who came and left before that time. That leaves us with twenty-three potential suspects.'

'Right,' Bjarne replies.

'Yes, this is a big care home. If we were to include everyone who worked here during that slot we're talking about sixty to seventy people. But I've made a list of the twenty-three visitors.'

Hagen hands Bjarne a sheet of paper.

'The names of anyone who visited someone in Ward 4 in that three-hour window are in bold.'

Bjarne studies the list and recognises the names of several people he spoke to the night before.

Fridtjof Holby
Astrid Solberg
Carl-Severin Lorentzen
Per Espen Feydt
Reidun Ruud
Maria Reymert
Markus Gjerløw – VS
Unni Kristine Fagereng – VS
Remi Gulliksen – VS
Petra Jørgensen – VS

Dorthe Arentz – VS
Ivar Lorentz Løkkeberg
Knut Bergstrøm
Signe Marie Godske
Trond Monsen
Janne Næss
Danijela Kaosar
Per-Aslak Rønneberg
Egil Skarra
Ole Edvald Åmås
Mette Yvonne Smith
Kristin Tømmerås
Thea Marie Krogh-Sørensen

'And the people whose names are followed by "VS" – they're the ones from the Volunteer Service?' Bjarne asks.

'Yes.'

'We should also take into account that not everyone signs themselves in,' Ella Sandland interjects. 'Especially not frequent visitors.'

Bjarne nods.

'It's also easy to move between floors here, using either the lift or the stairs,' Hagen continues. 'But we're starting with anyone who is known to have been to Ward 4.'

'And do you have a list of staff members?'

Hagen nods.

'Plus the patients, of course.'

'Okay,' Bjarne says as he visualises an endless queue of interviewees. 'Discovered anything interesting yet?'

'Might have,' Hagen says, shifting his weight from one foot to the other. 'One of the cleaners told me she heard an argument up here yesterday afternoon. She didn't know if it was between patients, staff or relatives, but she thought she heard doors slamming. And that it was on this side of the corridor,' Hagen says, taking a step towards the nursing station and pointing down the corridor in the direction of Erna Pedersen's room.

'She couldn't give me the exact time, but she was sure it was in the afternoon. We haven't spoken to anyone else so far who has seen or heard anything,' Hagen finishes and licks his upper lip.

'Which might suggest that the killer is known to most people here.'

'You mean he works here?'

'Could be. If you pass someone you see every day, you don't really notice them. Take you, for example, I know that you come to get water from the water cooler outside my office every day. If I asked you if the water cooler was half or quarter full, would you be able to tell me?'

Hagen thinks about it for a few moments before he shakes his head.

'So the killer could have been here so often that people didn't question his presence.'

'Or hers,' Sandland says.

Bjarne raised an eyebrow.

'Do you really think that a woman could have done this?'

'Why not? You don't have to be especially strong to strangle an old woman who was half dead already.'

Bjarne quickly rubs the bridge of his nose.

'Incidentally, the manager was very chatty about a lot of other problems they're having here,' Hagen continues. 'But I don't know how important they are.'

Another furrow appears in Bjarne's brow.

'Why do you say that?'

'The question is how relevant they are,' Hagen muses.

'Right now everything is relevant. What did he say?'

'She,' Hagen says, jutting out his chin a little.

'Eh?'

'The manager is a woman.'

'Oh.'

Hagen looks down at his notes.

'Her name is Vibeke Schou,' he informs them. 'She talked about relatives who moan and complain, patients who steal, broken equipment, medication going missing.' Hagen throws up his hands. 'You wouldn't believe it, everything was a problem. That's what they call care for the elderly today, eh,' he tuts and sighs.

'Medication going missing?' Bjarne asks.

'Yes, apparently. But she told me something that is quite interesting now that I think about it. Not all that long ago they had to introduce house rules in the TV lounge over there.'

Hagen points with his thumb over his shoulder.

'House rules?' Bjarne says.

'Yes, about who gets to decide what they watch and when. Some of the men were hogging the remote control a little too much and the women got upset about it. Erna Pedersen was one of them.'

Sandland tries to keep a straight face, but fails to suppress her smile.

'I can't imagine that those rules went down terribly well with the men.'

'No. Especially not with one particular resident, a—'

Hagen glances down at his lists again.

'Guttorm Tveter,' he says.

Bjarne looks over at Sandland.

'I'll see if I can find him,' Sandland says.

'Great,' Bjarne says.

Sandland walks past both of them, past the TV lounge and turns left into the corridor. Both officers turn to follow her with their eyes. Her uniform seems to fit her figure exactly.

'Have you seen Daniel Nielsen around?' Bjarne asks and shakes his head to dispel the image. Hagen licks his lips.

'Who's he?'

'Erna Pedersen's primary care worker. I've tried calling him several times today, but there's no reply. He's not returning my calls, either.'

Hagen takes out a fresh sheet of paper from his jacket pocket. His eyes skim it a couple of times before he replies: 'No. He's not in today.'

'Okay,' Bjarne says and nods. 'I'll talk to some of the others instead. Who do you suggest I start with?'

Chapter 18

It's not often that Trine drives herself these days, but it feels good to be behind the wheel again, alone and in perfect silence. The steady sound of tyres against tarmac makes her feel drowsy, something that surprises her. She would never have thought she could feel sleepy now after what has happened and given what she is doing now.

Resign or the truth will come out.

Replying to that email was not an option. She would never agree to enter into an email exchange that would be difficult to keep private. But neither could she stand staying in her office, being interrupted every five minutes by new problems, new statements, new media stories and new demands. The walls were starting to close in on her. She needed to be alone for a while; she couldn't bear the thought of fighting her way through a media scrum every time she tried to get in or out of a building. Not without knowing what to say or do.

She told Katarina Hatlem that she thought she had been set up, quite simply because she couldn't keep her suspicions to herself any longer. But she said nothing about the email because she didn't want Katarina to initiate her own investigation. Katarina can be quite headstrong once she gets the bit between her teeth.

Trine has a red baseball cap pulled down over her eyes and is wearing different glasses. She takes care not to look at any of the drivers in the oncoming traffic, but she thinks it's unlikely that anyone would recognise her. She realises how tempting it would be to try to shake off her bodyguards who are in the car behind her, but she daren't, she can't. It would have repercussions not just for her, but also for Katarina.

It was Katarina who helped Trine leave the Ministry of Justice unnoticed less than an hour ago through the concrete tunnel under Building R5 where a man was waiting to take her to a hire car in which she drove off. Katarina had also bought some food, clothes and a new mobile phone, since it would be easy for the police to trace Trine's old one.

Trine drives into the Lier Tunnel while she remembers the first question she was asked by a journalist when William Jespersen's newly formed government stepped out on to Slottsplassen for the very first time. 'Will you still have enough time for your husband now that you're going to be Justice Secretary?' Trine was completely taken aback; she had imagined she would have a chance to promote her core issues. No one had prepared her that the media would be more interested in her private life. Afterwards she wished she had been able to come up with something pithy and clever, but all she managed to stutter was: 'Yes, of course.'

And now she is running away from Pål Fredrik too. She sent him a text message right before she left to let him know that she wouldn't be coming home tonight, but she hadn't got a reply by the time she had to leave.

The new mobile rings. She recognises the number.

'Hi, Katarina,' Trine says.

'Hi. Where are you?'

'I'm close to Drammen.'

'Are you all right?'

'Yes, of course, Katarina, I'm all right.'

'Now this isn't unexpected, but I thought I should draw your attention to it anyway. As you can imagine, the opposition is having a field day with this, but what's worse is that the leader of the Labour Party's youth branch is saying that if the allegations are true then it's a very serious matter.'

Trine sighs.

'You know what the media are like. Every headline is now going to preface the allegations with "very serious". The disclaimer won't be mentioned until halfway down the story.'

'Typical. Anything else?'

'No. That's all for now.'

'Okay.'

'Call me when you get there.'

'Mm.'

But Trine doesn't want to call or talk to anyone. She just wants to get out of Oslo.

She glances up at the rear-view mirror and sees the black Audi behind her with the two men in the front. *I bet they're sweating*, she thinks, *given the situation and the job they have to do*. They are going to an unnamed location and haven't been able to secure it yet. She sympathises with them. What if something were to happen to the Justice Secretary on their watch?

Chapter 19

He studies the colours and the contrasts on the screen. He can see that he needs to brighten the surroundings, intensify their colour. Or maybe it's fine as it is.

He likes the mood in the picture. The early morning mist lying across the ground at the nursery. The trees around it, wrapped in nature's floating cotton wool. He should have taken some pictures of that as well, not just of the boy who has sand around his mouth. He is not smiling in this particular picture. He sits on the ground, lost in a world of his own. His waders keep him dry and warm. He is blissfully ignorant that the world only seems to be a safe place. Anything could happen to a boy of two and a half.

He selects the boy, increases the contrast so his colouring stands out more sharply against the dim morning light, and plays with various filters. Even though he doesn't need to, he prints out the picture. Soon a long, whooshing sound starts up under his desk. And the boy appears, clear and bright.

He studies the face, the cheekbones he can barely make out under the chubby toddler cheeks. Looks at the nose and the mouth. The teeth.

Does he bear any resemblance to me?

He knows the thought is absurd, but he can't help himself. And he imagines her, imagines them, hand-in-hand, the way she often drags the boy along, usually because she is late for work. But she can't have been late for work today given the leisurely pace with which she walked. And always so beautiful. Still so bloody beautiful. And the boy. Small and untouched.

At least for now.

He sits down in front of his computer again and feels the soft latex around his fingers when he rubs them together. He goes on Facebook to check the latest updates. Shakes his head. Everyone is so bloody happy and successful. He starts to play a computer game, but finds it impossible to concentrate.

He thinks about yesterday and how it all happened before he had time to savour it. The old woman died almost immediately. He didn't really know what he had done before he had done it and so he never saw the light go out. He never felt the struggle, no matter how short and feeble it would have been, in her fingers.

Four intense beeps from his mobile snap him out of his reverie. He picks up the phone and heaves a sigh.

He visualises his mother on her lunch break at work calling him to find out what he is up to, if he would like to come home for dinner tomorrow. He can't be bothered to reply. Nag, nag, nag. Every time the same questions: 'Have you been down to the job centre yet?' 'How do you pass the time?'

If only you knew, he thinks. And he won't be coming home for dinner tomorrow. He has plans. Big plans.

He looks at the boy again. Then he scrunches up the print-out and throws it at the wall, finds his USB-driven mini Hoover, points its nozzle at the keyboard and removes any breadcrumbs or dust that might have settled in the last few days. And especially any DNA.

When he has finished, he pushes himself away from the

desk, opens the desk drawer and looks at the open envelope with the large, green 'G' on the outside. He takes it out and puts it next to a wrap – slightly bigger than a street dose – of morphine capsules.

He can hardly wait until the next struggle. He is desperate to experience that. He wants to see the light. Especially when it goes out.

Chapter 20

Back at the offices of *123news* Henning sits down at his desk and reflects. Did he actually glean anything from his meeting with Pia Nøkleby?

Only a professional liar can control the reflexes of their facial muscles when confronted with compromising information. The tell is in the movements of the eyes. But rather than getting nervous or appearing ill at ease, Pia looked inquisitive and alert.

Is she really that good a liar?

If that's the case he has to find another way of solving the Indicia problem. And he thinks he has.

According to *6tiermes7*, Henning's secret Internet source, a man called Andreas Kjær was the officer on duty on the night of the fire. It's not unthinkable that he might remember something from that night. Perhaps he can provide Henning with information about which patrol car he despatched to investigate what Tore Pulli was doing in Markveien around 8.30 p.m. Perhaps the officers in that patrol car could be traced. It's definitely worth following up, especially now when Henning has some free time. The police investigation at the care home is trundling along and the online newspapers are focusing mainly on Trine.

Henning discovers that Directory Enquiries list several

Andreas Kjærs, but only one who lives in Oslo. Henning steps inside an office the size of a telephone booth and calls the number. A deep, male voice answers after just two rings.

'Hi, my name's Henning Juul. I'm looking for Andreas Kjær.'

'That's me.'

'Hi,' Henning says again. 'I'm calling because two years ago you were working at Oslo Police's control centre. Is that right?'

'Yes, that's correct. I'm still there.'

'Okay. Fine. I have a question that might be a bit – which might not make sense straightaway, but I ask you to bear with me because it's important.'

Henning gets no reply and takes it as a sign that he should keep talking.

'On 11 September in 2007 there was a fire in my flat in Markveien in Grünerløkka. You were on duty that night and I know that a patrol car was despatched to Markveien 32 shortly before the fire started.'

Henning stops to make sure that Kjær is keeping up with him.

'Okay?' Kjær says, sounding unwilling. 'I'm sorry to hear that. But why are you calling me?'

'Because you were on duty that night. I also know that it was—'

'How do you know that?'

'I lost my son in that fire,' Henning says and clears his throat. 'And apart from being more than understandably keen to know what happened, I'm also a journalist. I have sources.'

Kjær says nothing. Henning decides to plough on.

'A traffic warden had observed a man sitting in a car several evenings in a row outside the building where I lived; he got suspicious, called it in and you despatched a patrol car to the address.'

Henning holds another pause.

'Ring any bells, Kjær?'

Silence.

'The man sitting in the car was Tore Pulli,' Henning continues when Kjær still doesn't say anything. 'You've heard of him, haven't you?'

'Yes, of course. But I don't remember the case.'

'Are you sure? It would be really helpful if you could try to think back. Like I said, it's very important to me.'

'I understand,' Kjær replies. 'But yes, I'm sure. And even if I did remember that case I wouldn't be able to discuss it with you.'

'Okay, I understand, but—'

'I have to go now.'

Henning is about to launch a fresh protest before he realises his words will have no effect. The line has already gone dead.

Chapter 21

Pernille Thorbjørnsen is perching on the edge of a chair and leaning forwards with one leg slung over the other. The care worker has a round face with dimpled cheeks. Her brown hair is swept back in a low ponytail. Bjarne Brogeland puts her at thirty, perhaps a few years older.

They are in a meeting room on the ground floor of the care home where a couple of IKEA tables have been pushed together. The light from two large windows casts a layer of something sallow across Thorbjørnsen's face.

'Thanks for coming in at such short notice,' he says.

'Don't mention it,' she smiles and leans back.

'When did you leave work yesterday?'

'My shift ended at five o'clock.'

'Okay. Did anything strike you as unusual? I'm thinking about anyone who might have been acting differently. Staff. Patients. Visitors.'

Bjarne flings out his hands.

'Anything and anyone is of interest,' he says.

Thorbjørnsen squeezes her fingers for a moment, brushes a few stray strands of hair behind her ears; then she folds her arms across her chest.

'I don't think so,' she begins. 'I can't really think of anything. I was working and I didn't realise I was meant to be looking out for something.'

'No, I know. But try to think back. Was anyone a bit more agitated than they normally were, or calmer than usual, or more exalted—'

Thorbjørnsen looks up to the left.

'I don't think so.'

Bjarne doesn't continue until he is sure that she has finished sifting through her memories.

'Were you here when the people from the Volunteer Service arrived?'

'Yes, but I didn't join in the entertainment this time.'

'Why not?'

'I had things to do. The residents here are ill, Officer. Not everyone is able to take part in the entertainment every time. And there isn't room for us all, either.'

'So you don't know if Erna Pedersen took part yesterday?'

'Yes, I do actually. Ole Christian told me that she didn't.'

'Ole Christian – you mean Ole Christian Sund?'

Thorbjørnsen nods.

'When did you talk to him?'

'Last night.'

Bjarne looks at her for several long moments. A hand shoots up to her cheek and her nails scratch a dark brown mole.

'I've been told that someone had an argument in Ward 4 yesterday afternoon.'

Thorbjørnsen quickly glances up at him, but when she doesn't comment on his statement, Bjarne continues: 'Did you see or hear anything about that?'

She shakes her head.

Bjarne tries to make eye contact, but Thorbjørnsen is looking down now.

'There's always a little bit of arguing here and there,' she says eventually and juts out her chin. 'That doesn't mean that anyone here would stick knitting needles through the eyes of our patients. You don't seriously think that any of the staff or one of the patients could have done it?'

'It's too soon to say,' Bjarne responds, surprised at the sudden resistance in her voice, but he doesn't have time to think about it further before Ella Sandland knocks on the door and pops in her head to signal that she wants a word.

Bjarne apologises, irritated at the interruption because it shouldn't happen during an interview. But because Sandland is aware of that and yet still interrupts him, he gets up and asks Thorbjørnsen to stay where she is. Then he steps out into the corridor and closes the door behind him.

'What is it?' he asks.

Sandland's gaze is serious.

'There's something I've got to show you.'

Chapter 22

Henning was sorely tempted to ring back Andreas Kjær immediately, but on second thoughts he decided against it. It was too desperate. Maybe Kjær was on his way to work, perhaps he was about to walk an impatient dog. Or maybe he is one of those people who don't like answering the same question twice. Therefore another call would only make matters worse.

Henning grew up in Kløfta, seven or eight kilometres south of Jessheim where Erna Pedersen originally came from. One of his childhood friends is called Atle Abelsen. They didn't really get to know each other until after sixth form when they discovered a shared love of music. They would meet up from time to time and try to put words to something that was supposed to be a melody. And where Henning's interest in technology has remained at the gifted amateur level, Atle's passion for cyberspace and computers fed and sustained him all the way into his choice of career. He now works as a programmer for a company in Lillestrøm, but every now and then he will take on work of a quirkier nature – as long as he considers it a challenge. Henning sends him an email and explains what he wants help with this time with the usual promise of a bottle of Calvados as a thank you.

Henning then thinks about Erna Pedersen's closest family. Surely no one is better placed to tell him about any former enemies that she might have had and he finds out that Pedersen has a son called Tom Sverre Pedersen who works as a doctor at Ullevål University Hospital.

Tom Sverre Pedersen has featured in the media a few times in recent years because he believes that the training of doctors is ripe for reform. If Henning is not mistaken, Pedersen took part in a debate on NRK on exactly this subject not that long ago.

Henning finds Pedersen's mobile number, but his call goes straight to voicemail. *I'm not the only one who wants to get hold of him today*, Henning guesses. For all he knows Pedersen could be being interviewed at the police station right now. Even so Henning leaves a message and asks Pedersen to return his call. He probably won't, but you never know, he just might. Sometimes people with a public profile are happy to speak to the media when the opportunity presents itself.

The buzz in the offices of *123news* hasn't diminished – on the contrary; Henning can't remember when he last heard his sister's name mentioned so many times in one day. And it occurs to him that he hasn't even bothered to find out why every news organisation in Norway seems to have gone overboard with this story.

He brings up the front page of *123news* where he encounters fat, bold typeface against a black background and large pictures of Trine standing on a podium with a hotel logo strategically placed as near the microphone as possible. 'Shortly after giving this speech she assaulted a young, male politician,' the lead-in says.

Henning clicks on it and learns that Trine took part in the Labour Party's annual conference on 9 October last year where she is alleged to have forced a young man to have sex with her. 'The worst abuse of power,' someone states. 'Shameful,' cries another. A third person says that Trine ought to be reported to the police. So far the police haven't taken action; they are waiting for someone to file a complaint, but the public prosecutor the newspaper has spoken to will not rule out that the police might launch their own inquiry.

The lead story is accompanied by background material, reactions, comments, blogs and quotes. There are several other pictures of her; Henning looks at the new Trine as he has slowly started to know her. Smooth skin, nice make-up, elegant clothes, excellent posture and political gravitas in her eyes.

Henning clicks his way through several articles. An unnamed source claims that the unidentified, up-and-coming politician had tried to resolve the issue with Trine, to get her to apologise unreservedly, but that she refused. There are also speculations as to whether the Party knew about the accusations and failed to deal with them.

Henning's attention is drawn to the TV screen to his right. The news channel is on and Prime Minister William Jespersen is seen getting out of a car. The footage is from earlier that morning and Jespersen is asked to comment on the story in today's edition of *VG*. But Jespersen merely says that he agrees with the Justice Secretary, that he, too, refuses to comment on anonymous allegations, and that is all he is prepared to say for the time being.

The camera cuts back to the studio where a news anchor and a commentator look gravely at each other. The anchor asks how toxic this issue is for Jespersen's government.

'It's highly toxic,' the commentator replies. 'Last year alone the Prime Minister had to replace several government Ministers and many have started to doubt his judgement when it comes to making appointments. Trine Juul-Osmundsen represents a huge headache for the Prime Minister since she – despite speculation to the contrary – has proved to be a very popular and effective Minister. The fact that even someone like her finds herself in hot water must cause the Prime Minister to lose sleep, I'm absolutely sure of it.'

'Talking about sleep,' the anchor continues, 'how do you think that Juul-Osmundsen is feeling? It's no secret that she struggled with mental health issues not all that long ago and that she had been on sick leave due to depression. How do you think all this is going to affect her?'

'It's far too early to say, but it clearly isn't going to be easy for her. I don't recall that we've ever had a case where a female Minister is alleged to have exploited her position in this way. Now we have to treat this matter with caution because we've yet to hear the Justice Secretary's side of the story, but I find it hard to see how she can continue in her post after this.'

Depression, Henning thinks and frowns. That comes as news to him, but perhaps it shouldn't. Until his return to work last spring, he had barely read a newspaper or seen any TV while he was in Haukeland Hospital or later at Sunnaas Rehabilitation Centre. But why was Trine depressed?

The screen blurs and an image of Trine as a little girl appears in Henning's head. She is jumping through a garden sprinkler at their home in Kløfta; she is probably no more than six or seven years old. Her hair is wet; it sticks to her back and neck. Excited, she races towards him with a triumphant smile across her face. She takes a run-up, leaps through the water, breaking the jets before they point up at the sky in an elegant arc once more. 'Come on, Henning,' she calls out in her childish voice. And for a moment her voice reminds him of Jonas.

Henning watches himself take a step towards her. Just one, then he stops. Trine shouts that he must have a go because it's such fun. Sitting on a flimsy director's chair nearby is their mother who is holding a cigarette and smiling. She follows her daughter with her eyes, but her expression changes as she looks at him as if to order him into the water. So Henning does it, he takes a run-up and jumps; the jets cut through him like icy knives and he hears Trine squeal and shout out: 'I told you it would be fun!'

Henning blinks and is back in the office. He sees all the people in front of him, he hears the noise, senses the mood, the chaos; everything springs to life again. And he understands, possibly for the first time, the kind of strain Trine will be under for days to come. People will follow her wherever she goes, demand answers, try to speak to anyone who knows her, friends, family. Opposition politicians will make statements, there will be opinion polls and the telephones won't ever stop ringing in the office of any Norwegian newspaper with more than ten readers. Every news organisation will try to catch up on the head start that *VG* currently has with its exclusive. This means high publication frequency and a low quality threshold for what is published. Single source journalism. And it won't be long before other stories will come out; anything even vaguely controversial that Trine has ever done will be re-examined.

But this isn't just about Trine, Henning thinks. There are other people to consider. So he gets up and walks away from the others. He takes out his mobile and sees that the time is 12.21. Then he rings his mother. But instead of a dial tone he gets a message telling him that the number is temporarily unavailable.

Henning nods happily to himself.

Chapter 23

'How is that even possible?'

Bjarne Brogeland is still standing outside the meeting room on the ground floor of Grünerhjemmet, flicking through the documents that Ella Sandland has had faxed over from the police station. Sandland shrugs.

'I mean – don't they run checks on people before they hire them? I thought anyone who wanted a job in the care sector had to disclose criminal convictions.'

Brogeland reads the document from the beginning again, and sees that the conviction of Daniel Nielsen, Erna Pedersen's primary care worker, dates back to May 2006. Nielsen suspected his girlfriend of being unfaithful and tried to beat the truth out of her. The fact that he was right wasn't regarded as a mitigating circumstance.

'So he has a temper and a predisposition for violence,' Bjarne says.

'But is it likely that Erna Pedersen could have provoked him in quite the same way?' Sandland wonders.

Brogeland grimaces quickly before he takes out his mobile and sees that Nielsen still hasn't returned his call. Brogeland rings the number again, but it goes straight to voicemail. This time he doesn't leave a message.

'When is he due in at work?' he asks Sandland and hangs up.

'Not until four o'clock this afternoon.'

'Okay,' Brogeland says. 'Let's pay him a home visit.'

*

The city is grey from the low hanging clouds when Bjarne starts the car and manoeuvres out into the traffic.

'What did she have to say in her defence?' he asks as he turns left into Søndregate. At the bottom of the hill the River Aker winds its way under several bridges, warbles between dense alders and weeping willows whose branches arch down and only just avoid getting wet.

'Who?' Sandland asks.

'The manager of the care home. I presume she was the one who hired Nielsen?'

'No defence,' Sandland says with a sigh. 'She was desperate for people, she said, and Nielsen came across as a good candidate at the interview. And you don't have a legal obligation to disclose criminal convictions before you start working in a care home.'

Brogeland shakes his head and drives up through Grünerløkka. The wheels find their own path between tramlines and potholes in the streets after years of cable laying and poor maintenance. The buildings they pass look like unwashed Lego bricks, square and painted a range of different colours.

The ground in Sofienberg Park is sated with foliage from the chestnut trees in between patches of wet green grass and dark brown, slippery paths. They continue driving in the direction of Sinsen where the green area of Torshovdalen lies like a deep ravine in between arms of criss-crossing roads leading out of the city. The car ploughs through the wind.

'Did you get a chance to speak to that angry man from the TV lounge?' Bjarne asks. 'Guttorm Tveter or whatever his name was?'

'I did,' Sandland says and a smile forms around her lips. 'It's a wonder I've got any voice left. The old guy's deaf as a post. And he refuses to wear a hearing aid.'

'Typical,' Bjarne says. 'Did he see anything? Did you get the impression that he might be involved?'

'It was difficult to get much sense out of him. I'm not even sure he understands that Erna Pedersen is dead.'

'Really?'

'He was much more interested in telling me about his childhood in Linderud. He could remember every single detail of that.'

'That's often the way it is,' Bjarne says. 'Old people can't remember what happened yesterday, but you try asking them about the war.'

Sandland laughs.

'Do you know what he asked me?'

'No?'

'He asked me to bring a bottle of cognac next time.'

Brogeland smiles.

'Braastad XO, preferably,' Sandland says.

'That's priceless,' Brogeland laughs. 'I think I have a bottle of that at home.'

There is silence between them again. Brogeland turns into Sinsenterrassen, says goodbye to an open, grey Oslo and hello to denser development where the cars drive closer to the pavements and people lean into the weather.

'But Guttorm Tveter must have had something to say about what happened yesterday. Doesn't he remember anything?'

'Doesn't seem like it,' Sandland says. 'He was more concerned about what time it was. There was something he wanted to watch on TV.'

Bjarne finds a parking space outside the supermarket and reluctantly leaves the car in favour of an uninspiring walk that puts an end to their conversation. They step out on the pavement where wet leaves cover the tarmac like a blanket, find the brown building where Daniel Nielsen lives and press a button with his name on. Brogeland stuffs his hands in his jeans pockets in a vain attempt to warm them up and looks up at the grey and white windows.

Soon they hear a voice saying 'hello?'

'Hello, this is the police,' Ella Sandland says. 'Are you Daniel Nielsen?'

A long silence ensues before the intercom on the wall finally buzzes to let them in.

The officers enter and take the lift up to the fourth floor where a man meets them in the stairwell. Dark hair falls to his ears from a messy centre parting and three-day-old stubble steals the light from his face. He is wearing a black T-shirt with a picture of Whitney Houston. Below the artist's face the caption says '*Houston, we have a problem*' in red letters. His trousers, also black, are sagging. Over his belt hangs a belly that would make Bjarne run to the nearest treadmill in sheer panic.

'Hi,' Daniel Nielsen says quickly and smiles at the investigators. 'Have you been trying to get hold of me today?' He laughs. 'I've been to the gym, you see, and I've only just got home this minute.'

'So you haven't managed to shower yet?' Bjarne says.

'No, I—' Nielsen runs a hand through his hair. 'I haven't got round to that.'

He rubs his hands on his trouser leg. He smiles at them again.

'Where do you work out?' Bjarne asks.

'Eh, Svein's Gym,' Nielsen says.

Bjarne nods.

'Could we come in, please?' Sandland asks.

Nielsen looks at her.

'Can't we just take it out here? My flat's a real mess and I – I—'

'We prefer to talk inside,' Bjarne says firmly and doesn't offer any explanation.

'Of course,' Nielsen nods and goes in first, holds the door open for them and kicks some shoes out of the way before they reach a narrow hallway. Pegs on the wall are taken by jackets, baseball caps and a sad-looking umbrella. They walk past a cracked mirror and a three-drawer white chest where one knob is falling off.

They step inside the living room. There is an open laptop on a desk. Next to it is a plate with a half-eaten sandwich. There are teeth marks in the saveloy. A full glass of milk is standing beside it. On the walls are big framed pictures. Snowboarders in a white mountain terrain. An angler in a river in water up to his waist. Some smaller close-ups of flowers in vivid colours.

'Let's talk about Caroline,' Bjarne says and takes a seat.

The old sofa cushions sag under him and he ends up sitting close to the floor. Nielsen's eyes widen. And then he slumps.

'Of course,' he says, looking down. 'I should have known you'd find out about her.'

Nielsen heaves a sigh and clenches his fist.

'Why didn't you tell your boss about your conviction?'

Nielsen looks at Sandland.

'Do you think I'd have got the job if I had?'

He shakes his head.

'I needed money and I—'

He shakes his head again. The officers let him take his time. Soon he looks up at them.

'But I've got nothing to do with what happened to Erna Pedersen,' he says. 'I give you my word.'

Nielsen does his best to give them a look that inspires confidence, but it is a staring competition that Bjarne wins easily.

'Did you know her?'

'No,' he says quickly and loudly. 'I mean, only through work, if that's what you're asking.'

'That was what I was asking.'

'No,' Nielsen repeats. 'Absolutely not.'

Bjarne nods slowly.

'Did you go to work yesterday?'

'Eh, no. I mean, I stopped off at work, but I wasn't working.'

'Why did you stop off at work?'

'I was just dropping something off.'

Bjarne looks at him, waits for a continuation that doesn't come.

'When was this?'

'Late afternoon. Four thirty, five or thereabouts.'

It grows quiet between them while Bjarne stares at him.

'Did you see anyone enter or leave Erna Pedersen's room

while you were there?'

Nielsen shakes his head in jerks before he wipes his nose with the back of his hand.

'Did you notice anything while you were there? Anything unusual?'

Nielsen scratches his nose vigorously with the nail of his index finger.

'No, I don't think so.'

High up his forehead along his hairline the sweat has darkened his brown hair.

Sandland looks around.

'Why did you need money?' she asks.

Nielsen looks at her. His eyebrows narrow.

'Do you know how much it costs to rent a one-bedroom flat in Oslo these days? Even up here?'

Sandland shakes her head.

'I'm paying just over 12,000 kroner a month before utility bills and phone charges. I have to have a job. Though I guess I'll get the sack now.'

Nielsen tears a tiny bit of skin off his thumb. It starts to bleed so he reaches out for a loo roll in the middle of the table, next to two lumpy stones that look glued together.

'How would you describe Erna Pedersen's behaviour recently?'

Nielsen hesitates, rips off a sheet and wraps it round his thumb.

'Difficult to say. I didn't really know her all that well. I've only been her primary care worker for a couple of months and I rarely got a sensible word out of her.'

'Okay,' Bjarne says and gets up. Sandland does the same.

'We'll probably want to speak to you later. And it would be good if you could pick up the phone the next time we call, that way we don't have to come up to your flat.'

'Yes, er, sorry, I—'

'Don't worry about it,' Bjarne says. 'You were at the gym. At Svein's Gym.'

Bjarne stares at him for a long time.

'Yes,' Nielsen says and laughs quickly. 'So I was.'

'Thanks for the chat,' Sandland says and leaves first.

Nielsen accompanies them to the door and closes it firmly behind them.

*

'I don't think he went to the gym,' Bjarne says once they are inside the lift.

'Why not?'

'Did you see a sports bag anywhere?'

Sandland thinks about it, but doesn't reply.

'And why was he wearing regular clothes if he hadn't showered yet? Where were his workout clothes?'

The lift stops at the ground floor. The officers get out.

'So what do we do now?' Sandland asks and turns to him with her hand on the front door handle. Brogeland thinks about it.

'I think he's hiding something. I'll call Svein's Gym to check if he really was there. If it turns out that he wasn't, we'll put him under surveillance.'

'There's no way you'll ever get a unit together at such short notice, Bjarne. Don't—'

'Oh, yes,' Bjarne says and smiles. 'I still have a few favours I can call in. And it would only be for a couple of hours. At least to begin with.'

He smiles, but Sandland merely shrugs.

Bjarne sighs to himself. She is still unimpressed.

Chapter 24

Atle Abelsen replies much more quickly than Henning had expected, but not by email, which is his usual form of communication.

'Yo,' Abelsen says when Henning answers the call.

'Hi, Atle. I guess this means you got my email.'

'No "how are you?" No "what are you up to these days?"'

'How are you, Atle? What are you up to these days?'

'Overworked and underpaid.'

'I'm surprised to hear that.'

'It's a tough life.'

'So I've been told. But I presume you've read my email since you're calling?'

Henning is about to ask Atle what he has found out when he remembers something.

'Before we start, did you know Erna Pedersen yourself? Did she ever teach you?'

'No, but I called my mother. She still teaches in Kløfta. She said she had heard about her.'

Henning straightens up a little.

'And what had she heard?'

'Erna Pedersen had something of a reputation, as far as I can gather. Positively terrifying. Old school, I mean. We're talking canes slamming against the desk, that sort of thing. Stand up when the teacher comes into the classroom, mind your manners and always say good morning.'

'Ah, the good old days.'

'Quite. But I know that wasn't the reason for your email. I've managed to find out a couple of things about Erna Pedersen that might be of interest. In 1989 she filed a complaint at the local police station because her house had been vandalised. The old witch had finally had enough.'

'I see,' Henning says, picking up and clicking on a pen lying next to him.

'She claimed she knew who the culprits were, but their names aren't listed in the report. I don't know if the police ever bothered investigating her complaint, but no one was convicted of anything.'

Henning ponders this for a moment.

'Did the report say anything about what kind of vandalism it was?'

'Eggs had been thrown at her house, basement windows had been smashed, that kind of thing. She used to cycle to school, I believe, but someone deliberately damaged her bicycle. Let down the tyres.'

'Right,' Henning says.

It sounds mostly like typical schoolboy pranks, he thinks.

'Then her husband fell off a ladder in the garden in 1991, I think it was, and had a heart attack. Or the other way round, I don't remember. I can't imagine that made her less strict and bitter.'

'No, I don't suppose it did,' Henning says while he mulls it over. 'Was there anything else?'

'No.'

'Okay. It would be great if you could email or text me

her old address.'

'Will do. But how are you, mate? Do you still play music these days?'

Henning hesitates before he replies.

'No, not often, I'm afraid.'

'For God's sake, man, you mustn't stop. You had talent!'

'Mm. Are you still drinking Calvados?'

'Oh, forget about that. Let's go for a beer the next time I'm in town.'

'Okay. Thanks for your help, Atle.'

'You're welcome, dude.'

Chapter 25

A short morning of freedom.

Ever since Emilie Blomvik had a child there is practically nothing she treasures more than that. Several hours in a row where she can do whatever she likes. She can go to the gym, she can read that magazine that has been gathering dust on top of the fridge, she can watch a movie that has taken up space on the recorder for ever. No one needs watching or looking after or checking in. Nor will anyone disapprove if she drinks a can of Coke on a weekday.

Quality time with a capital Q, that's what it is. However, it continues to surprise her that she rarely ends up doing any of the things she had planned, just like today. She was going to waste some time on the computer, possibly look for some lovely holidays, start one of the books she was given last Christmas. But if she tries to reconstruct the morning, remember what she actually did after taking Sebastian to nursery, she is stumped for an answer. She doesn't remember anything other than reading the newspaper and tidying up the kitchen. The rest is one big fog of nothing.

Even so it has been bliss. No one needed her to do anything. The sheer knowledge that such moments exist gives her precisely the breathing space she needs.

She only wishes that Mattis would call soon. It has gone eleven now. Perhaps the meeting with the partners didn't go as well as he had expected?

She hopes he won't get disappointed or upset. Children hurting themselves or not getting what they want is one thing. It's part of growing up, meeting resistance and maturing as a result. Adults sulking is another matter. She just can't deal with it. And Mattis is one of the worst offenders when things don't go his way. The whole house becomes enshrouded in a thundercloud she can't get away from soon enough. On this specific point she has very little patience. One child in the house is enough.

Emilie has barely had this thought when the phone rings. She jumps, gets up from the kitchen chair and fetches her mobile from the worktop next to the bread bin.

It's Mattis.

'Hello?' she says with expectation in her voice.

'You're speaking to Mattis Steinfjell, partner in Bergman Hoff, Solicitors. Am I speaking to Emilie Blomvik, the most wonderful girl in the world?'

Emilie clasps her hand over her mouth.

'Is it true?' she screams.

Self-satisfied laughter bubbles away quietly before Mattis gives up trying to suppress it. He starts laughing out loud.

'But that's wonderful, darling. Congratulations.'

Emilie doesn't know what else to say. Neither does Mattis, or so it seems.

'So go on then, tell me all about it.'

'Well, there's not much to say except that I'm moving up the food chain, sweetheart. You know what that means.'

Emilie shakes her head to herself, but she says 'yes' all the same. And then she lets him brag to his heart's content and she has to pull herself together in order not to cry. One of several things she dislikes about herself since she became a mother is that she cries at the slightest thing.

'That's absolutely fantastic, Mattis,' she says when he finally stops talking. 'Once again, congratulations.'

'We're going to celebrate, sweetheart. I'll buy some champagne we can open tonight. We'll order a takeaway and get drunk.'

Emilie doesn't reply immediately.

'I'm on nights this week, Mattis. Don't you remember?'

'Can't you swap with someone?'

'It's too short notice,' she replies, but what she is thinking is that she could have asked someone if she really wanted to. And yet there is a part of her that doesn't want to be with Mattis in his moment of glory. She realises she is worried what he might ask her while he rides his happiness wave. Like, for example, if she will marry him.

'You'll just have to celebrate without me,' she says trying to sound kind, happy and exuberant. And she is, she really is, for him.

'So when is it official?' she asks. 'Can I tell my friends the good news?'

'Of course you can,' he says. 'But I've got to go now, darling. Love you.'

Emilie doesn't reply straightaway. Then she says, more quietly than she had planned to: 'I love you too.'

Chapter 26

The doorbell rings.

He turns around and frowns. He doesn't remember the last time he had visitors.

Probably someone trying to get into one of the other flats, he thinks. Or one of his neighbours who has accidentally locked themselves out again. That must be it.

He turns his attention back to the computer monitors. *World of Warcraft* on one. Facebook on the other where he has clicked on a profile he visits every day even though it always hurts.

The doorbell rings again. He tilts his head slightly and gets up from his chair reluctantly. Shuffles towards the door and looks through the spy hole.

A man he doesn't remember seeing before is standing outside next to a woman. *Plainclothes police officers*, he thinks, and is immediately gripped by panic, but he forces himself to think rationally. *Even if they are police officers, this can't possibly be about that old witch.*

Or can it?

The man looks like a local politician. Long and lean with thin, grey hair. Can't be too difficult to knock out. The woman doesn't look very tough, either. Maximum 1.65 metres. Practically flat-chested. Skinny arms.

He opens the door and is blinded by the light outside. He

has to shield his eyes with one hand in order to see them.

'Hello, we're from the bailiffs.'

The man introduces himself and the woman beside him, names he instantly forgets.

'Perhaps you know why we're here?'

He looks at them and shakes his head. He leans against the door frame and feels the pointy, cold edges of the steel lock.

'You haven't paid your rent for a long time and as a result you were issued with an eviction notice in accordance with the Eviction Act paragraph 13 section 2. This notice was sent to you and you were given fourteen days to move out. But I can see that you're still here. Haven't you packed your stuff yet?'

He had completely forgotten that notice. He has been lost in a world of his own in the last few weeks. And before that he always thought that he would find a way out, that he would be able to get hold of money from someone other than his mother.

The debt collector tries to look over his shoulder, but he blocks his path.

'I'm sorry, but there is no way around this.'

The debt collector's words fall like hammer blows. A taste of metal has settled on his tongue. He hugs himself, looks at the young woman with her blonde, shoulder-length hair. There is a hint of contempt in her eyes. And he feels the urge to—

'So am I right in thinking that you're not able to move out today?'

He turns his gaze to the debt collector again.

'No, I – I—'

'Okay,' the man says turning to the woman next to him. 'You're lucky; you've a very kind landlord. He has said he's willing to give you another three days, but that's the absolute final deadline. We'll come back at ten o'clock on Thursday morning and change the locks. So you've got three days. That should be more than enough.'

The debt collector seems to be expecting some kind of response, but it is not appropriate to nod or to thank him. So instead the man nods by way of goodbye and they start walking back to the stairwell and the lift. He takes a step back inside and closes the door behind him.

Three days, he thinks when everything around him is quiet again. What the hell is he going to do? He certainly can't ask his mother if he can move back home again for a while.

With heavy footsteps he plods back to his desk and the computer monitors. The back of the chair creaks as he sits down. It creaks in his brain as well as if the bones inside his head are stretching.

Again he stares at her Facebook profile and the status she posted just after eleven o'clock this morning. Now with forty-nine likes and thirteen comments. Another one is added while he watches.

And that's when the rage overwhelms him.

Just as well you ended up with Mattis. It could have been much much worse ☺ ☺ ☺. *Looking forward to hearing all about it tomorrow. Hugs and kisses. JK*

He shakes his head, feels a lump in his stomach and clenches his fists. Something cold pricks him in the back of his neck and turns into a restless itch he has to scratch. A light he just has to extinguish.

Chapter 27

To dread coming home is the worst thing.

Or rather, Johanne Klingenberg doesn't dread it because Baltazar will be there waiting for her, always happy, always eager for her company, but she has been on edge since the break-in – how long has it been now – two weeks ago?

She returned home after a lecture and got a strange feeling that someone must have been in her flat because Baltazar acted so out of character when she went up to greet him. As if he wasn't sure that she was someone he recognised or that she was a friend. It wasn't until she poured him a little milk and gave him some treats that she was allowed to stroke his neck and back.

She didn't get truly scared until she saw the damaged picture on the wall. And the red stain next to Baltazar's basket. It looked as if someone had smeared blood across the floor. She immediately checked the cat and discovered that he hadn't hurt himself.

Johanne proceeded to check out the rest of the flat, tiptoeing as quietly as she could from room to room and brandishing a kitchen knife. She wrenched open cupboards and doors in case someone was hiding behind them, but she found no one. Even so she called the police. She knew that these days they can identify a criminal from only a single hair or a trace of blood, but the officers who turned up told her she would just have to be patient. Such tests took forever to carry out. And when the sample finally got to the front of the DNA queue, it would only prove useful if they found a match – something for which there was absolutely no guarantee.

It might have been easier to forget the whole thing – after all nothing was taken. But there have been other incidents. On several occasions she has been absolutely sure that she was being followed, both when she has been for a night out or making her way home after a lecture. Once she saw a man in a khaki army jacket press himself against the wall one hundred metres away from her. He had been staring at her and he had had a camera. The strange thing was that she was sure she had seen him somewhere before, she just couldn't remember where.

Fortunately she doesn't believe anyone is following her today. Or yesterday, now that she thinks about it. Perhaps that is why the lecture is still buzzing around her head. Though to call that a lecture is insulting to lecturers. Reading out loud would be a more accurate description. Like sleeping tablets without the need for a prescription.

Johanne had hoped that she would start the new term invigorated after a long warm summer, but from day one she could feel it, the weight of something starting to oppress her. She didn't want to be there. She was quite simply fed up, fed up with marketing and the crackle of stiff new books being opened for the very first time. But she made herself get out of bed the next day and the day after and decided to put it down to a post-holiday depression that would lift of its own accord once she got back into the routine. But it hasn't passed. Everything just gets drearier and more exhausting.

It's no help, either, that the dreaded thesis is lying in wait for her like a troll under a bridge. And her useless supervisor who is always busy and never interested in hearing what she thinks or believes. He is the expert, not her. She is just a student, one of many who have filed through his office over the years. Fresh perspectives, hah!

She has no idea how she will find the strength to get through the last few terms. She recognises the feeling from her time at sixth form when she came to hate everything to do with school. She just wanted to finish the course as quickly as possible. It showed in the grades she got, something that prompted her to try to improve her academic results when she reached her early thirties. And to begin with, going back to school was fine. The partying from her teenage years came back, with all that entailed. And perhaps that's the only thing that has kept her going.

Her thumb glides up and down her mobile as she walks. She is on Facebook and she feels a warm glow when she reads Emilie's last status update. Johanne presses 'Like' and writes a comment. Only occasionally does she look up to see where she is going.

Luckily the college she attends in Oslo is not far from her flat and it feels good to get home and see that everything is still the same, that Baltazar lies in his basket just as he did when she left him. Black, white and happy.

Johanne Klingenberg throws down her keys, takes out her mobile and goes back on Facebook to update her status.

Home.

Safe at last.

Chapter 28

Henning looks at the clock. The working day has come and gone without Erna Pedersen's son returning his call. Henning has sent him a text message as well, but has had no reply. Nor does Bjarne Brogeland appear to have had the time to return his calls. Things are moving slowly.

Henning files a story about how Erna Pedersen was strangled, a story he illustrates with a photograph of her that the police have issued to the media. The story reads well even though it is far less sensational than the stories being written about Trine.

The online version of *VG*, *VG Nett*, has managed to track down an old boyfriend of his sister's when she was a law student who can tell the newspaper's readers that 'Trine Juul, as she then was, was known for her excessive partying. It certainly wouldn't surprise him if she is guilty of the accusations being made against her.' None of the newspapers has a single new picture to publish. The most recent ones they have are from this morning when she hurried inside the Ministry of Justice and didn't make eye contact with any of the cameras. A headline repeated by several papers is TRINE HIDES.

Henning would have expected that the identity of the young Labour Party politician would have become known during the day, but even though online speculation is rife, no one has yet come forward, nor has any particular name taken more hold in the public imagination than others. As far as Henning can work out, most members of the Labour Party's youth branch who took part in last year's conference must have been interviewed by now. All of them are denying that they went to Trine's hotel room.

The picture the media are creating of her now is very far removed from the little girl he grew up with. He remembers how every Christmas Eve they would sit in front of the television with bags of sweets and watch Christmas movies. They also used to have some bean bags; Trine's was pink, while Henning's was mint green. Some evenings he would go to her room just to give her a goodnight hug, and he would stay there and chat for a long time until there would be a knock on the wall from his parents' bedroom because their talking was keeping them awake.

They also used to play and exercise together down in the basement passage on the grey, knobbly carpet. Often there would be an acrid smell of urine because local cats favoured the foundations of their house. Trine and Henning had a foam ball and switched between playing handball and football; the door to the lavatory and the door to the larder served as goals. One Christmas they were given Adidas shorts, which they wore when they played and their game appeared to improve because they felt they looked so much smarter.

He wonders if Trine ever thinks about those days.

Perhaps they started drifting apart as teenagers when they developed different interests. Once he had finished sixth form and joined the army to do his national service, he barely spoke to her. Whenever he called home, it was always his mother who answered the telephone. Trine never called. Never gave him a welcome-home hug when he visited; instead she would usually go out straight after dinner and come back late.

Despite the lack of contact between them, there is something about her plight that moves him. He doesn't like to see her bleed. But no matter how tempting it is to get involved, he can't report on a story about his own sister. Besides, he would meet with closed doors everywhere. He doesn't have any contacts in the world of politics. And what could he really do? So far her young accuser hasn't even been named.

Leave it alone, Henning tells himself. *It's not your story*.

Chapter 29

Bjarne Brogeland doesn't know when he will be able to leave the office and anyway the weather doesn't encourage him to go outside, so he texts Anita to apologise for missing dinner yet again and tells her to eat without him. There is no reply.

The investigation team is about to hold another meeting when Bjarne receives a call from the unit that has spent the last two hours watching Daniel Nielsen's flat.

'Yes?' Bjarne replies.

'You wanted to know if the subject moved,' says the voice down the other end.

'Yes,' Bjarne replies again.

'He came outside a little while ago and was picked up by a red BMW with a massive hole in the silencer.'

'Go on?'

'They drove up to Holmenkollen via Majorstua and Smedstadkrysset, but we lost him at a red light. And we can't hear the noisy silencer any more.'

'Holmenkollen?'

'Yes.'

Bjarne wonders what Nielsen's car could be doing there.

'We've checked the registration number. The car belongs to a Pernille Thorbjørnsen. Do you know her?'

Bjarne thinks about it.

'Yes,' he replies.

'But she wasn't driving the car. The driver was a man with blond, shoulder-length hair.'

A man with blond, shoulder-length hair, Bjarne thinks, and tries to recall all the people he has spoken to recently. It doesn't take long before he gets a hit.

Could the man have been Ole Christian Sund, the care worker who found Erna Pedersen dead?

*

The bodyguards offered to carry Trine's bags of food and clothing, but she declined. The pain burning in her arms and spreading up to her shoulders is something she has to endure if only because it makes her feel vaguely alive. She hasn't felt that for the last couple of hours. She has merely existed, almost in a state of weightlessness, without being able to sense the ground beneath her feet.

Pål Fredrik doesn't like the sea, he prefers the mountains. His objection is that nothing ever happens by the sea. No, precisely. That's exactly why she loves it, because nothing ever happens. It's about being at one with the wind, the breeze and the sea. Because they never look at her with accusing eyes.

She finds the key where she left it the last time she was here – God knows how many years ago – under the bench by the door to the log cabin. The smell that comes towards her as she enters floods her with memories. Everything is as she remembers it from her childhood. The white, open fireplace in the corner, still in one piece. The crumbling old log basket beside it. The small, dusty portable television, the white display cabinet with glasses and bottles. The sofa bed up against the wall. The table in the middle, which can be extended to almost twice its size if she can be bothered to attach the flaps. Old, worn chairs with blue seat cushions.

She recalls one spring when they came here to get the cabin ready for the season; it might have been the middle of May. They found mouse droppings everywhere. The mice had nibbled the pillows, the bed linen, the wax candles; there were tiny black dots of mouse droppings all over the place. Another time they found a wagtail, completely stiff, but just as beautiful as if it had still been alive. It was lying under a bed. How it had got inside after they had locked up the cabin, nobody could explain. Not even Henning, even though he tried.

Trine sees that as usual the mice have sought refuge inside the cabin. Lots of them. And she discovers that she looks forward to cleaning, moving her body and concentrating on something completely different than the sword hanging over her. She draws the curtains, opens the door and lets in the sea breeze. The clammy, stuffy atmosphere of stale dust will soon be gone. The walls will come alive again. Already she feels what a good idea it was to come here. The constant waves even ease her breathing.

Trine turns on the water. The pipes gurgle and splutter a little before a steady, cold stream comes out of the tap above the utility sink. She puts on water to boil and takes out some cleaning supplies.

Trine has been scrubbing away for an hour when her mobile beeps in her jacket pocket. It's a text message from Katarina. She wonders if they have arrived yet and if everything is all right. Yes, Trine replies to both questions, surprised that the message goes through as mobile coverage in the area has always been poor. But it takes only a minute, then she gets a reply.

> I don't know if you have a TV where you are, but there will be debates both on NRK and TV2 tonight. The subject is: Has society done too little to prevent sexual harassment – and both male and female incest victims will be in the studio.

Of course, Trine sighs. They're already having a debate based on the assumption that the allegations are true. But what on earth does incest have to do with anything?

And that's when she feels it. The pull of the white display cabinet in the corner, next to the TV. She goes over to it and opens the door. A stuffy smell wafts towards her. Glass after glass, neatly lined up. And at the bottom – the bottles. Liqueurs. Cognac.

She recalls that her parents always drank cognac when they went to the cabin. It was part of the whole experience, they said. Coffee, cognac and chocolate. The holy trinity.

Trine takes out a bottle and looks at it. St Hallvard's liqueur, half empty. She sits down at the table and gazes at the bottle. And she wonders at what point you turn into your parents, no matter how hard you try to fight it.

She fetches a glass from the cabinet, blows the dust out from its bottom and fills it with St Hallvard's. Finds a cigarette from her bag and lights up. *Like mother like daughter*, she thinks. And she raises the glass to her lips and proposes a toast to yet another member of the Juul family who has stepped off the cliff while staring down at the bottom of a bottle.

Chapter 30

Above him the wind nudges the grey, dense clouds along. Around him the swallows screech, loud and piercing.

How strange that they never crash into each other, Henning thinks, and tries to follow one of them with his eyes. It flies from side to side, it soars and it plummets. Choppy, sudden turns. A free display of inexhaustible energy. All its movements seem random, as if its entire existence is ruled by impulses, in sharp contrast to the migrating birds that will soon start their annual trip to the south in V formations.

It must be a lovely life, Henning decides, and takes a swig of his daily ration of liquid black sugar. Whether it be living exclusively on whims or having a fixed plan with your life. Right now either option seems equally attractive.

Henning takes another sip of his Coke while he thinks. And thinking is what he always does best in Dælenenga Sports Park. There aren't many people around yet, but it's still early afternoon. And even though the weather forecast is bad, he knows they will turn up eventually. Children, teenagers and adults.

So Erna Pedersen was a strict and unpopular teacher. But what was she apart from that? Did she have any interests? Did she get involved with anything?

He believes she enjoyed knitting. Perhaps she had joined forces with people with similar interests, in a club or in an association of some kind. Someone must have known her. But according to Bjarne Brogeland, she hadn't had a visitor at Grünerhjemmet for ages. There is more and more evidence to suggest that she lived an isolated life while she waited for death to find her.

Henning is halfway through another mouthful when his mobile rings. He is surprised to see that the caller is Tom Sverre Pedersen, the victim's son. Flustered, Henning puts down the Coke can and takes out his notepad from his inside pocket while he answers the phone.

'Tom Sverre Pedersen here. You've been trying to get hold of me?'

'Yes, I – yes I have,' Henning says, biting off the plastic cap of his pen. 'I'm sorry for your loss.'

'Thank you.'

Henning makes himself comfortable, wedges the phone in between his ear and shoulder and tries to find a position that means he can make notes at the same time. Not easy on the cold, hard planks.

'And I'm sorry for disturbing you at such a difficult time.'

Pedersen makes no reply even after Henning has given him an opening.

'I work for *123news*, and I— '

'I know who you are, Juul. I follow the news.'

'Er, okay. Then you can probably guess why I've been try-ing to contact you. I want to write a story about your mother. The kind of person she was. The idea is for our readers to get to know her a little better.'

'I'm not so sure that they would want to.'

Henning is temporarily wrong-footed by the unexpected answer.

'What makes you say that?'

'Listen, Juul, I don't know how much you've found out about my mother, but if you're looking for a fairy tale to splash across your front page, you're wasting your time. My mother was no Mother Teresa.'

Henning presses his pen as hard against the paper as he can without tearing it, but no ink comes out. He tries, without success, to shake the pen alive.

'Strong words coming from her son?'

'Strong, yes, but true. My mother wasn't terribly popular.'

Henning gives up, puts down his pen and accepts he will just have to try to memorise the conversation to the best of his ability.

'I've been told she could be quite strict. As a teacher, I mean.'

'Hah, that's just for starters. She wanted things her way, and she was extra hard on the hard kids.'

'She and The Phantom both.'

'Yes. I'm sure you can imagine what it was like for me to grow up when my friends had my mother for a teacher.'

'All the kids wanted to come home and play at your house?'

'Not exactly. It's hard to separate the apple from the tree, if I can put it like that.'

'I understand.'

'I'm not sure that you do, Juul. And the reason I'm telling you this is that I've read some of your articles. You seem like a reporter who wants to get to the truth. My experience with the media is that not many of you are. And people in

Jessheim will laugh at you if you paint a pretty picture of my mother's life.'

'So your mother had many enemies?'

Pedersen snorts.

'My mother was a real bitch. It's a miracle that my father managed to stay married to her for all those years. Don't get me wrong – she was my mother and I loved her in my own way. I made sure that she got a place at Grünerhjemmet because I had neither the time nor the inclination to look after her myself. Now that last bit you don't need to include in your story, but despite her behaviour I wanted her to end her life in comfort. And with the exception of her actual death, I think she was really quite happy where she was.'

Henning nods to himself as he senses the temptation of handing over the responsibility for his mother to someone who can do a better job than him.

'I've heard that there was quite a lot of vandalism done to your mother's house while she lived in Jessheim?'

'Yes, at one point it almost seemed as if it had become a sport.'

'Did you ever find out who did it?'

'No, but I know that my mother had her suspicions. And there were several different gangs of kids who could have done it. You only had to look at the graffiti on the walls of Jessheim School.'

'Do you happen to know if anyone hated her more than others?'

Pedersen is quiet for a few moments.

'Not that I can recall. Don't forget it's a really long time ago.'

Henning raises his gaze in the pause that follows. He spots Adil walking towards the Astroturf with a bag slung over his shoulder.

'I presume the police have interviewed you?'

'They have.'

'Then they've probably asked you if you suspect anyone of murdering your mother.'

Pedersen waits a little before he replies.

'They have.'

'And do you?'

Long pause. Henning doesn't push him.

'No. But I'm concerned that someone might have a grudge against me too.'

Henning sits up.

'What do you mean?'

'I'm thinking about the damaged photo in my mother's room.'

Henning doesn't interrupt, but lets Pedersen tell him the story in his own words. And when he has finished, Henning feels a slight chill down his neck.

'So do you have any enemies? Someone you've reason to be scared of?'

'No. And that's what I told the police.'

'Okay.'

At that moment Henning sees another boy walking towards the football pitch, holding hands with his mother. And suddenly he remembers who the boy's father is.

'Thank you for being so frank with me, Pedersen. I really appreciate it.'

Henning gets up and looks at the boy.

'You're welcome. So will you be writing about my mother?'

Henning thinks about it.

'Yes, I hope so. But right now I don't know what kind of story it's going to be.'

Chapter 31

The incident room is filled with officers and investigators. As usual everyone's attention is focused at the head of the board-room table where Arild Gjerstad is reviewing the discoveries, evidence and facts of the murder case.

'How far have you got with interviewing people at the care home?' he asks.

Emil Hagen clears his throat.

'We've yet to cross the finishing line.'

'Does anyone stand out?'

Hagen shakes his head.

'Many people have alibied each other and most of them say that they didn't see anything. We're going to have to be a little more thorough in our interviews.'

Gjerstad nods. 'Forensics have finished analysing the crumbs and the dust they found on Erna Pedersen's clothing,' he informs them, running his index finger and thumb over his moustache. 'It's rock, that's all. Tiny rock fragments, probably from the other weapon that we've yet to trace.'

'The weapon used to whack the knitting needles into her eyes?' Ella Sandland asks. Gjerstad nods to confirm it is.

'A few wool fibres were found on one of the fragments. Wool with a tiny speck of glue.'

'Wool?' Emil Hagen says in disbelief and licks his upper lip.

'Rock, wool and glue,' Gjerstad says, looking around. 'What does that make?'

The officers stare at each other.

'Hair,' Sandland says.

More baffled expressions.

'Didn't you ever make stone trolls when you were little?'

'No,' Hagen says quickly and snorts at the same time.

'You take two stones,' Sandland explains. 'You glue them together and decorate them with straw or wool or something like that to make the hair. Then you paint on the eyes, the nose and the mouth. It's a very popular activity in nurseries and schools.'

'That's what Ann-Mari Sara thought as well,' Gjerstad says. 'So we're probably looking for a stone troll that has lost a little hair and has dents or marks from knitting needles.'

Hagen shakes his head.

'Do people normally make stone trolls in a care home?' he asks and looks at Sandland.

'I haven't seen that particular activity before, but it's not uncommon for patients to take part in different kinds of art and craft work – if they feel up to it. But I asked one of the care workers about leisure activities and it's not something they do very much of.'

'So how did the stone troll end up there?' Pia Nøkleby asks.

Bjarne coughs and looks at Sandland.

'Daniel Nielsen had something similar on his table when we visited him earlier today, but I didn't notice if it was dented. And I don't think he would be stupid enough to keep a weapon in plain sight. Incidentally, it was right next to a loo roll.'

'Perhaps he's one of those guys who gets turned on by that,' Hagen suggests.

'Turned on by what?' Sandland frowns.

'The guy lives alone. Murder weapon. Loo roll.'

Sandland still looks clueless. Hagen sighs in despair.

'Perhaps he was sitting there looking at his weapon, reliving the whole episode and got so excited that he needed something to wipe up the mess afterwards,' he says.

'I know what you meant. I just wanted to see if you had the guts to say it out loud,' Sandland replies with a mischievous smile.

'It might have been the little boy who made the stone troll,' Bjarne suggests. 'According to his father the boy came with him to work quite often. He was a popular visitor. Perhaps he made several stone trolls at school and brought one with him as a present. You know how kids love giving away things they've made themselves. He could have given one to Erna Pedersen and that's another reason to surmise that the killing wasn't premeditated. The use of the Bible also suggests that. Erna Pedersen always had it lying on her bedside table.'

Bjarne can feel that he is starting to warm to his subject.

'So you're saying the killer simply used whatever he found in the room?' Gjerstad says.

Bjarne nods.

The room falls silent for a few seconds.

'It's a good theory,' Gjerstad then says.

'There's something else about Nielsen,' Bjarne says and quickly summarises Nielsen and Sund's trip up to Holmenkollen earlier that day.

'And you're quite sure it was Ole Christian Sund driving

Pernille Thorbjørnsen's car?' Nøkleby asks.

'Absolutely,' Bjarne nods.

'But you don't know the address they went to or what they did when they got there?'

'No. But there is something fishy about Daniel Nielsen, I'm sure of it. I've already caught him lying to me once. He never worked out at Svein's Gym that morning, like he told me. I checked.'

'What an idiot,' Hagen sighs.

'Yes, but that's just it,' Bjarne says. 'It seems like a white lie to me. He doesn't want to tell us where he really was or what he was doing. So he says the first thing that comes into his head.'

'In which case he's unlikely to be a hardened criminal,' Nøkleby says. 'If he lies about something we can quite easily find out.'

'I agree,' Bjarne says.

But the point Nøkleby has just made troubles him. Only a total amateur would drop himself in it like that. It's not the action of a man capable of bashing knitting needles into the eyes of an old lady. It is too crude and too brutal. But the care workers at Grünerhjemmet are up to something, he just doesn't know what or how he can get to the bottom of it – or indeed if it has anything to do with Erna Pedersen's death.

'Do we have anything else?' Gjerstad says.

No one says anything.

'Okay,' Gjerstad says, getting up. 'What do you think, Pia – Nielsen's flat first and the care home afterwards?'

Pia Nøkleby nods.

Chapter 32

Henning's hips ache as he gets up from the rough seating planks. His legs feel stiff and he shakes them to boost his circulation.

He stops at the entrance to watch Adil and his friend who have sat down on the ground. They are not talking to each other; they just watch others play football on the Astroturf.

Henning turns and looks around for the boy's father, the man he met behind Grünerhjemmet yesterday, the man who was in such a rush to get home to his son. His son, who was the first person to realise that something was terribly wrong with Erna Pedersen.

Henning bends down, slips through a gap in the fence and carefully approaches the boys.

'Hi, boys,' he says. Only the boy with the blond fringe turns to face him. Henning smiles as he takes another step forwards.

'So you're a United fan too?' he says to Adil, pointing to the sticker of Wayne Rooney on his sports bag. The name of the football club makes Adil glance up at Henning.

'Is Rooney your favourite player?'

It takes a few seconds, then he nods.

'Mine too. But then again I'm a big fan of all the Man U players.'

Henning smiles and sees a tiny twitch reflected in the

corner of Adil's mouth.

'Boys, I've been watching you practise. Can I show you something?'

The blond boy continues to sit motionless on the ground. Adil looks up at him; this time his gaze is more alert.

'Come on then, up you get.'

Adil hesitates.

'Come on,' Henning says again. 'It works, I promise you.'

He holds out his hand to help Adil to his feet, but the boy doesn't take it. Instead he looks at his friend before he gets up unaided.

'Do you have a football in your sports bag?'

Adil slowly loosens the strings and takes out a ball. Henning smiles.

'A Man U football. Good heavens,' he says and looks at the ball, which is printed with pictures of the whole team. He squeezes it. Not enough air. But it will have to do.

'Right, let's get started,' Henning says, putting the ball on the ground. 'Can you see that wall over there?'

He points to a high wall at the end of the football pitch. He takes care not to look at the other boy.

'The best way to practise passing and gaining possession of the ball is to kick it against a wall. That way you have a fellow player who never moves. Watch me.'

Henning kicks the ball quite hard. It hits the wall and bounces back.

'When the ball comes back towards you, you stick out your foot to meet it and then you use your foot to slow it down. You have to move your leg or the ball will simply slip under your foot. It'll be much harder for you to regain possession of the ball. Do you understand?'

Henning demonstrates again and stops the ball with his foot.

'Your turn.'

Adil is still a little reluctant. Then he takes a step back, kicks the ball, but has to move to the side to stop it as it comes back. It jumps out from under his foot, just like before. He looks at Henning.

'Okay, not bad. But you saw what happened if you don't kick the ball straight to your teammate, didn't you? It forces him to move to one side and makes it more difficult for him to control the ball. Have another go. And remember your foot is there to slow down the speed of the ball, not to stop it completely. Your foot is not a wall. Come on, try again.'

Adil sets down the ball on the ground, kicks it, it hits the wall and this time he doesn't have to move; it comes straight back towards him. He sticks out his foot again. Same result, the ball escapes.

'Try to exaggerate the movement to start with so you learn how the ball behaves. And try to relax your foot, let your leg be loose and flexible when the ball comes towards you.'

Henning demonstrates again and then it's Adil's turn.

This time the ball doesn't roll quite as far away from his foot as it did before.

'Great,' Henning shouts out a little louder than he had intended. 'Good job! Now do the same again. And relax your leg even more.'

Adil kicks the ball against the wall one more time. Then he sticks out his foot and slows down the speed of the ball so it comes to a halt against his trainer.

Henning says nothing; he just waits for Adil to look at him.

'I don't think even Wayne Rooney could have managed that.'

Adil smiles shyly.

'So all you have to do now is to practise this again and again until you can do it in your sleep.'

Adil smiles. Henning goes over to him and ruffles his hair.

'You did really well.'

Adil doesn't say anything, but this time he looks straight at Henning. Henning turns and looks at the blond boy.

'So how about you? Do you fancy a go?'

Chapter 33

Not only does Henning show the boys how to practise passing, he also teaches them how to improve their technique by keeping the ball in the air with either foot, not just their better one. He also shows them basic techniques for side foot passing, again using both their left and their right feet. Standing in a triangle, they kick the ball back and forth to each other. And Henning can see that the boys pay attention to his instructions.

They have been practising for about an hour when Henning says he is tired and needs to sit down for a little while. Adil and his friend do likewise; their brows are sweaty.

'Doesn't your coach ever show you things like that?' Henning asks.

The boys shake their heads.

'Nobody gets better from being yelled at,' Henning says. 'Don't you agree?'

The boys nod.

Henning leans back on his elbows. It's a long time since he last played football. He has lost count of the number of times Jonas and he would come down here on a Sunday morning where they would have the whole pitch to themselves. Jonas in goal. Jonas taking penalties. Practising side foot passing, doing ball tricks using both feet. He could have kept going all day if Henning had let him. Without even stopping for food.

Henning looks over at the boy whose name he has learned is Ulrik, a boy who reminds him a little of Jonas. Same facial colouring, same hair. But where Jonas was a powder keg, frequently exploding, Ulrik is withdrawn. He is more of a thinker and not quite so chatty. Jonas talked the whole time. He used to ask all sorts of questions.

'Do you know what happened to me today?' Henning says, and doesn't continue until he is sure that he has the attention of both boys. 'I saw a bird get hit by a car in Mark-veien. It didn't die; the car just clipped it so the bird rolled over and landed near the kerb.'

Henning pauses.

'What happened?' Ulrik asks.

'Well, I went over to it and picked it up. I saw that it had broken its leg, poor thing, so I put a splint on it. Do you know what that means?'

They both shake their heads.

'It means making sure the fractured bone is kept com-pletely rigid. So it has a chance to heal.'

Henning looks at them.

'I couldn't just leave it there. Some cat would have got it.'

The boys nod. Henning stretches out on the ground even though it is damp. He stares up at the ominous grey sky, which will soon turn black. He stays where he is. Right until Ulrik says: 'I saw a dead person yesterday.'

Henning tries not to lift his head too quickly.

'Did you?'

Ulrik nods.

'It was an old lady in a care home.'

Henning sits up and leans forward across his knees. His

heart starts to beat faster and he has to force himself to stay calm.

'She just sat there in her wheelchair. It was really gross.'

Henning waits until the boy looks at him. Then he nods without saying anything.

'I had been to see her the day before and she told me that she was scared.'

Henning is sorely tempted to bombard the boy with questions, but he manages to restrain himself.

'And she sat like this,' Ulrik says, holding up an index finger. 'Pointing at the wall.'

'At a picture or something?' Henning tries.

The boy nods.

'And she kept saying: "Fractions. Fractions. Fractions."'

Ulrik imitates her crow-like voice.

'Fractions?'

The boy nods.

'What a strange thing to say,' Henning remarks.

'That's what I thought.'

'Was that all she said?'

'Yes. And when I came to see her the next day, she was dead.'

Henning can no longer control himself.

'Was anyone else there?'

Ulrik shakes his head.

'Did you see anyone else who had been to her room?'

Same response.

Hm, Henning says to himself. *Interesting.*

He thinks about the photograph of Tom Sverre Pedersen and his family, the photograph that had been smashed. Surely she couldn't have been pointing at that? What connection

could there be between a family photo and some fractions?
After all Tom Sverre Pedersen is a doctor, not a teacher.

So what was she pointing at?

Chapter 34

The stone troll in Daniel Nielsen's flat proved to be free from dents and scratches, exactly as Bjarne had predicted. Before they entered the flat, Nielsen told them that it had been a present from Sund's son; he got it a couple of weeks ago after the boy had made several stone trolls in a science lesson after a school trip. Nielsen also confirmed that Ulrik had given one to Erna Pedersen as a thank you for all the toffees she had given him.

They found nothing else of interest in Nielsen's flat, only signs of a family-free life. Nor did his finances suggest anything other than his income was his monthly salary from Oslo City Council and that he had bills to pay like everybody else.

They are currently checking all his electronic traffic, but something tells Bjarne that it's a dead end as well.

He is about to get back in his car when his mobile rings for the umpteenth time today. It's Henning Juul. Bjarne looks around. Ella Sandland is still inside Nielsen's flat so he takes the call.

'How many pictures were on the wall in Erna Pedersen's room?'

'Eh?'

Henning repeats the question.

'Why do you want to know that?'

'I might have something for you. But first answer my question.'

Bjarne sighs.

'None. That's to say there had been a picture, but someone had torn it down.'

'Was that a photo of Tom Sverre Pedersen and his family?'

Bjarne freezes.

'How the hell do you know that?'

'Take another look at the wall. See if you can find anything to suggest there might have been other pictures.'

'What makes you think that?'

'Because I think you're missing one.'

*

Bjarne hangs up after talking to Henning and immediately calls Daniel Nielsen. This time he fully expects Nielsen to pick up – even though he is at work. It takes only a couple of seconds before Bjarne is proved right.

He tells Nielsen about the evidence – or lack of – in Nielsen's flat.

'That's what I kept telling you.'

'I know, but we still had to check it out. However, I want to talk to you about something else. You're very interested in photography, aren't you? I noticed that you have a lot of pictures on your walls at home.'

'Yes, I suppose I do,' Nielsen replies unwillingly.

'And no one went to Erna Pedersen's room more often than you in the last few months?'

'No, that's . . . probably true.'

Bjarne waits a moment before he continues.

'If I were to say there were two photographs on her wall,

next to the chest of drawers – what would you say?'

There is silence for a few seconds.

'That you would be right. Or at least there used to be two until recently.'

Bjarne sticks a finger in his ear to block out the background noise.

'What do you mean?'

'When I started looking after Erna Pedersen, there was only one picture on the wall, a photograph. But not all that long ago a second photograph appeared. Why do you ask about that?'

Bjarne makes eye contact with Ella Sandland, who realises the conversation is important. She comes up to him.

'I want you to think carefully, Nielsen. One photo was Erna Pedersen's son and his family. The other one – do you remember what kind of picture it was?'

'It was a school photo,' Nielsen replies immediately.

Sandland makes a *what's going on* movement with her head, but Bjarne ignores her.

'A school photo?'

'Yes, you know – a typical group photo of everyone in the same class.'

'Aha?' Bjarne says.

'But it was taken quite a few years ago.'

Bjarne nods while he thinks about Erna Pedersen again. She was a teacher and she muttered something about fractions before she was killed. And someone recently put up an old school photo on her wall, a picture that wasn't there after she died. Which means it's highly likely that the killer took it with him.

Why on earth would he want to do that?

Tuesday

Chapter 35

The press release had been sent by fax late last night and it caused frantic activity in every newspaper office, both before and after their deadlines. The first paper versions hitting the streets of Norway didn't have time to include the news that a young Labour politician had made contact with every editor in the country, but that was about to change.

Fresh editions with new front pages went to press; a few newspapers also increased the number of pages to give both the press release and various follow-up articles sufficient space as it had now become obvious that it was going to be the story of the week. In the press release the unnamed young man announced that it would be his final word on the matter. He doesn't want a sexual assault by one of the country's best-known politicians to be brought up every time he himself features in the media as he has major political ambitions of his own. Nevertheless, in his statement he challenges the Secretary of State for Justice and he also gives a brief summary of the incident.

It started with a glance. At first, the man felt honoured that a Minister – and a woman he has always liked – and yes, in that way, too – would be interested in him. During that evening one glance turned into many. And when he spilled a little red wine on his white shirt and went up to his hotel room to change, he suddenly found Trine standing right behind him.

She asked if he wouldn't rather change in her room instead, and the rest, he wrote, people could work out for themselves.

Afterwards, when she had practically shoved him out of the door, he had felt used. And when he contacted the Minister a couple of weeks later to get her to admit that she had crossed a line, he was coldly dismissed with 'Plenty of men would count themselves lucky to have been in your shoes.'

VG has twelve pages about Trine, *Dagbladet* has nine. *Aftenposten* devotes practically its entire front page and four pages inside the newspaper to the alleged assault and there are reactions and commentaries about them in addition to a series of pictures of Trine. The sexiest and most seductive photographs have been dug out and reproduced. Newspapers carry editorials that demand that Juul-Osmundsen either resign as soon as possible or come up with an explanation, 'and a good one at that'. No one can understand why she hasn't yet resigned and they mock her for apparently running away from the Ministry of Justice yesterday to escape the media.

Several newspapers have visited Hotel Caledonien, they have discovered which room was registered in Trine's name on the night in question, and they have – as usual – photographed the door. '*It happened behind this door,*' reads the caption. The media have contacted every single member of the Labour Party's youth branch who was present that night to ask if they know the identity of the victim. No one does. But the media keep speculating. They have also spoken to other party members who were there, but no one remembers seeing Trine during the dinner. A revelation that causes several media commentators to conclude that 'she probably had other things on her mind'.

When Henning gets to the offices of *123news*, he realises that Trine won't be able to ride out this storm. Too much negative publicity about her has appeared in the wake of the initial story. She is accused of having doctored a working environment survey in the Justice Department because it made her look bad. Sacked a member of staff, apparently for no reason. Failed to produce receipts for her travelling expenses. Accepted gifts without declaring them or paying tax on them. During an official trip to India, her Indian counterpart presented her with a rug, which she brought back and put in one of the guest bedrooms in her house in Ullern. Last Christmas she was given a 3.5-litre bottle of whisky by the Parliament's Press Association, which she failed to declare.

The press has also resurrected a story from two years ago when she travelled to the US and flew business class, even though economy class tickets were available on the same flight. Travelling too often and too expensively never enhances a politician's popularity. And what about that cookery course she was given by the famous Norwegian chef and food writer, Arne Brimi?

The house, which Trine and her husband bought for 17.8 million kroner last year, becomes a story in itself. Several papers have included photo montages and added catty captions to the effect that Labour politicians don't usually live in mansions. A quote from an unnamed Labour Party politician helps to pour petrol on the flames: 'How many of us can afford to live like this? And I've heard she has a cleaner as well.' And a chalet in the Hafjell ski resort with four, possibly even five bedrooms? Shame on you. Nor does it help Trine's case that her husband drives a Porsche Cayenne, a hugely polluting car.

And since when is it appropriate for a Minister to wear such short skirts or be allowed to borrow jewellery for free for three months at a time from one of Oslo's most prestigious jewellers?

Opposition politicians also make sure to stick the knife in with a 'what she promised but failed to deliver' list. Anything she has done in the last three years that can be interpreted even remotely as a failure is dumped in a box labelled 'character assassination'. And more is to come. The fact that she doesn't get on very well with the head of Norway's police force gives especially the Conservative section of the opposition yet another reason to demand that the Minister be replaced at the earliest opportunity. If the opposition hadn't already lost confidence in her over the Hotel Caledonien scandal, then they certainly will now. In an opinion poll on the front page of *123news*, 97 per cent of readers demand that Trine resign immediately, 2 per cent disagree, while 1 per cent 'don't know'. These figures are practically identical in every other publication that Henning checked before he went to work.

Instead of sitting down at his computer, he walks over to the national news desk where he finds the fax that was sent to them along with every other newspaper late last night and locates Kåre Hjeltland. The news editor's gaze is focused on a PC screen a few workstations away. His hair stands straight up as usual and he looks as if he slept at the office and hasn't had time to shower before new stories appeared and demanded his undivided attention.

'Do you have two minutes, Kåre?' Henning says and stops in front of him. Hjeltland registers Henning's arrival, nods, bashes the keyboard hard for thirty seconds before he gets up so abruptly that his chair rolls several metres backwards.

'What is it?' he asks.

Henning waits until Hjeltland's eyes stop flitting.

'You know it's a stitch-up, don't you?'

Hjeltland folds his arms across his chest and looks at him for a few seconds.

'The whole case against Trine bears all the hallmarks,' Henning continues. 'Ever since yesterday morning *VG* has been drip-feeding stories to its readers, stories it couldn't possibly have written in just one day. It must have known about this for a while and planned it carefully.'

Hjeltland gives Henning a baffled look.

'Yes, and so what?'

'So what? Don't you think it's just a little bit suspicious?'

'No, not at all. We would have done exactly the same if a big story like this had landed in our lap.'

'It doesn't worry you that the story was deliberately leaked to Norway's biggest newspaper, and that Trine wasn't even offered the opportunity to respond to the allegations before the first articles went to print?'

Hjeltland is about to say something, but Henning has no intention of letting him get a word in yet.

'And don't tell me that *VG* didn't try because that's bullshit. It's had every opportunity to confront Trine *before* it started this smear campaign against her, precisely because it's known about it for a long time. It's obvious what *VG* wants. And the rest of the media will blindly follow its lead while doing everything they can to come up with their own take on the story.'

'But—'

'I haven't seen a single article that tries to defend Trine or examines the story from her point of view. No, that's not true, I saw a two-liner saying one of her Junior Ministers is one hundred per cent behind his boss. No one has yet managed to establish what exactly happened in that hotel room.'

'But she's refusing to say anything,' Hjeltland protests. 'What do you want us to do, Henning? Not cover the story?'

'No, but it has got completely out of hand. Trine might well be guilty of the things she's accused of, but that's exactly why it would have been refreshing to see a newspaper or a TV channel take a step backwards and assess the story from a balanced point of view. Or at least acknowledge that there could be more to it.'

'Did you read the press release he issued last night?'

Henning shows him the two fax sheets he is holding in his hands.

'Your sister is a powerful woman, Henning. She exploited her position to pressure a young man into having sex with her.'

'She might well have done, but all the media care about now is that Trine resigns and that she apologises. It doesn't matter what she says or what she did because no one is going to believe her. Especially not now when the press has dug up all kinds of dirt on her.'

Hjeltland scratches his head. Then he looks at Henning with editorial disapproval.

'I understand how you must be feeling, Henning, since it's your sister who's being hounded, but—'

'It's got nothing to do with Trine being my sister,' Henning says with an unexpected touch of anger in his voice. 'It's about how history repeats itself whenever a public figure is alleged to have done something wrong. We go for the jugular straightaway, and I can see it in people's faces – also here in our office – when yet another story is revealed that supports the impression that has already been created. It's a mixture of indignation and glee, and it's not just here, Kåre, I've seen it in every editorial office I've ever worked in. It makes me sick.'

Henning is aware that the blood is rushing to his head. Around them other staff members have noticed his outburst, but they keep their distance. Henning doesn't care about them; instead he makes a second attempt to get his point across and tries hard not to sound emotional or angry.

'Besides, Trine has been on sick leave. Not all that long ago. Doesn't anyone think that perhaps this is more than she can cope with?'

Even though he keeps his voice low, his words are explosive and he can see the effect on Hjeltland's face. The muscles tighten like wire.

'So what do you think we ought to do, Henning?'

'Investigate the allegations,' he says. 'Rather than just repeat them.'

Hjeltland emits a sigh from the depths of his chest.

'You know very well we don't have the resources, Henning. And our circulation figures, they've gone completely through—'

'And you wouldn't want to ruin that, would you? You'd rather bank on the story being true?'

'No, but right now we have to produce a story based on the information currently available to us.'

Henning can feel a fuse burning behind his eyes, but he

knows continuing this discussion is pointless. So he shakes his head and says: 'I'm going out. I can't stand being here.'

'Where are you going?' Hjeltland calls after him.

'Jessheim.'

Chapter 36

The sound of footsteps wakes up Trine Juul-Osmundsen. At first she is startled and wonders where she is before she remembers it could be one of her bodyguards who might have gone outside for some fresh air. But she doesn't recognise the noise. It's a small, hard stomping not made by shoes.

She sits up on the sofa bed in the living room and instantly feels the pounding in her head. Even getting to a sitting position is enough to make her nauseous. She groans and touches her temples. She screws up her eyes and sees the empty bottle of St Hallvard's in front of her. Her stomach churns at the sight. Nevertheless she gets up and opens the curtains. A grey hare hops away. It was sitting on the hilltop, Tissetoppen, as they used to call the little mound on the side of the cabin that overlooks the sea where Henning used to go for a pee in the evening before they climbed into the bunk beds in the narrow bedroom.

The light outside is sharp and hurts her head. Her mouth is filled with dry cotton wool and the taste of cigarettes lingers on her tongue. Her laptop is open on the dining table. Last night, in between shots of liqueur, she tried to reconstruct her movements on 9 October. She remembered how she sneaked out of Hotel Caledonien and got into a car that was waiting at the goods entrance, a car that took her straight to Kjevik Airport. How she arrived at a different hotel an hour and a half later. The run she went for that same evening to rid herself of some of the anxiety that was coursing around her body at the thought of what she was going to do the next day. Trine even looked up her running profile on a street map, just to assure herself that her memory was correct.

She also tried to find a name and face among all her enemies, but she couldn't think of a single one. Or, that is to say, the more she drank, the more potential candidates sprang to mind, but not one of them struck her as more plausible than the others. None of them is capable of gambling with such high stakes. It made her wonder if perhaps several colleagues have ganged up on her.

Trine groans and opens the door to let in the sea air. She walks outside in the clothes she fell asleep in. She is tempted to stick two fingers down her throat, so she won't have to spend the rest of the day recovering from her hangover. On Tissetoppen she has to take a step to the side when a gust of wind almost knocks her over while she looks for the hare. It would appear to be hiding.

Sometimes, when they opened the cabin early in the spring, the hares would come unusually close to them. They hadn't yet remembered to be wary of people after a long, lonely winter. Once she was sunning herself, wrapped up warm in a rug, when a hare hopped straight past her. It stopped only a few metres away. And it stood there, for a long time, just staring at her. While Trine stared back.

Now all she can see is the sea. An endless horizon, heaven and water united far, far in the distance without a clear dividing line, where one merges into the other. The spray rises behind the rocks of Svartskjær and Måkeskjær. Eider ducks dive under the surface of the water.

Trine goes back inside the cabin to get her mobile phone and brings it out with her to Tissetoppen where mobile coverage is usually better. There are no new text messages from Katarina Hatlem. Her core staff probably haven't held their morning meeting yet, Trine thinks, while she wonders how long her friend with the curly red hair will manage to hold out. Trine is well aware that the press office is snapping at Katarina's heels, even though Katarina wouldn't admit to it when they spoke last night. And they are not the only ones. Trine dare not even think about what people must be saying about her in her department, across the whole Labour Party and in the Prime Minister's office.

A large ship appears behind the rocks and slides past Rakke towards the foamy crests that are waiting for it. Trine turns towards the wind. The fast, blue colossus slices neatly through the white horses without rocking while her own little boat is listing and taking in water.

Further down the uneven hillside the hare peeks out from behind a bush. It stands still for a few seconds and sniffs before it runs off to hide from its enemies. And she thinks how easy it would be just to disappear out here among the rocks, the crags and the knolls, something she has been fantasising about in the last twenty-four hours. She could go for a walk along the coastal path and then just ...

Trine closes her eyes and imagines it. And realises that she isn't scared of the pain or of the darkness. The door is open. All she has to do is go in.

Chapter 37

The investigation team return to their activities straight after the morning briefing. The information about the missing school photo is a welcome development in the case and much of their work now revolves around it. They contact the three schools where Erna Pedersen taught. Ultimately that could mean hundreds of photographs, thousands of pupils, but at least it's a place to start. They have also requested pupil registers starting from 1972 and up to 1993 when she retired.

Other officers are busy searching the care home for a stone troll with a dent. There is a remote possibility that the troll might still have fingerprints or contain other forensic evidence that justifies expending resources on it. Meanwhile, they continue interviewing everyone who was at the care home at the time when Erna Pedersen was killed. Bjarne is responsible for interviewing the five people from the Volunteer Service.

Bjarne can't imagine that he could ever do what they do and visit people who are lonely but complete strangers. Accompany them to the doctor or the hairdresser. He wouldn't know what to say to them. What little time he has outside of work is spent on family and exercise. Quite simply, there isn't room for anything else.

He reads the first name on the list, Markus Gjerløw, and runs it through the criminal records register. No hits. So he rings Gjerløw's number and waits for a reply. The ring tone is interrupted by a bright voice saying 'hello'.

Bjarne introduces himself and explains the reason for his call.

'Yes, I wondered when you would get to me,' Gjerløw responds with a voice laden with haughty contempt. Bjarne suppresses a sudden rage and coughs into the palm of his hand instead.

'I'm trying to find out what happened at the care home on Sunday afternoon. Do you remember when the volunteers arrived and when they left?'

'I don't know when the others arrived, but I got there between three and three thirty, I think. And I guess I was there until around five o'clock. I didn't check what time it was when we left.'

Bjarne makes a note of the times.

'You said when *we* left. Did you all leave the care home at the same time?'

'Yes, I think so. I wouldn't know if anyone stayed behind as we didn't share the lift down. It isn't big enough for all five of us.'

Bjarne nods and gets a flashback to Sandland and him in the narrow space, a little too close for her comfort zone, too far apart for his. The silence that follows gives way to an impatience that prompts him to ask: 'Have you been to these singalongs before?'

'Yes, certainly.'

'Did anything last Sunday strike you as a little unusual?'

Gjerløw falls silent.

'Well, I'm not really—'

'Did anyone behave differently, a patient, a staff member or . . . or anyone else?'

'Not that I recall.'

Bjarne lifts his pen from the paper while he thinks.

'How well do you know the other volunteers?'

Gjerløw sighs again.

'I only know Remi. I don't know what it's like with the rest, if they know each other.'

Bjarne nods to himself and looks down at his notepad. Depressingly few notes.

'What made you volunteer in the first place?' he asks.

Gjerløw doesn't reply immediately.

'Helping others is a good thing to do,' he says eventually. 'Making a positive difference to someone's day. You ought to try it sometime.'

The words smart like an unexpected slap to the face. Bjarne is lost for an answer.

'Was there anything else?' Gjerløw asks. 'I'm about to go out.'

'No,' Bjarne says. 'Thanks for your help.'

*

Bjarne spends the next hour calling the other four names on the list from the Volunteer Service, but none of them can add a single new detail. All of them confirm that they left the care home around the same time as they normally do.

Bjarne shakes his head while he tries to sum up the case for himself. First Erna Pedersen is strangled in her own room, then her eyes are pierced with her own knitting needles; the killer proceeds to smash a picture of her son's family, which was on the wall, and takes with him a school photo from the crime scene without anyone seeing or hearing anything.

The only thing he can think of that could have distracted an entire floor in a care home is the Volunteer Service's singalong that afternoon. Someone could have stolen away from the entertainment, gone to Erna Pedersen's room, killed her and then returned to the singalong. It need not have taken more than a couple of minutes and no one would have noticed. Pedersen wouldn't have been capable of making very much noise and her room was quite a distance from the TV lounge where the singalong was taking place. And it's fairly easy to hide a framed school photo. All you need is a bag or jacket with big pockets.

But what was the point of mutilating her eyes? And what about the missing picture? Was Pedersen meant to look at it before she was killed?

His train of thought is interrupted by Ella Sandland knocking on his door and popping her head round.

'I've just had a call from Forensics,' she says, sounding agitated. 'They've found a fingerprint on the knitting needles that doesn't belong to Erna Pedersen.'

Bjarne looks up at her.

'Okay? So who does it belong to?'

Chapter 38

A layer of grey clouds hangs across Jessheim and refuses to let in the sun, but Emilie Blomvik doesn't even notice it when she drops off Sebastian at nursery, just in time for him to join in the trip to the Raknehaugen burial mound. Inside his Lightning McQueen bag are two packed lunches, a clear blue plastic bottle of tap water and a green apple. She sends him inside with whispered instructions to have lots of fun today because that's exactly what she intends.

As expected the morning started slowly after she came home late from work last night and found Mattis asleep on the sofa under a blanket. On the table stood a bottle of red wine that he had clearly consumed single-handedly because his dry cracked lips were stained blue. Next to the bottle was a note saying 'Wake me when you get home ...' followed by three x's – as if the first hint could be misunderstood.

But she didn't have the energy. A long night shift at the airport had worn her out. The luggage belt had broken down – again – which meant it took longer to check in passengers, whose bad mood increased in line with Emilie's. When she finally got home, well past midnight, she had only one thought in her head and that was to go to bed. So that was what she did. She fell asleep the moment her head hit the pillow.

Mattis was woken up by his mobile, which on weekdays makes an infernal noise at quarter to six in the morning.

She heard him get in the shower, but when he returned to the bedroom to get dressed, she pretended to be asleep. She didn't really know why she did that. He came over to her just before he left, but by then she had buried her head under the duvet and curled up in a ball.

As usual Sebastian woke up around seven o'clock and Emilie plonked him in front of the television for an hour, expertly ignoring all the voices in her head that called out: *you're a bad mother, you're a bad mother*, and went back to bed. She set the alarm for eight o'clock and woke up with a panicky feeling of being late for something. Fortunately she found Sebastian right where she had left him with his Lightning McQueen car in his hands and the remote control right beside him.

Television.

The world's best invention, surpassed only by a baby's dummy and the dishwasher.

But the mood of the day changed completely when she remembered that she was going to Oslo to have lunch with Johanne.

*

Emilie thinks about her friend's gentle face as she leaves the nursery and walks out into a day that is waiting just for her. She is so looking forward to seeing Johanne again, hearing the latest news in her life since they last saw each other, what she did last summer, if she has met a new man, what's going on with her.

Emilie drives towards the motorway while she wonders

about Mattis. If anyone can make sense of the thoughts and feelings that have started to appear about the man she thought she loved, then it has to be Johanne. She has always given her such good advice.

*

He blinks and carefully opens his eyes.

It is a new day. It means he only has two days left.

The realisation makes him feel dizzy. The pills he took last night always have that effect on him. They slow him down. But the thought of what he is going to do today makes him leap out of bed and go over to the computer. Has she told the whole world where she is? And what she is doing?

Of course she has.

He goes to the bathroom and washes his face. Puts on his clothes and gets ready. Takes some pills with him, different ones that make him stronger. Then he goes outside. Out into a day, the number of which is decreasing.

But it makes no difference. All he can think about is how it will feel. If he'll be there this time, all of him. When the light goes out.

Chapter 39

Henning made a point of asking if the rental firm had a yellow car, but had to settle for a small white vehicle that hasn't even clocked up 3,000 kilometres. Now it has clocked up another forty and his first stop is Jessheim School – one of Erna Pedersen's former employers.

It's more than sixteen years since she stopped working there and Henning realises there is a limit to what he can hope to achieve in just one morning. Even so he parks the car and enters the school's playground, an area that has changed considerably since Henning was last in Jessheim. He played a football match here when he was in Year Five. It was a big deal at the time for a class from Kløfta to come all the way to Jessheim to play. It was rivalry at its best – and at its worst. On the lumpy pitch behind the school they played two halves of twenty minutes each and won 5–2. Henning scored three of the goals. He can still remember being lifted up on the teacher's shoulders after the match.

If Tom Sverre Pedersen was right and the school walls used to be covered in graffiti about his mother, there is no trace of it now. The paint on the walls look fresh and the school has been extended since Henning took part in the legendary football match back in the eighties.

He walks around to the rear of the school. Everything looks much better than he remembers it. Back in his day the place was unloved and filthy. Today there are green areas. A new volleyball sand court. The football pitch that Henning used play on now looks like something a reasonably well-off football club would use for training purposes. It feels a little odd to be retracing his footsteps now that the past has been erased and replaced with something better. But he tries to visualise them, the pupils who detested Erna Pedersen, what they did, what they thought. The graffiti on the walls would probably have been removed as soon as it was discovered and the culprits probably wouldn't have been hard to find. But would the kid who hated her most have done something quite so obvious?

Maybe. Maybe not. People differ. But if Henning had wanted to hate, he would have picked a spot where he could nurse his hatred. A specific place that no one could destroy, erase or restore.

Henning looks around. None of the pupils is outside. The sun shines on the school's windows, but he can see activity behind them. There are some trees at the end of the playground close to the fence separating it from the grey high-rise buildings on the other side. Trees of various heights. Trees you can climb.

Henning studies them as he walks over to them. The branches stretch up high and spread to the sides, some of them have become tangled up in each other. He reckons there are ten or twelve trees clustered together.

He looks around for the thickest branch, tests it and starts to climb. He can find no carvings in the tree trunk after the first or the second metre, so he climbs back down again and tries the next tree. Same result. An elderly woman with a

Zimmer frame walks past on the pavement outside the fence. Henning smiles to her before he scales yet another tree; he manages to climb quite high; he swings one leg over the biggest, fattest branch, leans into the tree trunk and looks around.

No.

Nothing.

And yet somehow he feels closer to the killer, or at least he can imagine having a place like this, a place where you can sit and think and feel and hate. The school photo that was removed from Erna Pedersen's wall and the word 'fractions' that she uttered in horror the day before she was killed both suggest that someone truly loathed her. And that her death is linked to her job as a teacher.

Henning climbs back down again and goes inside the school just as the bell goes for break; a small boy helps him find the head teacher's office. The head teacher isn't there today, a helpful secretary tells Henning, but perhaps she can help?

'Yes, perhaps,' Henning says and smiles to the friendly woman with the long, black hair. 'Tell me, how does it work – do you keep old yearbooks here?'

'Yes, indeed we do,' she smiles. 'But we don't have very many of them. We didn't start producing yearbooks until the mid-noughties, I think.'

'So if I were to ask you to find me a school photo that includes Erna Pedersen then you wouldn't have it?'

The secretary's smile freezes.

'Oh,' she says. 'So that's why you're asking.'

Henning realises that news of the murder of Erna Pedersen

has obviously reached her former employer. He introduces himself and explains the reason for his visit.

'I'm trying to find someone who knew her when she worked here. Do you have any teachers who were hired before Pedersen retired in 1993?'

The secretary thinks about it.

'We have quite a young team here, so I don't think so. But if you're looking for a photo of her, you're better off trying one of her former pupils. If you can find one, that is.'

Another smile.

'Yes, that's just it,' Henning says. 'Anyway, thanks for your help.'

Chapter 40

The uneven tarmac rumbles under the car. Bjarne looks across to the passenger seat where Ella Sandland is gazing out through the window.

'I've been thinking about the care workers at Grünerhjemmet,' he says. 'Nielsen, Sund and Thorbjørnsen.'

'What about them?'

Bjarne holds up one finger.

'We know that Daniel Nielsen lied about what he had been doing when we visited him in his flat yesterday. He hadn't been working out at Svein's Gym as he claimed. We know that he stopped by the care home last Sunday to drop something off and that the time of his visit fits with the time of the killing. And none of the staff knew the victim better than him.'

Bjarne holds up a second finger.

'We know that Ole Christian Sund was at work when Erna Pedersen was killed and that he was most likely the man who drove Daniel Nielsen up to Holmenkollen yesterday for reasons we've yet to establish. So they're more than just colleagues. They could be protecting each other.'

'Don't forget that Sund's son was present at the care home that evening,' Sandland objects. 'Surely you don't think that Sund took part in a brutal murder while his son was just around the corner?'

'Hush, I'm on a roll here. And then we have Pernille Thor-bjørnsen,' Bjarne says, holding up a third finger. But the train of thought that was so clear in his head has been derailed.

'What about her?'

'I don't know,' Bjarne says. 'But it was her car they used to drive up to Holmenkollen yesterday. Sund and Nielsen, I mean.'

'But that's not exactly a crime.'

'No, but I've had another thought. What kind of temptation might staff in a care home be exposed to?'

Sandland shrugs.

'Not money, certainly.'

'How about medication?' Bjarne suggests.

Sandland looks unconvinced.

'The manager of Grünerhjemmet did say yesterday that quite a lot of medication has gone missing.'

'I don't think that's particularly unusual, Bjarne.'

'No, you may be right, but prescription medication has a certain street value no matter what part of Oslo you live in. And Daniel Nielsen, you remember, has already admitted needing cash.'

At the entrance to Birkelunden Park the car rattles as it crosses the tramlines. Three trams are queuing at a tram stop. There is an endless flow of passengers getting on and off.

'But what does that have to do with Erna Pedersen?' Sandland asks while Bjarne manoeuvres in between two cars at the pedestrian crossing. 'Could she have seen them pilfer medication and threaten to expose them?'

Bjarne doesn't reply immediately.

'I don't know,' he says, pressing the accelerator. 'But let's see if we can find out. There has to be a reason why Pernille Thorbjørnsen's fingerprints are on Erna Pedersen's knitting needles.'

Chapter 41

The dots signposting the route aren't quite as blue as she remembers them. Nor does she have a clear recollection of the coastal path, only that they used to walk it and that it was a great walk. Cocoa and gooey brown cheese sandwiches. Perhaps a bar of milk chocolate – on special occasions. Plastic bottles filled with yellow squash.

While she put some food in a rucksack she found in the cabin, she told her bodyguards to prepare themselves for a bit of a walk today. But when she announced where she was planning to go, they insisted on positioning themselves in front and behind her, so they could check the path first and warn her should anyone appear. If she really didn't want anyone to know where she was, then that was what they had to do, they said. Besides, there was a security risk that couldn't be ignored and which she obviously understood and accepted, but she still insisted that they keep their distance.

They have been walking for one and a half hours in spitting rain when Trine's mobile rings. She takes it out from her anorak and stops on a knoll that reminds her of a bald head.

'Hi, Katarina,' she says. 'I was wondering when you'd call.'

'Yes, there has – there has been quite a lot to do this morning. Have you seen today's headlines?'

'No.'

'It's—'

Trine's Director of Communications sighs heavily before she tells her about the press release that was issued last night.

'You're joking,' Trine says.

'I wish. The Permanent Secretary came up to me this morning and asked me what the hell you think you're doing. "She's holding us hostage," those were her exact words.'

Trine closes her eyes. That incompetent, sour-faced bitch.

'I don't know for how long we can keep putting out the same statement, Trine. The press office is very frustrated. I think that Ullevik can weather the worst of the political pressure, but—'

'What about the Prime Minister's office? Have they said anything?'

'Their Director of Communications called me this morning wanting to know what our strategy was. I said I would have to ring him back. That was some time ago now.'

Trine opens her eyes again and stares across the surface of the water where ripples are starting to form.

'By the way, where are you?' Katarina asks.

'I've gone out for a walk. I'm trying to clear my head.'

'That sounds like a good idea. And I don't want to pressure you, Trine, because I know how hard it is for you. But have you given any further thought as to what you're going to do?'

Trine sighs and takes a step nearer the edge of the knoll. There is a drop of several metres down to a pile of stones that leads on further to some rocks which are getting a thorough and constant wash from the waves. She feels the wind take hold of strands of her hair, which have torn themselves loose from under her red baseball cap.

'No,' she says.

Trine turns away from the wind, which makes the mobile howl. But it's not true. She has thought about what to do. She's going to do the only sensible thing she can. There is no other way out.

Chapter 42

Brinken is a residential development the size of a small village. It lies to the left of the main road when you approach Jessheim from the south.

Henning has driven past it many times, but he has never driven through it. Once he does, it's exactly as he imagined it would be. Criss-crossing streets, detached houses in a grid, tarmac roads and pavements. Not so many new builds, most of the houses seem to have been built in the seventies and eighties.

After entering the address he got from Atle Abelsen, Henning follows the instructions provided by the sat nav. Atle was also able to give him a plot number as well as a detailed description of the house Erna Pedersen used to live in – a terraced bungalow with two bedrooms.

As Henning pulls up he can see that the house is well maintained. It is timber-framed, clad with wooden panels and painted mustard yellow. A flat roof. A tarmac drive. There is a garden with a well-kept lawn, hedges, flowerbeds, an apple tree and a terrace.

The property has clearly been renovated.

Henning parks outside and rings the bell. No one is in. It's to be expected; he imagines the owners are probably at work. Henning takes out a business card, writes on the back that he would like to speak to them and pushes the card under the front door before it strikes him that the new owners might not have known Erna Pedersen.

So he decides to call Tom Sverre Pedersen.

'You again?' says the doctor.

'Yes, me again,' Henning replies. 'Listen, I'm in Jessheim now and I've just had a thought. I know that you said that your mother was unpopular, but do you know how she got on with her neighbours?'

Pedersen doesn't reply immediately.

'I know that some neighbours will chat over the fence for hours, especially in the summer. I was wondering if your mother liked or knew some of her neighbours better than others.'

'Then it would have to be Borgny,' Pedersen says. 'But I don't know if she still lives there.'

'What's her full name?'

'Borgny Ramstad. I know they belonged to the same knitting club a lifetime ago. Give her my best if you manage to track her down.'

'Okay. Thanks for the tip.'

Henning ends the call and walks up to a row of letterboxes nearby. He reads the name 'RAMSTAD' on one of the boxes with a clumsy number '25' written below. Henning looks around, finds a house wall with the same number and rings the bell. Again, no one answers so he slips yet another business card under the door.

Henning is on his way back to the car when a text message from the paper's breaking news service arrives. Henning clicks on the link.

He reads on and learns that Trine didn't come home last night. Nor did she turn up at her office at the usual time this morning. No one in the department has been able to contact her. All media requests are being passed through Katarina Hatlem, Trine's Director of Communications, but she is playing everything down. She repeats yesterday's statement that Trine doesn't wish to comment on anonymous allegations and she has gone into hiding due to the enormous media pressure. 'Surely most people can understand this if they just take a moment to think about it.' But Hatlem refuses to say if she knows where Trine is.

Nor have any witnesses seen his sister. No one has spotted her at a petrol station, in a shop or in the lobby of a hotel. Though the Security Service say that they are aware of Trine's movements, many people don't believe them. The questions don't change. Where is she? What is she doing?

Henning might not have been so worried if he hadn't learned yesterday that Trine had been on sick leave suffering from depression. A story that triggers this level of media witch hunt can affect even the most resilient. There isn't a bodyguard in the whole world who can prevent Trine from doing something drastic if she makes up her mind.

And that changes everything.

Henning thinks about his brother-in-law, Pål Fredrik Osmundsen. He might know something. According to the article no one, including *VG*, has been able to get hold of him in the last twenty-four hours.

Henning gets into the car; he has forgotten all about Erna Pedersen. Before he drives back to Oslo, he finds Osmundsen's mobile number on the website of Predo Asset Management and sends him a text message:

> *Hi. I know everyone wants to talk to you right now, but I'm probably the only journalist who wants to help Trine. Can we talk? Preferably face to face. Henning Juul (Trine's brother)*

Henning drives to Oslo as fast as he dares. When his mobile buzzes, he snatches it up. It's a text message from Pål Fredrik Osmundsen:

> *Can you meet me in Stargate in half an hour?*

Chapter 43

Johanne Klingenberg tends to do a weekly food shop. She was due to go shopping yesterday, but when she realised that the leftovers from the ready-made lasagne she had on Sunday could be reheated in the microwave, there was nothing she really needed to get. Now she is wishing she had done her big shop as planned because then her arms wouldn't have been hurting as much as they are right now. The carrier bags weigh a ton.

You shouldn't have given Emilie those dumbbells for Christmas, she mutters under her breath. *You should have kept them for yourself.*

But when she finally approaches the building where she lives, the fear creeps up on her. The fear that someone might have broken in again, that someone might be lying in wait for her in the stairwell or in her flat. She has grown more anxious recently. Before she goes to bed at night, she checks every cupboard and every room. She even looks under the bed before she climbs under the duvet and listens out for strange noises that never come. Eventually, far too late, she slips into a restless sleep.

Perhaps she should have mentioned the break-in to Emilie, but she didn't want to worry her, didn't want their lunch to be all about that. They hadn't seen each other for such a long time and they had so much other news to share even though she had secretly been a little cross with Emilie. Emilie has always had her pick of men. And now when she has finally settled down with a good-looking guy, she can still find fault with him.

Look at me, Johanne felt like saying. I haven't had a steady boyfriend for years. I would be on cloud nine if I had someone to love. If only someone would be prepared to look past the exterior and give me a chance.

She knows she is overweight and that she talks too loudly, especially when she is drunk. But she has lots of love to give. Lots! Emilie has always been blessed with men ready to give her anything she wants.

There is no justice in the world.

Johanne feels the sweat press on her brow. And, of course, the carrier bags manage to get caught on bicycles and push-chairs as she makes her way up the narrow stairwell.

It takes time, but eventually she reaches the second floor. Panting heavily she lets herself in, dragging the heavy bags behind her. A fire has started under her jacket that spreads to the rest of her body. She feels the need for a shower, but right now she only has the energy to collapse in a chair in the kitchen.

She sits down while her heart tries to resume its normal rhythm. She looks around for Baltazar, the little rascal, but he is not in his basket. Nor does she get a meow in response when she calls out his name.

It takes a few minutes before Johanne is able to get up and go into the living room. She calls out his name again, but there is no reply this time, either. Is he hiding under the sofa again? Johanne gets down on all fours, sees a lot of stuff that ought not to be under the sofa, but no cat. She gets back on her feet and heaves a deep sigh.

Then she senses movement right behind her.

Johanne spins around and her eyes widen.

'What are you doing here?'

If she hadn't recognised him straightaway, she would have screamed. But there is something about his eyes. They are empty and cold. And they don't shift from her until he says: 'Cute kid.'

He nods towards the wall. Then he takes a step closer. Johanne moves back, but her retreat is blocked by the coffee table.

Then she realises it. He is the man who broke into her flat two weeks ago, who has been following her and waiting for her outside the lecture hall.

She looks at him, at his eyes. And she realises she has never been more scared in her life.

*

He takes a step closer. Somewhere deep inside his ears he can hear the steady beating of his heart, strong and fast. He tries to see clearly, but everything blurs. It's as if he is watching her through a veil; he swallows and blinks, he tries to breathe as calmly as he can, but the room doesn't change. The details don't come into view.

Wait, he says to himself. *Be patient.*

He clenches his fists, but he can't feel a thing. There is no pain. The pills are working. And that's wonderful.

He blinks a second time. Suddenly he can focus.

'You owe me an apology,' he says.

Her eyebrows shoot up.

'Me? What for?'

Then his sight grows fuzzy again; he doesn't feel his hand punch the picture on the wall, all he can hear is the shattering of glass. Johanne raises her hands up to her face to protect herself. When she takes them away, he lashes out again; he is not sure what he hits, but he hopes it's her head this time. Whatever it is, it makes her fall backwards across the glass coffee table; she lands on the sofa and bangs the back of her head against the wooden armrest. Then she goes quiet.

Not yet, he tells himself, *wait for the veil to fall. Wait until you can see*. When his eyes can focus again, he sees that although the years have changed her, it's still there. Her contempt for him. She still despises him, the boy who saved her life that cold night in 1994.

It had been a Friday like any other Friday in Jessheim. Emilie and Johanne had been to Gartneriet Bar and as usual were high on life. They staggered along the pavement, arms linked. On their way home they had stopped at the takeaway by the Esso petrol station, right by the junction, for something to eat. And as usual Emilie was surrounded by boys.

He was there with some friends and they watched as the girls' behaviour, giggling and eating drunkenly, changed completely when Johanne choked on some food and couldn't breathe. Emilie freaked out and screamed at the top of her voice for someone to please help Johanne. In the light from the takeaway he could see everyone freeze to the spot while Emilie's shrill voice hurt his ears. A strange calm came over him. What he really wanted to do was stay where he was and watch Johanne's light go out. But what about Emilie. Sweet, lovely Emilie, who was running around wailing and shouting.

So he went over to Johanne who was clutching her throat. Her lips were starting to turn purple. He had to make an effort to snap out of his trance and remember the first-aid course they had been taught at school; the soft, revolting plastic doll he had pressed his lips against and that had tasted grotesquely sterile, and he thought about the other procedures they had learned, the bit about the Heimlich manoeuvre and he couldn't quite remember how to do it, but he positioned himself behind her and half lifted and half squeezed her, and suddenly Johanne was able to breathe again. She stood there, spitting and coughing, hawking and crying.

Emilie threw herself around his neck and stayed there. She stayed there for a while. And, he supposed, that was what Johanne had never been able to accept. That someone could get between her and her best friend for more than a few weeks.

Seriously, Emilie, it'll never last. You're not going to marry him, are you?

And he knows now that she won't ever apologise to him. She is another one of those who won't. So he bends down and waits until signs of life return behind her eyelids. The moment she regains consciousness she tries to escape, but she is trapped. Frantically she looks around; she kicks and screams so he squeezes her neck. A little harder while he tells himself to stay calm. *Remember, you want to watch. You want to watch*, he repeats to himself while he straddles her midriff. Her legs hit his back and thrash in the air, her arms flail wildly and she claws at his jumper and gloves. But when he tightens his grip around her neck and feels her sinking into the sofa like a balloon slowly deflating, that's when he sees it.

He sees it.

And it's the most incredible sight ever.

Chapter 44

Two journalists are hanging around outside the entrance to *123news* when Henning parks the hire car and gets out. He doesn't recognise them and tries to ignore them by looking up at the autumn clouds, but one of the reporters blocks his path when he walks past them.

'Hey,' says the journalist, a small, fat man with very little hair and thin, round Harry Potter glasses. 'Do you have anything to say about what your sister has done?'

Henning stops and smiles.

'Forget it, I'm not going to throw you a bone.'

The journalists glance at each other.

'No, no comment,' Henning says and pushes his way past them.

'But—'

The journalists' voices rise behind Henning as he walks out through the gates, but he shrugs them off. Instead he walks as quickly as he can in the direction of Grønland towards Stargate. The pub isn't far away, but he makes a few detours to be sure that he isn't being followed.

Henning sees that the rundown watering hole has just opened when he arrives and it strikes him that this choice of meeting place was really quite clever. The press has laid siege to both Pål Fredrik's office and his private home, but no one would ever suspect him of frequenting a dump like this.

Henning orders a cup of coffee and takes a seat in the furthest corner of the room. The dark interior suits him fine; it makes it easy to hide, to disappear in a fog of stale alcohol and sweat against which soap and water stand no chance. A man with stubble and faded clothes comes out from the gents with his trousers still hanging halfway down his knees. On the loudspeakers Johnny Cash reminds the customers that pain is good.

Pål Fredrik Osmundsen arrives fifteen minutes after Henning. His grey suit is elegant and, in view of his red eyes and the bags under them, he could have come straight from a late-night drinking session at the more upmarket Aker Brygge. Henning barely recognises him from the photos in the newspapers.

Pål Fredrik Osmundsen is a business economist who graduated from BI Norwegian Business School. He has worked for Tvenge Brothers Investment, been a consultant and a private investor, but he is now in charge of an asset management fund specialising in European property. Henning doesn't know how many millions Osmundsen is worth, but it's a lot. He has also gained a reputation for himself as a bit of a modern-day explorer. The magazine *Vi Menn* featured him a couple of years ago when Osmundsen gave them access to some of his private photographs from when he climbed K2, Kilimanjaro and crossed Greenland on skis. He has taken part in the Trondheim to Oslo bike ride many times as well as other popular endurance events such as Birken.

Henning waves to the athletic man who weaves his way through chairs and tables.

'Over here,' Henning calls out.

Osmundsen takes Henning's outstretched hand and presses it firmly. They sit down. A silence ensues. Quick glances sweep across the table.

'Funny way to meet you, brother-in-law,' Osmundsen says at last.

Henning smiles briefly.

'Are you here as a journalist or as her brother?'

Henning doesn't reply immediately.

'I'm automatically disqualified from writing about Trine because I'm her brother.'

'So why are you here?'

'Because I—'

Henning thinks about it.

'Because there's something about the story that troubles me, only I don't know what it is. Perhaps it's this alleged victim, who ...'

Henning searches for the right word.

'I just don't buy it,' he says finally.

A waiter comes over and takes Osmundsen's order, a cup of coffee and a glass of water.

'But if you can't investigate the story,' Osmundsen begins, 'how will you be able to help Trine?'

Henning hesitates.

'I don't know,' he says and flashes a cautious smile. 'I haven't even started thinking about it.'

Osmundsen nods calmly. An ambulance with howling sirens drives past outside; the sound fills the room before fading away like a dying lament.

'She's going to kill me if she finds out that the two of us have been talking,' Osmundsen then says.

Henning tilts his head.

'Why?'

'Well, you're not exactly the best of friends.'

Henning lowers his gaze, stares into a past that rises from the table like a multi-coloured fog. And in the midst of it – a sad and lonely truth.

'No, we're not,' he admits. 'I don't really know why, but—'

'Is it true?'

Henning nods.

Images of Trine that have started to surface recently come back to him like uninvited guests. He hears her voice, small and fragile. He sees her gaze, dull and distant. And he wishes he knew, that he understood when and why they grew apart.

'Has she ever talked about it to you?' he asks.

Osmundsen shakes his head.

'I've asked her several times, but every time she just gives me a hard stare and that's the end of that conversation.'

Henning nods slowly.

Osmundsen takes out his mobile and puts it on the table with the screen facing up.

'In case Trine calls,' Osmundsen says by way of explanation.

'Have you heard from her?'

'She sent me a text message yesterday saying she wasn't coming home. She wouldn't tell me where she was because she needed to be alone, she said.'

'So she hasn't gone missing as some papers are speculating?'

Osmundsen hesitates.

'That rather depends how you look at it.'

Osmundsen lowers his gaze again. A dark shadow falls across his coarse, weather-beaten face. Even though he is tall and big, he looks small as he sits there. As if the strength in his upper body, the strength that kept him upright, has gone.

'It's happened before,' he says eventually. 'Her disappearing, I mean. It happened one Sunday a few years ago, I think it was, and I didn't find her until late in the evening, far away in Nordmarka Woods. She sat under a tree and was completely out of it. She came to when I touched her, but she couldn't remember anything of what had happened.'

'What did her bodyguards say?'

'Trine didn't have bodyguards in those days.'

'But—'

The words stop in Henning's mouth.

'There's a name for it,' Osmundsen continues. 'For what happened. Dissociative fugue,' he pronounces it clearly. 'A person will leave their home or their job, apparently with a sense of purpose, but afterwards they remember nothing.'

The waiter brings Osmundsen's coffee cup in one hand and a pot in the other. Henning covers his cup with his palm.

'So what causes it?' he asks when the waiter has left.

Osmundsen puts his head on one side.

'No one really seems to know, but it's usually trauma of some kind that the body is trying to protect itself against. Trine denies that she has ever experienced something that could trigger a reaction like that, so I guess we've agreed that it must have been due to work pressure. I could tell from looking at her in the days and weeks leading up to it. She was exhausted. And something was weighing her down.'

'And still she carried on as Justice Secretary?'

'Yes, anything else would have been unthinkable.'

'And the media never got wind of it?'

'No, they called it depression. The media write whatever you want them to write. Or they do some of the time.'

Henning tries to digest the information he has just been given.

'Do you think that's what has happened now?'

Osmundsen raises the coffee cup to his lips, takes a sip and puts it down with a clatter. Then he throws up his hands.

'Trine has always been a tough girl. I would have thought this kind of challenge would only have made her stronger. But who knows. And I don't like the fact that I can't get hold of her.'

'She has probably just switched off her mobile.'

Osmundsen nods helplessly and lowers his gaze again. Another silence descends on the table.

'So what do you make of all this?' Henning says. 'Did Trine do what they say she did?'

Again Osmundsen flings out his hands.

'She told me yesterday morning that the story isn't true. That the accusations against her are false.'

'But if that's the case,' Henning says, 'why doesn't she defend herself? Why has she run away?'

'I don't know,' Osmundsen replies and lowers his gaze again. 'It's not like her. I've no idea what's going on.'

The next moment the mobile on the table between them starts to vibrate. Henning sees hope and fear rise in Osmundsen, who quickly picks it up. Only to put it down and let it ring out.

'Journalists?' Henning asks.

Osmundsen nods.

'I think I must have got two hundred calls in the last

twenty-four hours. They just refuse to give up.'

Henning feels the need to say something, but the words won't come out.

'Do you have any idea where Trine might be?' he asks instead. 'Is there somewhere the two of you go when you want to be alone?'

Osmundsen thinks about it again, but Henning can see that he has given up. Shortly afterwards Osmundsen makes his excuses, explains that he has to get back to work where he is taking part in an important video conference. Henning shakes his hand and says that he'll pay, obviously. And the tall man disappears outside, out into a miasma of uncertainty.

Henning doesn't know why, but the sight of Pål Fredrik reminds him of his own father. In a rare TV profile he found about Trine last night, she talked about how hard her father's death had been for her, how it shaped her as a person. And he wonders how Pål Fredrik will cope if Trine doesn't recover.

This line of thinking leads him straight to his mother. He wonders if the caretaker in the block where she lives has managed to do him that favour he asked him.

Henning decides to find out.

Chapter 45

Pernille Thorbjørnsen and Ole Christian Sund are sitting down when Bjarne Brogeland and Ella Sandland enter the staff room. Their chairs are close together and they are leaning in towards each other, but both jump back when the officers greet them.

'Hello,' Sund says with a stiff smile. He looks across to Thorbjørnsen who immediately lowers her gaze and folds her hands in her lap. They don't stay there for long; she fiddles with her hair, tries to sit upright and glances quickly at the officers who have yet to ask them any questions.

Bjarne bides his time because he has a hunch about the two care workers, prompted by the first conversation he had with Thorbjørnsen after Erna Pedersen had been found dead. It started when she told him that Sund had called her *after* the murder.

Now it might just have been a conversation about a traumatic incident at the place where they both work. But given the looks they exchange and the closeness of the chairs, Bjarne suspects that their relationship is more intimate. Not only do they share a staff room, they also share a bed.

The room is so small that the police officers remain standing.

'Who would have thought we'd find you both here at the same time,' Bjarne says and looks at Thorbjørnsen. Her defences were intact the first time he met her. Now he can practically see the cracks. Her face has lost some of its colour.

'Have you finished arguing?' Bjarne says.

Thorbjørnsen's gaze shoots up at him, then shifts to Sund who starts picking at a callus.

'There's nothing wrong with having a quarrel, all couples do from time to time. I'm more interested in why you argued here, in Ward 4, on the afternoon Erna Pedersen was killed.'

Bjarne sees the beginning of the protest form in Sund's face.

'And why we found your fingerprints on Erna Pedersen's knitting needles,' Sandland interjects and points at Thorbjørnsen.

'Mine?' she frowns.

Sandland nods.

'There's nothing suspicious about that. I used to help her cast on and finish her mittens and socks. She couldn't do it herself, poor thing, her hands weren't what they used to be.'

Bjarne looks at his colleague. *It's a plausible explanation*, he thinks, and looks at the flame red colour in Thorbjørnsen's cheeks.

'What was your car doing up in Holmenkollen on Monday afternoon with you behind the wheel,' Bjarne points at Sund, 'and Daniel Nielsen in the passenger seat?'

Thorbjørnsen's lips part.

'Holmenkollen?' she exclaims and looks at her boyfriend. 'You told me you were going to Storo?'

Sund tries to look her in the eye, but can't stand up to his girlfriend's sudden, intense scrutiny.

'I thought you were meeting a mate to see if he could fit

my car with a new silencer?'

Sund makes no reply, he simply bows his head.

'Heaven help us,' she snorts and shakes her head.

Bjarne gives them a little more time. Thorbjørnsen, who had briefly assumed a more upright posture, collapses again with fresh anger in her eyes.

'Perhaps one of you can tell us what's going on?' Sandland suggests.

Thorbjørnsen's face gets even redder. Finally Sund starts talking.

'Please leave Pernille out of this. She's got nothing to do with it.'

'And what is "this"?' Sandland asks.

Sund sighs.

'You're right,' he says, looking at Bjarne. 'We did have an argument at work on Sunday. Daniel came by to drop off Pernille's car because she needed it to drive herself home and he asked if he could borrow it again the next day for another job up in Holmenkollen.'

'Another job?'

'Well, you see—'

Again Sund looks away. When he doesn't start speaking immediately, Thorbjørnsen continues the story for him.

'I was really upset about it,' she says and lifts her head. 'Upset that they kept using my car for their scheme. I wanted out, pure and simple; I refused to be their accomplice any longer.'

'Accomplice to what?' Sandland asks, sounding tired.

Sund braces himself.

'I'm a care worker,' he starts tentatively in a low voice and looks up at Sandland, now with a little more defiance in his gaze. 'All I've ever done is help people in need.'

Bjarne looks at him in disbelief.

'You're telling me you help people by selling them drugs that you steal from your employer?'

Sund glowers at him.

'Drugs? What are you talking about?'

Sund puts on his most indignant face.

'Just what exactly are you accusing us of?'

Bjarne doesn't reply.

'We visit people in their own homes and give them the care they don't feel they get enough of from social services.'

Bjarne doesn't realise that his jaw has dropped. This particular development has taken him completely by surprise.

'Have you any idea how many people are let down by the health service in Norway today, Brogeland? Here in Oslo alone? How many people have watched relatives, people who helped build this country, be treated like rubbish? Like—'

Sund can't even find the words.

'I'm sure it's bad,' Bjarne says. 'But are you telling me that you care for elderly people in their own homes?'

Sund nods.

'And you get paid cash?'

Sund looks away.

'That's against the law,' Sandland says.

'Don't I know it,' Sund says, sounding cross.

'And you've never stolen medication from the care home?'

'Our clients have plenty of medication; they can get whatever they need for free on prescription. I don't know why so much medication goes missing from Grünerhjemmet, but it's something that happens in every care home. But care isn't just about giving someone pills, Brogeland. Care is so much more.'

'Mm,' Bjarne says again. 'So this was a business you were running on the side?'

Sund nods.

'How long have you been doing this? When did you start?'

Sund looks up at him again. The outrage he had worked up appears to have deserted him. His head hangs heavy.

'My father had a stroke when he was only fifty-seven years old. He relied completely on full-time care for the rest of his life. I looked after him right up until his death a couple of years ago. My mother had died when I was little. Many of those who knew us also knew how I had cared for my father and they asked me if I might consider doing the same for their relatives. Not all the time, of course, but whenever I could. They would pay me. In the meantime, I had managed to get a job in the care sector and I was all too aware of the problems and the dissatisfaction people felt. So I said yes.'

'And it took off?'

Sund nods.

'Daniel and I met through work and had become friends. I knew that he needed money so I asked him if he might be interested in a second job. Yes, we don't declare it and yes it's illegal, but neither of us has a guilty conscience. Not for one second. People live better lives because of what we do.'

'As do you.'

Sund snorts.

'I can pay my rent, yes. Just about. Something you would think was owed to a highly skilled man like me. But I guess you have to follow procedure,' he says, now sounding grumpy. 'Lock me up. And when you get home tonight, look in the mirror and ask yourself if Oslo is a better place because you did. If we can all now sleep safely in our beds?'

Bjarne says nothing; he sees no point in embarking on a discussion with Sund. So he thinks about Erna Pedersen again. His initial theory was that she must have seen something, but she hadn't. Ole Christian Sund has nothing to do with her death. Nor would it appear do Daniel Nielsen and Pernille Thorbjørnsen.

So who does?

Sandland's mobile starts to ring in her jacket pocket. She takes it out and signals to Bjarne that she will take the call outside. Bjarne is left alone with the care workers who don't say anything, nor do they look at each other.

Sandland reappears shortly, but she stays in the doorway and summons him outside with her right index finger. Bjarne does as she asks. Sandland leans towards his ear and whispers: 'We've got to go. There's been another murder.'

Chapter 46

Two cars are parked quite a distance from each other outside the apartment block in Helgesensgate. Henning knows that reporters have been trying to call his mother and that they have rung her doorbell.

He also knows that gaining access to a block of flats is easy, as is knocking on every available door until you find the person you are looking for. But when Henning lets himself in and walks up the stairs, he can see that the caretaker, Karl Ove Marcussen, has done his bit to make the job more difficult for the vultures. He has unscrewed the name plate saying 'Christine Juul' and hopefully disconnected her doorbell and telephone as well. In addition he unplugged the aerial to make sure she can't watch television. Henning's mother is one of the few people left who still swears by landlines.

He lets himself into her flat, but doesn't call out her name until he has closed the door behind him. As always he is met by the stench of cigarettes, but the smell isn't as pungent as usual.

He walks in without first taking off his shoes, but pulls up short when he spots his mother in the kitchen. Or rather, slumped on the kitchen table, her cheek pressing against the surface. Next to her are an empty bottle and a shot glass.

She's dead, Henning thinks, and a mixture of grief and relief washes over him. The first emotion surprises him. The second fills him with shame. But then one of her fingers twitches and she moves her head. It looks as if she is trying to lift it, but she fails.

His initial relief changes into disappointment while he tries to convince himself that it isn't caused by the fact that she is still alive. Even so he can't help wishing that she, for her own sake, would soon let go. She is trapped in her body, plagued by chronic obstructive pulmonary disease as she is.

With a feeling of dismay he helps her up, but she has no strength left in her arms. And he realises from the smell of her breath that there is no point in trying to talk to her. She is quite simply too drunk.

For a brief moment her eyes light up, she manages to focus, but then she sees who it is. Her excitement turns into contempt.

'And here I was hoping it would be Trine,' she slurs.

Henning looks at her. He sighs and allows yet another of her hurtful comments pass. He tries to lift her up, but she fights him like a child. Henning lets her slump back down on her chair. Her upper body falls forwards again. He takes hold of her shoulders; she makes a pathetic attempt to shake off his hands, but this time he keeps hold of her.

'The radio,' she says still slurring. 'It's not working. Can you do something about it? I haven't been able to listen to the radio for two days.'

Henning nods and promises to fix it.

'And the TV,' she adds.

'I'll have a look at that as well. Come on,' he says, lifting her up again. 'We've got to get you to bed. You can't sleep here.'

Once again she fights him.

'Come on, Mum. Work with me here.'

He realises she doesn't just smell of cigarettes and alcohol. Her clothes haven't been washed for weeks. He dreads to think when she last had a shower.

'Come on. Don't be difficult now.'

At times Henning had to resort to bribery when Jonas acted up and refused to go to nursery, get dressed or go to bed. Sometimes Henning would bribe him with films, other times with pancakes or sweets. And when none of the usual inducements worked there was only one option left.

Force.

And Henning thinks about Jonas as he picks up his mother, ignoring the protests she spits at him. She mentions Trine again, she mutters something about cigarettes and her glass, but he just carries her out of the kitchen and into the bedroom. And when her struggle to free herself leads to nothing, but only wears her out and makes her breathless, she starts to gasp and point. Henning realises what she wants and puts her down on the bed. He fetches her breathing apparatus and sees her grab the mask with the desperation of a drug addict. She closes her eyes and inhales the medication that loosens up the slime and relieves the gurgling in her chest.

And it strikes him how desperately we cling to life no matter how much each heartbeat hurts.

Gradually she regains control of herself while the machine whirrs and hisses. And when her body has calmed down and her lungs are once more in a tolerable condition, she releases her grip on the plastic tube and sinks further on the bed. A few seconds later she is asleep.

Chapter 47

It's like trying to get up after a knockout only to be punched in the face again. Just as they have eliminated suspects in one murder inquiry, news of another comes in. And now they have to focus all their resources on that, at least for the next forty-eight hours. It's not always like this, fortunately, but it happens more and more often. The cases are starting to pile up.

Bjarne parks outside the police cordons next to several patrol cars and stays in his car while a grey light falls across rooftops that still show traces of days and nights of precipitation. And the rain continues to fall.

As usual curious onlookers have congregated nearby. It looks as if they are holding a bizarre vigil and there is an aura of morbid expectation in the raw air. Bjarne finds Emil Hagen at the entrance to the block of flats.

'What's happened?' Bjarne asks.

Hagen stuffs a piece of chewing tobacco under his lip.

'Woman in her mid-thirties, strangled. There appears to have been a struggle.'

Bjarne looks up to get an impression of the building. Grey walls. Black gunk from spray cans on the walls. The windows overlook the city, but they are dark as if there is nothing behind them. The whole building has been cordoned off. Blue lights are flashing all around them. It's a grim day in Oslo.

'The victim's name is Johanne Klingenberg,' Hagen continues.

'Who found her?' Bjarne asks.

'A neighbour, her landlady, heard the cat whimper,' Hagen explains. 'I believe it's been a problem before and she knocked on the door to ask her to put a stop to the noise. When there was no reply, she tried the door. And found it was open.'

'Had she heard anything leading up to that point?'

'No.'

'Did anyone else see or hear anything?'

'Don't know yet,' Hagen says. 'I've only just arrived myself.'

Bjarne takes another look around.

'I think I'll go upstairs and view the crime scene.'

'Okay,' Hagen replies. 'I'll find Sandland and start speaking to the other neighbours while you do that.'

Bjarne can smell mould as he climbs the stairs. A wall lamp is askew. No light bulb. *The rent is probably in the same league as Daniel Nielsen's*, he thinks, even though the hessian wallpaper is a little more faded and grimier.

The door to the victim's second-floor flat is open. He enters and nods to familiar faces. Ann-Mari Sara, the crime scene technician, is already there.

'Always working,' he says.

'As long as people keep dying in this city, then—'

Sara takes a photograph as Bjarne steps inside the living room. There are definite signs of a struggle. There is a cushion on the floor. The glass coffee table has been knocked over, but not damaged. The remote controls lie scattered; the batteries from one of them have fallen out. The rug under the coffee table, brown and threadbare, is bunched up as if someone quickly pushed the table away. Shards from a broken mug are smeared with thin and sticky brown dregs. Bjarne thinks it must be tea, he can see black flecks in it. Tea leaves, possibly. Or cigarette ash.

The victim is lying on her back on the sofa. Her long hair spills out in a wreath around her head. A hair band from a ponytail lies next to her, brown just like the sofa. One leg hangs over the front. She is still wearing her trousers and her blouse, white, but wet. Sweat, possibly. The upholstery under her is also damp.

Bjarne detests the thought that the bladder empties itself at the moment of death. The loss of dignity at the end of life. One of nature's little cruelties. *But at least she's dressed*, he thinks, which makes it unlikely that the motive is sexual, *if* the struggle is related to her death. And the fact that there has been some kind of fight in the living room gives him some encouragement. The chance of finding DNA evidence is considerable. And God knows they need an open and shut case right now.

'Did she live alone?' he asks.

'Looks like it,' Sara remarks. 'Only one toothbrush in the bathroom.'

More flashlights go off, which blind Bjarne for a second before he can see properly again and take another look around. There is a candle stuck in a red wine bottle on the windowsill. He would have expected a woman in her thirties to have had flowers here and there, but all he sees are lamps and candlesticks. Pictures on the wall.

Sara's camera flashes again and it's as if the sharp, artificial light makes the pictures stand out more clearly. Bjarne goes over to the wall and looks at one of the framed photographs.

The glass has been smashed.

He takes a step closer as a chill runs down his spine. Even the broken glass can't hide the smile of a boy who can't be more than two years old.

Chapter 48

He doesn't come here often. But now that Henning has un-locked the door to the attic room and looked inside, he wishes he hadn't come at all. There are so many memories stored up there, in everything he sees. Boxes of clothing, toys, shoes that would have been too small for Jonas today. An old scooter, a pair of skates. He can't bear to let them go. It's as if Jonas will be even further away from him if he were to throw out his things. Just thinking about it feels like a violation.

Even so he enters the attic room and finds the box he is looking for; he carries it down to his flat and wipes off the dust before he opens the lid. He stares at the piles of photos and photo albums. He deliberately avoids looking at pictures of Jonas. What he is interested in right now are photographs of Trine and him, the identical collages their mother made for them the Christmas when they were ten and twelve years old respectively.

The idea came to him when he saw an old photograph of Jonas, Nora and himself on the mantelpiece in his mother's flat. It made him realise there is so much about Trine he has forgotten. He blows hard into the box and the dust whirls back in his face. He instinctively recoils before he starts rifling through the photographs. It doesn't take long before he finds the album he is looking for.

He opens it so that the light and the air can reach it. The

233

first page is blank. Then – a photo of Trine and him as babies, eighteen months apart. They are lying on the same blanket, with the same open gaze aimed at the camera. Henning can see how much they looked like each other as babies.

He turns the page and sees more baby pictures of them together on the floor. Henning's back is ramrod straight and his hand reaches out to Trine, who is lying on her back with her legs in the air. They play. They smile. There are pictures of them in their cots, pictures of them lying under a duvet on the sofa with dull eyes and feverish foreheads. Pictures of them growing bigger. Pictures from birthday parties, Christmases, from the pebble beach near their cabin in Stavern of them trying to skim stones. Two '1' candles on a birthday cake the year Trine turned eleven. Trine puffing up her cheeks ready to blow out the candles.

I wonder what I did, Henning thinks to himself. *What did I do that made Mum hate me and worship Trine?*

Henning looks at the photo album again, the pebble beach, the rocks, the ships in the Skagerrak. He can't remember when he last visited the cabin, but it must be many years ago. He remembers how the small community and the holiday resort seemed to die every year in mid-August. Their sun-loving cabin neighbours would disappear before the schools started again. When Henning's family came back in September to shut down the cabin for the winter, their neighbours would already have left. The sea could carry on gambolling without an audience. And it occurs to him that if Trine has gone somewhere to be alone right now, then that has to be the place.

It has started to rain again when Bjarne comes back outside, a cold shower with big, heavy drops. But neither the wet nor the cool autumn air has any effect on him. An uneasy gut feeling has brought on a fever that is spreading to the rest of his body.

Two crime scenes in the space of just a few days presenting with very similar evidence. *Is that a coincidence?* he asks himself, and answers his own question immediately. Photographs can easily get broken in the heat of a struggle. Murder by strangulation is not uncommon. And only Erna Pedersen was mutilated after her death.

But even so.

Shortly afterwards Bjarne sees Emil Hagen outside the entrance to the apartment block. Because of the heavy rain they get into one of the patrol cars, but don't start the engine. The raindrops batter the windscreen. Big curtains of water are blown across the bodywork.

'I checked with the emergency services,' Bjarne says. 'There were no calls to them from the victim's mobile.'

Hagen runs a hand over his wet face and wipes it on his trousers.

'I've spoken to those neighbours who were at home,' he says. 'Nobody heard anything.'

Bjarne tries looking out through the windscreen. It's starting to mist up. Outside two police officers walk past, chatting to each other, but their words can't be heard inside the car.

'But there was one interesting thing,' Hagen says. 'The victim reported a break-in two weeks ago.'

Bjarne turns his head to his colleague whose jaw looks even more tightly clenched than usual.

'Nothing was taken, but she said – if I've understood this correctly – that someone had been bleeding in her flat.'

'Bleeding?'

'Yes. She found a blood stain right next to the cat basket, I believe. And someone had smashed a photo on the wall.'

Bjarne looks at him.

'Two weeks ago?'

'Yes.'

'The same picture hanging there now or a different one?'

'I'm not sure, but I think it was the same one. It's possible she hadn't replaced the frame. Or the glass yet.'

'And left broken glass on the floor?'

Bjarne shakes his head.

'I highly doubt that.'

Hagen doesn't reply. A smell of wet leather rises from his jacket.

How bizarre, Bjarne thinks. *Someone broke a picture in the victim's home two weeks ago and the same thing happens again today?*

This is definitely not a coincidence. And it bears witness to a deep-seated rage.

'Who handled the investigation?' Bjarne asks.

Hagen looks at him.

'It was low priority. Nothing was stolen. And nobody got hurt.'

'Except, possibly, the man who broke in.'

'Perhaps.'

'But what about the blood? Can that help us?'

'I don't know,' Hagen says. 'I guess it's at the back of the queue at the lab, like everything else.'

Bjarne shakes his head and sighs.

'What kind of blood was it?'

'What do you mean?'

'Are we talking drops, blood spurts – what was it?'

'A smear. Like if you have a cut, but you don't know it and then you accidentally touch—'

'I know what a smear is, Emil.'

The investigators sit in pensive silence for a few seconds while the rain lashes the windscreen. Bjarne puts his hand on the door handle.

'Well,' he says, 'I guess we'll have to do what we always do.'

'I guess so.'

Chapter 49

Henning loves autumn. In the summer only the copper beeches and the bright yellow rapeseed fields stand out from all the lush shades of green. But in the autumn nearly every tree and bush changes colour. It's as if the year has matured. And yes, the colour palette warns of darker times, and yes, there is something sad about the dying plants and withering leaves. But even so Henning has always welcomed it.

Nora could never understand why halfway through Edvard Grieg's Piano Concerto in A minor, Henning would sit there with tears in his eyes and yet expect her to believe that the salt-water was a sign that he was enjoying himself.

Now autumn rushes past outside the car window. The fields lie shorn and dormant, like a memorial to bright, warm summer evenings.

Henning remembers that the drive to Stavern used to take two and a half hours, but that was going from Kløfta. It was also in a different car, in another age. They would pack the small, blue VW Beetle to the rafters and, had they been spotted today, the police would have pulled them over for careless driving. Just being back on the same road – or almost the same road because motorways have been built since – reminds Henning how he used to be squashed on the backseat, barely able to reach out to undo the small latch that opened a window to get rid of the cigarette smoke in the car.

His mobile rings when he is almost halfway there. It is the *123news* national news editor. He is tempted to ignore the call, but capitulates in the end.

'Hello, Heidi.'

'Where are you?'

As usual, his boss skips the small talk.

'I'm in the car.'

'A woman has been found murdered in a flat in Bislett. I want you to go there straightaway.'

'Sorry, but that's going to be difficult. I'm on my way to—'

Henning stops himself; he doesn't want to reveal his destination.

'On your way to where?'

'I've almost got to Tønsberg.'

'What on earth are you doing in Tønsberg?'

'There's just something I need to check.'

Heidi sighs heavily into the telephone.

'So when do you think you'll be back?'

'Don't know. Later tonight, hopefully.'

Another sigh.

'Okay.'

She hangs up without saying goodbye.

*

For the next hour Henning concentrates on the road. All he has to do is remember to turn off at the crazy golf course at Anvikstranda Camping, which they were allowed to visit once every summer, and he'll be there. It's a trip down memory lane.

He remembers too small hands trying to grip too big golf

clubs. He remembers the bumpy road, which hasn't grown less bumpy over the years, how they practically had to drive off-road to make way for any cars coming towards them. But he doesn't need those memories now.

Past the grove a large grassy area opens out. This is where they used to play football in the summer. Where they tried to fly kites. Where they would practise cartwheels, throw Frisbees and forget to eat because they were having so much fun. And on the horizon lies the sea, big, blue and beautiful.

Henning drives past the rubbish bins and continues until the road stops at the end of Donavall Camping with rows of trailers with picket fences, decking and locked plastic crates containing garden furniture. Everything is exactly as he remembers it.

The parking space allocated to their cabin appears a short distance ahead of him. But there is no car in sight. Trine isn't there. No one is.

So he was wrong after all.

A little further along the gravel track he spots tyre tracks. Fresh. As if a car, or two, drove halfway into the space before turning around again.

Whenever Henning's family went to the cabin, they would park as near the footpath as they could to unload the car. Then there would be the strenuous hike through the forest laden down with rucksacks, bags and food shopping. Trine and Henning were always made to carry something, even when they were little, and they would walk through the trees whose viper-like roots snaked down towards the footpath where they were. And every time there was a noise in the thicket, they would jump a mile, spooked as only children can be.

But it was also an incredibly beautiful landscape where the trees grew close, vines wound their way around them and white anemones, almost luminous in the spring, covered the forest floor like a duvet. And the view when they reached the top of the hill, when the sea opened out before them, and they could see ships draw white trails in their wake on the mirrored, blue surface of the Skagerrak.

He remembers everything now.

And seeing that he has driven all this way, he decides he might as well go down to the shore. Henning loves the sea. He has always loved throwing stones at the rocks to see if he could hit them. He loved snorkelling, looking for flounders on the seabed, the way the seaweed and bull rushes wafted around him in slow motion when he went swimming.

Henning parks the car and walks down the footpath where everything has changed, while at the same time nothing has. He still looks out for vipers, just in case. And the feeling when he reaches the top of the hill and the sea spreads out in front of him hasn't changed, either. It's as if something in him lets go. He stops and looks across the water; the distant sky has acquired a pink evening glow, which in a few places is reflected in the almost motionless surface of the sea.

He remembers how they used to play on the pebble beach, him and Trine, how they would pick bog whortleberries and crowberries that looked like blueberries and which Trine insisted on calling blueberries for years. Trine would always boss him around, like the know-it-all she was. This is how he remembers her, even though she is eighteen months younger than him, her constantly wagging finger and a tone of voice that would frighten most people into doing what she told them. This extended to when the family played cards. She learned new games and strategies very quickly. Their mother, however, never played to win; she always let her children beat her. And Trine hated that.

Henning inhales the sea air deep into his lungs before he starts walking down towards the row of blue cabins. He remembers the mound where he used to go to pee because the cabin only had an outside toilet and no power on earth could make him step inside the tiny cubicle that was riddled with flies, spiders and cobwebs. And he remembers the seagulls they fed with prawn shells and fish waste. Cormorants, oystercatchers and swans that always caused a stir whenever they flapped past. The eider ducks.

Tvistein Lighthouse stands just as staunchly on the horizon as it always did. On clear summer evenings they could see all the way out to the island of Jomfruland. If he tries really hard, he is sure that he can conjure up the smell of his father's cigar smoke, the smell of holiday. And nowhere in the world do the stars twinkle more brightly.

Henning comes to a standstill when he sees that the door to the cabin is open. At first he thinks there must have been a break-in; he has read countless newspaper articles over the years about cabins closed down for the winter that have had uninvited, light-fingered guests, but his initial concern soon gives way to profound relief when he notices a plate and a glass in the sink outside.

So he was right after all.

Trine hasn't scattered breadcrumbs for the wagtails with which they always used to share their breakfast, but the washing-up bowl is still there. Square and made from faded red plastic. And he sees the old gulley in the hillside that their father dug to divert rainwater away from their cabin. Their mother always took great care to weed around it. He can't imagine that anyone has done any weeding here for years.

Their plot is relatively inaccessible from the surrounding footpaths so people rarely walked straight past their front door – even in the summer. It meant that they hardly ever had to lock the cabin, a tradition Henning notes to his satisfaction that Trine has upheld.

He enters the cabin tentatively.

'Trine?'

It feels strange to say her name out loud and there is no response. The cabin is silent. But he sees a laptop on the table. Clothing thrown over the dark blue sofa. The curtains are still the same blue and white ones, in case anyone should forget that they are by the seaside. He looks across the juniper bushes that cover the hillside in front of the cabin; the thicket below. The irregularities in the terrain. And he remembers the cream buns they used to eat, radio plays on Saturdays, the television that never worked.

He remembers everything.

He leaves the cabin and walks up to the small mound and it feels as if the whole world is spread out in front of him. All he has to do is reach out his hand to touch it. And the wind, he hadn't noticed it until now. Or the smell from Firsbukta, either – a smell he hated when he was little – of seaweed and rubbish that the sea has washed up and which has been rotting in the sun.

He wonders if that's what makes him take a step back to stop himself from falling over. How can all this have been buried inside him, all these lovely memories that are now coming back to him? He closes his eyes and lets them in. He stands like this for a long time.

Then he walks back inside the cabin and sits down at the table where Trine's laptop is open. He bumps into a table leg, and as he does so he causes the screen to wake up. A detailed city map appears. Blue, yellow, white and beige colours dotted across the page. A slightly thicker line runs through the streets along some water. He is about to read the street names when a shadow flits across the window. His gaze darts to the door frame where his sister is staring at him with frightened eyes.

'Henning? What the hell are you doing here?'

Chapter 50

Trine is wearing muddy walking boots and a green, white and red anorak. A baseball cap covers her hair.

All he can do is stare at her. She has their mother's features around her mouth and her eyes; nothing about her has changed except that she has aged a little. She is Trine, his sister. To whom he hasn't spoken for God knows how many years.

'Hi,' he says at last.

Two men, whom Henning presumes to be Trine's bodyguards, appear either side of her. He can see that they are about to rush inside, but Trine stops them with a gesture and mutters – with her face turned away from him – that it's only her brother.

Then she turns to him again. And he doesn't know how to interpret the look in her eyes. Whether it's anger, fear or something else. But there is definitely something. Hostility, possibly.

'Have you come here to gloat?' she asks.

'Gloat? No. I'm here to—'

Henning stops and thinks about it.

'I came because I was worried about you.'

Trine starts to laugh.

'A lot of people are worried about you, Trine. No one has been able to contact you for thirty-six hours.'

'So you decided to come here? To find out if this was where I was hiding?'

'Yes.'

'That's just like you,' she mutters to herself. Henning is about to ask her what she means by that remark, but Trine interrupts him.

'So what's the deal now? Were you hoping to interview me?'

'The thought hadn't even crossed my mind.'

'So why—'

Trine swallows the rest of the sentence. Henning looks at her for a long time before he says: 'I've come to see if I can help you.'

'I don't need your help,' she pouts.

Henning continues to look at her, at her fingers which fidget, at fingernails which haven't been left alone for one minute. If he knows anything about her at all, she has been biting them right down to the quick. When she was little she used to get told off about it all the time.

She still refuses to look at him. If he hadn't known better, he would almost have believed that she was scared of him.

'I didn't see your car in the car park,' he says. It's both a question and a statement.

'No, you don't think I'm that stupid, do you? I parked elsewhere. And I didn't come in my own car, either.'

Trine turns her head slightly and, for a brief moment, Henning makes eye contact with her, enough to see his mother in them. The same anger. The same contempt. As if she finds it loathsome even to be in the same room as him.

'Neither did I. But then again I don't have a car of my

own,' he says, trying to laugh. Trine is not even close to being mollified.

'Have you been out for a walk?'

Trine glances at her watch, then she shifts her gaze towards the sea.

'Did you find the blue dots?'

Henning smiles at the memory, how they used to compete to be the first to spot the blue dots placed along the coastal path for guidance. At that time they cared little about nature, the point of the game was winning. And Trine always wanted to win. Always.

'How far did you walk?' he asks. Trine turns to him again.

'To Stavern,' she says in a low voice.

'Stavern?' Henning exclaims. 'You walked all the way there? And back again?'

She nods, but only just.

'That must be miles.'

Trine automatically checks her watch.

'12.21 kilometres,' she says. 'Each way.'

'So you've walked—'

Her impatience gets the better of her and she sighs.

'What do you want, Henning?'

He looks at her. Some of her hair, wet and dark, has come loose under her baseball cap. The wind takes hold of it and blows it in front of her eyes.

'Please can we just talk, Trine?'

'No.'

The reply is firm.

'I don't want to talk to you.'

Henning searches her eyes for an explanation, but finds

only hostility. Again, she looks out at the sea before she steps inside the cabin. And that's when she notices that her laptop is on.

'Have you been snooping on my computer?'

'No, I—'

Trine marches up to the table and slams shut the laptop.

'Get out,' she demands.

Henning is about to protest, but he sees that it will serve no purpose.

'Get out,' she orders him again.

Henning gets up and holds up his palms. He starts to walk, but stops and turns around; he looks at her windswept, ruddy cheeks. He tries to think of something to say, but the right words refuse to come.

'Please, just let the world know that you're still alive,' he says. 'People are worried about you.'

'Yeah, right.'

'No, I mean it, Trine.'

Trine laughs again.

'Yes, I guess you all feel really bad now.'

Henning still can't think of anything to say.

'You've seen for yourself that I'm alive,' she says, pointing to the door. 'Now you can go home.'

'But—'

'Please, Henning. Just go.'

Suddenly he can see the hurt in her eyes; it's only for a second or two, but it's long enough for him to notice. Trine walks back to the doorway and stands facing the sea with her back to him. Henning watches her for a few seconds before he does as she asks. He walks around the cabin and past his father's overgrown gulley. Once he gets to the top of the mound he stops and turns around again. He looks across the roof of the cabin and out at the sea, now just as black as the approaching night. He hears seagulls screech, sees a ship in the distance, tiny against the endless background. And he thinks that the big, open sea contains as many questions as answers.

Chapter 51

Trine watches Henning disappear up the mound. She waits. Listens out until everything is quiet again. Then she waits even longer until she is absolutely sure that he has gone.

Henning.

She knew that he had returned to work, of course. She has even read some of his articles, the most recent one only last week, about Tore Pulli and how he was killed. She always gets a lump in her throat when she reads his stories and sees the small byline picture of him with the scars. But this time she can't just click a button to make it go away.

Now that she has seen him again, in person, she is unable to block out the images that pop up in her head even though she is awake and should be able to suppress them. It's the middle of the night and she is woken up by noises coming from nearby. A low sound repeating like a rhythm. Something squeaks. Mild scraping from a chair. Followed by more squeaking.

Trine gets out of bed and goes to the door; she sees a soft light spill out from Henning's room. The noises grow louder and she hears breathing that quickens. She tiptoes closer to Henning's room. And the sight that meets her when she peeks inside—

Trine closes her eyes.

She could never look at her father or Henning afterwards.

She had hoped that it might get easier in time, but it was just as difficult today as it always was.

Trine tries to shake off the images and the memories. Now she regrets that she didn't ask Henning to keep his mouth shut about having found her and get him to promise not to reveal the location where she has been hiding for the last thirty-six hours. But something tells her that Henning won't say anything. He understands.

Trine sits down; she takes a sip from her water bottle and feels the soreness in her legs and the blisters on her heel. Even the soles of her feet hurt. She's in need of a shower. She would have gone for a swim in the sea, except that the water temperature is probably only thirteen or fourteen degrees in September. What she ought to have done was jump in the sea and drown herself. But she couldn't step off the cliff when the thought occurred to her on the coastal path. She just couldn't make herself do it.

Perhaps she didn't want it enough. Or perhaps she was still clinging to the hope that a brilliant solution would present itself during her long walk.

Trine takes out her mobile and reads the last text message she got from Katarina Hatlem almost an hour ago, a message Trine has yet to reply to.

You can't hide any longer, Trine. Clear message from the PM's office: 'She needs to come out and kill this story or she has to resign.' Can you think of any other solution?

Again Trine weighs up her options. She can either confront the allegations, reveal where she was and what she was doing that night and then wait for the public outcry that will exile her from politics for good. Or she can roll over, play dead and resign quietly out of fear of losing the best and finest person in her life.

You'll lose him anyway, she thinks, *if you don't tell him*. Both options are equally impossible.

Once again she rages at herself because she wasn't brave enough to end her problems at the bottom of the sea or at the foot of a cliff while she still had the chance. *You're a coward*, she reproaches herself.

But running away is also the act of a coward, fleeing your problems as she is doing now. It's not her style, it never was. Yes, it has been necessary to bury certain things from the past, but that was different. Piling earth on top of something that stinks to make the smell go away. And so far the press hasn't managed to uncover what is rotting underneath.

But what guarantee does she have that her accusers would tell the truth once they get what they want?

None.

Trine shakes her head. No matter what she does, it'll be wrong.

Chapter 52

The incident room on the fifth floor of Oslo Police Station is busy as always with uniformed and plainclothes officers whose attention is directed at the end of the boardroom table where Arild Gjerstad raises a coffee cup to his mouth. The table is covered with files, coffee cups and half-full water bottles. On the smart board on the wall the name JOHANNE KLINGENBERG appears in capital letters. Preliminary forensic evidence is listed in bullet points under her name.

Gjerstad puts down his cup and walks up to the smart board.

'The killer is likely to be known to the victim,' he says. 'Do we have a list of everyone she knew?'

Gjerstad looks across the assembly. Fredrik Stang, who has dark hair in a crew cut and a face whose expression is always grave and tense, speaks up.

'If the calendar on her laptop was up-to-date, she had lunch with someone called Emilie earlier today at twelve noon. The victim had a public profile on Facebook and according to her friends list she has only one friend called Emilie. Emilie Blomvik.'

'We need to talk to her,' Gjerstad says. 'Today.'

'I can do that,' Bjarne volunteers.

'Good,' Gjerstad replies.

Stang runs his hand down his tanned, muscular arm before he continues.

'The victim was a mature student at Oslo University's College of Applied Sciences; she was quite active on the online dating scene with profiles on both match.com and sukker.no as well as various other sites. We'll check out anyone she has been or is in contact with to see if some of the relationships were more serious than others. But I'm not sure that's the lead we should be prioritising since the victim was found fully clothed. There were no signs of sexual assault.'

'Even so,' Gjerstad says, 'check it out.'

Stang nods.

'Talking about friends, she had over 1,800 Facebook friends. In the last two days alone she made more status updates than I have in a whole year.'

'That might explain how the killer knew that she wouldn't be at home two weeks ago,' Bjarne says. 'And when he would be able to break into her flat.'

'In that case the killer has to be one of her Facebook friends,' Sandland concludes. 'That narrows down the list of suspects.'

Stang nods and puts down his notepad. Silence descends on the table. Bjarne picks up the pen in front of him and clicks it on and off in a quick rhythm.

'I have a theory I'd like to try out on you,' he says when he has given it some thought. 'Last Sunday eighty-three-year-old Erna Pedersen was murdered. She was strangled before being mutilated with her own knitting needles. Her killer smashed a photo on her wall and took another picture with him. A picture that hadn't been there for very long. None of the people we've interviewed at the care home can explain how it came to be on the wall in the first place. In which case it's possible that the killer put it there himself. This would mean that he had been to the care home before and that he knew the victim.'

Bjarne pauses briefly to make sure that everyone can follow him.

'And today Johanne Klingenberg was found dead in her flat. She, too, was strangled and again someone had smashed a picture on her wall – the same picture, incidentally, that was smashed two weeks ago when someone broke into her flat. I think it's likely that she was strangled by the same person who broke into her flat.'

'Are you saying that the killings are connected?' Gjerstad asks.

Bjarne pauses briefly.

'I think there's evidence to suggest it, yes. Not only were both victims strangled, but it seems as if the killer in both cases has a particular obsession with photographs. They mean something to him and they trigger a rage in him. And this particular obsession is something I've seen much too much of in murder inquiries in recent years.'

'It's just a random coincidence,' Pia Nøkleby objects. 'The pictures, I mean. Anything could happen in the heat of a struggle.'

Bjarne is about to continue putting forward his theory, but Ella Sandland looks up from her documents and beats him to it.

'There's actually another coincidence,' she says. 'Both victims are originally from Jessheim.'

Silence descends on the water bottles and the coffee cups. Bjarne lets his gaze wander from investigator to investigator and sees that his theory has stirred their interest.

'That doesn't necessarily mean anything,' Nøkleby insists. 'I'm sure many people from Jessheim move to Oslo. We're only talking about a distance of – what is it – fifty kilometres?'

'Forty,' Bjarne says. 'But three coincidences mean we have to examine if the two cases are connected.'

Bjarne sees Hagen and Sandland nod in agreement.

'And there's one more point that I think is worth noting,' he continues. 'In both murders the killer appears to have planned his approach in advance.'

'What makes you say that?' Emil Hagen says.

'Why break into someone's home when they're not there – if you don't intend to steal anything or harm them?'

Bjarne looks around. There is no reply.

'Because you're doing research,' he says. 'You're doing the groundwork. The killer must have been to Erna Pedersen's room at least once before he killed her – if we surmise that he put up the missing picture. When it comes to Johanne Klingenberg, then, I think that the killer checked out her flat, looked at what opportunities there were for him and what difficulties might arise, and came back when he had finalised his plan.'

'He could have been stalking her?' Sandland suggests.

Bjarne fixes his gaze on her.

'Why would he then have smashed a picture of a toddler on her wall? Twice?'

'Because he thought the child was hers?'

Bjarne shakes his head.

'If he had been stalking her, he would have known that she had no children. And then we would probably also have

256

found evidence of a sexual assault at the crime scene.'

'Not necessarily,' Sandland says.

'No, but it's likely.'

Sandland lowers her gaze.

'However, there are a couple of things that militate against my theory,' Bjarne continues.

'Such as?' Nøkleby asks.

'While the murder of Johanne Klingenberg appears to have been premeditated, I'm not sure that the murder of Erna Pedersen was. It's seriously risky to kill someone in a care home where any number of people might see you. But he did it when the whole floor, with one or two exceptions, was busy with this visit from the Volunteer Service – a visit Erna Pedersen would normally have enjoyed and taken part in, but which she wasn't well enough to attend last Sunday. That means he took advantage of the situation that arose there and then. And I'm not sure that his plan was to kill her. The murder seems rushed and messy, if you know what I mean. And remember: Erna Pedersen had one foot in the grave already. She would have died soon anyway.'

'So why did he kill her?' Gjerstad says.

Bjarne expels the air from his lungs hard.

'I don't know. But the killer appears to have been angry with her. Killing her wasn't enough. He also had to whack knitting needles into her eyes. But Erna Pedersen had dementia and dementia sufferers have poor short-term memory. Things from the past, however, are crystal clear.'

Bjarne looks across to Sandland who nods.

'Is it possible that the killer tried to make her remember something from the past? The missing school photo could suggest that. And since he ended up killing her, it's tempting to think that she hurt him a long time ago.'

'So we're talking about an ex-pupil of hers?' Fredrik Stang says. 'Since the missing picture was a school photo, I mean?'

'It could be anyone, really. A pupil, a colleague, an angry family member or an enraged neighbour who cared about the person or persons Pedersen had harmed.

Bjarne's mouth is dry from talking so he sips some water. He studies the faces in the room for signs that his arguments have swayed anyone. He has no sense of whether he has been successful.

'But there are aspects of the killer's MO that match in both cases,' he continues. 'And if we treat the murder of Erna Pedersen as a clumsy first attempt, then the killing of Johanne Klingenberg suggests that this time the killer had much more control over his actions. It might mean that murdering Erna Pedersen was what got him started.'

'So you're saying we could be dealing with a serial killer?' Nøkleby asks. She sounds sceptical.

Bjarne looks at her for a few seconds before he replies. His voice sounds a little more feeble than he intended: 'Possibly.'

He scans the room for support and receives a nod from Gjerstad. Nøkleby follows shortly.

Bjarne is pleased with his reasoning, but two questions immediately present themselves. Why did the killer damage the picture of Erna Pedersen's son and the little boy whose picture Johanne Klingenberg had on her wall? And if they really are dealing with a serial killer who has now finished warming up – might their friends and relatives be his next victims?

Chapter 53

Once he killed a bird with his bare hands. The feeling of life ebbing away between his fingers made his heart beat faster, but it never came close to a thrill. Neither did suffocating the neighbour's cat, which had strayed into their house and refused to leave.

He was home alone that day, sick under the duvet and watching videos on the sofa; there was no way he would tolerate the presence of a cat, which would stink up the whole house with its pee. So he tossed the duvet over it and trapped it. And even though he had a temperature, he experienced the intoxicating sensation of being master of life and death.

But in neither of those instances had he seen the actual death, observed the precise moment when the spark is extinguished and time stops. He thought he might see it with the fish he caught down on Vippetangen where all the East Europeans go to fish, when he held the slippery creatures, alive and wriggling, before slowly twisting their necks. He saw the blood and felt their frantic death throes between his fingers, but there was never any change in the eyes of the fish. He never *saw* them die.

He didn't have time to see it in the eyes of that old bat, either. She was dead before the veil lifted and he could see clearly again.

But now he has seen it. And now he understands.

This is what it's all about. This is what he has been looking for.

And he can't stop thinking about the light that faded from her eyes when she looked at him, pleading. It was as if the light travelled into him and started radiating from his own eyes and illuminated the path that lay in front of him. The path he had been wandering recently suddenly felt clearer and wider. He felt a sense of purpose. Something inside him slotted into place.

For that reason he is going home.

For the last time.

When he was a boy, he liked travelling by train. He also liked watching them. Before taking their bicycles across the level crossing they always had to look right and left and then right again. Or perhaps it was the other way around. The coolest and scariest thing he knew was standing on the platform on Nordby Station, as close to the tracks as possible, waiting for the trains to whizz by. And when they did, it was so loud, so powerful and with so much air passing right in front of him that he almost lost his balance.

He looks out at the small village of his childhood, which is no longer small. Everything has changed. The houses, the people, cars; he feels at home, but at the same time not. Everything is bigger, everything is different. *He* is different.

Some passengers get off, others get on. The doors close and the train moves on. He doesn't feel like leaving the train at the next station; he would prefer to stay where he is and watch the world go by, watch autumn settle over the rooftops and colour the sky. But he can't do that, either.

The train slows down again and he gets off at Nordby

Station. Nor is this place anything like he remembers it. Gone is the old station building where they wrote rude graffiti, misspelt because they hadn't quite mastered double consonants yet. The new building is bigger and made from glass. Even the platform has been replaced. Wooden boards have turned into concrete.

He walks past Østafor Care Home where she would probably have lived now, the old crone, in her retirement, had she stayed here. She could have sat on the veranda and watched the trains go past. Perhaps they would have made her forget about fractions.

A few minutes later he stands outside the door to his childhood home. It has been a while since he last visited. Before he goes inside, he takes a look at the garden and remembers the shovel, the snow that whirled around them that day, the cave that collapsed on top of Werner and squeezed the life out of him. It happened so quickly, but even now, so many years later, it still makes the hairs on his neck stand up.

He opens the front door and enters; he sees how she jerks upright in the green leather Stressless armchair where she sits embroidering, a hobby of hers, but it doesn't take long before her confusion turns to delight. And, for a brief moment, he thinks that this is exactly how it ought to be. That's how people should react. This is what it feels like to be part of a normal family.

He wonders what kind of father he would have made; if his child would also have stood close to the tracks to watch the trains whizz by. If his son might have conquered his stutter and made something of himself. There must be qualities you pass on, surely, or traits, in the same way you pass on hair and eye colour. Perhaps Sebastian would have broken free, been his own man, his father's direct opposite, the person he tried so hard to become when he was little? First he wanted to be a pilot; no, a butcher actually, he longed to look into the stomachs of dead animals. But then he wanted to be a hunter and later a professional football player. And then he stopped wanting to be anything at all.

She comes to greet him, her arms wide open and she pulls him close. And he stands there, he doesn't put his arms around her, he just recognises the smell of her, the familiar smell of something sweet mixed with the aroma from the kitchen. Lamb and cabbage, black pepper and potatoes; the smell of stew usually makes his mouth water, but today it just makes him feel nauseous.

'How nice that you were able to come after all,' she practically shouts and holds him out away from her.

And everything is all right until his father enters the room, his father who had always favoured Werner. He says nothing; he just stops in front of the mirror where the telephone used to be in the days before they got a cordless one. The floorboards always used to squeak so badly right there.

'I thought you said he wasn't coming?' he says, addressing his wife.

'I know, but – he changed his mind. Isn't it wonderful?'

'Couldn't he have let us know?'

She tries to say something, but no words come out before he marches past them. No welcome hug. No outstretched hand.

Not this time, either.

'I hope you're hungry,' she says as she goes into the

kitchen, eager for him to follow. 'See,' she adds, pointing to the saucepan. He nods and looks at her.

Everything is as it always was and everything is different.

Soon they sit down to dinner, but he struggles to swallow the food. He thinks about how much has been said in this room and how little.

'Could you pass the salt, please?'

He looks at his father. Gives him the salt shaker, but as he does, he knocks over his own half-empty water glass. The water splashes across the table cloth and drips down on the floor. His father's knife and fork hit the plate on the other side of the table. His father sighs heavily.

'Are you just going to sit there?'

He makes no reply. His mother, who is sitting next to him, tears off several sheets of kitchen towel and presses them against the table cloth.

More sighing. More snorting.

'Are you just going to sit there like a brat? Aren't you going to apologise?'

Slowly he turns his head and looks at him. He makes no reply.

'Eh? Aren't you going to say sorry?'

No, he thinks to himself. *Not any more.*

The next moment his father pushes his chair back. The chair legs scrape against the floor as his hastily scrunched-up napkin lands on the table.

A veil settles over his eyes. And, as he feels a strong hand clamp down on his own, he stops seeing clearly. He just does.

And he does.

And he does.

Chapter 54

Emilie has been to many funerals over the years, but the pain she felt at losing someone can't compare to what she feels now. It's completely different when someone is murdered. And what torments her the most is the thought of what must have been going through Johanne's head when she realised that she was going to die.

Emilie has gone to bed and closed the door. She desperately needs to be alone. All she can think about is who could have taken the life of her best friend. A woman she could talk to about everything. She remembers all the wonderful things they used to do together. It's impossible to understand that they will never do anything together again.

There is a knock on the door and Mattis opens without her having said 'come in'.

'It's the police,' he says, holding up Emilie's mobile. 'They want to talk to you.'

Emilie feels punched in the stomach at the mere thought of having to talk to someone now. She hoists herself upright. Mattis comes in, hands her the telephone with a cautious, friendly smile. Emilie wipes the tears from her face, her cheeks feel red hot; she takes the telephone and waits until Mattis has closed the door behind him. Then she says 'hello'.

'Hello, this is Bjarne Brogeland from Oslo Police.'

'Hi,' she says in a feeble voice.

'I'm sorry for your loss,' he says. 'I understand that you were one of Johanne Klingenberg's best friends.'

'Yes,' Emilie stutters. 'I was. Thank you.'

'I'm sorry for disturbing you, but I need to speak to you.'

'I understand,' she says, and straightens up a little more. *He has a nice voice*, she thinks. *Warm and reassuring.*

'You and Johanne met at a café today, am I right?'

'Yes. At Café Blabla on St Hanshaugen.'

'How did she behave while you were together? Was she anxious about anything? Nervous?'

Emilie thinks about it.

'No, she was just as she always was. Joking and laughing as usual.'

'She didn't give you the impression that she was scared of anything or anyone?'

'No,' Emilie almost laughs and wipes her nose. 'She was in a good mood.'

She hears the policeman making notes.

'Did she mention what she was going to do after you'd had lunch together?'

'No, she was going home, I think. She might have had some shopping to do first.'

'Nothing apart from that? Did she say anything about what she was doing with the rest of her day?'

'No, we didn't talk about that,' Emilie replies.

'Did you notice if anyone was watching you at the café?'

Emilie tries to search her memory, but not a single face comes up.

'What time was it when you left?'

'About one o'clock, I think.'

Emilie can hear that her voice is still weak so she clears her throat in an attempt to make it firmer.

'How much do you know about your friend's life?'

'What do you mean?' Emilie asks.

'Would Johanne tell you everything?'

'Yes, or at least I think so.'

'Do you think she would have told you if she was in any kind of trouble?'

A stinging feeling starts in her stomach and spreads to the rest of her body. Even the thought that Johanne might have kept secrets from her, problems Emilie could have helped her solve, makes the tears well up again. She squeezes her eyes shut and feels the teardrops run in parallel down her flushed cheeks before dripping from her chin.

'Yes, I'm sure of it,' she stammers.

'What about men, then? Boyfriends.'

Emilie coughs again.

'Yes, we did used to talk about men.'

The policeman stirs and the chair he is sitting on squeaks.

'Was she seeing anyone at the moment?'

'No. She hasn't had a boyfriend for ages, but I know that she would go on dates from time to time. But it never got serious.'

'So she never mentioned anyone who was obsessed with her – or vice versa?'

Emilie shakes her head before she remembers that the officer can't see her.

'I can't think of anyone,' she replies.

'Okay,' the officer says, pausing again. 'How long has it been since you last visited her flat?'

Emilie tries to remember.

'It has been a while. We usually meet for lunch once a month or thereabouts, but we don't visit each other at home nearly as often as we used to. I live in Jessheim, I have a young child and I work full-time, and she's busy with her life in Oslo. Well, that's to say,' Emilie says and grief takes over her voice again. 'She's not busy with anything any more.'

Her voice breaks and she starts to sob; she loses control of her facial movements. A wave of anger and anguish overcomes her and she clutches the duvet while unintelligible noises escape from her mouth. The officer says nothing while Emilie calms herself down.

'I'm sorry,' she says eventually.

'It's all right; just let me know when you're ready to continue.'

'I'm ready, it's just so—'

Emilie doesn't know how to complete the sentence.

'I understand,' the officer says and pauses briefly before he asks the next question.

'In your friend's living room there was a picture of a small boy on the wall. Do you know which picture I'm talking about?'

Emilie thinks about it.

'That must be the picture of Sebastian,' she says.

'Sebastian?'

'Sebastian is my son,' Emilie continues. 'Johanne is – or she was – one of Sebastian's godparents. We gave her a picture of him last Christmas.'

She switches the phone to her other hand and wipes her face with the duvet.

'My next question might sound very strange, Emilie, but I have to ask it. Do you know if anyone might have a reason to be angry with your son?'

Emilie looks up.

'With Sebastian? Why do you want to know that?'

'Please just answer the question.'

'What does my son have to do with this?'

The officer doesn't explain. A sudden rage takes over her voice.

'No,' Emilie snaps. 'Sebastian is two and a half years old. He hasn't lived long enough to upset anyone yet, apart from me and his father.'

'I understand,' the police officer says.

Her head feels as if it's going to explode and she realises that she hasn't eaten for a long time. But the very thought of putting something in her mouth makes her stomach churn.

'Johanne and you are both from Jessheim, I understand. If I mention the name Erna Pedersen to you – what would you say?'

Emilie rubs her cheeks with her knuckle.

'Erna Pedersen?' she repeats, but gets no reply. 'We had a teacher called that, I remember, but it's quite a common name, isn't it?'

'Yes, you're right,' the police officer says quickly. 'But I believe you're thinking of the right Erna Pedersen. What do you remember about your old teacher?'

'Far too much,' Emilie says and laughs before she feels guilty for laughing in a situation like this. 'No, she was . . . strict, I suppose you'd say. What about her?'

But the officer gives her no answer.

'You were at school together, you and Johanne?'

'Yes.'

'When was this?'

'The whole time, we grew up together.'

'So when did Erna Pedersen teach you? Do you remember?'

Emilie thinks about it.

'Towards the end of primary school, I think it was. The last two or three years, possibly.'

'Did you have any school photos taken?'

Emilie tries to remember.

'I'm not sure. I think we might have had one taken in Year Six.'

There is a moment of silence.

'Do you still happen to have that photo, Emilie?'

She thinks about it.

'Yes, I think so. Somewhere.'

'Do you think you could find it?'

Emilie hesitates for a second.

'I can try looking for it, of course, but—'

Then she realises why the officer wants to know.

'Was it . . . was it Erna Pedersen, who was—'

Emilie clasps her hand over her mouth.

'I read something in the newspaper about an Erna Pedersen who had been—'

She is unable to complete the sentence.

'Yes, that was her,' the policeman says. 'And we wouldn't be doing our job if we didn't investigate the possibility that there might be a connection between the two deaths. That doesn't necessarily mean that there is. But can you think of anyone you went to school with who had unfinished business with Johanne *and* Erna Pedersen?'

Emilie doesn't reply at once. She is thinking, or trying to think, but too many questions are hurling themselves at her at the same time.

'Teachers are never very popular,' she says. 'But I can't imagine that—'

She stops again.

'No,' she says quietly. 'I don't know of any.'

'If you do think of any, please call. You have my number?'

Emilie checks the display on her mobile.

'Yes.'

'Good. I think that's it for now. Please try to find that school photo. It might be important.'

'I'll see what I can do.'

'Good. Thank you. And once again, I'm sorry for your loss.'

Emilie smiles a feeble smile.

'Thank you,' she replies.

Chapter 55

Henning hasn't driven far before he pulls over in a lay-by. He is thinking about the map he saw on Trine's laptop. The date in the top right-hand corner.

It did say '9 October', didn't it? The day when she, according to every newspaper in Norway, allegedly made the biggest blunder of her life. What kind of map was it? And why had she looked it up on her laptop?

Henning starts the car again and drives on. He stops at a Statoil petrol station in the centre of Stavern and helps himself to a handful of paper towels without buying anything. He finds a pen in the car's glove compartment and clicks it ready while he tries to remember what he saw.

When he was at school, his friends used to tease him about his photographic memory. To some extent they were right, even though he always corrected them and said that it wasn't about memory. He took a screen dump with his eyes and later he would note down what he had seen – a skill he has often found useful as a reporter.

Henning makes himself comfortable in the car, closes his eyes and summons up the image from the laptop, concentrating on its major features. First the parks and the lakes. Then he starts to draw. When he was little, he loved drawing city maps. It gave him a satisfying sense of order. Seeing the big picture. He sketches in any other streets that he remembers and the thick line that represented a kind of running profile – it looked like a malign virus under a microscope. When the sketch is done, he starts the car and drives on, pleased with the likeness he has managed to re-create.

When he gets home, he takes a long shower. While soap and shampoo settle in a foaming circle around the drain, he ponders his unfortunate tendency to irritate every woman he meets. In the past he could usually charm his way out of awkward situations, but there is very little left of that side of him. These days he is surrounded by women with problems, women who create problems, women who are the problem. Nora, Trine, Pia, Heidi.

Is that all his fault?

Now that he thinks about it, it's not only the women. He has managed to fall out with everyone he knows; he couldn't honestly say that he has a single friend left. Not a real one. No one came to visit him while he was in Sunnaas Rehabilitation Centre, though there might be a perfectly good reason for that. Before Jonas died, he might have gone for a drink or two with colleagues, but he never let anyone get close. He never felt the need to tell anyone about himself. Sometimes they would ask how things were with him and Nora, and every time he would say that they were fine, even though they weren't.

Friendships and acquaintances are fleeting. You get close to people you see every day, and when your studies are over, when you move or get a new job, you say goodbye with every intention of keeping in touch. But new people take their place, time passes and it becomes harder to remain a central part of each other's lives. It's not because you don't care any more. It's just the way it goes.

The closest Henning has to a friend right now – and he is struggling to name even one – is Iver Gundersen. Even though Henning is loath to admit it.

Half naked, he walks into the living room. He stands there staring at all the photographs that are spread out on the floor. The thought of tidying up fills him with dismay and as he intends to work on the map he sketched in the car, he decides that clearing up will just have to wait. But then he spots a picture of Jonas, a big picture where his son is smiling. Henning bends down and picks it up.

It's a lovely picture.

And though he tries as hard as he can, he can't stop the pain from welling up inside him. Usually he can suppress it by trying to think of something else, looking at something else or forcing another image to appear in its place. But it's not working now. Jonas is inside him, inside all of him, his eyes bore into him like a laser sight. His knees start to wobble.

I should have tried harder to cover myself up, he thinks. I should have thought about it for one more second, just one, then perhaps the flames would have burned me in a different place. It might have made all the difference. My eyes wouldn't have glued themselves together and I would have been able to see properly before I got ready to jump off the railing and not slip just as I was about to escape. Everything could have been different. And Jonas would still have been alive.

Henning strangles a sob while he looks at the picture. *You should be on the wall,* he says to his son. *You should have been on my wall all this time. But I can't bear to have you there. I'm so sorry, my darling boy, but I just can't bear it.*

A rumble outside his window makes him take a step to

one side. He looks for something familiar, something to fix his eyes on as the storm draws near. The sweat trickles down between his shoulder blades and he imagines tasting salt-water as he breaks through the surface of a shimmering, dark pink sea. Sinking like a sounding lead. He turns into a shadow and a dry noise is forced out of him. But the only part of him that gets wet is his eyes.

Chapter 56

His legs feel strangely jelly-like as he walks down the road, which he can barely see in the darkness. The headlights of an oncoming car sweep towards him and he steps on to the verge and bows his head as the car passes him. He doesn't want anyone to know that he has been back home.

Home.

Where is his real home now? He is about to be evicted from his flat. And given what he has just done to his father, he can never go home to his mother again.

How strange, he thinks, *that you can do something and not see it.* It wasn't until the display cabinet got knocked over that his sight returned and he realised what he had done.

Smoke is coming from a chimney on one of the houses he passes. The smell drifts down towards him, even though the smoke itself is rising. He is reminded of something he learned at school. After a forest fire everything regenerates. New plants and flowers will grow from under the ash as if the flames have pressed a reset button that makes everything default to the start position.

And, as he stands on the platform at Nordby Station, he wonders if anything will rise from his ashes when the time comes. If he has a reset button.

Fortunately there is no one around so he takes a step closer to the edge of the platform and looks at the thick, rough-hewn stones between the railway sleepers and the tracks. It is very quiet. He closes his eyes and recognises the buzz he used to get as a child though no trains are approaching. And he doesn't know how long he has been standing there, how long it takes before the rail tracks start humming, charging him up and preparing him for what comes next. The alarm bells start to ring, the lights on the plate change from white to red, and the barriers hesitate for a second before they begin to lower. The ringing that was steady to begin with ends up out of time, just like when he was little and it takes maybe thirty seconds before the barriers at the level crossing have come down and the ringing stops.

But it doesn't stop inside him; he can feel it in his head. And then a light appears; a glow deep inside the forest as if the trees are the walls of a tunnel that gradually comes alive. And standing here now, so many years later, it feels even better; he can see the rail tracks glisten in the darkness. They look like shiny, white ski tracks.

Then the eyes appear, fierce and beckoning, huge like the eyes of a troll. And the train doesn't slow down, the tracks become even more alive, they hiss, they snarl, they make themselves look sinister and dangerous, and he takes another step forward, feels his foot touch the edge of the concrete. The train is coming and the driver sounds his horn, perhaps he has seen him. But it doesn't stop him from sticking out his foot. He lets it dangle over the edge; the gleaming rail tracks are just one metre below him as is the light in the lovely, big eyes that will devour him.

*

Henning shakes off his distressing thoughts and finds the paper towel with the sketch he drew in the car. He copies out the map on an A4 sheet, paying more attention to the details this time and before long a clearer image emerges in front of him.

He has seen this map before.

He goes to the kitchen, opens his laptop and starts a search engine. Types in the name of the city and clicks on the first map that comes up. And as he sees the characteristic canals, bridges and parks, he realises that his memory was correct.

It's a map of Copenhagen.

Henning thinks about Trine's watch that told her how far she had walked along the coastal path. He has heard of fitness fanatics who log their exercise efforts, who wear pulse and distance counters and God knows what. The fat line that looked like a worm on her laptop was the route she had run and walked. In Copenhagen. At 20.17. The same evening she was supposed to be at a party conference in Kristiansand sexually assaulting a young man. The same evening no one remembers seeing her during dinner.

Bloody hell.

The young politician's statement is false. And Henning starts to get an inkling of what is going on. The reason why the politician doesn't want to be named, but chose to write an unconvincing account of a 'sexual assault' and sent it anonymously by fax.

It's because it never happened.

It's because that person doesn't exist.

And since the media appear to have accepted that they will never be able to interview him, they have turned their attention to all the other stories being written about Trine instead. The sex scandal was the perfect detonator. The character assassination destroying her reputation was only the beginning.

This is the work of someone who is an expert in media manipulation, who knows which buttons to press to trigger an avalanche of negative publicity about a Minister who has made too many enemies along the way.

But there is one thing Henning can't understand. Why doesn't Trine speak up? And since she was studying her running profile on her laptop, she would appear to be aware of the evidence that would clear her name. So why doesn't she defend herself? Why doesn't she fight?

There must be more to this than meets the eye, Henning thinks. And the only thing that makes any sense to him is that Trine is protecting someone or something. Herself, possibly, from anything else that the media might uncover. That could also explain the nature of the attack. Her enemy knows that she knows. He knows her secret, knows that she can't defend herself because then the truth of what she was really doing that day will come to light.

So the question is: who else knows? And what on earth was Trine doing in Denmark?

Wednesday

Chapter 57

Henning falls asleep around three o'clock in the morning, slumped over the kitchen table, but he wakes again three and a half hours later. The first thing he does is make himself a cup of coffee. Then he sits down with the printout of the map of Copenhagen.

If the fat lines he saw on Trine's laptop match the lines he has just drawn on the printout, it would mean that Trine's run on the evening of 9 October started in Nørre Søgade, a long, wide street that runs parallel with Peblinge Lake.

Henning opens his own laptop, retrieves the map and zooms in on the area. More details appear. Bridges, parks, buildings. *What was Trine doing there?* he wonders again. *Apart from going for an evening run?*

Kristiansand isn't that far from Copenhagen. Flying from Kjevik Airport would probably take forty-five minutes, possibly less. She could have been at the party conference until the afternoon and then left.

But surely someone would have seen her?

Of course they would. Unless she took steps to avoid being seen. But why would she do that? Because no one must know. It's the only explanation Henning can come up with.

Right. What is so important about Nørre Søgade or its surroundings?

Henning does a quick Internet search and finds only one

hotel in the same street. Kong Arthur, four stars. She probably stayed there. He finds a nearby spa. Hardly the reason she would leave Norway. The Catholic Apostolic church. No. Belldent Dental Lab? Unlikely.

Then he sees it.

StorkKlinik.

The fertility clinic. The place you go if you have tried and failed to get pregnant. Henning knows that Trine wanted children. He remembers seeing a feature about her in *Se og Hør* magazine in his mother's flat once where Trine gave childlessness a face. He knows that more and more Norwegian women travel to Denmark for fertility treatment. It's usually not something people broadcast to the world. Trine could have gone to Denmark in secret to remain anonymous. And the procedure could have taken place the day after the conference. Perhaps she went for a run when she arrived the night before to release some of her tension.

Even so, something doesn't ring true. How likely is it that someone had found out what Trine was doing in Denmark and then – almost a year later – thrown her to the wolves? Why the delay? Didn't they know until now? And what's so terrible about travelling to Denmark to try to get pregnant?

Henning doesn't think it adds up. Nor can her trip to Denmark have been particularly successful because Trine is still childless. Though that in itself is not unusual. Fertility clinics don't offer guaranteed success.

Henning tries to work out who would stand to gain the most if Trine were to leave politics. It's a long list. It could be a rival in the Labour Party, someone in her department or someone who quite simply doesn't like her. *But someone is pulling the strings here*, Henning thinks. Someone who has it in for his sister.

But who?

Chapter 58

Once Bjarne had repeated his conversation with Emilie Blomvik to the team, his theory of just one killer was elevated from 'possible' to 'highly likely'. Even Pia Nøkleby had to admit that the similarities could no longer be ignored and the investigation was reorganised on that basis. The job of identifying Erna Pedersen's former pupils was prioritised and their names cross-referenced with anyone the police had been in contact with in the investigations of both murders. In addition, covert protection was arranged for Pedersen's son and family, and the family of Emilie Blomvik – especially for two-and-a-half-year-old Sebastian.

Bjarne Brogeland, however, has no intention of sharing this information with Emilie Blomvik when he goes down to meet her. It's already ten o'clock in the morning and he gets her a visitor's sticker, which she puts on her dark blue jacket before he escorts her through security and up to his office on the fifth floor.

'How are you?' he asks when they have sat down.

It takes a while before Blomvik answers.

'I didn't sleep much last night, to be honest.'

She smiles feebly. Her cheeks are drained of colour.

'So perhaps you did some thinking instead?' Bjarne asks to encourage her.

'I did little else,' she says and brushes aside a strand of hair that has fallen down in front of her eyes. 'But my mind is completely blank. I haven't got a clue who could have done this.'

'There's no ex-boyfriend who might have cause to be mad at Johanne because of something she said or did a long time ago?'

Blomvik turns down the corners of her mouth.

'Well, Johanne has had hundreds of boyfriends. I mean, not literally, but it's possible that some of them were more interested in her than she was in them. But I find it hard to believe someone might be upset with her now. As I told you yesterday, it's been a long time since Johanne saw anyone.'

Bjarne nods and moves a little closer to the table. The ensuing silence prompts Blomvik to put her hand into her shoulder bag.

'This is all I could find,' she says, placing a photograph in front of Bjarne. 'It's from Year Six at Jessheim School.'

Bjarne takes the photograph and studies it. A much younger version of Erna Pedersen is standing at the back to the left, several heads taller than any of her pupils.

'Johanne is sitting there,' Blomvik says, pointing to a small girl with big dimples and long plaits on a chair at the front. 'And I'm next to her.'

Bjarne looks up and senses her embarrassment.

'It was a very long time ago,' she says by way of explanation.

Bjarne continues to study the faces. He sees no similarities to anyone he has met in the last few days.

'If you're anything like me, you'll be able to remember the names of most of the people in this picture,' he says, sliding it back to her. 'Please would you write down as many names as you recall?'

Bjarne finds a sheet of paper and a pen for her.

'I'll try,' Blomvik says.

'Please start at the front row from the left.'

She nods and starts writing. She can only remember the first names of some pupils, but most of those sitting in the front get their full name, including their middle name.

Then she looks up.

'Yesterday you asked me if someone might have reason to be angry with my son,' she says. 'With Sebastian.'

Bjarne nods.

'Why did you want to know that?'

Bjarne hesitates for a second before he takes out a crime scene photograph from a file and shows it to her.

'This photo was taken in Johanne's living room yesterday afternoon,' he says. 'As you can see, the picture of your son has been destroyed. Or at least the glass has been smashed.'

Blomvik studies the photograph.

'And you're quite sure that it didn't just happen in . . . in the heat of the moment?'

'Absolutely,' Bjarne replies.

Blomvik scratches her head with the pen.

'It all seems very strange,' she says. 'I fail to see why someone would get so angry with a little boy. And how Johanne could have anything to do with it, it – it—'

Blomvik shakes her head.

Bjarne says nothing; he gives her time to think things through. But she doesn't come up with anything. Soon her attention returns to the school photo and a few minutes later she puts down the pen.

'Right,' she says. 'I think those are all the names I can remember.'

'That's great.'

Bjarne takes the sheet back. Studies the names and the faces. Row one – no names he recognises. Middle row – no hits there, either. In the back row—

No.

He swears under his breath. Surely he is due a break now. Then he thinks back to his own childhood and the girls he had crushes on when he was growing up. To begin with the girls were his age, but eventually they started to be younger. One year, two years. In sixth form he was head over heels in love with Henning Juul's sister. And as for the girls, they wouldn't even consider going out with you unless you were a little older than they were. Or at least many wouldn't. And Erna Pedersen taught a lot of pupils.

We need to go through the years she taught when the pupils were one, two and three years older than Emilie Blomvik and Johanne Klingenberg, Bjarne realises. *If nothing else, it might limit our search.*

'Okay,' he says, gets up and extends his hand to Emilie Blomvik. 'Thank you so much. You've been a great help.'

Chapter 59

Trine's legs are killing her after yesterday's coastal walk. Her head feels leaden too. She hasn't managed to eat very much in the last few days. Nor has she had enough to drink. Not water, anyway.

Though she still doesn't know what to do, she feels better for having spent time out here. It has been good to have only the sea, the wind and the rocks for company. Feeling small again. She realises she would like to return to the cabin as soon as possible, but knows she will have a hard time persuading Pål Fredrik to join her. She will have to bribe him with at least fifty kilometres of main road cycling every day; though whether she will still have him after recent events remains to be seen. Perhaps that is why she feels so drained of energy. So terrified.

Trine locks the cabin, returns the key to the nail under the bench and says a quiet 'goodbye for now' in her head. Then she walks up the mound and rings Katarina Hatlem, who answers after just a few rings.

'Hi, it's me,' Trine says. 'I'm coming home.'

The voice of her Director of Communications sounds instantly relieved, but Trine adds that she won't be returning to her office today. She probably won't come in until tomorrow.

'Okay.'

'But you can tell anyone who might be wondering that I

288

intend to make a statement soon. I have to. I just don't know when.'

'That's great, Trine. But what are you going to say?'

Trine stops, turns to look at the sea, at Tvistein Lighthouse and the endless blue.

'Well, that's the thing. Whatever will do the least damage.'

*

At the morning meeting, Heidi Kjus is in a foul mood because Henning isn't up to speed on the Bislett murder and even more annoyed because *123news* are still having to quote NTB. Henning has been told to cover the Bislett murder as well, but he has little interest in it as he finally appears to be making headway in the mystery surrounding Trine.

He thinks about the fax that was sent to every newspaper in the country a couple of days ago. The death blow to his sister's career. Surely it must be possible to trace where that fax was sent from?

Trine's enemy probably wouldn't be stupid enough to send it from their own office. They might have got someone else to do it, of course, but that would be risky. If you want to keep a secret, tell no one.

Henning's gaze is drawn towards the desk where Kåre Hjeltland is clapping his hands for joy.

'Sign of life from Juul-Osmundsen!' he shouts.

Hjeltland turns to one of his staff.

'Great,' he continues. 'Issue a short version. Two lines maximum and put it on the front page.'

The news desk assistant nods.

'Tuva, what other cases are we waiting to publish?'

Henning cranes his neck; he can just see the head of the girl who looks down at the screen in front of her. Henning blocks out her voice while he shakes his head. *Business as usual*, he thinks. *Nothing ever changes.*

And if it hadn't been the equivalent of banging his head against a brick wall, Henning would have contacted the *VG* journalists himself and asked them straight out who had sold them this pathetic pile of tosh that they have been happy to splash across several front pages without a second thought. But no journalist ever reveals their sources and certainly not to another journalist. And no newspaper would ever admit that they had allowed themselves to be used to bring down a government Minister.

Instead Henning retrieves the notorious fax from the huge pile of documents and newspapers on his desk. At the top of the printout he sees a fax number. It takes only minutes to discover that it belongs to an Internet café in Eiksmarka Shopping Centre. He decides to give them a call.

'Hello,' he says and introduces himself. 'I'm wondering about something: do people have to show ID when they want to use one of your machines?'

'People have to give their name and mobile number, which we register in our database, yes. If the FBI, for example, were to discover that someone had sent a threatening email to the US President from one of my machines, then I'm obliged to tell them the name of the person who used it.'

'So if I were from the FBI, you'd be able to tell me who came to your café Monday evening sometime after ten o'clock to send a fax?'

'Not exactly; the fax machine is available to anyone who comes here. But it's probably going to be a short list. There weren't that many people here that night.'

'Great,' Henning says. 'Thank you so much.'

Chapter 60

Fredrik Stang races into Bjarne's office without knocking.

'We've got a hit!' he exclaims. 'We've gone through some of Erna Pedersen's registers from Jessheim School. We've got a hit!' he says again.

'Who is it?'

'Markus Gjerløw,' Stang says with jubilation written all over his face.

Markus Gjerløw, Bjarne mutters to himself. The man he spoke to only yesterday. He was one of the volunteers who visited Grünerhjemmet.

'He was two years above Emilie Blomvik and Johanne Klingenberg,' Stang continues.

It has to be him.

'Okay. Fantastic, Fredrik. Good job.'

Bjarne rings Emilie Blomvik immediately.

'Markus Gjerløw,' he says, pronouncing the name with exaggerated clarity when she answers. 'Do you know who he is?'

Blomvik doesn't reply immediately. Background noise from Oslo intrudes on the line.

'Markus? Yes, of course I know him.'

'Were Markus and Johanne ever friends?'

Bjarne sticks a finger in his ear in order to hear better.

'They were an item at school, I think. I went out with

Markus as well, but only for a short time in sixth form.'

Bjarne can barely sit still.

'Emilie, this is very important. Can you remember why Markus and Johanne broke up?'

'Yes,' she says and laughs. 'They were thirteen or fourteen years old. At that age it's a miracle if anyone stays together for more than three weeks.'

'So it wasn't very serious, is that what you're saying?'

'That's exactly what I'm saying, yes.'

'And what about your relationship with him?'

Another short pause.

'I don't suppose I could have been more than seventeen or eighteen years old. Far too young for a serious relationship. And anyway, he was off to do national service, and so—'

Bjarne nods slowly while he digests the information.

'Do you know what his relationship with Erna Pedersen was like?'

'No, he was a few years older than me. But why do you want to know about that? Is he the man you're—'

'We don't know yet,' Bjarne interrupts her.

But his gut feeling tells him that Markus Gjerløw is his man.

*

A child, Henning ponders. How strange that such a blessing can cause so much destruction. His life is ruined by the death of a child. Trine's life might be falling apart because of a child she never had. And he thinks about how his family slipped through his fingers without him doing anything about it. But could he really have prevented it? Was he even interested in stopping it happening?

He doesn't think so. Not after he met Nora, not after Jonas. When he had his own family and became preoccupied with them. He didn't think much about Trine or their shared past, he just accepted that it was a closed book for them both. He never made any attempt to patch up his family. Yes, he makes sure that their mother has cigarettes and alcohol, and that her flat is reasonably clean, but that's the limit of his involvement. And now, as he sits here alone, knowing full well that Trine lives her life independently of him, independently of him and their mother, it's tempting to think that the breakdown of the Juul family is his fault. He was the man of the house after his father died, he should have done something. Taken steps to uncover the problems and then fix them. Instead, he just let it fall apart.

And perhaps it's too late now. Trine made it perfectly clear that she didn't want his help. There was so much remoteness in her eyes in the cabin, so much hostility. It was hard to admit it, but it felt good to see her again even though she threw him out. Away from the newspaper interviews and the TV debates where she always comes across as so confident and self-assured. She had been her old self. Just as temperamental and just as bossy as when she was little.

*

Henning hasn't yet returned the rental car, something he is pleased about as he parks outside Eiksmarka Shopping Centre with the front of the car practically inside a florist called Blåklokken. The centre is deserted this early in the day, as is the Internet café. There is not a single customer around when Henning enters and introduces himself to a balding, dark-skinned man with a moustache who is chewing vigorously on something.

'I'd like to speak to anyone who worked here Monday evening,' Henning says.

The man carries on chewing.

'Do you know who was working here that night?'

'Possibly. Why do you want to talk to them?'

'Because I'm trying to find out who sent a fax from that machine,' Henning says, pointing left where the room's only fax machine is located. 'It's important to a person who . . . who's important to me. I'd be really grateful if you could help me.'

The man carries on chewing while he gives Henning a sideways glance. Then he looks across the room. There is no one at the computers. Outside the entrance a man with a walking stick shuffles past.

'How much?'

Henning hesitates for a second before he takes out a 500 kroner note from his back pocket. The man takes the money. Studies it. Then he wanders off to the back room and stays there for a long time. Henning is starting to feel awkward when another man comes out. Same skin colour. Same short hair and a moustache.

He nods quickly to Henning, something Henning interprets as a green light so he asks if the man whose badge states his name is 'Sheraz' could check on his computer to find out who visited the café Monday evening. Sheraz looks languidly at him and shakes his head.

'It's against the law,' he says.

'Is that right?'

Henning never really thought that it would be that easy. Over to Plan B.

Henning opens his shoulder bag and takes out a pile of paper he printed out before he left the office. He has lost count of how many pictures he printed out from the home pages of the Justice Department and various political parties, but it was a lot.

'I'm going to show you some pictures,' he says, 'and I want you to say stop if you recognise the person who came here Monday night. Is that all right?'

Sheraz waits a little, then he nods without enthusiasm.

'Okay, let's begin.'

Henning puts down the shoulder bag. He pushes the first printout across the counter. They go through a number of politicians – government as well as opposition – political advisers and past and present members of the Justice Department. All he gets by way of response from Sheraz is a shake of the head. Henning flicks through the printouts while Sheraz keeps on shaking his head, more and more reluctant and increasingly hostile in his demeanour.

Suddenly he says: 'Stop.'

Henning stops.

'Go back.'

Henning removes the top sheet. Sheraz plants his index finger right in the middle of the sheet, but says nothing.

'And you're sure?' Henning asks.

Sheraz nods.

'Okay,' Henning says, taking back the pile of paper and stuffing it into his shoulder bag. *Well worth 500 kroner*, he thinks to himself, and quickly leaves the café.

Chapter 61

The atmosphere in the incident room is like the area behind the starting gate right before a skiing race. Everyone is eager to push off as quickly as possible. But it's essential to do things in the right order.

'Okay,' Arild Gjerstad says, 'this is what we know about Markus Gjerløw so far: he's thirty-seven years old, he lives in Grorud and he's unemployed. No wife or girlfriend, nor does he have any children. His parents live in Jessheim. Gjerløw's mobile is switched on right now and we know that it's in the vicinity of a mast close to his home address. So it's likely that he's at home. The armed response unit has been alerted and the whole building must be hermetically sealed before we go in.'

Several people nod.

'Okay,' Gjerstad says. 'We're going in. We've been given permission to enter by force.'

*

The patrol cars drive without flashing lights so as not to alert Gjerløw that they are on their way. Bjarne peeks furtively at Sandland and sees that she, too, lives for moments like these. For the action. Taking that six-month vacancy with Vestfold Police would feel like a step backwards, at least to begin with. More paperwork. More time spent at his desk.

Is that really what he wants?

The drive to Grorud takes them less than fifteen minutes. At this speed the raindrops smack against the windscreen. They park on the pavement only one street away from the large tower block where Gjerløw lives and jog to the entrance. Some officers shelter from the rain under the covered area outside.

A uniformed officer from the armed response unit opens the front door and enters followed by several officers. Two men position themselves outside the lift, while another four take the stairs. Bjarne and Sandland follow. Soon they have reached the seventh floor. Behind him Sandland is panting heavily.

One of the uniformed officers knocks on Gjerløw's door. The sound fills the stairwell with short, sharp bangs. There is no reply. He knocks again, harder this time. Calls out Gjerløw's name. Still no response.

Several officers from the armed response unit have now joined them. One of them has brought a battering ram. The others stand aside. He hits the door with full force and the door gives way at his second attempt. The officers burst into the flat, holding up their weapons and shouting words no one is meant to understand, but are intended to shock.

The reports come in quickly.

'Clear!'

'Clear!'

Then there is silence.

It takes a few minutes before an officer comes out and takes off his helmet. He looks gravely at Brogeland and Sandland.

'I'm fairly certain that the man inside is Markus Gjerløw,' the officer says, jerking a thumb over his left shoulder. 'And I'm absolutely certain that he's dead as a doornail.'

*

Markus Gjerløw is leaning back in the Stressless armchair with his arms flopping to each side; his glazed eyes stare vacantly into space. An almost empty bottle containing a clear liquid is standing on the table beside him. And on the floor under the same table they see it – a small, transparent bag with capsules.

Bjarne knows morphine capsules when he sees them.

What he first took to be a living room turns out also to be the bedroom. The duvet lies bunched up on the bed. Clothes have been flung over a chair and piled up on the floor. Bjarne's gaze glides across the empty walls, a desk with newspapers, books, papers and randomly scattered food packaging. On the floor, mostly along the skirting board, various cables have been trailed, white as well as black, leading to a home cinema unit in the corner. A vast TV screen is mounted on the wall with satellite speakers on either side. Two laptops are turned on. Facebook on one, a shooter game on the other.

'He can't have been dead long,' Sandland says as she scrolls down his Facebook profile. 'He updated his status—'

She checks her watch.

'Two hours and fifteen minutes ago.'

Bjarne takes a step closer to her.

'What did he write?'

'"Sorry".'

Bjarne stops.

'He has had comments from some of his friends asking what he means, wondering what has happened, but he hasn't replied.'

'So he felt remorse,' Bjarne concludes.

'Yes. We've got the guy,' Sandland says, looking relieved. 'It's over.'

*

The crime scene officers soon take charge of the room, but Bjarne doesn't want to leave before he has had some more answers. It takes a long time before Ann-Mari Sara comes out to him. She is carrying an evidence bag, which she hands to him.

'This was lying at the top in one of his drawers,' Sara says.

Bjarne takes the bag. There is an envelope inside it.

'Check the logo,' Sara says.

Bjarne turns over the bag, recognises the logo, a green 'G' surrounded by flowers in the top left-hand corner.

'Grünerhjemmet,' he says.

'As you can see the letter is addressed to Tom Sverre Pedersen in Vindern. Erna Pedersen's son.'

'So Gjerløw stole his mail,' Bjarne declares. 'That was how he found out where Erna Pedersen went to live after she left Jessheim.'

Sara nods.

But why smash the picture of the family? What sparked his rage? Bjarne wonders.

'Did you find anything else in there?'

'Pictures,' Sara says. 'Numerous pictures on his laptop of Johanne Klingenberg and of Erna Pedersen's room at the care home. But while the pictures of Klingenberg were sharp and almost professional, the photographs at the care home were taken with a mobile phone.'

Bjarne heaves a sigh and tries to get the pieces to fit together. Markus Gjerløw had unfinished business of some kind with Erna Pedersen and Johanne Klingenberg. He finds them, kills them – and then commits suicide? So killing them didn't help? Did he not recover the balance in his life once he had got his revenge? And what part did Emilie Blomvik's little son play in all this?

The only thing that appears clear is that Markus Gjerløw will take no more lives. Exactly what turned him into a killer will have to be discovered in due course.

Chapter 62

Heidi Kjus marches towards Henning as he is about to help himself to a cup of freshly brewed coffee to take back to his desk. Her speed does not bode well.

'Where have you been?' she barks and stops right in front of him.

'I had to return the hire car,' he says.

'I thought you were working on the Bislett murder?'

'I am.'

'They've got him,' she announces.

'Got who?'

'The man who killed Johanne Klingenberg. He has been found dead. Suicide, I believe.'

Henning blows carefully into the cup and walks past her on his way back to his desk.

'Great, so the case has been solved then.'

Heidi doesn't say anything immediately, but she follows him.

'I had hoped that we could write our own story,' she says. 'All we have so far are five lines from NTB. You know I hate using agency material.'

'Mm,' Henning says. 'I'll see what I can do.'

'Okay, fine. And it wouldn't hurt if you went out and took some pictures, either.'

Henning sits down, runs his hands over his face and is

struck by a sudden realisation. He is actually missing Iver Gundersen. Iver could have shared the workload with him or at least he would have had a sparring partner. Too much is happening at once.

But he has to prioritise and right now helping Trine is more important, even though he hasn't decided what to do with his discovery. It's not proof as such, but it should give Trine the ammunition she needs to fight back. The question now is how to communicate it to her and if she will even listen to him.

Even so, Henning makes a quick call to the duty crime editor and gets a summary of what happened at Grorud. He pads out the NTB story and inserts his own byline even though it goes against the grain when he is so far behind the other reporters. He also rings Bjarne Brogeland, but his call goes straight through to voicemail.

Right, I've done everything I can on that story, he says to himself. *At least for now.*

Now what do I do about Trine?

Perhaps I could give the information to a colleague, he thinks. *Is there anyone here who could make use of the damning evidence I've found?*

He shakes his head. The story is too important for him to delegate it. And if it's to have any impact at all he needs irrefutable, physical proof, legally acquired. Trine is Justice Secretary, after all. Secondly, he must make sure that she is informed, preferably without revealing his own involvement. Trine made it clear that she didn't want his help, a point she emphasised with a hard stare.

How does he do that?

He can't go to the police, either. They need reasonable grounds to subpoena the records from Eiksmarka Internet café.

And one big obstacle remains, the biggest of them all: Trine must be willing to face her accusers. There has been no sign of it so far and Henning has no idea why. And as long as he doesn't understand that, it's impossible to know if what he has found out will help her.

You'll just have to risk it, he says to himself. *Trine deserves to know who is trying to ruin her career. Then it's up to her what she does with the information.*

Chapter 63

Trine takes a deep breath and keeps her eyes firmly on her front door. She knows that the moment she leaves the car, it will be impossible to hear anything other than a cacophony of noise. Questions will be fired at her, it will be claustrophobic. But she will just have to get through it.

She braces herself and shuts everything out. While a blitz of flashlights turns the front door blinding white, she keeps telling herself that she will be inside her own home in a moment.

Pål Fredrik is waiting for her in the doorway. He ushers her in and closes the door behind them. But the sound of the media scrum continues to penetrate both the keyhole and the air-conditioning ducts.

She looks at him. He looks back at her.

'Hello,' she says at last, quietly.

But Pål Fredrik says nothing. He just comes closer and stands right in front of her. Then he pulls her towards him. And Trine disappears into his arms. Rests her head against his chest. Hears his heartbeat. Her big, strong man. She could try pushing him away, but she knows that he wouldn't budge an inch.

They stand like this for a long time without saying anything. Finally, she takes a step back from him.

'How are you?' he asks and helps her take off her jacket.

'How are you?' she counters.

He smiles feebly.

'I've been better.'

'Me too.'

They exchange quick and guarded smiles.

Trine enters the living room first; she stops when she sees the soft lighting. The dining table is set for two. A bottle of red wine is open and breathing.

'I've had a go at cooking,' he says.

Trine blows air through her nostrils and smiles tenderly.

'You know what a great cook I am,' he quips.

Trine can't help laughing.

'It'll be ready in ten minutes, I think. Or it will be if Nigella knew what she was doing when she wrote this book.'

Trine had forgotten how good it feels to laugh, how good it is to be home. How much she loves this handsome man, how much she longs to give him everything he wants, right now, because he is so kind to her. Because he doesn't press her for answers, but is willing to wait until she is ready.

They eat slowly while they talk about work. That is to say, Pål Fredrik talks and Trine listens. She takes a few bites of the marinated chicken, sips the chambré wine. But though she tries, she can't manage to eat very much. Eating doesn't feel right. Nor does drinking or talking. To think about what she has done and look him in the eye at the same time is torture.

You can't tell him, she thinks to herself. *You just can't.*

After dinner they sit down on the sofa with some more wine. Listen to music. Chet Baker. Trine has never liked jazz all that much, but the sensitive trumpet-playing goes well with the soft lighting. They don't turn on the TV. They don't ask each other anything. Their teeth turn dark blue, but when Pål Fredrik returns with another bottle of red wine, there is a harder and more determined quality to his footsteps.

'I have a plan,' he announces and sits down. 'I'm going to get you very drunk.'

He isn't smiling or laughing. The light in his eyes bores into hers.

'But it's not so that you'll blurt out the truth. I'm actually not that interested in what the papers say. I believe you when you say that you didn't do the things they're accusing you of.'

He pauses before he goes on.

'But we've been married quite a long time now, Trine. And though I might know you better than anyone, I don't think I can say that I know you all that well.'

Trine bows her head.

'We live our lives in the public eye. I signed up for it, I've enjoyed it. But not any more. Not after this. You owe me much more explanation than what's written in the papers, Trine.'

He pauses again.

'I'll only say this to you once.'

He waits until she looks up at him.

'I love you. I'll probably always love you. But if you want me to stay, then you have to give me all of you. I want all of you. It's about time that you tell me who you really are, Trine. Who Trine Juul is. Who Trine Juul was before she met me.'

He tries to penetrate her gaze, but she shuts him out.

'You can start by telling me about your family,' he says firmly. 'Tell me about your parents. Tell me about Henning.

What happened to you? Why are you no longer in touch?'

Trine lifts her head and looks at him anxiously.

'Henning?' she says. 'Have you been talking to him?'

Pål Fredrik is about to reply, but he stops. And Trine sees that she is right.

'He came to me, Trine. He also sent me a text message last night to tell me that he'd found you and that you were still alive.'

Trine stands and starts walking over to the living-room window. She turns her back to him. Pål Fredrik doesn't follow her. Trine stops at the piano.

'He was only trying to help you,' Pål Fredrik says and gets up. 'And now you're doing it again.'

He comes over to her.

'Every time I ask you about Henning and your family, you shut me out. I asked Henning why, but he says he has no idea why the two of you fell out. So what's really going on here?'

She spins around to face him.

'Is that what he said? That he doesn't know?'

'Yes.'

Again, she walks away from him, but Pål Fredrik follows her. Neither of them says anything for a long time. He positions himself in front of her, takes her by the shoulders and tries to look into her eyes. She can't manage to look back at him so she wriggles free and goes over to her wine glass and swallows a big gulp. She puts down the glass hard.

Pål Fredrik continues to follow her. He says nothing. He just looks at her.

Trine thinks about all the things she doesn't want to think about. Events she has been trying to forget. What she saw that night. The subject of some of her nightmares.

It takes a long time before she can look at him.

'I've never told anyone,' she begins. 'And you must take this with you to your grave. Will you promise me that?'

Pål Fredrik nods quickly.

Trine sighs and drinks another mouthful of wine. She massages her temples. Then she sits down. The room is silent. Chet Baker stopped playing long ago.

She lowers her gaze. She knows she won't be able to look at him while she talks. So she picks a spot on the coffee table in front of her. And she says: 'I've told you about my dad?'

Pål Fredrik nods.

'He died when I was fifteen years old.'

She can barely hear her own voice. She pauses again.

'You want to know why we don't talk to each other in my family?' she says and looks at Pål Fredrik. 'Why I can't bear to have anything to do with Henning?'

Pål Fredrik nods again.

'I need to tell you a couple of things about my dad.'

Chapter 64

Henning stays at the office until late that afternoon. He spends most of his time in the small telephone cubicle where he can talk undisturbed.

He finally realised who to call. And when he has finished, he has a good feeling about it. Things have been set in motion. He has done everything he can do. The rest is up to Trine.

There are still people left in the office, but most have gone home. Henning sits down in his chair, unlocks his mobile and sees to his immense frustration that no one has called him back yet. Neither Ole Christian Sund nor Erna Pedersen's old neighbours.

But there's nothing new about that. A journalist casts his line hoping to get a bite. Usually he ends up with nothing.

Henning is about to try Bjarne Brogeland again when a number further down his call list catches his attention. It's the number for Andreas Kjær. The man who was on duty on the night Henning's flat burned down. *There was something curt about the way he spoke to me, wasn't there?* Henning asks himself. *Kjær couldn't wait to get rid of me especially once I mentioned Tore Pulli's name.*

And again Henning thinks about priorities. What is more important – the suicide in Grorud or the fire in his own flat?

He puts down the telephone, goes online and discovers

that the Kjær family lives in Tåsen Allé. He leaves the office and finds the nearest bus stop.

*

Forty minutes later Henning is standing on the drive outside a large, red house. The roof tiles might once have been orange, now they are dark brown. The ridge tiles are sagging.

Henning walks past a trailer with a pile of shingle and up some stone steps staying close to the black painted railings, and presses the doorbell. He takes a step back, waits and checks the time on his mobile. 5.30 p.m. No one answers. He rings the bell a couple of times and waits again. He hears no footsteps coming from inside the house.

Henning swears under his breath, then he steps back down on the crunchy gravel in front of the house. He takes a brief moment to decide before he walks out on to the dewy grass, continues past the garage and around to the rear of the house. He stops next to a tall hedge. The smell of freshly mown grass reminds Henning of his childhood garden back in Kløfta, big with lots of pine cones, a peat bog and tall trees.

A boy of twelve or thirteen and wearing the obligatory earphones is raking up the freshly cut grass. Henning holds up his hand, puts on his I'm-not-a-pervert face, but isn't convinced if the boy is able to see past his scars.

'Hi,' Henning mouths.

The boy removes the earphones and grips the rake harder.

'I wanted a word with your dad. Is he in?'

The boy doesn't say anything.

'My name is Henning Juul. I'm a reporter for an Internet

newspaper.'

The boy loosens his grip slightly.

'My dad's not here,' he says in a surly voice.

'Do you know where he is?'

'At work, I guess. I don't know.'

Henning nods, irritated with himself for not calling ahead.

'So you don't know when he'll be home?'

'No.'

'No, I guess not,' Henning says while his gaze sweeps across the large garden, the small strawberry patch, the redcurrant bushes, the hedges that provide privacy from the neighbours. He is about to leave when his eyes are drawn to something white sticking out of the ground under one of the cherry trees nearby.

'Is that for your hamster?' he asks, pointing to the homemade cross. The boy follows Henning's finger.

'No,' the boy mutters before he carries on raking.

'It's our dog.'

The tiny voice makes Henning jump and he turns around abruptly. A little girl, eight years old possibly, is standing right in front of him.

'We were allowed to bury her over there,' she says, pointing towards the white cross.

'Aha?' Henning replies while he looks at the children in turn. The boy forces the rake angrily across the grass as if scratching an itch.

'One day we found her dead on the steps to the veranda,' the girl continues.

Her brother glowers at her. A humid smell rises from the grass cuttings. Henning can't stop himself so he asks: 'On the steps, you said?'

'Yes. I saw blood on her.'

'Ylva,' her brother warns her.

'But I did.'

The boy starts to rake the grass again. Henning stands still and waits.

'Here,' the girl says, pointing to her own chin. 'I know it, because I was the one who saw her first.'

'Shut up, Ylva.'

'And Dad has never let us have another dog,' she continues now almost on the verge of tears. 'I want a new dog.'

Henning tries to sift through his thoughts. He knows what he wants to ask the children, but he doesn't think he needs to.

'Okay,' he says and feels his heart beat faster. 'I'll come back another time when your dad's home.'

Neither of the children says anything. Soon the girl picks up her skipping rope and skips past him as if the conversation they have just had never happened. Henning follows her with his eyes, but his gaze is instinctively drawn to the white cross. It glows, even in the diminishing evening twilight.

Chapter 65

Bjarne stares at the sheet in front of him with keywords from interviews they have carried out in the last couple of hours. Discoveries, facts.

He just can't get it to add up.

Gjerløw's parents were in shock. Though they had only sporadic contact with their son, neither of them could understand why he would do what he had done. They believed they had given him a good, Christian upbringing. As far as they were concerned he had no traumas that involved either Erna Pedersen or Johanne Klingenberg. They remembered the names, but had to be reminded who the women were. And though few children tell their parents everything that happens at school, she would have known if there was a problem, Gjerløw's mother assured him. Markus was a popular boy, he had lots of friends, he was good at football, usually played in goal and was selected for the regional team for several years in a row. He was a happy-go-lucky person most of the time. He had lots of girlfriends as a teenager, though he had been unsuccessful in later life, on both the girlfriend and the job front.

The absence of success in adulthood, Gjerløw's parents admitted, had probably affected or upset him, but not to such an extent that he would go and kill people he knew twenty years ago. Nor had he ever shown much interest in photography.

Bjarne just can't understand what it was about Emilie Blomvik's son that had so incensed Markus Gjerløw. When Bjarne called Emilie, she told him she hadn't spoken to Markus for years. So why did Gjerløw decide to act now? Rather than when the little boy was born?

An event of some sort must have triggered this, Bjarne thinks, and leans back in his office chair. At the same time it occurs to him that they might never know what turned Markus Gjerløw into a killer. Sometimes it's just the way it is, unfortunately.

Bjarne looks at his watch. It has been a long time since he was last home in time to have dinner with Anita and Alisha. A long time since the three of them sat chatting around the dinner table.

He doesn't have time to finish his reflections before there is a knock on the door. Pia Nøkleby pops her head around.

'Hi,' she says. 'Are you busy?'

'Not more than usual,' he replies. 'Come in.'

Bjarne can't remember when she last came to his office. Nøkleby takes a seat on a chair by the wall and crosses her legs. She folds her hands in her lap.

'You know Henning Juul, don't you?'

Bjarne nods.

'I had a chat with him recently,' Nøkleby continues. 'He said something that got me thinking. He asked if anyone could access Indicia if they knew my username and password. And sadly, these days, that's not very difficult. What I don't understand is why he wanted to know.'

'Didn't you ask him?'

'Yes, but—'

Nøkleby moistens a dry upper lip and sends her eyes on a voyage of discovery around the room.

'I'm beginning to get to know Henning. He would never have asked me that question unless he had a very good reason. It roused my curiosity. I logged on to Indicia to check my account and I discovered something disturbing. I found one search that I'm absolutely one hundred per cent sure that I didn't do.'

'So someone had your login details and accessed the program remotely?'

'Yes, so it would seem. And I don't know which is worse: that it happened or that Henning knows it did. Nor do I know if it would be wise to pressure him about it. After all, he's a journalist who'll never reveal his sources or explain how he came to be in possession of such information. He would rather go to prison.'

It begins to dawn on Bjarne where she is going with this.

'So you were hoping that I might—'

Bjarne breaks off; he can tell from her reaction that he is right.

'I'm afraid it's a serious security risk, Bjarne. Obviously I changed my password immediately, but in theory someone out there could be sitting on extremely valuable intelligence. I don't know what we're going to do. We can't go public with it; there would be an outcry and years of work would go straight down the toilet. And the last thing we want is for Henning to write a story about it.'

Bjarne nods slowly.

'I don't know how much I'll be able to get out of him. Or if I can prevent him from writing anything.'

'No, but I have an idea that I'll tell you about if you promise me that you won't mention the security breach to anyone else in the investigation team.'

She suddenly lowers her voice. Bjarne pricks up his ears and moves closer to her.

'Henning is a bright guy. And I'm thinking – perhaps *we* could make use of *him*?'

Bjarne watches as Nøkleby struggles to phrase her suggestion.

'Massage his ego,' she says. 'Include him a little in what we're doing – off the record, of course – and make it clear that you're doing him a favour, not the other way round. Make him feel that we're on the same team. Though the breach is regrettable, I don't think Henning is interested in damaging the police in any way. That has certainly never been his agenda before.'

'He's going to see through me,' Bjarne objects.

'Perhaps. But I think it might be worth a try. We're fire fighting here, but I don't want to call the fire brigade. It would only aggravate the situation.'

Bjarne's shoulders tense up. A vein throbs in his temple.

'I'll see what I can do,' he says, attempting to sound confident though he isn't sure Nøkleby buys it. Nevertheless she gets up, smooths her skirt and smiles. Bjarne gets up too; Nøkleby puts her hand on his shoulder and sends him a gaze laden with expectation.

'But I can't promise you anything,' he says. 'I can't just ask Henning a question about Indicia out of the blue. I need time.'

'Of course, I understand. Use your analytical skills. I know how good you are at extracting information from people.'

Bjarne beams; he feels effervescent. Pia Nøkleby hardly ever praises anyone. And though she probably only said it to flatter him, it still worked.

She smiles once more before she leaves the room. Bjarne sits down again and exhales noisily. As if he didn't have enough on his mind already.

Chapter 66

Henning doesn't feel the soft, rocking movements of the bus as it makes its way back to the centre of Oslo. Nor is he aware of the darkness that is descending on the city. Stripes of dark blue change into purple before finally mutating into grey and black.

Did the Kjær family's dog have an accident? Or did someone kill it?

You have to be one unlucky dog to die from such a relatively minor injury. And why wasn't the rest of its body damaged?

The dog was killed, Henning concludes, *and it was left on the veranda steps in the Kjærs' garden so that everyone – especially the children – would see it. And that,* Henning thinks, *is brutal. It's twisted. And it's impossible not to interpret it as a direct threat to the family. Kjær must be in some kind of trouble. A policeman can have many enemies.*

Henning forgot to ask the children when their dog died, but he will have to do that later. He gets off the bus at Alexander Kiellands Plass, but rather than go home, he goes to Dælenenga Sports Park and gazes at the football pitch. He sits there until it's completely dark in the west. And though he can't see any clouds, it feels as if the air is pregnant with raindrops only waiting to be released.

Once he gets home, he sits down with his laptop and tries

to contact *6tiermes7*, but again he is unsuccessful. He heats a ready-meal in the microwave and eats it in silence. Sated, he paces up and down the living-room floor while he thinks. As always when he passes the piano, he thinks he ought to try playing a little, but he doesn't know how to make himself do it.

He stops in front of the IKEA bookcase, which is packed with CDs. Bands and artists lined up and organised alphabetically. Henning can remember the tunes, of course, but not how they sound here, in his new flat. He can't remember playing a single CD since he moved in just over six months ago when a flat with a balcony facing his old flat became available to rent.

He selects the soundtrack to *The Thin Red Line* and feeds the disc into a dusty CD player. He presses 'play' and sets the volume to 3; he doesn't want it to start too violently. The soundtrack begins as low, soft vibrations in the floor; the sound rises out into the room and soon a repetitive keyboard chord is keeping him company. Slowly Hans Zimmer's violins take over.

It feels so strange to stand there, in his new flat, listening to music again. It's as if the room changes and becomes alive. And he can't understand why he hasn't listened to music until now.

He sits down on the sofa, quietly taking in the first track. Then he lies down and closes his eyes, but not to sleep. Track two begins, a lovely, unhurried and lyrical piece of music. And as he hears the score again, he is convinced that *The Thin Red Line* is the best war movie he has ever seen.

Track three is his favourite. In the movie US forces race to

the top of the ridge on the small Japanese island they are trying to take control of. The scene starts low-key, almost sub-
dued, then the soundtrack grows louder. At the end – when
the soldiers are shooting and killing and running around in a
kind of blood lust – only the music remains. Not a gunshot,
a death cry or the sound of a single explosion is heard. Only
the music.

Only the magic.

The moment is ruined when the doorbell rings. Henning
turns down the volume, plods over to the intercom by the
front door and asks who it is. A familiar voice answers from
the pavement: 'Hi, it's Nora.'

Henning doesn't reply immediately, but his breathing becomes more laboured.

'Can I come up?'

Henning hesitates before he says yes, of course she can. He
can hear her footsteps against the tarmac in the archway. The
sound gives him butterflies in his stomach.

Nora rings the bell at the bottom of the stairs to his flat.
Henning lets her in. Half a minute later she reaches the
second floor. Henning waits for her in the doorway. Nora is
out of breath after the stairs and stops right in front of him.

'Hi,' she says again.

They stand there looking at each other for a few seconds
until Henning opens the door fully and invites her in. At that
very moment he is struck by the urge to tidy up until he realises that the place is actually quite neat already. His shoes are
lined up against the wall. His jackets are on pegs. He has also
cleared away his plate and glass, and washed up everything he
used for dinner.

Nora enters.

From the living room Zimmer's bewitching notes float towards them. It feels like he is visiting someone else and yet at the same time it doesn't. It feels strange. It feels very strange indeed to have Nora back in his flat again.

She kicks off her shoes and hangs up her jacket, then she follows him into the kitchen. Henning doesn't sit down; he just stands there looking at her. Clammy and tense. Warm and disturbing. There is something in Nora's eyes that Henning doesn't like. At the same time he likes it all too much.

'How are you?' he asks.

'Well,' she says, still breathless. 'All right. I think.'

The pitch of her voice rises as she speaks.

'Lots to do,' she adds. 'Especially now.'

'There's always lots to do,' Henning says.

'Yes,' she laughs.

Silence. Oppressive and awkward.

'Can I offer you something to drink?' Henning asks.

Nora's face looks pensive.

'Yes, why not?'

'What do you fancy?'

Henning goes over to the fridge, opens it and looks inside. Cans of Coke. A carton of milk that is definitely well past its sell-by date. Three bottles of Tuborg. A bottle of white wine he won in a Friday lottery he didn't even know he was taking part in.

'I'll have a glass of white wine, please, if you're having one,' she says.

Henning can't remember the last time he drank wine. But he takes out the bottle, finds a corkscrew and removes the cork, not without some difficulty.

'Is not exactly Chablis, but—'

Henning smiles apologetically, remembering Nora's favourite wine, which they would often share a bottle or two of on Friday evenings when they had eaten their tacos and Jonas was asleep.

'I'm sure it'll be fine,' she says.

Henning finds two glasses, pours and gestures towards the living room where they sit down on separate sofas. Their glasses find the table at the same time. Then everything falls quiet again. Henning looks at her, waiting for her to begin.

'So,' she says. 'How are you?'

Before Henning has time to answer, she says: 'And I don't mean what are you up to, because I think I probably know that. But how are you, Henning? Really?'

Henning is tempted to ask why she wants to know, but he can't make himself.

'Well, I guess I ... function,' he replies. 'I'm busy at the moment with Trine and with . . . with—'

'Tore Pulli?'

Henning looks up at her.

'Yes,' he replies. 'Or rather, there's not much going on with him, or at least not right now, but—'

Henning realises he is on the verge of telling her about Indicia and murdered dogs, and manages to stop himself. It's too soon.

'I understand,' is all she says and sips her wine; she smacks her lips and makes a contented, wordless sound. Henning lets his glass stay where it is, untouched. He is pleased that the music is keeping them company, but even with Zimmer's violins, there is something claustrophobic and weird about sitting so close to Nora again. She takes another sip from her wine glass, leans back in the sofa and crosses one leg over the other. Then she changes her mind and leans forward again.

'Sorry,' Henning says. 'It's a rotten sofa.'

'Oh,' Nora says and smiles awkwardly.

Once again there is silence between them. Henning watches her.

'Was there anything in particular you wanted to . . . talk to me about, Nora?'

She looks up at him suddenly as if he had caught her red-handed.

'No, I was just—'

Nora casts down her gaze again. Henning waits. She takes another mouthful of wine.

'Last week or whenever it was,' she begins. 'When you were lying in that grave, I—'

She looks up hoping the rosette in the ceiling will come to her rescue. 'I thought you were dead,' she says at last without meeting his eyes. 'I thought that – that I would have to bury you too.'

She is still not looking at him.

'And—'

Then she sighs and shakes her head.

'Why do you live here, Henning?'

Her question takes him by surprise.

'What made you choose this place?'

Nora throws up her hands, taking in the room.

'I mean, from your bedroom you have a view of – if that is your bedroom in there,' she says, pointing to a white painted door. 'You can look right out at . . .'

Nora doesn't complete the sentence.

'You even have a balcony exactly like the one we had in the old flat.'

Nora doesn't continue; she simply looks at him. It's Henning's turn to stare at the floor.

'Well, I—'

'Why do you do this terrible thing to yourself?' she asks. 'To torment yourself? Is it a form of punishment because—'

Henning holds up his hand.

'Don't say it,' he begs her. 'Please don't say his name.'

Nora's eyes start to moisten. As do his.

'Please don't say his name,' he repeats in a voice close to breaking. The moment expands, there is a pause between two tracks and for a few seconds the flat is very quiet. Henning can hear his own heavy breathing. He sees the pulse beat in Nora's neck, her necklace against her thin, white jumper. He doesn't remember seeing that necklace before.

Then another song begins and it's as if they are both roused from their nightmare. Nora doesn't say anything else, but knocks back her wine with an uncharacteristic urgency.

'I've got to go,' she says and gets up. Henning follows her back to the kitchen, out into the hallway where she puts on her shoes and her jacket. Then she straightens up and looks at him. Really looks at him.

And then she comes towards him and she doesn't stop before she is standing very close to him. He puts his arms around her and she clings to him as if she doesn't ever want to let go. Henning can't remember the last time he held Nora like this. He places his hand tenderly on her neck and strokes her hair. He closes his eyes. Her soft, lovely hair. Just like he remembers it. The scent of her. Also just like he remembers it.

And when she pushes herself away from him a little later, her feet refuse to follow. So she stays where she is, close to him. They are separated by only a few centimetres. He can feel her breath on his face, a cloud of alcohol that lingers around his nose. Henning doesn't know whether he pulls Nora close to him or Nora glides imperceptibly towards him, but again he feels himself trembling at her magnetic power, which has never lost its hold over him. And he realises with all his being that he has never loved anyone the way he loves Nora.

And that's why he pulls away.

He sees it in her eyes; how she, too, feels that what they are doing is wrong. They look at each other for many, long moments.

Then she turns around and leaves.

Thursday

Chapter 67

Trine can't remember the last time she had such a good, dreamless sleep. After they had talked late into the night, she cuddled up to Pål Fredrik and didn't wake up until her mobile started to buzz on the bedside table. She has heard people say how therapeutic it is to make a clean breast of things, to share the secrets that were eating them up, but she would never have believed that it could feel like this.

But though it helped to tell Pål Fredrik about her father and what she saw that night, she didn't tell him everything about herself. She didn't even come close. And she doesn't know if she will ever manage it.

Trine gets up at the same time as Pål Fredrik though she doesn't intend to go back to work yet. They eat breakfast together, read the newspaper, discuss the news – at least any news that isn't about her. When Pål Fredrik goes to the office, Trine finds herself alone once again in a silence that festers around her. She feels the urge to exercise, to run away from it all, but she doesn't; instead she reflects on how the media have wallowed in every revelation about her that has come out in the last few days.

She hasn't read even half the stories that have been published, but the biggest headlines seem to have taken root in the public's imagination. As an elected politician and a member of the government, she had known that her life would be subject to constant, close scrutiny. And she has yet to meet someone who has never made a single mistake. She accepted that she would always be under the microscope.

But she hasn't deserved this.

She bloody well doesn't deserve this.

With the benefit of hindsight, it's easy to see that she should not have done what she did. Life would be so much simpler if we never had to deal with unintended consequences.

Talk about things being simple.

Trine realises she hasn't allowed herself to think simple thoughts in the last few days. When she tried to identify the person who could have known what she did in Denmark, her initial conclusion was that a friend might have mentioned it to someone and thus inadvertently started the rumour. But the simplest explanation hasn't occurred to her until now. There is one person who knows everything, who helped her, got her out of Hotel Caledonien discreetly, arranged a car and a plane ticket, booked a hotel and packed some clothes for her so she could travel incognito from Kjevik Airport. Who made the appointment that enabled Trine to deal with her little problem. It's someone she has worked closely with during the three years she has been Justice Secretary. The person she trusted the most.

Trine picks up her mobile, which is lying next to her coffee cup, retrieves a number from her contact list and rings it.

'Hi, Trine. How are you?'

'Good morning. I want to hold a press conference later today. Please would you set it up?'

A short pause follows.

'Yes, of course, but—'

'Great. Make it two o'clock, that gives me time to prepare. But first I'd like to have a little chat with you. Let's say my office twelve o'clock?'

Another silence.

'Eh, okay?'

'Great. I'll see you at twelve noon.'

Chapter 68

Henning looks at his watch. He is early.

He doesn't mind. Whenever he visits the Olympen café, he prefers to sit by the window. In the past he would make up stories about people walking by outside based on only a quick glance at their face, their eyes and their clothing. He regarded it as training in his quest to become a better judge of character, which in turn would make him a better journalist. And it was something to do when he was bored or waiting for someone, as he is now. It occurs to him that fear has stopped him undertaking many other activities he enjoys. Wine, friends, music. He has even stayed away from the sea. An amateur psychologist might say that he is scared of feeling anything ever again. Henning doesn't know. He just knows that a lot is happening with him right now though he finds himself unable to take it all in.

Henning's mobile rings. *Talk of the devil*, Henning thinks when he sees that the caller is Iver Gundersen. Henning immediately experiences a rush of guilt because of what nearly happened with Nora last night. *Perhaps that's why Iver is calling? Did she say anything to him?*

Reluctantly, Henning puts the phone to his ear.

'Hello?' he says, sounding a little less confident than he had hoped.

'Hey, man,' Iver says in his usual cocky voice. Slowly the air escapes from Henning's lungs. 'How are you?' his colleague continues. 'Are you busy?'

'Fairly,' Henning replies. 'I'm waiting for a source, but he hasn't shown up yet.'

'Oh, so it's a he,' Iver laughs conspiratorially.

'Mm. And now you obviously know who he is.'

'If you tell me where you are, then I can guess.'

'Yes, I'm not going to do that, obviously.'

Iver laughs again. Henning realises that he is beginning to smile.

'How are you?' he asks Iver. 'Are you coming back to work soon?'

'I hope so. I'm going for a check-up at Ullevål Hospital in a couple of days, and then we'll see. I'm getting cabin fever from sitting around all day doing nothing.'

Henning remembers how he felt in the weeks and months before he decided to return to work. He spent most of his time at home, staring at the wall, watching a bit of TV. The world had ground to a halt. Then he started going for a walk every day. He would sit in Dælenenga Sports Park in the evening. Gradually he got used to being around people again, though he hardly ever spoke to anyone.

'Sorry for not stopping by last week at the hospital,' Henning says.

'Ah,' Iver snorts. 'Sod that.'

'Only there was so much to do after the Pulli case. I didn't have a single—'

'Forget about it, I said. Isn't that what you're always telling me?'

'What?'

'To forget about it?'

'Yes, I . . . I suppose I do.'

'Well, then, forget about it.'

Iver laughs again. Henning smiles and gazes out at the street where a woman with three shopping bags trundles along the pavement.

'So how are you?' Iver says. 'Anything happening in your life?'

'You can say that again.'

'So what's going on? I mean apart from the stuff I can read in the paper myself.'

Henning would have liked to share some of his thoughts with Iver, but he hesitates before he replies. Perhaps because of Nora. Or perhaps he clams up like he did in the past when he sensed that someone was getting close to him.

Across the street he sees Bjarne Brogeland coming towards him.

'My source is here,' Henning says. 'I've got to go.'

'But—'

'Sorry, Iver. I'll tell you all about it later.'

'Do you promise?'

Henning doesn't reply immediately. Then he says: 'I promise.'

*

In time Olympen has become Bjarne and Henning's regular meeting place when they need to talk shop. Usually at Henning's request, but this time it was at Bjarne's initiative. Henning didn't mind, not in the least; the morning had come and gone without him finding anything he could feed to his editor. Nor had he spotted any developments in the story about Trine, other than more negative publicity about her.

Henning gets up from the table and greets Bjarne with a firm handshake. They find a table further towards the back and order coffee.

'You look tired,' Henning says as they sit down.

'Thanks, mate,' Bjarne grins and runs a hand across his face. 'I didn't sleep very well last night. There's something about this case that—'

He fumbles for the words before he continues.

'We're still in the dark, to tell you the truth,' he says. 'And I thought that perhaps you could, that you—'

Bjarne looks around.

'Everyone knows you have a sharp eye for detail,' he says.

Henning smiles quickly while he studies the police officer with mild curiosity. Bjarne looks as nervous as a teenager on his first date.

'And your bosses have obviously given you their full support for this conversation?'

Bjarne shakes his head slowly. The aroma from their coffee cups wafts towards them.

'No, I didn't think so,' Henning says. 'So, tell me, what's really going on here? Normally I have to play the jester to get a seat at the king's table, and suddenly it's the other way round? Don't tell me you're banging your head against a brick wall already? The guy killed himself less than twenty-four hours ago.'

Bjarne's face hardens.

'A fresh perspective is always useful,' he says.

Henning takes a sip of his coffee while he looks at his old school friend. Bjarne's dark hair appears to have gone grey at the temples during their short conversation. His cheeks are clean-shaven as always, but his skin, usually golden from a summer tan, looks pale now.

'But you obviously can't report any of what I'm about to tell you,' Bjarne continues.

'So you want me to help you, but you're not going to give me anything in return?'

Bjarne's brow furrows.

'Let's agree on the things you can report. Not all of it is sensitive.'

Henning looks at him for a while.

'Okay,' he says eventually and shrugs. 'Go on then. Tell me about the pieces that don't fit.'

Bjarne heaves a sigh, then he glances around again before he leans forward and tells Henning about Gjerløw's past connection with the victims. He tells him about the crime scenes, the broken pictures on the walls, the photos of the victims on Gjerløw's laptop, his visits to Grünerhjemmet, the envelope they found in his flat addressed to Tom Sverre Pedersen. The Facebook apology.

'But nobody understands why Gjerløw did it,' Bjarne concludes in exasperation. 'We haven't found any evidence that links the adult Gjerløw to any of his victims, apart from the fact that he was friends with Johanne Klingenberg on Facebook, and that he volunteered at the care home where Erna Pedersen lived. I quite simply can't discover a motive.'

Henning, too, has moved closer to the table. It comes as a

surprise to him that the murders were carried out by the same killer. It also intrigues him in a way he hasn't felt for a long time.

'And there are a couple of other oddities. One of Gjerløw's two laptops was completely clean. The one with the photographs. There wasn't a single fingerprint or a speck of dust on it. The other one, a more recent model, was covered in grime. Plus Gjerløw sent a text message to a friend shortly before he died, saying he was busy playing a computer game. "*Hate the graphics, but love the sound.*"'

Bjarne looks at Henning for a few seconds, then he lowers his gaze.

'I just don't understand,' he says and shakes his head.

'What did Gjerløw do for a living?'

'He was unemployed. Or he was at the time of his death.'

'What kind of jobs did he used to do?'

'Casual jobs. He had worked in a nursery school, for example, mostly here in Oslo. He also did a bit of removal work, I believe. He has a lorry driver's licence and worked for Ringnes Brewery for a couple of months, delivering beer.'

Henning rests his chin in his hand.

'And there's something about that little boy that sends shivers down my spine,' Bjarne continues.

Henning tries to visualise the killer, sees him lose his temper in Erna Pedersen's room and smash a picture of her son's family. He sees him go berserk in Johanne Klingenberg's flat and smash the photograph of her godson.

And he remembers the emotions that welled up in him last night when he looked at the lovely picture of Jonas. The guilty conscience that nearly choked him, how he would never, ever, be able to bear having Jonas's eyes look out at him from the wall. That could have been the reason why Gjerløw put up that school photo he was in on Erna Pedersen's wall. Perhaps he wanted her to remember something. Perhaps he wanted her to feel guilty.

Henning shares his thoughts with Bjarne.

'It's possible,' Bjarne admits. 'But what would cause him to smash the other photo?'

'Maybe he wasn't angry with the people in the pictures. Then he would have hurt them instead. And the little boy couldn't possibly have upset anyone, that goes without saying.'

Again Henning thinks about the information Bjarne has given him.

'If you're right in suggesting that Gjerløw had a particular relationship to the pictures, they might have represented something to him.'

'Such as what?'

'I'm not sure. Perhaps he was lonely? Didn't you say that he hadn't managed to have a family of his own?'

'Yes?'

'Then he might have been jealous. Otherwise why get mad at a picture of a happy family? He didn't know them personally, did he?'

'No, or at least we don't think so. But don't forget he smashed a photo of a little boy as well. Surely he can't have been jealous of a toddler?'

Henning doesn't reply immediately, but he is aware of a thought, an answer somewhere deep inside him that is just out of reach.

'What if the little boy symbolised the same thing as the

happy family?' he says eventually.

'What do you mean?'

'Gjerløw had no children of his own. Perhaps he longed for one?'

'So it's not necessarily the boy himself who is the problem,' Bjarne says. 'It's what he represents?'

Henning opens up his hands.

'Why not?'

Bjarne sits in pensive silence for several seconds. Then his mobile rings. He picks it up. Henning studies his friend's facial expression while he listens. His pupils start to expand. His mouth drops open.

'Okay,' he says. 'I'll be there right away.'

He hangs up.

'What was that about?' Henning asks.

'It wasn't his blood,' Bjarne says.

'Whose blood?'

'The blood Johanne Klingenberg found in her flat two weeks ago. It doesn't belong to Markus Gjerløw. He's a different blood type.'

Chapter 69

It's about pulling yourself together. Finding a special room for grieving in your heart, but using the other rooms as well. Remembering that life must go on.

Emilie Blomvik spent the night in the freezing cold guest bedroom in the basement. She even managed to sleep for several hours. And when she was woken up by footsteps running across the parquet flooring above, the sound of her son's pitter-patter as if he is incapable of doing anything at normal speed, she made up her mind. Enough is enough. Yes, you can feel sad, but don't let grief eat you up.

So she went back upstairs and told Mattis that he could go to work today. He had been kind enough to take a day off to look after Sebastian and her – even though he had just been made partner. And she realised how good it felt to get back to normality. Make Sebastian's packed lunch. Get him dressed. Sebastian, poor kid, knows nothing about what has happened; he knows nothing about death. But he knows his parents. And when one of them acts out of character, he can sense it. Of course he can.

Emilie finds him in his bedroom, subjecting Lightning McQueen to his usual brutal treatment. She smiles. Sebastian barely looks up when she says 'hi'. There is a vroom. Then some screeching and crashing. Recently she has noticed that her son has started to close the door to his room. He wants to be alone. He opens it and he closes it. She hadn't expected him to do that yet; after all he is only two and a half years old.

'Right, I'm off,' Mattis shouts out to them from the hall-way.

'Daddy is leaving now,' she says to Sebastian. 'Let's go and say bye bye to him.'

Sebastian drops the car with a crash. Emilie is about to tell him not to treat his toys like that, but she stops herself. Today is not a day for rebukes. Today is all about the path of least resistance. Getting back on her feet.

They send Mattis off with hugs, kisses and waving. When the door slams shut, she asks Sebastian if he has had his breakfast yet. She gets a vigorous headshake by way of response.

'Okay,' she says, 'then we'd better get you something to eat. What would you like?'

'Cornflakes.'

'Cornflakes it is.'

Emilie is heading to the kitchen via the living room when an object on the wall next to the stuffed reindeer head makes her stop. It's a picture. A picture she hasn't seen before. Two footprints in the sand, one halfway across the other, on pink photocopier paper. *When did Mattis put that up?* she wonders. *And since when does he care about interior design? What on earth is the meaning of the two footprints in the sand? Could it be a subtle kind of marriage proposal?*

There is something familiar about the image. She knows she has seen it before.

A long, long time ago.

A cold prickling begins in her neck and spreads to the rest

of her body. She is about to fetch her mobile to call Mattis when her eyes are drawn to the front door.

She can hear footsteps outside.

*

Bjarne hurries out of Olympen and into the street where the wind takes hold of his jacket and flaps it open.

It wasn't Gjerløw's blood. The blood didn't have to belong to Klingenberg's killer, of course, but it was an obvious thought. According to the police report, Klingenberg hadn't noticed any blood near the cat basket until the day her flat was broken into. She was adamant. And though the intruder might not be the same man who killed her, it's likely. It's much more than likely.

Markus Gjerløw didn't kill Johanne Klingenberg.

And the squeaky clean laptop continues to trouble Bjarne. When they examined it they discovered that the computer's serial number was registered to Markus Gjerløw and that he had bought it in Spaceworld twenty-six months ago. So far so good. Then they examined the second laptop, a computer of a more recent design that showed every sign of being in daily use. Why treat the two computers so differently? And why did Markus Gjerløw kill himself?

If indeed that was what he did.

Questioning his suicide seems absurd. There is nothing to suggest anything other than Markus Gjerløw chose to take his own life. But Bjarne thinks about the killer's MO and the earlier visits he made to Erna Pedersen's room and Johanne Klingenberg's flat. He could have planned the murder of

Markus Gjerløw as well. He could have planted the evidence that would point the police to Gjerløw so that the suspicions would be directed at a dead man. So that he himself would go free.

So that he could kill again?

Bjarne decides to ring Emilie Blomvik straightaway. While he waits for a reply, Henning catches up with him.

'What's going on?' he asks.

But Bjarne doesn't reply. His head fills with fresh thoughts while he crosses the road, still pressing the phone to his ear and navigating the traffic. He hangs up when Emilie Blomvik doesn't answer.

Come on, he says to himself. *You know what you have to do. Analyse the information quickly, accurately and effectively. Make the right call. If you hope ever to become Head of Investigation, you have to deliver in situations like this one.*

If his theory is correct, the killer has to be someone close to Gjerløw. Someone who would know that Gjerløw would be at Grünerhjemmet that day.

He stops in his tracks.

Of course.

Chapter 70

Henning follows Bjarne across the street, but his police friend is deep in thought while at the same time trying to get hold of someone on the phone. At that moment, Henning's own mobile rings; it's a number he doesn't recognise.

He takes the call.

'Hello. Am I speaking to Henning Juul?'

It is an old person's voice. Henning stuffs a finger in his ear to shut out the noise from the street.

'You are.'

'I'm sitting here with your business card,' says the woman down the other end.

'Oh, right,' Henning says, now remembering Erna Pedersen's old neighbour in Brinken. Borgny Ramstad, that was her name, wasn't it?

'I've been visiting my daughter in Bergen for a couple of days and I've only just got back. I caught the night train. And the first thing I saw when I came home was your card stuck in my front door. I hope you're not going to try to sell me something?'

'No, not at all,' Henning assures her. 'I wanted to talk to you because you knew Erna Pedersen.'

'Indeed I did. We were neighbours for twenty-four years.'

Henning looks across to Bjarne and sees him take out his notebook and check something.

'Mrs Ramstad, I want to ask you about something that happened quite a few years ago. It's to do with Erna Pedersen.'

Henning tells her that Erna Pedersen has been murdered.

'Oh, how dreadful,' Borgny Ramstad says. 'I haven't been following the news recently. My grandchild has colic, you see.'

'I understand,' Henning says. 'What I'm particularly interested in is the vandalism done to Erna Pedersen's house while she was still working as a teacher. Did she ever talk to you about it?'

'She certainly did. Erna was in such a state about it.'

'I know she had her suspicions about who was behind it. Did she ever tell you?'

There is silence for a moment. Henning watches Bjarne press the phone to his ear again.

'I don't really—'

'As far as I understand there were several culprits. But do you know if Erna was scared of any of them?'

There is another silence.

'Well, in that case, it must have been the boy who—'

Silence again.

'Oh, I can't remember his name.'

'Please try—'

'Oh, now I remember!' she exclaims. 'It was the brother of the boy who died in that snow cave accident, wasn't it?'

*

Bjarne remembers what Markus Gjerløw said to him on the telephone.

'I only know Remi.'

Bjarne pulls out the list of names that Emil Hagen gave him. Sees that there is a Remi highlighted in bold.

Remi Gulliksen.

Bjarne takes out his mobile and calls Fredrik Stang.

'Hi, it's me,' Bjarne says. 'Can you check if a boy called Remi Gulliksen went to school with Markus Gjerløw?'

'Okay, hold on.'

It has to be Remi Gulliksen, Bjarne thinks while he listens to Stang flicking through documents down the other end of the phone. Of the people who were at Grünerhjemmet on the day that Erna Pedersen was killed, Gulliksen was the only person Markus Gjerløw knew. As a friend of Gjerløw's, Gulliksen would have been able to gain access to Gjerløw's flat, force him to swallow the morphine capsules and then write a cryptic apology on Facebook that would make everyone think that Gjerløw was apologising for the lives he had taken.

'No, I can't find a Remi Gulliksen,' Fredrik Stang says. 'But there is another Remi in his class. A Remi Winsnes.'

Bjarne tastes the name a little. It rings no bells.

'Okay, can you look up both Winsnes and Gulliksen for me? Try including Jessheim in your search as well and see if you get any hits.'

He hears clicking and keyboard sounds in the background. The seconds pass.

'I've found a Nils Jørgen Winsnes and a Susanne Marie Gulliksen. They live in Jessheim at the same address.'

'They must be Remi's parents.'

'Looks like it. He must have changed his surname as an adult.'

It has to be him, Bjarne thinks.

'And it says here that they lost a child,' Stang says. 'In a snow cave accident in Jessheim in the eighties.'

Bjarne makes no reply; all he can think about is that he couldn't get hold of Emilie Blomvik a few minutes ago. He is still very unhappy that Romerike Police decided to call off the protection Bjarne had requested for Blomvik and her family once Markus Gjerløw was found dead.

'Call Romerike Police and ask them to go to the home of Emilie Blomvik,' Bjarne says to Stang. 'And tell them to hurry up.'

'What's going on?'

'Just get them to check that everything is okay with her and her family.'

'Okay.'

They end their calls. Henning comes up behind him.

'I think I might know the name of the man you're looking for,' he says.

Bjarne spins around.

'Do you now?'

'It wouldn't happen to be Remi, would it?'

Chapter 71

Remi can still remember it. Her birthday.

Eighteen years. The portal to adulthood. Old enough to drive and finally able to get into most bars without fake ID. Not that Emilie ever needed to. She got in everywhere, even though the doormen knew that she wasn't old enough.

He gave her a very special present on that momentous day. A picture of two footprints, partly covering each other, on a beach. To let her know what he thought about the two of them and their future. He also gave her eighteen long-stemmed red roses, though the man in the florist told him that even numbers and flowers didn't go all that well together.

Memories.

Memories are crap.

He wishes he had never opened the local newspaper that day when the past suddenly became the present. The years had left their marks in her cheeks, time had done something to her chin and her eyes, but he could see that she was the same girl. Just as lovely. She still had that special light in her eyes, which beamed into him and turned everything it found upside down. And it was as if the smile she sent the readers of *Eidsvoll Ullensaker Blad* was aimed at him. He wanted the ground to open and swallow him up.

They used to talk about what they would call their children if they ever had children together. Emilie had said

Sebastian if it was a boy, and Johanne if it was a girl. Remi didn't really mind, he just wanted Emilie to be happy. And suddenly, there she was, in the newspaper with a child on her lap. A little boy called Sebastian. He could no longer remember what the article had been about, only that the picture had been taken at the boy's nursery.

And hey presto, they came back.

The memories.

Not only had they come back, he could physically feel them in his body, he started reliving the past, he felt the butterflies in his stomach when he walked past the places where it had happened, the place where – according to Emilie – absolutely nothing had happened. But he knew that it was all a lie.

They did it in the grove between the junction and the school playground where houses have since been built. Markus and Emilie hadn't even been able to wait until they got home, but they were seen – at least so the rumour went. And this at a time when she was supposed to be his girlfriend, when life was meant to be good, but it became a living nightmare.

Some people are just like that; they covet what others have. If Markus saw someone with a cool jumper or jacket at school, he had to have the same – or preferably something better and more expensive. He had to have the latest thing. For some reason he had always been popular with the girls. And, to top it all, he was Erna Pedersen's teacher's pet.

So when Remi started going out with Emilie, Markus obviously couldn't help himself. He had to have her, too, couldn't bear that someone else had something so wonderful. And as for Emilie, she was out of control and just wanted to party all the time.

Emilie had pleaded innocence, of course, and blamed it all on common gossip in Jessheim. She managed to sow just enough doubt in Remi for them to get back together. And that was when it happened with the worst possible timing; she missed her period. And he remembered what it had been like, when he hoped it could have marked a fresh start for them, that everything would be different. We'll erase the past and start over. We'll be a family, build a life together. And we'll call our child Sebastian.

Remi tightens his fists when he remembers the conversation they had a few days after she had told him about the pregnancy. Though she never said so outright, he realised that Johanne had been whispering in her ear and told her no, you can't do this, Emilie. Don't throw your life away. It's too soon to have kids.

So what are you going to do? You're not going to marry him, are you?

Johanne had never liked him much even though he had saved her life when she choked on that kebab outside the takeaway. He could see it in her eyes.

He finally got his proof a couple of days ago in the form of the message Johanne had sent to Emilie on Facebook.

Just as well you ended up with Mattis. It could have been much much worse ☺ ☺ ☺

*

A red ride-on tractor is parked on the shingle outside the garage. All Remi can think about is what it would have been like to live in this house, in its warmth. With her and Sebastian. It should have been like this. She said it would be.

The front door opens and a man comes out. A man who shouldn't be there. He walks down the steps and smiles to himself, he looks so bloody smug, just like Erna Pedersen's son in the picture the old hag had hanging on her wall.

Then something clouds Remi's vision. He can't see that he has started to move, he just feels it, he hears the shingle crunch under his feet. He doesn't say anything, either; he can just about make out that the garage door glides open and something shiny and expensive appears behind it. He doesn't feel his hands, his arms or his head, doesn't feel them make contact, doesn't hear the punch or the crack. And he doesn't know what he has done before he realises that his knuckles are red.

Chapter 72

'How the hell did you know that?' Bjarne asks as he starts to run.

'Forget it,' Henning says, trying to keep up. 'What's going on?'

The distant between them grows with each step.

'Where are you going?'

Bjarne turns his head, but increases his speed. Henning tries to follow, but his body protests.

'Are you going to Jessheim?' Henning calls out after him, but Bjarne just keeps on running. 'Can I get a lift? I think I've earned it, don't you?'

Henning stops outside the entrance to the police station's underground car park and watches Bjarne disappear inside. A few seconds later a car starts up in the darkness below. Tyres squeal. A fan belt complains. Then a grey Volvo estate comes towards Henning at a furious pace and brakes abruptly right by his feet. The window is already down.

Henning looks inside and meets Bjarne's wide-open eyes.

'Go on then, get in!'

*

Emilie looks up from Mattis's bloodied face and stares at the man who appears right behind him. With a hard push he shoves Mattis into the hallway, follows him and locks the door behind them.

'Remi?' she exclaims.

Remi keeps pushing Mattis towards the living room and stares at her with glazed eyes.

'You,' he says, pointing at her. 'Come here.'

Emilie stands rooted to the spot.

'But—'

'Come here,' Remi demands again, louder this time.

From the kitchen they hear the sound of quiet weeping. It grows and becomes increasingly desperate. Emilie sees the look Remi sends her little boy. A look that is seething with rage.

Emilie blocks the door.

'Please,' she says. 'Don't—'

But Remi interrupts her by raising his index finger, grabbing hold of her and forcing her into the living room. Mattis tries to stop him, but he has never been much of a fighter, nor is he particularly strong and Remi wards off the attack with a punch that hits him in the mouth. Mattis crashes on to the floor.

Sebastian cries even louder.

'Please,' Mattis stutters through split lips. 'Take whatever you want. Only please don't hurt us.'

Remi says nothing.

'Just leave us alone. Please,' Mattis implores him.

Emilie has no idea what is going on. And then there is Remi, who—

Remi's army jacket. It's khaki. Remi was the man with the camera outside Sebastian's nursery the other morning. Her gaze shifts to the wall, to the framed picture. The two footprints in the sand.

Emilie clasps her mouth with both hands while her eyes well up. Remi grabs Mattis and pushes him towards the dining table. In his hands he holds a thick green rope that Emilie recognises from the garage. He orders Mattis to sit down.

Mattis does as he is told and sits on the floor next to a table leg. The sweat pours from his forehead and mingles with blood that stains his bright white shirt. A sob escapes from Emilie's lips as she sees the madness in Remi's eyes, a wide-eyed expression that is new to her, as if he has become someone else. She watches him tie single, double and triple knots, criss-crossing the rope and tightening it so hard that Mattis groans. Sebastian is still crying in the kitchen.

'Get that kid to shut up,' Remi snarls and wags an angry finger at her. 'Make him shut up, or I will.'

Emilie sniffles, turns around and goes out into the kitchen. She kneels down to Sebastian, wipes his face, hushes him, says it'll be all right, it'll be all right, you just have to be very, very quiet, listen to me everything is going to be all right if you can just be very, very quiet. But it's no use. Mattis, too, tries to call out words of reassurance to Sebastian from the living room, but to no avail. Sebastian keeps crying, his wailing rises and falls. Emilie looks around for a dummy. Finds none.

'Where is his room?' Remi says in a harsh voice as he comes up behind her. He grabs hold of her arm and holds her tight. Emilie tries to wriggle free, but his grip is so hard and so vicious that resistance only causes her more pain.

'Where is his room?' Remi says again, now louder.

'In there,' Emilie sobs and nods her head in the direction of the hallway.

Remi releases his hold on her.

'Put him in there, I don't want to listen to that bloody—'

Emilie picks up Sebastian, puts his head close to her own and strokes his back while she tries to console him. She walks down the hallway, past the door to the bathroom and into Sebastian's room.

'You need to be quiet now,' she says, trying to control herself, but even she can hear that her pleading voice is close to breaking. *Be strong*, she tells herself, *for Sebastian's sake. It's up to you to stop him from experiencing even more trauma than he already has.*

Fortunately Sebastian seems to calm down at the sight of his things and his bed, the pale blue wallpaper, the action figures, the stuffed toys and Lightning McQueen – they all help to make him breathe more easily and he finally stops wailing and sobbing.

This in turn makes Emilie weep even harder. Her little boy. So small and vulnerable.

'And you,' Remi says to her when she comes back out. 'Stop your bloody crying.'

Emilie nods, even though the tears keep flowing.

'Close the door.'

Emilie does as she is told. Remi nods in the direction of the living room where Mattis is frantically trying to free himself. Emilie rushes over to him, she tries wiping away some of the blood on him, and doesn't care that her hands and clothes get wet and sticky.

She turns to Remi, who has followed and stopped right in front of her.

'What are you doing, Remi, why—'

He wags an angry finger at her.

'I think you know if you just think about it.'

Emilie stops.

'No,' she says. 'I don't.'

'Then you're a stupid cow.'

Again Emilie tries to understand, but she can feel the effects of not having eaten for two days. Her brain quite simply refuses to work and the frantic thoughts make her dizzy.

'You may be right, so why don't you tell me? Explain it to me.'

Remi inhales and clutches his head. He massages his temples. Then he looks up at the wall, at the two footprints.

Emilie's mobile rings. Her eyes automatically seek out the sound.

'Is that yours?' Remi asks.

Emilie doesn't reply.

'Is that yours?' he demands to know.

Emilie nods.

Remi walks towards the sound and finds her mobile on the large, black coffee table. He takes it, checks the display and lets it ring. However, she can see that the noise troubles him. With a brusque, panicky movement he blocks the call and tosses the mobile aside.

Then he sits down on a chair. Rubs his fingertips against his temples again. Something glides across his face. An expression or an emotion, Emilie isn't sure. But she's quite sure that she doesn't like what she sees.

*

Remi tries to think clearly.

It proves to be difficult.

He has only been inside the house once before and he hadn't planned on doing this. He doesn't know what he had hoped to get from Emilie. Just something. That she would say she was sorry and mean it, rather than merely say it. That she would understand.

He should have taken some more of the pills he swallowed before he went to Johanne's flat, then he wouldn't have been able to feel anything. But now he feels everything. The pain in his hand and in his head. It's as if the walls are closing in on him and threatening to crush him.

So what's he going to do now?

What next?

He lifts his head and looks around. His gaze stops on the stuffed reindeer head mounted on the wall. The eyes are dark and shiny. As if the light is still on in them.

'Do you hunt?' he asks, looking at Mattis.

Mattis nods reluctantly.

'Then I guess you keep guns in the house, don't you?'

Chapter 73

Bjarne mutters curses under his breath. Emilie Blomvik still isn't answering her phone. And worse, she has just blocked his call.

He swears loudly and drives as fast as he can in the direction of the Trafikkmaskinen interchange roundabout to get out of Oslo. While he weaves frantically in and out of the traffic, he finds a white cable, which he plugs into his mobile. He sticks the earplugs into his ears and calls Fredrik Stang again.

'Did you get hold of Romerike Police?'

'Yes, they're despatching a patrol car to the address now.'

'Just the one car?'

'Yes, they said that was all they had available.'

Bjarne rolls his eyes.

'Okay, I'm on my way there now. Have you found out more information about Remi Gulliksen?'

'Yes, a bit. He was born and grew up in Jessheim, but now lives in a small flat in Tøyen.'

'Have we sent people over to his address?'

'We have. Gjerstad has got everyone working on it.'

'Great.'

'By the way, Remi was due to be evicted from his flat today.'

'Really?'

'Yes, that could have been what set him off.'

'Hm. Keep me posted.'

'Will do.'

Some high-risk driving enables Bjarne to get out of Oslo in the rush-hour while he calls Directory Enquiries and asks to be put through to Nordby Nursery. There he learns that Sebastian Blomvik failed to show up today.

Bjarne calls Emilie again, but this time his call is cut off immediately.

'Damn,' he says and hits the accelerator.

*

Emilie Blomvik.

She was his first, his only one. Now, when he thinks about it, he doesn't know why he loved her, only that he did. He couldn't explain it. Perhaps it was just that she made him feel loved and valued. He believed that she admired him. That's what she told him, she praised him, called him nice and good. No one had ever said that to him before.

But he should have known that it couldn't last. Emilie wasn't that kind of girl. She got bored easily and hated staying in. She liked going to parties and having fun, while he just wanted her all to himself. At first when the rumours about Markus and her started to circulate, he refused to believe them. He was in denial.

Right until that became impossible.

Emilie was his first, his only one. He could never erase her; no one would ever surpass her. It had started with Emilie and it would finish with Emilie.

The doorbell rings.

He is startled, as are Emilie and Mattis. Both of them are about to cry out, but Remi points the gun at them.

'Hush,' he says. 'Not a sound.'

Chapter 74

Bjarne has barely left Oslo when his mobile rings again.

'Yes?'

It is Ella Sandland.

'I've just spoken to Remi Gulliksen's mother,' she says. 'Remi visited them Tuesday evening. She says he went berserk.'

'In what way?'

'He beat up his father.'

An articulated lorry pulls out in front of Bjarne. He sounds the horn and flashes his headlights while he says: 'Why?'

'His mother wasn't sure. It came out of the blue. Remi had knocked over a glass of water and refused to clean it up. And when his father told Remi to apologise, he went crazy.'

'Just because he knocked over a glass of water?'

The articulated lorry refuses to get out of his way.

'So it would seem. They don't sound like the world's happiest family.'

Bjarne opens the window and places a blue flashing light on the roof, though technically he should have requested permission first. It takes only a few seconds before the lorry pulls over. Bjarne accelerates and sends the driver a long hard stare before he overtakes him. The speedometer is close to 150.

'We need to send officers over to Remi's parents' address,' he says.

'I think that's already happening.'

'I'm seven or eight minutes away from Jessheim.'

'Thanks for letting me know.'

*

Bjarne exits the motorway at Jessheim, turns right at the first roundabout, drives past a bank and across the new roundabout left of the bridge. He continues towards the industrial estate and speeds through more roundabouts and sleeping policemen until he reaches a residential area. He follows the sat nav instructions on the screen and it doesn't take long before he spots the patrol car from Romerike Police parked outside a red house. Bjarne parks his car alongside the local officers and looks across to Henning.

'Stay here. And don't even think about leaving the car—'

He pushes his index finger very close to Henning's face.

'Okay.'

Bjarne gets out and introduces himself.

'It doesn't look as if anyone is in,' says one of the officers.

'Have you rung the doorbell?'

'Yes. No one came to the door.'

Bjarne checks the windows for signs of movement and listens out for sounds. The house glistens in the sunlight that has broken through the layer of clouds. The garage door is open. A stroller is parked outside. A green garden hose is stretched across the shingle.

'There!' Bjarne exclaims.

'Where?' the officer asks.

'The curtain in the small window. It twitched. There's someone inside.'

'Then why doesn't she open the door?'

Bjarne doesn't reply.

'I'll try calling her again,' he says and takes out his mobile. He lets it ring for a long time.

Finally the call is answered, but he hears only static.

'Hello?' Bjarne says.

There is no voice down the other end.

'This is Detective Inspector Bjarne Brogeland from Oslo Police. Who am I speaking to?'

The silence continues.

At last a dark voice says: 'Go away.'

Bjarne freezes.

'Remi?' he stutters. 'Is that you?'

'I want you to leave.'

Bjarne hears a chill in Remi's voice that he doesn't like the sound of. Bjarne says Remi's full name, but gets no response.

'Is Emilie there?' Bjarne then asks.

Silence.

'Emilie isn't here,' the voice replies eventually.

'I know she's in there, Remi. I want to talk to her.'

'No.'

Pause.

Bjarne starts to feel hot.

'Please could you just tell me if she's okay?'

No reply.

Bjarne places his hand over the telephone and looks at the others for assistance, but all he gets in return are blank stares.

'Remi,' Bjarne begins.

'Just drop it,' Remi interrupts him. 'And don't try to come inside or I'll shoot.'

It takes Bjarne a moment before he is able to respond.

'What did you just say, Remi?'

'I've got a gun and I'm not afraid to use it. Don't – come – in.'

Then he hangs up.

Chapter 75

Trine Juul-Osmundsen looks at her watch and sighs. In just a few hours she will be facing the pack of wolves. She has tried writing a statement, but her fingers just hovered over the keyboard. She has heard about writer's block and believed that it was restricted only to writers, but now she understands its true meaning. Not being able to put down a single, coherent thought. Stare at the screen and get nothing but emptiness back. It's like living in a vacuum.

She has gone through her emails and fortunately not found any more messages from biglie0910. It confirms the conclusion she reached earlier this morning. The sender knows that there is no point in sending her emails she can't read or reply to.

There is a knock on the door and Katarina Hatlem peeks in.

'You wanted a word with me?' she says and enters Trine's office. Her long red curls are coiled around her neck.

'Yes. Close the door behind you,' Trine says.

Katarina does as she is asked and approaches the desk. Her steps are normally brisk. Her face is usually alert. Now it looks haggard. As if she has been crying or not slept for several days.

'How are you?' Hatlem asks her cautiously.

'Sit down.'

Katarina hesitates a second before she does as she is told.

'I've been doing a bit of thinking recently,' Trine begins. 'Or more accurately, I wasn't able to think very much until I came home last night. It has been a little – how can I put it – difficult to focus on anything other than negative thoughts.'

'I understand,' Katarina says, nodding vigorously.

'But this morning I remembered something.'

Trine drums her fingers on the desk.

'Whoever started this smear campaign against me must have known that I wouldn't defend myself. He or she must have known why I couldn't tell the public what I really did on the night of 9 October last year, or rather what I did the following day. It means that this person must have known that I was in Denmark and what it would do to me if the truth came out.'

Katarina Hatlem lowers her gaze.

'I confided in one person,' Trine says, locking her eyes on to Katarina. 'One person who helped me with the arrangements. And that person, Katarina dear, was you.'

Katarina makes no reply. She just stares at the floor.

'Either you're behind all of this or you told someone what I did.'

Trine pre-empts Katarina's potential protest.

'I'm going to give you one chance – just one – to explain yourself. And spare me the outrage; don't tell me it wasn't you, because you must have had something to do with it. Because I certainly didn't tell anyone else.'

Katarina can't even look her in the eye, but Trine sees the colour flare up in her cheeks. It doesn't take long before the corners of her mouth start twitching.

'Please believe me,' she whimpers. 'I never thought that it would go this far.'

'Didn't you?' Trine replies tartly. 'Few people know the media better than you, Katarina. You knew exactly how to play it.'

Katarina shakes her head frantically.

'It wasn't like that,' she says. 'It was my fault, but I promise you, Trine, I had nothing to do with this.'

'Then I suggest that you start talking. The press conference begins in less than two hours.'

Katarina breaks down and sobs. She cries for a long time until Trine orders her to pull herself together.

'I'm sorry,' Katarina stutters while she closes her eyes and lets the tears run free. 'I'm so, so sorry.'

Trine doesn't reply, she just looks at someone who has been her closest colleague for several years. A colleague she regarded as her friend. And the tender feeling she gets inside surprises her. But she can't make herself say that it's okay. It's very much not okay. The damage can never be undone.

'I'm waiting,' she says and juts out her chin.

Katarina Hatlem sniffs, puts a finger under each eye and lets the skin absorb some of the moisture, but to no avail. When she finally starts talking, her voice no longer trembles.

And Trine thought she knew how bad getting hurt could be. Dull pain punctured by tiny pulsating pricks, words driving splinters of pain into her heart and forcing all the air out of her lungs. She thought she knew how bad getting hurt could get.

She was wrong.

Chapter 76

As soon as Bjarne has finished the call, he rings a new number. It takes only a moment before the call is answered. He quickly explains where he is and what has happened.

'This is a hostage situation,' he repeats to emphasise the gravity of the situation. As he ends the call, he looks up at the house.

'Do you have any experience with hostage situations?' he asks.

The local police officers exchange glances.

'I mean, apart from what they taught you at the police academy?'

'No,' one of them says.

'Would it be okay with you if I take charge until the armed response unit arrives?'

'Yes,' they reply in unison.

'Okay,' Bjarne begins. 'We need to set up an inner cordon so that the hostage taker can't escape if he decides to leave the house. Next we set up an outer cordon that will stop outsiders entering the area. We're lucky, only one road leads in here and it starts around the bend over there.' Bjarne points to a grey house with tall walls. 'There's a footpath over there. One of you, you for example,' he says, pointing to the man on his left, 'go over there and stop everyone from getting through. And I mean everyone.'

The police officer nods.

'I noticed another footpath on my way here, over by the post boxes. You go over there,' Bjarne says, pointing to the other officer. 'You should still be able to see inside the house, but act discreetly. We mustn't do anything to provoke the hostage taker. Take off your jacket, there's always a chance he won't realise you're a police officer. See if you can get an idea of how many people are inside. We also have to assess whether we need to evacuate any of the neighbours, certainly anyone we see outdoors. We have to get them out of here.'

The officers nod.

'I'll stay here in front of the house. We'll do what we can, and wait for backup.'

The officers nod again.

'Okay,' Bjarne says and waves them off. The officers quickly take up their positions. Bjarne watches the house closely, sees the curtain twitch again. A head pops up and then disappears.

Bjarne has been present at two previous hostage situations. The first took place in an asylum centre. A staff member at reception called the police himself to say that he was being held against his will by a resident threatening him with a knife and a can of petrol. An ambulance and armed police officers attended immediately, and initially there were fears that the resident might burn down the whole centre. But everything was over in thirty minutes. The resident was arrested without drama.

The second time was a woman in a house out in Lørenskog and the call they got was similar to this one, that a man inside had a weapon and that he wasn't afraid to use it. The hostage taker even stepped out on the veranda and fired a shot in the air to prove his claim. The police arrived in full force, took up positions around the house, and the hostage negotiator made contact. Again, it didn't take long before the hostage was released. The man was arrested inside the house after a short raid.

What both hostage situations had in common was that Bjarne felt strangely disappointed afterwards. There was no action, no adrenaline rush. No messages on the police radio about an arm, a shoulder or a head in the middle of quivering crosshairs. But though Bjarne felt a little cheated then, he realises now with all of his being that he hopes this hostage situation will have the same outcome. That it will play out just as quickly, end just as undramatically and with as few injuries as possible.

Bjarne jumps when his mobile rings. He looks at the display. The call is from Emilie Blomvik's phone. Bjarne stands frozen for several long seconds. Reluctantly, he presses the green button.

'Hello?'

'Didn't you hear what I said?' says the heavy, dark voice.

'Yes, Remi. I heard everything you said.'

'So why are you still there? I told you I had a gun. Do you need a demonstration?'

Bjarne closes his eyes and thinks hard.

'No, Remi, I don't.'

'Then I suggest that you get out of here now.'

Bjarne rubs his forehead, his hand gets wet from sweat and he realises he has no source of advice, he is on his own. Police academy training means nothing; he can't access the calm, the sensible advice, the gentle voice that tells the hostage taker that the negotiator is now in charge.

'Let me help you,' he says and immediately hears a snort down the other end.

'The only thing I want you to do is keep your mouth shut and listen to me. I know that you're going to call for backup now; negotiators and armed officers will turn up and everyone will want to help me, isn't that right, everybody's going to be ever so patient and understanding. Well, you can forget about it. I don't want to talk to some bloody hostage negotiator.'

There is silence again. The sweat is dripping from Bjarne's forehead.

'Okay,' he says. 'So who do you want to talk to?'

*

The police officer's voice echoes in Remi's head. He looks at the TV screen where the news channel is on. A red dot is flashing as if a tsunami warning is being broadcast.

Next to the dot it says that Justice Secretary Trine Juul-Osmundsen has called a press conference later today and that she is expected to resign. But the experts Remi can hear, the reporters in the television studio, think that no one should expect her to apologise for what she has done.

So she is another one of those.

'I want to talk to the woman on the TV,' Remi says. 'The Minister for Justice. I want to talk to Trine Juul-Osmundsen.'

Chapter 77

Though Henning has been told to stay in the car, he can see that something is brewing. He has already called *123news* to alert them when Bjarne comes over and wrenches open the door.

'You can't stay here,' he says, his voice laden with police gravity while he summons him outside with his index finger.

'Okay,' Henning says, getting out. 'So where can I be?'

'Anywhere,' Bjarne says. 'Just not here.'

'What's going on?'

'Much too much,' Bjarne replies, but offers no further explanation.

Henning retreats discreetly while he watches Bjarne and the two other officers. Their faces are grim, their footsteps purposeful. If you put two and two together, you usually get four. Their presence must indicate that Remi is inside Emilie Blomvik's house. And that he has no plans to come quietly.

Henning finds a spot further away where he still has a view of the house. He takes out his mobile and rings *123news* again.

*

The armed response unit is in place thirty minutes later. A tall, dark-haired man called Simen Krogh is in charge of the

374

operation. He has long sideburns, a strong jaw and a thick bull's neck.

'Right, people, listen up,' Krogh says, summoning the officers closer to him. He allocates some of them to a detention group tasked with catching Remi if he comes out or tries to escape. Krogh tells them that he has requested a trained hostage negotiator who will be with them in fifteen minutes.

'We have one objective right now,' Krogh says earnestly. 'And that is to get the hostage taker to come out with the hostages alive. And remember, we have all the time in the world. We can drag out events to try to wear him down. Unless there's an emergency and the hostages' lives are in danger, then we don't take action. We don't storm the house unless we absolutely have to. But we'll still prepare as if that was exactly what we were going to do.'

Krogh turns.

'That hedge there,' he says, pointing to one side of the house. 'It's dense. It'll provide cover. There is also a veranda close to the hedge. I want two men up on that veranda, but do it quietly. I don't want him to hear your footsteps and panic.'

The officers Krogh is pointing at nod.

'On the other side, to the right of the garage, you can get across the fence and access the back garden. There are no windows on that side, something that will help us get closer. But the house has several windows on its long sides. So stay out of sight. See, but don't be seen.'

Krogh then goes over to two men who are assembling rifles.

'If you see the hostage taker aim his gun at the hostage and declare an intention to shoot, then you must await orders from me before you can take him out. No heroics. Understand?'

The marksmen nod.

The rest of the officers take up positions, both outside and inside the white picket fence.

'Okay,' Krogh says, walking towards Bjarne. 'What do you make of the hostage taker's demand?'

Bjarne shakes his head.

'Difficult to know. Even the lunatic in there must know that you can't just pick up the phone and, hey presto, the Justice Secretary comes running.'

'Well, I think we should alert her,' Krogh says. 'So that at least she's aware of the situation.'

'I've tried getting hold of some of her aides, but it's chaos at the Ministry right now. As far as I can understand the Minister is about to hold a press conference.'

Krogh nods.

'The hostage taker wants to talk to her. He has a gun, which he says he's not afraid to use. I think that a call to a Minister is a small price to pay to save someone's life.'

Bjarne takes a deep breath.

'I'll get my boss to put some pressure on the Justice Secretary's staff.'

Chapter 78

The words from Katarina's mouth were like a punch to the stomach. Trine had never thought that the sound of a name could cause her so much pain. The years they have spent together. The plans they have made. Their dreams. The foundations underpinning everything they had done – blown away. And she understands it now; she sees how the traps were set for her and how she walked into each one without even thinking about it. Just because he told her to.

It was fiendishly clever. And now it's too late. He has won. Or has he?

Trine looks at the clock on the wall, gets up and rolls her shoulders. She goes to the cloakroom and looks at herself in the mirror. Tiny needles of anger prick her at the thought of what she is about to do. In the last half hour alone she has been to the lavatory three times. An hour's run would be welcome now, she thinks, to drain the stress from her body. She is still suffering the after-effects of the liqueur she drank too much of in the cabin.

Trine removes a strand of hair from her forehead, adjusts her jacket and turns around in the full-length mirror. She looks okay, doesn't she?

Yes, she assures herself. *You look fine.*

She inhales, stares into her own eyes and then closes them. She knows she is going to hate every second of this press conference. She returns to her desk, picks up the pages she printed out, though she is not sure if she really needs them. She has always been comfortable giving speeches and lectures without notes. Nevertheless it's good to have something to look at, just in case. Something to do with her hands.

She is about to step outside when Katarina Hatlem rushes in. After she had made a clean breast of everything to Trine, Katarina said without prompting that she would obviously clear her desk immediately and not come back. Now she is waving her arm in the air and holding a mobile in her hand.

'Trine, wait,' she calls out.

It is as if the confrontation they had only a couple of hours ago has been wiped from her face. There is a sense of urgency to her movements that Trine has seen many times before. It means that something has happened.

Katarina stops right in front of Trine and puts her hand over the microphone on the mobile.

'I've got a policeman on the line,' she says. 'There's a hostage situation in Jessheim.'

Trine gives her a look of exasperation.

'I'm just about to give a press conference, Katarina, I can't—'

'Two seconds,' Katarina implores her. 'Just listen to what he has to say for two seconds.'

Trine looks at her ex-friend for a moment before she takes the mobile and says 'yes'. A man introduces himself as Arild Gjerstad.

Trine says nothing while she listens to his briefing. Her thoughts are racing. When Gjerstad has finished, she says: 'Tell the hostage taker I'm on my way. Tell him that he will get to talk to me, but that I want something in return. Such as a hostage.'

Trine hands back the mobile to Katarina without ending the call.

'I want you to go to the press room,' Trine says as she walks past her. 'Tell the reporters that the press conference has been postponed until further notice.'

Trine asks her secretary to inform her driver that she will be downstairs in two minutes. She doesn't even put on a coat before she goes over to the lift and hits the down button several times. Four minutes later, after having fought her way through a throng of noisy reporters who can't understand why she is leaving without talking to them, she is on her way to Jessheim in her ministerial car, a perk she thought she had enjoyed for the last time. The driver asks if he should request assistance from the police to get out of the capital as quickly as possible, but Trine doesn't think that will be necessary. She regrets her decision once they get stuck in the Trafikkmaskinen interchange roundabout, but the traffic eases up as they approach the Vålerenga Tunnel. Then it slows down again near Furuset, and again at the exit to Olavsgård. Trine looks at her watch. The call came in thirty minutes ago. She hopes she won't be too late.

The drive to Jessheim takes almost fifty minutes, but the location proves easy to find. Crowds of curious neighbours and news-hungry journalists have gathered behind the police cordons. A reporter from TV2 is holding a microphone in her hand while talking to a camera; her face is solemn as if she were about to announce a death. Then her gaze is drawn to the car in which Trine is travelling. It takes only a few seconds before the blonde reporter recognises the ministerial car and realises who has arrived.

Trine tries to find something to focus on while her driver looks for a place to park. She gets out of the car and instantly feels everyone's eyes on her so she picks a spot above them and concentrates on that, ignores the murmur of voices and makes her way through the crowd and over to police cordons. The TV reporter calls out to her.

'Minister, what are you doing here?'

Trine doesn't reply, but identifies herself to the uniformed officer standing guard and is let through immediately.

Her heels make a steady clicking sound against the damp tarmac. Everyone she meets looks at her and follows her with their eyes. She finds the car marked 'Head of Operations' and nods to some of the uniformed officers outside.

'Hello,' she says. 'Who is in charge here?'

A tall, dark-haired man turns around.

'I am. My name is Simen Krogh,' he says, holding out his hand.

Trine shakes it.

'Have you had any more contact with the hostage taker?'

'No,' Krogh says. 'He hasn't called us in the last forty-five minutes, and we haven't called him. But we're prepared, we have people ready to go in – should it become necessary. All lines of communications are open. The Police Chief is following the situation and will decide whether or not we take action.'

'I'll make that decision,' she says. 'I'm still Justice Secretary.'

'Er, yes, of course. That's your right. Have you been briefed about the hostage taker?'

'I know a little, yes,' she says and nods. She didn't follow the news much when she was young, but she does remember the snow cave tragedy in Jessheim. She read about it in the local paper. Remi's brother who died under the snowdrifts. A terrible, tragic accident.

'Okay, good,' Krogh says. 'Before we get started, I'd like you to talk to the hostage negotiator from Lillestrøm. Follow me.'

Krogh leads Trine through a crowd of police officers. Then he stops at a mobile incident truck, gives an order Trine doesn't catch and a few seconds later a woman in civilian clothing gets out. She is wearing a bullet-proof vest on top of her thin, dark blue raincoat.

'Hello, my name is Tonje Tellefsen,' the woman says. 'I'm the hostage negotiator for Romerike police district.'

'Trine Juul-Osmundsen.'

They shake hands and quickly smile at each other.

'I'll be with you the whole time listening to every word that's being said. Situations like these are always unique and you can never know in advance what will work. There's one thing that is important and it might seem obvious, but you mustn't say or do anything that could make the hostage taker even angrier than he already is. Don't remind him why he is here. And don't speak to him in any way he might perceive as threatening. Listen to what he says and make sure your voice sounds as gentle as possible.'

Trine nods.

Tellefsen gives her a warm smile.

'It's highly unusual,' she says. 'For a hostage taker to demand to talk to a Minister. We're very pleased that you've come. It's a brave thing to do.'

'Thank you,' Trine smiles and gets a warm feeling inside. 'Which house is it?'

'The red one over there,' Tellefsen says and points.

Another mobile incident truck is parked outside. Trine can see that members of the armed response unit in their dark uniforms are strategically positioned around the house.

'Okay,' she says and starts walking towards the truck. 'Let's get going.'

Chapter 79

The agonies of choice. What to do.

Emilie Blomvik sits on the floor a short distance from Mattis. She is shivering even though she feels hot. Remi paces up and down in front of her, sits down, gets up again. Closes his eyes and writhes. It looks as if his head hurts. And now the police are outside.

The question is, should she do something or simply wait for them to sort it out? Can she trust them to handle it?

Yes, she decides at first. They've been trained for this. But then Remi started talking about the Justice Secretary. Threatened to use the gun. It made Emilie think she might have to do something as well. She can't just sit there and wait.

Do something, yes. But what?

Fortunately Sebastian is still playing in his room, bashing away at his hammer board toy. He turns over the board and starts whacking the other side. It is a game that usually sends him to sleep. She hopes he is starting to feel sleepy now.

'Remi,' she says with warmth in her voice. 'Why don't you sit down for a moment?'

Emilie can't gesture to him because her hands are tied behind her back. So instead she makes a come-hither movement with her head. Remi looks at her.

'Do you remember when we used to skive off school and spend the whole day at home just watching movies?'

Emilie attempts to produce a smile she knows usually has an effect on men.

'I can't remember how many sweets we ate. I feel almost sick just thinking about it.'

Mattis stares at her, but Emilie ignores him. She sees that the memories start to come back to Remi. The time when they were good together. Life was fun. It was quite a wild time as well, she remembers. A lot happened.

'We could be like that ... again, you know that, don't you?'

She has barely spoken the words before he snorts with derision.

'What is it you want from me, Remi? What can I do to make all this go away?'

He lifts his head and looks at her.

'I want you to say that you're sorry,' he says. 'I want you to look at me and tell me you're sorry for ruining my life.'

Emilie nods softly, before she realises what he has just said.

'Me? I ruined your—'

'Yes, you. You, Johanne, that vicious old—'

Remi bites his lip.

Emilie doesn't say anything immediately, but she realises that she can't stop herself.

'Remi,' she says. 'What happened between us. It was a hundred years ago.'

Her voice is calm even though she is seething on the inside.

'You're not seriously telling me that you're still upset about what happened back then?'

Remi makes no reply.

'I was eighteen years old, Remi. Eighteen! Dear God, we

were just kids. We did crazy stuff all the time.'

'*You* did crazy stuff all the time.'

'Yes, okay, but so what? We're allowed to make mistakes when we're young.'

'Right and who cares if anyone gets hurt while we make our mistakes? Anything goes as long as *you're* having fun?'

Emilie doesn't respond immediately.

'Remi, everyone has done things they regret. If I had the chance to live my life all over again there are many things I would do differently, and if that's what you want me to say, then yes, I'm sorry for what happened between us. So here goes: I'm really sorry I hurt you. I apologise. Okay? Now can we please get on with our lives?'

'I can tell from your voice that you don't mean it.'

Emilie rolls her eyes, but Remi just sends her an icy glare.

'Okay,' Emilie says with a sigh. 'Fine. But don't come back later and say that I didn't apologise.'

'It's too late now, anyway.'

The next moment the phone rings. Remi looks at it for a long time before he presses a button and puts it to his ear. But he says nothing. Emilie presumes it's the police trying to talk him down.

But Emilie's intuition tells her that talking won't help; only action will do. And there is something in Remi's eyes that terrifies the life out of her. There is no hope left in them. Only hatred.

You have to do something, she thinks.

Chapter 80

Trine is given a telephone and a headset, which she puts on and exhales.

'I'm ready,' she says and looks at the hostage negotiator who nods back in return.

'We need to go inside the truck,' she says. 'You can't stand out here and make yourself a target. This is a man who clearly wants attention, and you—'

'I get it,' Trine interrupts her.

They step inside the mobile incident truck. Trine is given a chair, an A4 pad and pen. The negotiator sits down next to her.

Trine has read the police contingency plan for situations like this, so she knows that every action suggested and executed will be logged. Everything she says will be subject to close scrutiny afterwards.

'Remember, I'm with you all the way,' the negotiator says. 'Look at me and any notes I write down for you while you talk to him. Be calm. Self-assured. Controlled. Don't let him know that you're nervous.'

'Is it that obvious?' Trine says and laughs quickly.

'I'm always nervous in situations like these,' the negotiator says. 'It usually brings out the best in me. And one more thing: use his first name, Remi. It might make him feel that you know each other. And, if you can, refer to the hostages by their first names. It'll make it harder for him to hurt them.'

Trine nods and closes her eyes in an attempt to focus her thoughts. What if this goes belly up as well? What kind of legacy will she leave behind? She can see the demands. APOLOGISE! the front pages will clamour. Again.

Trine's chest is pounding. Her pulse is 190. Adrenaline. A feeling she normally loves, but this is nothing like a high. She closes her eyes for a moment. Then she rings the number.

*

Remi looks at the phone vibrating on the worktop in the kitchen. The police have stopped ringing Emilie's phone. And started calling his.

It means they know who he is now. They must also have discovered what he has done. But how could they? Where did he screw up?

Once more he reviews the murder of Erna Pedersen in his mind. She didn't remember him the first time he rolled her wheelchair back from the singalong in the TV lounge, not until he showed her pictures from the year he was in and reminded her about the fractions.

Remi had never been much good at maths. One day, she ordered him up to the blackboard, told him to reduce a fraction she had written. And he stood there, staring at the confusion of numbers without understanding anything at all. Later, he suspected that had been her intention all along, make him go up there so they could all have a good laugh at his expense, the whole class. What she did afterwards, as the volume of her voice rose, certainly caused some of his fellow pupils to snicker. She ordered him to crawl under one of the desks in the front row and screamed while she hit the desk with her cane, 'This is a fraction. And you can't have a nothing under a fraction!'

Another time she had turned up with three large bars of chocolate and told them that if every single pupil in the class could work out an equation she had taught them, they could have the chocolate. As expected Remi failed and, surprise, surprise, she made a big point out of stressing how he had ruined it for everyone. Then there was the way she always looked at him. Her scornful laughter.

When he held up the school photo to her and pointed himself out, she showed signs of recognition, but she said nothing. And he felt the urge, right there and then, to extinguish the light in the eyes he had hated ever since his school days, but he couldn't do it. Too many people had seen him wheel her in. Markus was waiting for him. So he left the school photo on the wall in the hope that she would remember what she had done. Perhaps she would say sorry next time.

But no. What he saw instead were traces of the same contempt she had treated him with at school. And though he had planned it, he didn't actually understand what had happened until after he had killed her. He had also destroyed the trophy on her wall, the photograph of her son's family displayed like a prize for successful mothering. Then he took the school photo with him and sneaked back into the TV lounge, took up position right behind Markus and sang along with 'Thine Be the Glory, Risen Conquering Son'.

Remi hadn't spoken to Markus since sixth form when one day they bumped into each other in the Storgata branch of

Spaceworld where Remi had gone to buy a computer. They got talking and it was actually quite amusing to hear what had become of the old Romeo: absolutely nothing. No girlfriend, no children. A hefty spare tyre had formed around his waist and most of his wavy, blond hair had been replaced with a shiny, bald circle at the top of his head. Nor had he been very successful at finding work.

But as neither of them had that many friends, they started hanging out together. It was awkward to begin with. Remi wasn't over Emilie and Markus made a point of never mentioning her name. Not voluntarily. They had to drink a whole bottle of Vargtass before Remi could ask Markus if he was still in touch with Emilie, a question that inevitably stirred up the past.

And if Remi's father has taught him anything, it is that apologies come in many forms. It wasn't until Markus's body was practically anaesthetised with alcohol that he produced a feeble, miserable apology. But saying sorry means only that you sympathise, not that you take responsibility for what you did. That was the night Remi made up his mind.

Markus must be made to take responsibility.

Remi knew that Markus had dated Johanne at some point. He had also discovered that Erna Pedersen lived at Grünerhjemmet and that the Volunteer Service would visit from time to time to sing and play to the residents. And even though Markus might have lapsed over the years, he came from a family where Christian values mattered. So when Remi suggested that the two of them did something other than play computer games and get drunk, Markus was surprisingly easy to persuade.

It was well over twenty years since Erna Pedersen taught

them and time had made her grey and lined. There was nothing to suggest that Markus recognised her when he saw her again. Remi knew that the police would check who had visited Grünerhjemmet on that day. If they were to discover that Johanne Klingenberg was another one of Erna Pedersen's former's pupils, they would start looking for a killer with a similar background. If they then tried to find out if any of Pedersen's former pupils had been present at Grünerhjemmet on the day in question, they would finally get a hit with Markus Gjerløw. Remi Gulliksen, as he had signed himself in the visitors' log, had never been one of Pedersen's pupils. Remi Winsnes, however, was the name he had been known by until he turned eighteen.

The laptop arrangement was also straightforward. Markus, who always had to have the latest thing, didn't mind selling his old laptop to Remi, a laptop Remi made sure to load with photos of Johanne and pictures taken in Erna Pedersen's room. If the police checked if the laptop really belonged to Markus, then they would find his name registered against the computer's serial number. All the evidence would point them to a man who, about to be exposed, had swallowed a blister pack of morphine capsules. Once again Remi saw the light extinguished in the eyes of someone he hated. And, as the perfect finish, Remi posted an apology on Markus's Facebook profile, a status that remained unexplained.

It was perfect, wasn't it?

So why are the police outside now?

Johanne's murder, Remi thinks. *Could Markus have had an alibi?* Remi shakes his head. *Halo 3* had just come out and Markus would have done nothing but play the game and play it 24/7. When *Killzone 2* came out, he didn't sleep for two days. Remi doesn't know for sure, but he thinks it was even worse with *Crysis*. It was a risk, obviously, but Remi sent a text to Markus just before he went to Johanne's flat to ask what he was doing. The reply was as he expected: Markus was playing on the computer. '*Hate the graphics, but love the sound.*' Everything was as it should be.

So what had he got wrong?

Not that it really matters now. There are only two ways out of this situation: either with his hands above his head or staring up at the inside of a body bag.

So what do you choose?

He picks up the phone from the worktop, presses the green button and puts it to his ear. He hears white noise and senses tension. It takes a few seconds before someone says:

'Hi.'

The voice sounds different, but he knows who it is.

'This is Trine Juul-Osmundsen, Justice Secretary.'

It feels weird to hear the voice of a public figure he has never met in real life. But everyone in Jessheim knows who she is as she comes from Kløfta and would often be seen in Jessheim when she was young. The local newspapers have followed her political career from the start. Somehow Remi feels that he knows her and right now he doesn't want to talk to a total stranger.

'You wanted me to come,' Trine says in a slightly harsh tone of voice that startles him. 'And here I am. It's my understanding that you haven't met the demand I made. If you want something, Remi, then you have to give something. This means that if we're to continue with this, talking, I mean, you and me, then you have to show good faith. You have to give me something in return.'

Remi snorts, but takes care that no sound escapes his nostrils. In view of the mess Trine Juul-Osmundsen has got herself into, he might have expected her to understand. But no. Instead, *he* has to give *her* something.

He knows what will happen if he does. The moment he opens the door, the police will storm the house and overpower him.

There is no way he will give her anything.

'How many people are inside with you?'

Too many, Remi thinks to himself while he shakes his head.

'I want you to release one of the hostages, Remi. No more, no less.'

Remi snorts again.

This was a mistake, he thinks. The day has been full of mistakes. And he knows what the rest of his life will be like. First he will be remanded in custody, then there will be mass vilification in the media and meetings with his lawyers in prison, and finally the trial. Even if they let him out in twenty years, everyone will know who he is and what he did. That's no kind of life.

So what do you choose?

He looks at the gun. Then he gets up.

'No,' he says, picking up the gun. He looks at Emilie.

'What did you say?' Trine asks.

'I won't be releasing anyone.'

'You have to,' she protests.

I don't have to do anything, Remi thinks as he squeezes

the gunstock.

'It doesn't matter,' he says quietly.

'Why not?'

'Because it's all over now.'

'No, Remi, it isn't.'

'Yes,' he says, cocking the gun. 'It's over. And now I'm going to kill us all.'

Chapter 81

If anyone were to ask Trine to recount what happened next, she wouldn't have been able to. Not in detail. She saw Simen Krogh make a thrusting movement with his hand and then she screamed. She doesn't remember what came out of her mouth, but whatever it was, it must have worked because he stopped and looked at her. And God knows what the hostage negotiator did. But the gunshot never rang out. Nor did the hostage taker hang up.

The hissing down the other end of the phone feels like piercing, high-frequency pain. Trine blinks, tries to focus and it helps, her vision improves, but she keeps staring at a point in front of her. The hostage negotiator says something to her, but Trine ignores her.

She filters out all noises and tries to imagine Remi Gulliksen and the terrified hostages who are with him inside the house. What they must be going through. Pressing Remi to release a hostage was a mistake.

'Remi,' she says quietly. 'I think I know why you wanted me to come.'

And this time she waits until he says something. It's not much of an answer, but there is a grunt, a signal that he is interested in hearing what she has to say.

'You and I,' she says and waits a little longer again. 'We've both done something we shouldn't have. We've both

394

been backed into a corner and we're desperate to find a way out.'

Trine holds another pause; her forehead gets hot.

'I think I know a little about how you feel,' she says and leans forward on her elbows, resting them on her knees. Some hair falls in front of her eyes, but she doesn't brush it away. She waits a little longer before she says: 'I've never let anyone dictate to me. I've fought injustice wherever I've come across it. But I've learned something in the last few days, Remi. Or, at least, I think I have. And I understand that sometimes it's pointless to fight the inevitable. You can stand in the sea with water up to your knees and tell yourself you'll stay where you are, even if a giant wave comes towards you. But no matter how strong you are, that wave will knock you over.'

Trine pauses.

'Do you understand what I mean, Remi? Do you hear what I'm saying?'

Pause. The silence gnaws at her insides. Trine holds her breath, clutches her fingers.

'I hear you.'

'I've got a suggestion,' Trine says, warming to her subject. 'I've never liked talking on the phone. I prefer being able to look people in the eye. So what I'm going to do now,' she says and looks up for a brief moment at the protests she can read in the faces of the police officers in the mobile incident truck, 'is to leave this truck and go and stand outside the house. I want you to walk to a window, so that—'

'Why? So you can take me out?'

'No,' Trine says emphatically. 'No one here will shoot you. I give you my word.'

She gets up and brushes off a police officer who tries to stop her.

'If you look up now,' she says, taking a step down on to the tarmac outside the truck, 'then you'll see me. I'd really like to be able to see you, too, Remi.'

There is silence.

Trine scans every window for signs of movement. She sees nothing. Hears nothing.

Then a curtain twitches.

'Like that, yes,' she says and feels a sense of agitation. She notices that it has started to rain, a soft, cool drizzle that lowers the temperature in her head and makes it easier to think. 'And I'd like to see the whole of you. Do you think you can do that for me?'

Remi makes no reply. But soon she sees the face of a man with dark eyes. The raindrops settle like tiny pearls on her glasses, but she can still see him clearly.

'Hi,' she says and smiles. 'Good to see you.'

No response.

'What I wanted to tell you,' she continues and locks eyes with Remi, 'is that I've realised that I have to let it happen. There's nothing I can do to make this . . . giant wave . . . disappear.'

Trine loses the thread for a moment. She shakes her head and a thought occurs to her. The fighter in her miraculously returns. There is no way she will accept that the winner takes all. There is no way she will be the only one who takes a beating. She will dish one out as well.

She feels all eager and excited, but then her mind returns to the situation in hand.

'Remi, I know it's tempting to just wait for the wave to sweep you away. God knows the thought has crossed my mind, too, more than once. I've raged at the people who made my life difficult and caused me pain, but at some point you have to let go of the past and start looking forwards.'

Trine tries to see through her misted-up glasses. It is becoming increasingly difficult.

'And I think starting with an apology is a good thing. Apologies matter, Remi. It's a—'

'What did you say?'

'Eh?'

'I said what did you say?'

Remi's voice has grown harsher.

'I said it's important to say you're sorry. It's the cornerstone of every human relationship.'

'Don't talk to me about apologies.'

'Why n—'

'You know nothing about apologies.'

Trine is temporarily wrong-footed.

'No, perhaps I don't,' she says and tries to find Remi's eyes through the beads of moisture on her glasses. 'But I know it's a thin line between love and hate. And I'm absolutely sure that you loved Emilie once, Remi, and that perhaps you still do. It's easy to love and to hate. But forgiving someone might well be the hardest thing of all. And I'm not saying that you have to forgive the people who ruined your life because no one can demand to be forgiven. But nor do I think you can force someone to apologise. If you say you're sorry, then you have to mean it. And you yourself have to recognise that you did something wrong and you must truly want to make amends. Wouldn't you agree with me, Remi?'

There is silence again. Trine listens out for the sound of his breathing, but all she can hear is white noise. Then he moves away from the window.

'Remi?'

No reply.

'Remi, are you there?'

Chapter 82

Emilie looks at Remi, she listens to the short grunts he makes, but she can't hear what is being said at the other end. She only sees him nodding from time to time, almost imperceptibly, and running his hands over his head. The words seem to have some effect on him, but it is only a few minutes ago since he threatened to kill them all. Though Remi seems to have calmed down a little, she has no idea if the rage will flare up in him again. And that could mean the end for all of them.

Emilie's hands are bleeding. She has been rubbing them against the thick rope the whole time, but the knots haven't loosened even a millimetre.

'I'm listening,' he says.

Again she wonders what they could be talking about. And who he is talking to.

The knocking in the bedroom has stopped. Sebastian must have fallen asleep. *Thank God*, she thinks, and hopes that it is so. Again she tries to wriggle her hands out of the rope, but it cuts into her flesh, sending shockwaves of pain through her. It's no use. She is completely stuck.

'How are you?' whispers Mattis a short distance away from her.

Emilie thinks about everything that has happened in the last few days, Mattis's new job, her negative thoughts about him that have started to surface even though she doesn't quite know why. Looking at him now and seeing how out-manoeuvred he is, how bloodied and how battered, she real-ises there is very little left of the man who came up to her at the check-in counter at Gardermoen Airport and invited her to go reindeer hunting with him. And she understands that if anyone is going to stop Remi in case the police don't, then it has to be her.

She tugs at the rope, feels the pain in her wrists again and grits her teeth. *Primal strength*, she tells herself. Only women know what that is. Pain is nothing. Not once you've given birth. But still it makes no difference. The knots refuse to budge.

From the kitchen she can hear Remi's angry voice. He says something about apologies. Then he falls silent again.

A noise makes her glance sideways. The door handle to Sebastian's bedroom is being pushed down.

No, she mouths silently. *Don't do it, Sebastian. Stay where you are!*

But he doesn't. The next moment the door opens and his little face peeks out. Emilie closes her eyes, desperately wish-ing she could shoo him away with her hands, but they are still trapped. She whispers to him to go back, but Sebastian doesn't react, he doesn't do as he is told, why can't he ever do as he is told? Instead, he comes running towards her as he always does.

'Mummy,' he shouts. 'I'm hungry.'

Of course he's hungry, he hasn't had anything to eat or drink all day.

'I know, darling. But I don't have anything for you right now. You'll have to wait a little. Why don't you go back to your room and play? I'll come and see you very soon and I'll bring you some food.'

Sebastian doesn't budge. He just stares at them.

'Hungry,' he repeats before turning.

And then he starts walking towards the kitchen.

'Sebastian,' Emilie says, louder this time. 'Don't go in there.'

But he does.

'Sebastian, don't go—'

'Sebastian,' shouts Mattis in a voice that cuts through everything. 'You're not allowed to go in there. Do you hear me?'

And Sebastian stops and turns around again. He is not used to being spoken to like that. The slightest change in pitch makes him burst into tears, especially if he thinks he has done something wrong.

'You mustn't go in there,' Emilie says, as gently as she can manage.

'Why not?' he demands to know.

'Because—'

The next moment a figure appears right behind him.

Remi.

He looks at them. At Sebastian. Then he grabs the boy's arm and drags him into the kitchen.

Chapter 83

Remi ignores the screaming that erupts behind him. He closes the door and sits down on one of the kitchen chairs.

The pressure on his temples has increased. He grimaces and closes his eyes, trying to ignore the pain.

When he opens his eyes again, Sebastian is standing in front of him. In his hand he holds a small, red toy car.

'Hungry,' he says indignantly.

Remi's mouth opens.

'Eh?'

'I'm hungry,' the boy repeats.

'A-are you?'

Remi continues to stare at him.

'I want some food.'

'Okay,' Remi says at last. 'What do you want, then?'

'Cornflakes.'

Cornflakes. His favourite cereal when he was little. Who is he kidding? It still is.

Sebastian, he thinks. *You and me both*.

'Then I'm going to need your help,' he says to the boy.

Sebastian goes over to the cupboard where they keep empty bottles on one shelf and finds the cereal box, then he fetches a small, blue spoon from the cutlery drawer and half runs back to Remi with both. Then he turns and races over to the fridge, opens it, tries to make himself as tall as he can, but he can't reach the milk. Remi gets it down for him, picks him up and puts him in his high chair and pours cereal and milk. He watches Sebastian eat his cornflakes; he slurps and makes a mess.

Somewhere far away he hears a voice. It's a woman. She says his name: 'Remi. Are you there?'

'Yes, *I'm* here. *We're* here. From now on it's just you and me, Sebastian.'

He gets up and takes the gun. He thinks about where he is going to do it. The bedroom, perhaps. It'll be messy, no matter where he does it. Best to wait until Sebastian has finished eating. You shouldn't travel on an empty stomach.

He goes over to the door and pushes it open. He thinks about how quiet it will be. How he will finally be able to do it, this time with Sebastian. How the two of them will stare right into the brightest of lights.

*

Emilie's body is convulsing. She is crying so hard that she can't breathe properly. When she finally calms herself down enough to take a deep breath, she resurrects the thought of primal strength and primal pain, and tells herself that pain doesn't really exist. She contorts her hands again, more desperate now, and only one thought keeps her going, the thought of Sebastian and what Remi might be doing to him in the kitchen. Every second counts. She wiggles and twists; she feels her back getting wetter so she tears, yanks, pushes and jerks. The blood acts as a lubricant and she feels the rope begin to give; she pulls as hard as she can and hopes that if she just keeps trying, just a little bit longer, then she will be able to free herself.

Emilie grits her teeth as her back grows bloodier, but she carries on tugging at the ropes and suddenly there is no more resistance.

She brings her hands round to the front, looks at them red and sticky with blood; she doesn't recognise them and they don't hurt. She is free and Sebastian is still with Remi. Mattis tries to say something to her, but she hushes him in order to listen out to noises from the kitchen. Her first instinct is to rush in before it's too late, divert Remi's attention away from Sebastian and on to herself. But she has no way of knowing what would happen then, Remi might panic and lash out and she can't run that risk because of Sebastian.

So now what?

Emilie looks around for a weapon, anything that can inflict injury. It's not enough to knock Remi out even if she does get the chance. She has to make sure that he can't get back up again.

My weights, she thinks. The dumbbells Johanne gave her for Christmas and which she keeps under the sofa in case she feels a sudden urge to exercise. Emilie rushes over to the sofa, lies down flat on the floor and spots the dumbbells in between dust bunnies, Lego bricks and an old grape that is turning into a raisin. She stretches out as far as she can, gets hold of one of the dumbbells and rolls it towards herself. Then she stands back up, raises the dumbbell to chest height and pledges that if she – and Sebastian and Mattis – get out alive, she is going to start exercising properly rather than just talk about doing it. She will take responsibility for her life.

Improve herself. Try to love all of Mattis and not just the reindeer hunter in him.

Emilie hurries over to the door and braces herself.

At that moment the kitchen door handle is pushed down.

*

Remi doesn't reply.

Trine turns to the hostage negotiator, to Simen Krogh, to the police officers and everyone in uniform who begin to move in almost robot-like unison. Trine knows why. A scream from a hostage means danger, that lives may be lost.

The officers from the armed response unit move closer, orders are issued, code words and warnings that make no sense to her. Everyone is standing by.

Trine closes her eyes.

Please, she says to herself. *Please let this end well.*

Chapter 84

Emilie raises the dumbbell over her head, ready to strike. She knows that Remi might be holding Sebastian so she hides behind the kitchen door when it opens. Remi takes a step forward. And she sees that Sebastian is right behind him, but neither of them has noticed her.

Emilie closes her eyes and lets her arm fall. She has only one thought in her head and that is to hit Remi and hit him again and again until there is nothing left to hit.

At that moment there is a bang. She has never heard such a loud bang before and when she opens her eyes, she realises at once that Mattis's rifle has been fired, but it doesn't stop her, she still lets the dumbbell fall and she feels that she hits something, but has no idea what.

She is about to strike again when one of the living room windows is smashed in. The floor starts to shake with the heavy footsteps of men in dark uniforms and her arm stops moving. There is a lot of shouting, but Emilie doesn't understand a word that is being said, she just concentrates on hitting Remi, but it's no use. Someone is restraining her.

Emilie exhales and then she sees Remi's feet under a pile of men and Mattis's gun trapped under a solid, black boot on the birch parquet floor. White powder scatters from the ceiling as if it has started to snow indoors. And that's when she realises it's all over.

The tiny, delicate crying of a toddler emerges from the pandemonium of loud, male voices and Emilie wriggles free. She rushes over to her son, who is looking up at her with wide-open, moist eyes. His cheeks are flushed. Lightning McQueen is lying next to a bowl of half-eaten cornflakes on the kitchen floor. There is mess everywhere. And Emilie doesn't really understand what has happened, but right now she doesn't care, either.

She puts her hand on Sebastian's head and hugs him tightly. And she thinks that nothing in the whole world will ever make her let go.

*

Trine doesn't notice that the drizzling rain has turned into heavy drops. It is as if she has a puncture. The air is escaping from her, making her heavy and empty. She feels a hand on her shoulder as someone speaks to her, but she doesn't hear what they say and she doesn't know who they are. It's not until now that she realises she is shaking all over.

Slowly she becomes aware of the uproar around her; someone starts to clap, a round of applause, born out of relief, which gradually gains momentum. But Trine doesn't join in. She just stands there panting.

It ended well. No one was hurt.

And she doesn't know where they come from, the tears that now engulf her. She hasn't cried for as long as she can remember. She didn't cry when she was accused of sexual assault and life became intolerable. She didn't cry when she lost a friend to cancer some years ago. She didn't cry when they watched *Atonement* on DVD, she and Pål Fredrik, even though he did. Nor did she shed tears of joy when Petter Northug beat Axel Teichmann in the last lap of the World Championship Relay Race in Liberec, though she was a little moved.

But she is crying now.

The heavy rain disguises her tears and Trine cries as if her body needs to make up for all the tears she never shed. She doesn't know for how long she stands there sobbing in the rain, but when she turns around and walks back to the police cordons, to the TV cameras and all the onlookers, knowing full well that she has another battle to fight before this day is over, she straightens up a little and juts out her chin.

And it strikes her that she hasn't felt this strong for a long time.

Chapter 85

Henning cranes his neck to see what is going on. Exactly what has happened doesn't require major analytical skills. Applause and cheers spread across the neighbourhood. The hostage situation has been resolved, clearly without the loss of life, otherwise people would not be cheering.

Henning sends a quick message to the news desk. To the extent it was possible outside the police cordons, he has kept the news desk updated and he knows that they have been feeding the readers of *123news* with an account of events as they happened.

But that the story would conclude with Trine coming to Jessheim to try talking Remi Gulliksen out of Emilie Blomvik's house, Henning would never have imagined. He should really have stayed away since conflict of interest means he can't write anything about his sister, but she wasn't the central character in the hostage drama.

Now she comes towards the police cordons. Her head is held high. Her stride is purposeful and her gaze is steady. *She looks confident again*, Henning thinks. Trine straightens her shoulders as she walks directly towards TV2's reporter Guri Palme, adjusts her clothing and pushes out her chest slightly.

Henning makes his way to the front and earns himself a look of disapproval from the other journalists, which he decides to ignore. Trine stops in front of the TV2 camera where Palme waits until she gets a message in her ear that everything is ready. Then she asks what happened and what part Trine played in it. And Trine gives plain and simple answers without dramatising or overplaying her own role; she stresses how delighted she is that there was no loss of life.

'But Trine Juul-Osmundsen, earlier today you were about to hold a press conference to tell your side of the sexual assault allegations. What can you tell us about that right now?'

'What I can tell you is that I've offered my resignation to the Prime Minister and that he has accepted it. We'll have to see what the King says when the Cabinet meets tomorrow.'

'So you're confirming that you'll be resigning as Justice Secretary?'

'I am,' Trine nods.

'Why are you resigning?'

'I don't think the Norwegian people need further information. Everything the media have written and said about me in the last few days should provide ample explanation.'

'So you're admitting that you're guilty of the allegations?'

'No, that's not what I said. But recent media coverage makes it difficult for me to carry on.'

'You need to elaborate,' Palme demands.

'No, I don't.'

Palme is briefly thrown, but quickly recovers.

'Can you tell me what the last few days have been like for you?'

Trine inhales deeply.

'They've been tough; to say anything else would be wrong.'

'Many people will view your resignation as an admission of guilt.'

'I realise that. People will have to interpret my resignation as they see fit.'

Palme hesitates. A few seconds pass before she continues: 'The identity of the young politician has yet to become known or confirmed. Have you spoken to him since this?'

'No,' Trine says.

'Is there anything you want to say to him right now?'

'No.'

'Are you going to apologise to him?'

Trine looks straight into the camera.

'I've got nothing to apologise for. I need to go now,' she says and starts walking. New questions are hurled at her by Palme and the other reporters, but Trine just carries on walking and shows no sign of wanting to answer them. She aims for her ministerial car, which starts with a vroom before she reaches it. A blitz of flashlights follows them around the first bend.

Chapter 86

After Trine's departure, Henning remains in Jessheim with the other reporters where one press interview follows another. Officials sing from the same hymn sheet. They can't praise Trine Juul-Osmundsen enough for the part she played in saving the lives of Emilie Blomvik and her family.

Henning leaves just before seven o'clock and catches the 7.30 p.m. train back to Oslo. A good hour later he is home in Grünerløkka.

Trine's problems in the past week remind him that he ought to look in on his mother. The last time he left her she was in bed, deep in a heavy, alcohol-induced sleep. He decides to check if her condition has changed.

The sky over Sofienberg is almost black when he lets himself into her flat. Again he is met with a disturbing silence, but the cigarette smell is back at its usual, intense level. He sees the disappointment in his mother's eyes when he enters the kitchen.

'Hi, Mum,' Henning says and attempts a smile.

She never replies, she never says hi, hello or good evening. Such pleasantries simply have no place in Christine Juul's vocabulary. As always she is sitting at the kitchen table. The ashtray in front of her is overflowing and a cigarette in it sends a steady column of thin, blue smoke up towards the ceiling. The small glass beside her is almost empty.

'You didn't fix the radio,' she sulks. 'You said you were going to fix the radio.'

'I know, Mum. I just haven't got round to it yet.'

'I want to listen to the radio.'

'I'll fix it.'

His mother takes a drag of her cigarette and stubs it out so hard the ash spills over the edge of the ashtray.

'And here was I hoping it was Trine coming,' she says, knocking back the last few drops in the glass and slamming it down.

Henning looks at his mother for a long time before he closes his eyes and tells himself to just let it go as usual, that there is no point in arguing with her, there never was. But he is hurt, deeply hurt by the venom she constantly spits at him as if the very sight of him gives her a bad taste in her mouth.

'Why do you always say that?' he asks.

Christine Juul raises her head towards him.

'Why do you always have to tell me that you wish it had been Trine instead of me?'

His mother's eyes don't move.

'Tell me,' he insists. 'How often does she visit you? Do you even remember when she was here last?'

'Yes,' she says. 'I do remember. I wrote it down.'

Henning splutters.

'And why on earth did you do that?'

His mother looks up at him.

'That's none of your business.'

'So you can flick through your diary and daydream about it? Is that what this is about?'

'Hah,' she snorts and looks away.

'You're a coward,' Henning continues. 'You sit here day in day out, mad at the whole world and me in particular – or so it seems. You smoke and drink and wallow in your own grief. Yes, I'm sure it was tough for you when Dad died, but it wasn't my fault.'

Christine Juul stands up on trembling legs and grips the back of her chair. She tosses her head and pulls herself up to her full height. Her eyes, normally glazed and heavy with alcohol, brim with a sharpness and a rage Henning doesn't remember seeing before.

'Yes, it was,' she says through clenched teeth.

Henning stares at her. His tongue swells up in his mouth and the words that finally seep out of him sound like a strangled whisper.

'What did you say?' he stutters.

'You heard me,' she barks without moving a muscle in her face. Henning can feel a red flush spread across his neck and upwards. He is only one metre away from his mother. The bitter words hang between them and her breath pricks him like needles. In the ensuing silence his legs begin to feel unsteady and it takes him a long time to compose himself.

'And just what the hell do you mean by that?' he asks her at last.

She is still clinging on to the chair while her gaze bores into his. She says nothing. She sits down and lights another cigarette, drinks some more liqueur. Henning demands that she explain herself, but Christine Juul has nothing more to say to him. Finally she points to the door and tells him to leave.

Henning steps out into a night that is still damp and cold.

People and cars rush past him. *Of course it's not my fault that Mum's life turned out the way it did*, he thinks, and shakes his head. *I was only sixteen years old when Dad died.*

So why would she say that?

Chapter 87

Trine enjoys the silence and the soporific motion of the car. Her driver always handles the vehicle so smoothly and skilfully. It is especially welcome now. The excitement at Jessheim, the intensity, the resolution, the relief – all induce in her a state of deep relaxation. At last she feels calm on the inside as well. And she knows that the media will write nice things about her this time even though she doesn't deserve them. All she did was turn up and talk. She didn't make Remi come out voluntarily. It could so easily have gone horribly wrong. But for once the odds were in her favour. And it felt good to announce her resignation in the TV2 interview. *There is no way back now. It's over. It's finished.*

Well, not entirely.

Just as she thinks this, her mobile rings. Trine checks it and slumps slightly. She lets it ring for a long time. Finally she capitulates.

'Hi,' Katarina Hatlem begins. 'I heard what happened. It was great that—'

'What do you want?' Trine interrupts.

Katarina sighs heavily.

'I want to try to make it up to you.'

'It's a little too late, Katarina.'

'I understand why you would say that. But even if you never want to speak to me again, I think you might be interested in hearing what I've been doing since you left the office.'

Trine straightens up.

'Go on?'

Katarina starts talking. Trine doesn't move. But her newly acquired peace of mind has evaporated.

When Katarina finishes some minutes later, Trine thanks her.

'Don't mention it.'

'How did you discover all this?'

Katarina doesn't reply straightaway.

'I had a tip-off,' she then says.

'Who from?'

'From . . . someone who wants to remain anonymous.'

'Is that right,' Trine says pensively. Katarina doesn't elaborate.

'And then there's one final thing,' she says. 'I'm prepared to go public to support you – in case he thinks you're bluffing.'

'I really appreciate that, Katarina.'

'Good luck.'

'Thank you.'

They finish their conversation. As the petrol stations on either side of the motorway at Kløfta pass by, Trine leans forwards and says to her driver: 'I'm afraid I have two more stops I need to make before the day is over. Is that all right?'

'Yes, yes, of course.'

'Great. First, we're off to see the Prime Minister.'

Chapter 88

The rain continues to fall though it is now reduced to a drizzle. But even if it had still been tipping down there is no way Trine would have accepted Harald Ullevik's invitation to come inside his warm, terraced house opposite Eiksmarka Tennis Club. She chooses to remain outside, looking hard at the champagne flute in his hand and the rising colour in his cheeks that indicates it is very far from the first glass of bubbly he has enjoyed that evening.

And she knows exactly why.

'I've just been to see the Prime Minister,' Trine says and looks at her friend and closest colleague in the three years she has been Justice Secretary. As always he is elegantly dressed in suit trousers and a white shirt that is without a single crease even after a long working day. He is leaning against the door frame and has loosened his tie.

'And I suppose I ought to congratulate you now that I know the Prime Minister asked you if you would like to take over from me less than an hour ago.'

Ullevik sends her an unconvincing smile. Trine sees what lies behind it. Anxiety and apprehension because he has never seen her like this before. Out in the rain and with a look that would make a tiger flinch. Trine has to control herself very hard not to scream at him. Attack him physically.

The new Justice Secretary.

'Yes,' Ullevik replies reluctantly. 'He did.'

'You declined, I trust?'

Ullevik wrinkles up his nose and tightens his grip around the stem of the flute.

'Eh, no. I accepted.'

Trine nods slowly.

Ullevik shifts away from the door frame, straightens up slightly and examines her with guarded eyes. Trine is tempted to slow clap him, but stops herself.

'There's no doubt that you should have got the job three years ago, Harald. You were better qualified; I'll be the first to admit that. And I'm quite sure you felt that you had been overlooked, who wouldn't have? A man with your background, and then I come along – little me, a nobody – I waltz in and go straight to the top. That must have hurt.'

Trine winks. Ullevik is about to say something, but no words come out.

'Was that when you decided to stab me in the back?'

Again he pulls a face.

'Did you start planning your revenge straightaway? And were you just biding your time?'

Ullevik's face assumes a look of blank incomprehension.

'Are you suggesting that – that I should have—'

'I'm way past suggestions, Harald, and I know that not even your good friends at *VG* will want to protect you if the truth about your duplicity comes out. And if you do become the next Justice Secretary, I'll make sure that everyone knows what you did.'

'Trine, I really have no idea what you're talking about.'

'Oh yes, you do. And if you don't call the Prime Minister

the moment I leave, then he'll be calling you. The Prime Minister knows that I went to Copenhagen during our annual conference in Kristiansand because I had an appointment the following day at a clinic that would remove the child I was carrying. Information that you found out from Katarina Hatlem one evening after the two of you had torn each other's clothes off in room 421 at Hotel Bristol.'

Ullevik spins around and looks into the house. Then he steps outside and quickly closes the front door behind him.

'She also told you that I hadn't told my husband. Katarina was a good friend, one of the few people I tell most of my secrets to. Armed with this information, you convinced me to tell the press that Pål Fredrik and I had been trying for a baby for a long time. That was a smart move. It increased my popularity in the opinion polls. But it was also cynical and calculated. After that statement, I couldn't possibly admit to having had an abortion. It would have been career suicide; me who has opened God knows how many children's homes around Norway and signed a convention to support children's rights across the world. Besides, there was a real risk that I would lose the man I love. And that was what you were counting on, Harald; you calculated that I wouldn't want to risk my marriage or my career. So you fabricated an allegation of sexual assault and gave it to Norway's biggest newspaper, a newspaper you've been leaking stories to for years. And I know the kind of feeding frenzy journalists engage in when they spot the chance of bringing down a member of the government. They don't give up until they get what they want.'

'This is completely absurd, Trine, I would never do anything like that to you.'

'You would and you did, Harald. And cut the crap, please, I know it was you. Let me give you a piece of advice. The next time you decide to send an anonymous fax, go further away. Go to a part of Oslo or to somewhere in Norway where people don't know you, so you can lie about who you are when you register your name and mobile number at an Internet café.'

Trine stops talking. Ullevik opens his mouth, but closes it a few seconds later. Only water dripping from a nearby gutter punctuates the silence.

Trine thinks back to the day her nightmare started, when Ullevik came to her office after the morning briefing and asked if there was anything he could do for her. *'You've done a brilliant job as Justice Secretary. You're the best one we've had for years.'*

Lies.

All lies, the whole time.

'Katarina has said she's willing to do whatever she can to make amends. Do you know what she suggested to me, Harald?'

Trine continues to speak before he has time to shake his head.

'She volunteered to take a peek at the department's log files to find out who sent me that nice little email I got on Monday morning, just before you came strolling into my office, incidentally. What are the odds, do you think, that she'll be able to trace that email back to your computer?'

Ullevik clears his throat.

'She's not allowed to do that,' he begins.

Trine scoffs.

'I really don't think you're in a position to lecture anyone on morality, Harald. And in case you've forgotten which department I've been heading the past three years – how hard do you think it would be for me to find out if you really did get a telephone call from *VG* that Monday morning, like you claimed, just before all hell broke loose?'

Ullevik continues to look blank.

'That was a lie too. Just like everything else.'

He makes no reply. He just lowers his gaze.

'Look at me, Harald.'

He does, but reluctantly.

'Look me in the eye. Do I look like I want to lose this fight?'

'No,' he says and tries to straighten up. 'But you'd never take it public.'

'That's where you're wrong, Harald. As soon as I get home I'm going to tell Pål Fredrik everything. Do you know why? Because I can't bear to go on living under the same roof as a man I've hurt without knowing what he feels about it. It might well be the end of our marriage, but in the long run we might have broken up all the same. My secret would have driven a wedge between us, I'm sure of it, I know all about how secrets can destroy a family. And just so you know it: I can document all my movements in Denmark. I still have the plane ticket, the hotel booking, I can even produce an invoice and a receipt for the abortion. Katarina has also stated that she's willing to confirm that she helped me with the arrangements. And who knows – perhaps she'll also tell the public how you came to be in possession of the information you so deviously used against me. And what about your wife?'

Trine says, pointing to the door behind Ullevik. 'What do you think she's going to say? What do you think your children will say?'

Trine has participated in many debates, in private as well as in public. Usually the duellers have been evenly matched. It's rare to be able to serve your opponent a death blow of this magnitude.

'I've no desire to go public with this, Harald, it wouldn't help either of us. It would hurt our families, it would hurt the Prime Minister, and not least, it would hurt the Party. But I'll come clean without a moment's hesitation if you become the next Justice Secretary. Nothing will be off-limits. And that's a promise.'

The rain has slowly gathered strength. Ullevik's cheeks are even redder now. He looks at her for a long time before he drains his glass and gazes across to the tennis courts behind her.

Trine can't resist the temptation to smile.

'You're caught between a rock and a hard place, aren't you? You know that whatever you do, your life will be hell.'

A part of Trine can't help wishing that Ullevik will call her bluff, so she can redeem herself in public. But something tells her he won't take that step. His body language betrays him. His shoulders are slouching. The muscles in his cheeks have slackened. He even seems shorter than usual.

Trine is tempted to deliver a final blow to intensify the obvious pain in his eyes. But enough is enough.

So she turns her back on him and leaves.

Chapter 89

Henning crosses the street at Café 33 and walks down Seilduksgaten, which is quiet as always, even though the street is in the middle of a bustling part of Oslo. Still, the area could be filled with noise without Henning noticing; he is completely lost in a world of his own.

That is why the man who comes up behind him has to speak to him twice before Henning reacts.

'Don't turn around.'

Henning turns his head instinctively, but doesn't recognise the man's face in the brief glimpse he catches of him before he does as he is told. But he noticed that the man had his hands stuffed in his jacket pockets and that the hood over his head cast dark shadows across his face.

'Just keep walking,' the man says. 'Walk straight ahead and don't turn around.'

Henning does as the man says while his heart jumps in his chest. As he walks, he tries to remember if he has seen the man before, but the face rings no bells.

Markveien appears in front of them, dark like a river at night. There is no traffic so he crosses the street and slows down outside the entrance to his own apartment block, but the man tells him to keep moving. Henning crosses Steenstrupsgate and continues towards Fossveien. He can barely resist the temptation to turn around.

Suddenly the footsteps gain on him and before Henning has time to react, he feels two strong hands pushing him into a dark archway and slamming him hard against a wall. A face is shoved right up in his; he smells garlic breath and a furious rage.

And that's when he realises who the man is.

Henning tries to lean back his head so he can look into the eyes of Andreas Kjær, but the concrete wall prevents him.

'What do you think you're doing?' Kjær hisses. 'Talking to my kids in my garden when my wife and I are out.'

Henning tries to stay calm, but struggles to reply because Kjær's hand is pressing his cheek into his teeth. Kjær glances furtively out at the street to see if anyone is watching them, before his eyes return with rekindled anger. He relaxes his hold on Henning's face and Henning tries to say something, but only gurgling sounds come out.

'Don't you dare come near my home again, you bastard,' Kjær snarls.

Henning is paralysed with terror and all he can manage is a nod. This makes Kjær let go of him. Henning touches his face and neck and realises that he hurt his back when Kjær flung him against the wall, but when he looks at Kjær's eyes, he sees not only rage.

He also sees fear.

The white cross in the garden, the dead dog on the veranda steps. Someone has tried to scare him. And they have managed to scare him so much that he doesn't want anyone to see or hear him when he confronts Henning.

'We're alone,' Henning says, surprised at how quickly he

rediscovers the composure in his voice. 'I think you know something about Tore Pulli. Is that why you decided to come looking for me?'

Kjær's defences are still intact and his eyes continue to smoulder.

'Is that why they killed your dog? So you won't tell anyone what you know?'

Kjær is about to say something, but he stops and takes another look around.

'Please,' Henning appeals to him. 'You're a father yourself; you fear for your children, that's why you're here. You want to protect them. But I lost my son that day, Kjær. So I'm sure you can understand why I need to know what happened.'

A car drives through the puddles in the street outside. Kjær's gaze flits.

'I promise you, Kjær, no matter what you tell me it'll stay between us.'

Again Kjær looks as if he is tempted to say something. His eyes search for a point on the ground.

'It . . .'

He looks up, he looks down. Out into the street and back again.

Then he fixes his eyes on Henning and stands with his back to the street.

'I don't know who it was,' he whispers.

'You don't know?'

'Hush,' Kjær hisses. 'That's all I can tell you.'

'Come on, Kjær.'

For the second time Henning is slammed hard against the wall.

'I don't know,' he says with his mouth close to Henning's ear. 'Okay? I don't know. And I don't want to know, either.'

Kjær glances around again before he lets go of Henning.

'But they spoke funny.'

'Funny?'

'Yes. They spoke Swedish, but with an East European accent. That's all I'm prepared to tell you. Now stay away from me,' Kjær says with renewed intensity in his voice. 'Stay away from my family. If I see or hear from you ever again, then—'

Kjær points an angry index finger at Henning's face. It stops, quivering, in front of his eyes.

Then he turns around and disappears out of the archway.

Chapter 90

Bjarne Brogeland savours the pleasant sensation of having solved a crime, of having tightened up the loose screws. It's like hunting for your glasses for a long, long time before finally finding them and putting them on. Suddenly the world comes into focus again.

In Markus Gjerløw's bank account they found a transfer of 3,500 kroner from Remi Gulliksen with the reference 'PC purchase'. The police concluded that Remi must have bought Markus's old laptop and uploaded pictures of his victims on it before leaving it in Markus's flat to incriminate him.

Bjarne takes out the photographs of Remi's childhood bedroom in Jessheim. His parents haven't changed it much over the years. The few times Remi stayed the night, he always slept in it. And the picture of his dead brother on the wall always kept him company.

Bjarne can't even begin to imagine what it must have been like to grow up with Werner's eyes resting on him every time Remi went to sleep. According to Remi's mother, his father always blamed Remi for his brother's death.

Bjarne is happy and exhausted and should be heading home, but he walks down the corridor and knocks on the door to Ella Sandland's office. She calls out 'enter' and smiles at him as he does.

'Hi,' she says.

'Hi. Fancy a beer?'

Bjarne can see that she is about to say 'no' out of habit, but she surprises him by hesitating before she replies.

'Actually, that's not a bad idea. Just you and me, is it, or are any of the others coming?'

'Everyone else has gone home.'

Sandland nods.

'Okay,' she smiles.

And Bjarne, who has been waiting to hear her say this for as long as he has known her, smiles and completely fails to disguise the excitement in his voice:

'Great! See you in five minutes?'

*

Henning is still standing in the archway, trying to calm himself down. A man glances at him as he walks past, but only for a second then he is gone.

Slowly Henning makes his way back to the street. A gust of wind whistles towards him, but he is too preoccupied to feel the touch of autumn it brings. Cars go past him at a snail's pace looking for spaces to park, but Henning doesn't see them. He just wanders along, pondering, while pebbles, cigarette butts and rubbish crunch under his shoes.

The people who threatened Andreas Kjær were from Eastern Europe. Now that could mean any number of countries, but it's a beginning. Tore Pulli was going to reveal what he knew about whoever started the fire in Henning's flat, but before he could do it, he was killed – a murder that was arranged by a man who had long been in cahoots with East

European criminals.

Ørjan Mjønes.

Could he also be behind the threats against Kjær?

Chapter 91

The car brakes slowly as if the driver is trying to make the moment last.

Trine knows the perks will disappear now that she is no longer Justice Secretary. She will miss the car in particular. And the driver.

Trine finds his eyes in the rear-view mirror.

'Thank you so much, Bjørn. It's been great sitting here with you.'

'You're welcome,' he says.

He sends her a pale smile. But instead of prolonging the agony, she steps out into an evening where drifting clouds liven up the darkening sky above her. She realises that she is already longing for tomorrow.

As she expected, several journalists have gathered outside her house, but this time she isn't intimidated by them. She holds up her head and nods to some, refusing to let herself be distracted by the questions they call out. She just aims for the door where Pål Fredrik is waiting for her as usual.

And perhaps none of this would have happened if she had told him the truth in the first place. She would have been able to convince him, wouldn't she?

Neither of them ever thought she would be able to get pregnant. They had tried for years without success. But then one day, she discovered she was. And she didn't really know what happened, but suddenly she no longer wanted a child. The child became much more concrete. A new life. She didn't know if she would be able to do it, if she would be a good mother. If Pål Fredrik had known then what he knows now about Trine's family, perhaps that wouldn't have been so hard to understand.

But she knew that Pål Fredrik desperately wanted to be a father and she robbed him of that chance. Without ever consulting him.

Now he takes her jacket, as he so often does, being the gentleman that he is. In a way she dislikes it, it makes her feel like a guest in her own home. And she is more than a guest. Or at least she wants to be.

He ushers her into the living room where music from hidden loudspeakers fills the room. But it is music for other, more cheerful occasions, so she switches it off and steels herself before she turns to face him.

*

Bjarne Brogeland and Ella Sandland arrive at Asylet. The café is always busy on Thursday evenings, but Bjarne manages to get them a table for two near the fireplace. He orders two beers and folds his hands on the table while he tries to make eye contact with Sandland. Her eyes keep slipping past him, out into the room.

'Hey,' Bjarne says and smiles. 'That's *my* occupational hazard.'

'What is?'

'Being on the lookout for villains.'

'Ah.'

Sandland is embarrassed and laughs.

'Always on the job?' he asks.

'Always.'

A waiter brings their beers.

'Are you hungry?' Bjarne asks her.

He realises that he wants to keep her to himself for as long as possible, but Sandland shakes her head. Bjarne nods to dismiss the waiter who disappears immediately.

Silence descends on the table. Sandland takes a sip from her glass, sends her gaze on a new voyage of discovery before she suddenly turns it on him.

'So – who will be our new Justice Secretary, do you think?' she asks.

Bjarne shrugs.

'It makes no difference to me. It won't affect how I do my job.'

'But the way she resigned was really very odd.'

Bjarne makes a 'whatever' gesture with his head while he thinks about Trine Juul-Osmundsen, his teenage crush.

'She can't have been a particularly good boss,' Sandland declares.

'No, perhaps not,' Bjarne says quietly.

'Sexual harassment in the workplace,' Sandland goes on and looks at him. 'I've got a friend in the force who was the victim of that. It was fairly low-key, but still very upsetting. Looks, comments, whispers and gossiping behind her back.'

Bjarne suddenly feels the need to undo the top button of his shirt.

'And she told her boss, but you think he did anything about it?'

Sandland shakes her head before Bjarne has time to answer.

'A good manager would have done something,' she says, without taking her eyes off him. 'A good manager nips that kind of thing in the bud.'

And now, for the first time, it is Bjarne's turn to look away. He seeks refuge in his beer where the foam clings to the inside of the glass. He doesn't know what to say next so he looks across the room. An early Thursday evening. Life and laughter. Good times.

Sandland raises her glass towards him.

'But cheers,' she says and smiles her most dazzling smile at him. Bjarne returns her toast and empties his glass.

A word has formed in his mouth when he looks at her again.

But he can't get it past his lips.

Friday

Chapter 92

Henning wakes up with a jerk, not entirely sure where he is. Then he recognises the walls of his living room, the ceiling, the matchbox and the Coke can on the table next to the sofa. And before he has opened his eyes properly, it comes back to him, the events of the last five days, everything he has found out. The past has risen like a multi-headed hydra and it bites and snaps at him from all sides.

Henning looks at the clock on his mobile and sees that much of the day has passed already. Fortunately he agreed with Heidi Kjus last night that he can come into the office late today. So he takes a long shower while he makes up his mind to deal with one question at a time. If the East Europeans who terrified the living daylights out of Andreas Kjær have links to Ørjan Mjønes, then someone must know who they are. *As long as I get a name*, Henning thinks, *then I'll be able to track them down.*

Henning has just switched on the kettle when his mobile beeps. He checks the message, sees that it is from the *123news* breaking news service.

> *Truls Ove Henriksen has been appointed as the new Justice Secretary following the resignation of Trine Juul-Osmundsen. Henriksen, who*

Henning has barely heard of Henriksen, but he still clicks on the link that follows the text message. The main text doesn't add much more information about the appointment itself, but Henning notices that Harald Ullevik, considered by many to be Trine's obvious successor, has resigned with immediate effect. No reasons given other than he 'has decided to leave the government'.

Henning smiles; he would love to be a fly on the wall in the Justice Department right now, but he has more important things to do.

*

Bjarne Brogeland's voice is sleepy when Henning finally gets hold of him. He, too, would appear to be taking it easy today.

'Thanks for yesterday,' Henning says.

'You're welcome.'

'I'm glad it ended the way it did.'

'Mm.'

'I've just got one question for you. The Swedish Albanian criminals Ørjan Mjønes used to work with. Have you caught them yet?'

Brogeland doesn't reply immediately.

'You're calling to ask me that now?'

'Yes.'

Again it takes a while before Brogeland says anything.

438

Henning hears him yawn.

'Rough night?'

'Are you sure that it's morning?'

'Quite.'

'Right, the Swedish Albanians,' Brogeland says. 'I can double-check for you, but the last time we spoke about them, they were lying low. I guess most of them have left Norway.'

'Scared that they would be banged up as well?'

'Probably.'

'So, in theory, they could be anywhere.'

'Yes, I think so.'

'Okay,' Henning sighs and they hang up.

But even if they have gone underground, Henning thinks, it must still be possible to find them. It's just a matter of asking the right people.

Chapter 93

Bjarne lay in his bed all night, wide awake, staring at the ceiling. At one point he got up, went to his study and sat down with the application he had prepared for Vestfold Police. He reread his bombastic statements, ambitions and visions. Then he scrunched up the pages and threw them in the wastepaper basket.

Now he walks into the kitchen where Alisha sits on her Tripp Trapp chair doing everything but what she was supposed to do, which is to eat her breakfast. He stops and gazes at her tenderly.

So big and yet still so small.

And he doesn't know if there is any point in him trying to explain to her why the evenings come and go without him being there for her bedtime. But he owes it to her to try, perhaps tonight, even though he isn't sure he knows the answer himself. If what he does makes a difference, if he helps make Oslo safer.

'Hi, girls,' he says and walks across to the cupboard by the window and takes out a bottle. He removes a few more until he finds the one he is looking for. Unopened and dusty. With a well-aimed puff he blows away a layer of grey household dirt and looks at the brown contents of the bottle that bears the good old Norwegian name Braastad Cognac.

'What are you doing with that?' Anita asks, sounding

alarmed. 'Surely you're not going to drink cognac at this hour?'

'Of course not,' Bjarne says and laughs, then he rubs his eyes and stretches his hands high above his head. He finds a bag for the bottle.

'Where are you going?'

Bjarne gives her a kiss on the cheek and is still smiling when he says: 'I'm off to see a friend.'

*

It is early evening when Henning makes another visit to the building where his mother lives, but this time he doesn't let himself into her flat. Instead he knocks on her neighbour's door. He hears footsteps and the door opens. The caretaker Karl Ove Marcussen, a man with a beer belly, thin longish hair and six-day-old stubble that gives his face scattered patches of colour, looks him up and down.

'Hi,' Henning says. 'I'm Christine's son.'

He jerks a thumb in the direction of his mother's front door.

'Ah,' Marcussen says and nods. 'You rang me the other day.'

'That's right.'

Marcussen nods again. His stomach wobbles.

'What the hell happened to your face?'

'Microlight flight accident,' Henning replies. 'Dangerous things.'

'Oh, right.'

'Thanks for doing me that favour I asked you for. I don't think my mother has been listening to the radio or watched

TV in the last few days. But it's safe again now.'

'So you want me to reconnect—'

'Yes, please. It would be great if you could, so she can carry on destroying her hearing. But here,' Henning says as he hands him a bag from an unnamed shop with black windows he visited on his way here.

'A contribution to your collection, in recognition of all your help.'

The caretaker hoicks up his trousers, takes the bag and looks inside it. He smiles when he sees what kind of movies they are. He is about to thank him, when Henning holds up his palms.

'Don't mention it.'

Henning makes a Scouts salute to Karl Ove Marcussen, thanks him again and starts making his way home. But as he realises it is coming up for 8.30 p.m., he is reminded of something his mentor Jarle Høgseth would often do when he was stuck on a story. He would return to the scene of the crime, usually at the same time as the crime had been committed, to take in the mood, see if a detail that wasn't clear when there were police cordons everywhere might suddenly stand out. And the fire brigade's report stated that the police had received a call about the fire in Henning's flat at 20.35.

So he walks back to his old flat and stops outside the entrance he would so often go in and out of, usually accompanied by Jonas. He looks around and tries to work out where Tore Pulli must have parked in order to keep an eye on the building's front door. There are several possibilities on both sides of the street. And Henning realises how suspicious Pulli's presence must have seemed to the sharp-eyed traffic warden who saw him sitting in his car in roughly the same place several nights in a row and why the traffic warden alerted the police.

Henning walks up and down the street, meets some people in party clothes with bottles that clink in carrier bags, a woman pushing a pram, and sees cars whose suspensions groan as they go over the speed bumps. *If I'd been Tore Pulli,* Henning thinks, *and I'd been sitting in my car, what would be my reason for being there? And why did Pulli get in touch with me while he was in prison? After all, we had never had anything to do with each other before the fire.*

Once again he comes to the same conclusion: Pulli was watching him. And that's when Henning gets a flash of inspiration. If *he* had been watching someone, how would he have gone about it?

He would have mapped that person's movements. Made notes. Taken pictures.

What if Tore Pulli did the same?

What if he photographed all the people who entered or left the building that night?

Henning walks as quickly as he can up to his new flat. He sits down at the kitchen table and calls Tore Pulli's widow, Veronica Nansen, whose delighted voice says that it's good to hear from him again. And though Henning is sorely tempted to cross-examine her immediately, he takes the time to ask her how she is. After all, it's only a few weeks since she buried her husband.

'I guess I'm all right,' Veronica says. 'All things considered.'

Henning nods; he can't restrain himself any longer.

'Listen, the reason I'm calling is that there's something I

wanted to ask you. Now I know that you're the photographer in your house, but did Tore have a camera as well?'

There is a short silence.

'Yes, he . . . did.'

'Why do you say it like that?' Henning asks.

Veronica Nansen sighs.

'Because someone broke into my flat last week. Stole some camera equipment. Including Tore's camera.'

Henning stands up.

'It was really quite creepy,' she continues.

'Was anything else taken?' he asks as his hope deflates.

'A few bits and pieces.'

'And the police haven't caught the people who did it?'

'Oh, the police. I could barely be bothered to report it. They wouldn't waste their time on it.'

No, Henning thinks. *They probably wouldn't.*

'Do you know what kind of pictures were on Tore's camera?'

'Holiday snaps, I presume. Why do you want to know?'

Henning is tempted to tell her the whole story, but he hasn't got the energy.

'Do you know if he'd backed up the pictures?'

'We always back up our digital photos, but I'm afraid they stole the backup disks as well. I'm really upset, to put it mildly. My whole life with Tore was on those disks.'

'I understand,' Henning says, resigned.

But he can't summon up much grief for her loss right now. He can think only of his own. So near and yet so far away. And he knows without a shadow of a doubt that those photos are gone forever.

It has happened again.

And once that thought has materialised, the next one follows close behind. Could that have been the information that was redacted from the Indicia report? That Tore Pulli was sitting outside his flat with *a camera*? Could that be the information that Andreas Kjær was too scared to tell him?

Saturday

Chapter 94

The morning has arrived with an unstable layer of clouds when Henning decides to go out and get some fresh air to clear his head. He spent most of last night on the sofa thinking. Then he got up and meandered around the room for a bit. Did some more thinking. Finally he was on the verge of losing his mind.

He buys himself a cold can of Coke and sits down in his usual spot below Dælenenga Club House. He thinks about Jonas again, about the evidence that slips away the moment he discovers it. Tore Pulli who might have had photographic proof of who entered Henning's flat. All gone. And someone with an East European accent who went to the trouble of threatening Andreas Kjær so he wouldn't disclose whatever it was that he knew. That evidence is probably gone as well. If Henning's theory about the deleted Indicia report is correct, it might even be that that was the information which Kjær had. That Tore Pulli had taken pictures of the person or persons who set fire to Henning's flat. He knows it's a long shot, but right now he is clutching at straws.

As usual he is frustrated with himself for not being able to remember more of the weeks leading up to the fire. He recalls that it said 'first and last warning' on the note someone had pinned to the inside of his front door after starting the fire. But a warning against what? Why does his memory keep failing him?

Knowing that his mind has a tendency to short-circuit when confronted with painful or traumatic events, perhaps he should do something about it. Seek professional help? At least he is starting to remember more from his childhood. His memories of Trine have grown more vivid in the last few days.

And that's the insight which makes him leap up.

Quickly he walks down from the seating planks, along the tarmac and through Birkelunden Park. He realises that it wasn't until he started thinking about Trine properly that memories of the life they shared before their father died came back to him. Without even trying to he grew close to her again, he recognised feelings he'd had, thoughts he believed were long forgotten.

It all goes back to the fire, Henning thinks, now getting agitated while at the same time dreading what he has to do next. It's the fire that is stopping him, the flames that are blocking his memories, and that is why he has to feel them on his body again. Just like his childhood memories started to return when he decided to help Trine.

He runs up the stairs and lets himself into his flat with only one thing on his mind.

To find the damned matchbox.

It is where he has tended to leave it recently, on the small table next to the sofa where he often sleeps. And he sits down, focusing all his attention on the rectangular box from hell, knowing that it contains an arsenal of weapons and that every single one of them is out to get him.

He realises that he has forgotten to replace the batteries in his smoke alarms, but the moment has passed and he knows it won't make any difference now. Henning closes his eyes and summons up all the courage he can. *Come on*, he says to himself, *you know what you have to do, just take out a match and strike it.*

Henning steels himself before he opens his eyes, shutting out everything but the matchbox. He picks it up and weighs it in his hand before he opens it and sees them lie there, every single one of them. The soldiers from hell.

Henning takes one out; he stares at the slim matchstick, which looks so tiny and innocent between his thumb and index finger. Then he puts the head to the side of the box, holds it there, senses the friction build up between his fingers and spread to the box, but the matchstick refuses to budge.

Henning pauses before he makes a second attempt and this time he feels the matchstick scrape against the strip before he lets go. But there is no flame.

Okay, he says to himself. *That's one all.*

He presses the head of the matchstick against the side of the box and again the box nearly wins. But suddenly he realises that the box and the matchstick are no longer in contact. And what he sees next makes him hold his breath.

A flame.

A proud, bright flame.

He stares at the red and orange tongue as it eats its way quietly down the wooden splinter. He can barely believe he has done it. At last he has slain one of his demons. But he still has one lap left. The most difficult. It's not enough to light the match. His body must feel the flames.

His fingers are starting to hurt as the heat approaches, but he has only one thought in his head and that is to endure. To grit his teeth. Fight his instincts and reflexes, and hold on.

And that is exactly what he does, he clings to the tiny bit of pine that is slowly losing its fight against the flame that creeps ever nearer the end, eating its way towards Henning's fingers, and he is shouting now, he screams because it hurts so much, it hurts like hell, but he doesn't let go. Not until the match has burned itself out. And Henning has large, red burns on his index finger and thumb.

He gasps for air. When he opens his eyes again and looks at the shrivelled, pathetic remains of a fallen soldier's brave fight, it is as if a curtain has lifted and the light shines on a blurred image.

And Henning sees.

He *sees*.

And now he remembers too.

'Tore Pulli,' he mutters as his fingers clench into a fist. 'You bastard.'

Also by Thomas Enger

Burned

Don't be Scared. I'll take care of you . . .

A Brutalised Victim

A solitary tent is found to contain the body
of a half-buried woman.

A Lone Voice

Physically and emotionally scarred,
journalist Henning Juul returns to work
two years after losing his son in a fire.

A Mystery Ignited

Assigned to the story, Henning begins to
suspect, unlike the police, that the case may
not be as simple as it first appears . . .

'Highly recommended.' *Shots*

'A fascinating addition to the "Scandinavian noir"
genre, I look forward to the series unfolding.' *Crimesquad*

ff

Pierced

Shortlisted for the Petrona Award 2013

**If you clear my name
I'll tell you who killed your son.**

A murderer who has information others would kill for.

Tore Pulli, once a powerful player in Oslo's underground scene, is currently in prison charged with a murder he has always denied committing. When he contacts journalist Henning Juul he offers him a deal: If Henning can clear his name then he will tell him who was responsible for the fire that killed Henning's six-year-old son.

But is he telling the truth?

Desperate to continue his own search for justice, Henning soon realises that Pulli's information may prove dangerous – to both of them as well as others. As events take a deadly turn, Henning finds himself on the trail of two killers, for whom the stakes have never been higher . . .

'[Enger is] one of the most unusual and intense talents in the field.'
Independent

'A dark and suspenseful blast of nordic exposure.'
Chris Ewan

Thomas Enger is the author of two previous Henning Juul novels, most recently *Pierced*, which was described in *Shotsmag* as 'excellent, another superbly compelling read'. As well as writing, he also composes music. He lives in Oslo and is currently at work on the fourth novel of the series.

Praise for Thomas Enger:

'Slick, compelling and taut, *Pierced* combines a sophisticated layering of mysteries with an intensely scarred hero embarked on a tragic quest. A dark and suspenseful blast of Nordic exposure.' Chris Ewan

'With tight plotting and short chapters, this stands out as something special in this crowded area. Highly recommended.' *Bookseller*

'One cannot help but root for Juul, the scarred and battered central figure with but one purpose in life: finding out who torched his flat and his life. The characters leap right off the page, and the relationship between them is as twisted and complex as the story itself . . . Recommended.' *www.shotsmag.com*

'Original and striking novel . . . a superior piece of fiction . . . highly recommended.' *Catholic Herald*

Also by Thomas Enger

BURNED
PIERCED